BRICK
LA

SECURITY

DAY

BY

MATT CRICCHIO

Jangi Spai Publishing House

www.notmfa.com

"Matt Cricchio brings a soldier's heart and a writer's pen to the story of four men—two Afghans and two Americans—during the American war in Afghanistan. *Security Day* is as beautiful as it is unputdownable, and the ways Cricchio subverts the American war novel will forever change how you think about American conflict overseas. Cricchio's prose guarantees him a place beside soldier-writers such as Elliot Ackermann and Kevin Powers, and helps us see that we've been reading and writing war novels all wrong. The story here is not about how war affects the lives of American men but how American men affect the lives of people who never asked for their help."

—Rachel Beanland, author of *Florence Adler Swims Forever*

"Written with extraordinary insight into the complexities of both modern warfare and the hearts and minds of those who fight them, Matt Cricchio's *Security Day* is worthy addition to the literature of our seemingly never-ending wars. I urge you to read it."

—Kevin Powers, author of *The Yellow Birds*

"Just appreciate *Security Day* for what it is–a well-constructed, twisting and turning tale...Fans of military thrillers, especially those set in Afghanistan, would be well served to pick up a copy of this novel."

—Steve Netter, Best Thriller Books

"*Security Day* is a must read for anyone who loves to read military thrillers. This was such a unique take on the genre, and I highly enjoyed it."

—Sarah Walton, Best Thriller Books

"A classic spy novel in the timeworn haunts of the Great Game which unfolds with all the ominous inevitability of a Greek tragedy, *Security Day* transcends genre. Cricchio has been there, done that, and it shows in every line. I really can't recommend this book highly enough."

—Stephen England, author of the bestselling SHADOW WARRIORS series

The Lord said to the Accuser,
"Where have you come from?"
The Accuser answered the Lord,
"From roaming through the earth
and going back and forth in it."
—The Book of Job

I am one of those subtle thieves
Who find a way up to the roof at night
When everything human beings love
Is there for the taking.
—Rumi

This book is dedicated to the following individuals who sacrificed their lives:

LT Thomas C. Fouke, Jr.
Staff Sgt. Kashif M. Memon
Sgt. Clinton K. Ruiz
SO1 (SEAL) Matthew G. Kantor
SO1 (SEAL) Kevin R. Ebbert
CDR Job W. Price
CTTC (EXW) Christian M. Pike
SO1 (SEAL) William B. Marston
CTICS (EXW) Shannon M. Kent

And to the Afghans who, whatever their reasons, helped us.

PART I

ISAIAH KHOST FINALLY KNEW HOW TO WIN THE WAR

Police Headquarters, Tarin Kowt City, Uruzgan Province, Afghanistan, 12 October 2012—

Commander Isaiah Khost sat alone in his armored vehicle, fidgeting with the strap of his helmet. The rough band of scar across his face—from a mortar splinter on his fourth deployment—throbbed. Khost had ten minutes to get inside the Afghan Provincial Police Headquarters for his first meeting with his Afghan equal, General Mir Hamza Khan, and his men were taking forever to secure the area. He wondered if it was on purpose.

Only twenty-seven hours after he had landed in Afghanistan, Khost already knew that everyone was against him. Small-minded, jealous, stupid—whatever it was. They called him fat behind his back and he could feel their gossip like razor wire. They trusted him least of all because, after thirteen deployments, Commander Isaiah Khost said that he finally knew how to win the war. All he needed was General Khan.

Through the vehicle's porthole, Khost watched his SEALs patrol the macadam streets of Tarin Kowt City, taking positions at the corners of buildings and on crumbling rooftops. Their sniper had climbed a rusty radio tower to pull over-watch. Khost hated all of it. Outside his vehicle there was a war on, sure, but really it was counter-insurgency. Counter-insurgency had become Khost's religion. He summed its first commandment up simply: avoid oppressing the populace.

Khost's men—crawling all over the city with their guns—were oppressive. Khost hadn't brought his rifle *or* pistol. He hoped this would show General Khan that he was a different kind of American. "It's not an invasion, Rick," Khost said over the radio to his Master Chief. Master Chief Rick Thompson, thirty-eight years old, skin tanned like a catcher's mitt, body chipped from stone, was setting security for Khost with the rest of the men. "Tell them to hustle up."

"Wait one, skipper. I'm outside your truck," Master Chief said back over the radio. The heavy, armored rear hatch opened. Sunlight poured through. Master Chief's eyes adjusted to the dark cab. "We're set, sir," he said. "Ready to meet Khan?"

"Yep." Khost stood and sucked his gut behind his body armor. "Born ready." Khost had studied General Khan, the intelligence reports and news articles. He had conducted interviews with previous American commanding officers in Uruzgan who had worked with General Khan and Khost knew—for sure—that General Khan was his guy. Strong, smart, rags-to-riches, a hard negotiator and judge. General Khan would make Khost's final deployment to Afghanistan the crown jewel of his long military career. "Hold on, Rick." Khost reached into his cargo pocket for a wad of tissue paper. "I gotta blow my nose."

Master Chief rolled his eyes and waited.

The American generals, far away in Kabul, were against Khost too. That morning they had ordered him to change the terms of Security Day—the weekly supply convoy conducted by General Khan's men to protect American and Afghan supply trucks from Taliban attacks as they crossed the Kandahari desert—by cutting the payments in half. General Khan had become rich from Security Day. American-made

Afghan millionaires were trouble, even dangerous. *Jesus, let the man make a living*, Khost thought.

Khost had a plan to appease General Khan: saffron. A cash crop. The price per pound was high, labor costs low, and the Uruzgani soil yielded plenty. General Khan could start saffron farms across Uruzgan. To make it happen, Khost had twenty thousand American dollars, shrink-wrapped and packed in a canvas bag, at his feet. Seed money for General Khan's saffron empire. A carrot for the stick, the second commandment of counterinsurgency.

Master Chief rapped on the running board. "Khan's waiting, sir."

"Okay, all right," Khost said. He threw the tissue on the ground, shouldered the bag of money, and jumped to the street. "Let's go."

The sun was already hot, the fifth day in a row without a cloud. Two men on a cart, drawn by a skinny donkey, stopped to watch the Americans. Their donkey shit on the street and a red-combed rooster, emerging from an awning of evergreen branches woven above an alley, investigated. Khost, his interpreter—a young Tajik they called Chamber because no one could pronounce his Afghan name, and Master Chief walked toward General Khan's Police Headquarters. The building, like all of the larger structures in Tarin Kowt City, had been constructed by the Soviets, and was three stories, drab and square, the cement walls peeling and veined with cracks. The Americans approached the guard shack and two Afghan Police Officers, leather boots polished to a high gleam, lifted a wood pike with a snappy flourish and allowed them inside.

The Americans lumbered up a narrow stairwell covered in fraying red carpet. Khost looked down at his feet, careful not to miss a step, trying to control his breath. Master Chief nudged him. Khost looked up and nearly stopped walking. General Mir Hamza Khan, tall and imposing in his sea-blue police uniform, stood at the top of the stairs, radiating a gentle power. A smile formed under his manicured beard. Khost took a deep breath and sucked in his gut again. Next to Khan was a small man. *Colonel Maziullah.* The intelligence reports had called Maziullah the Robin to General Khan's Batman. It was difficult to tell the age of most Afghan men, the wear of their life premature, but General Khan looked forty. Maziullah was craggy and ancient. *There's victory looking right back at us.*

Khost raised his hands, bag of money swinging, calling out in Pashto "*as-salaamu' alaykum, ta sanga yee jordia phakeyr*" almost correctly. "I hope everything is good, general," Khost continued, switching to English and letting Chamber translate. "It's nice to finally meet you."

"Yes, it is, commander! How are you? How was the trip through the city? You took a long time to finally come inside." General Khan ushered the group into his office without waiting for a reply.

A heavy walnut desk, a gift from an American Congressman, dominated the room. A green Iranian carpet and two leather Queen Anne wingback chairs, from the Australian Prime Minister, filled out the rest. In the corner, leaning barrel up, was a blue AK-47. General Khan ignored the chairs and desk and went right to the carpet where five empty glasses and a bowl of dried blackberries were arranged in a circle.

The Americans peeled themselves out of their armor—Master Chief and Chamber leaning their rifles against a Queen Anne chair—and Khost placed the bag of money in full view beside him. Maziullah brought over a white porcelain teapot decorated with gold-leafed finches. He filled the glasses then stood at the edge of the carpet like a servant. Khost made a show of enjoying the tea, swirling the *chai* around his glass.

"How is the tea, commander?" General Khan said, slurping his own.

"It's good, general."

"And how is your family?" General Khan leaned over and touched Khost's hand. "They must miss you."

"They're good, thank you for asking," Khost said. He hadn't talked to his wife or kids since he'd arrived. He gulped his tea and put the glass down. "There's an issue with Security Day, General."

"Business first is not the Pashtun way but I understand," General Khan said. "My family is also doing well, *hamdulillah*. Thank *you* for asking."

Master Chief kneaded his hand without looking up.

Read the room, Khost said to himself. "I apologize, General. Tell me more about your family?"

"You want to get directly to important matters, yes? That's what the Americans like to do." General Khan stared at Khost. "Americans come and go from Uruzgan. There's not much time to get things done."

"But this time we'll get the job done." Khost balled his fist. "I promise that."

"How many times have you been to Afghanistan?"

"Thirteen." Khost calculated for a moment. "Almost five years, altogether."

"Wonderful!"

Khost brought his hand down on the bag of money to remind himself to give the carrot after the stick. "Like I said, I'm here to talk about Security Day."

"Where else have you been in my country?"

Khost looked over at Chamber. Chamber shrugged. "Five deployments to the north and seven to the south."

General Khan pointed to the groove of Khost's wound. "Is that where your scar came from? Fighting in my country?"

Khost touched his face reflexively. He caught another glimpse of the blue AK-47 in the corner. "I almost lost my eye fighting for you and your people."

"But then you went home? To America? I've been to America and it is very safe." General Khan looked at Maziullah. "Everyone there eats well too."

Maziullah jiggled his torso as though he had a fat belly. General Khan laughed.

"General, have I offended you in any way?" The third commandment of counter-insurgency: have no pride. Apologize for every offense. "It's not intentional."

"Commander, please!" General Khan went to his desk and picked up a large knife with a bone handle. The Afghan flag was embossed on its polished blade. "This knife has the flag of my country. The one I cannot leave if something bad happens to me." He handed the knife to Khost. "A gift for all you have sacrificed for Afghanistan." General Khan smiled. "And because it appears that you have forgotten your rifle. You need weapons in Uruzgan."

Khost's faced turned red. He slipped the knife into the webbing of his body armor. From the corner, the blue AK-47 flashed. Khost pointed. "Is that your weapon, General?"

"The rifle?" General Khan went over and lifted it. "This is a special rifle. A holy one. It's how we won the wars." He put the blue rifle down and walked back to Khost. "It belongs to Colonel Maziullah."

Isaiah Khost didn't know how that rifle could've won wars—*which ones?*—but he wished General Khan had let him hold it. "It's beautiful."

16

General Khan sank down onto the carpet and waved his hand. "More tea?"

"No, thank you," Khost said. He squeezed the money bag for reassurance. "I have to cut the cost of Security Day. In half."

General Khan paused to sip from a fresh, hot glass. "Do the Americans feel I have done a poor job?"

"No. The route isn't as dangerous anymore. Your prices are too high for the current situation. It's a compliment, General."

General Khan smirked. "And because you are withdrawing. Less men and bases. You don't need as many supply convoys."

"Yes, but that doesn't mean we won't still be in business together." Khost unzipped the bag. A bit of the cash peeked out. He lifted it. General Khan didn't move. Khost put the bag between them on the carpet. "I've done my research. Saffron is the new gold. Take this money and start saffron farms. Our gift to you."

General Khan looked at Maziullah and they both looked at the bag of money as if it were a bomb or a pile of animal shit. "I'm not a farmer," General Khan said.

"I know but you can hire men from the local economy to work the farms. They have jobs and you make a profit. It's very good for the entire community."

"Our community needs Security Day," General Khan said. Security Day didn't just move American supplies, it brought all the food, medicine, and fuel that the entire city of Tarin Kowt needed too. No one, American or Afghan, would eat, heal, or move without Security Day. General Khan reclined and pushed the money away with his foot. "I don't know how to farm. I know how to fight."

"So I'm supposed to tell my generals that you refuse our new offer?"

"Tell your generals to keep their agreement. Promises matter in my country." Khost held out his glass for more tea. General Khan took the teapot from Maziullah and poured. "Are there any other issues we can work on?"

"I didn't come here today to only ask for favors but there is something else I need your help with, General."

"Anything."

"Noorzai, your police chief in Chorah District."

"Yes?"

"He executes prisoners without trial. We'd like him removed from his position."

General Khan studied Khost's face, as if the long, ragged scar was an opening through which he could see the working of Khost's mind. "But he fought alongside your men when you invaded. The Americans loved him then."

"That was a long time ago. We're different Americans, General."

General Khan sighed. "I must keep a man like Noorzai in place. I've promised him his position. I always keep my promises." General Khan stood. Maziullah gathered the empty teapot and glasses. "Let's continue this conversation another time."

"General." Khost searched for something to give, say, do—anything to create a better rapport. He remembered the fourth commandment of counter-insurgency: share intelligence with local partners. "We're doing an operation tomorrow. In a village called Safad Khare." Master Chief looked surprised. "I should keep that secret but this is your province and you're my friend."

"I know Safad Khare village well. Are you doing a raid there?"

"Of course not, we're sending doctors to treat sick people."

General Khan smiled. "The people will like that."

Khost looked at the blue gun again before leaving. Neither General Khan nor Maziullah followed them out to the stairwell.

At their vehicle, Khost told Master Chief to put the money in the safe when they returned to base. "You don't think I should've told him about Safad Khare," Khost said, taking off his helmet and putting it under his arm. A motorcycle, three men riding it, buzzed by. "I saw your look in there."

"We don't know this guy very well," Master Chief said. The men setting security for Khost and Master Chief were peeling back from their positions. Two kids chased a dirty dog, throwing rocks at the animal. Master Chief climbed into the thundering cab and Khost followed. "It's only a matter of time before he remembers we own him."

Khost's face filled with blood. *We don't own General Khan.* He strapped into his seat and stared straight ahead without talking for the entire ride back to the American base.

GENERAL HAJI MIR HAMZA KHAN: THE HERO OF PEACE AND UNITY

Tarin Kowt City, Tarin Kot District, Uruzgan Province, Afghanistan, 12 October 2012—

Mir Hamza Khan sat on the roof, his favorite resting place in his palatial compound, waiting for Maziullah. For safety, they had driven separate vehicles from their first meeting with the American Commander to Khan's mansion. His mansion was like no other in Uruzgan—there were no other mansions—protected by fifteen-foot walls inlaid with jade-colored tile from Dubai, every turreted corner manned by a guard behind a machine gun.

The courtyard below was ringed with rose bushes, honeysuckle, cannabis, purslanes, and the season's last watermelons, fat on the vine. Four buildings—a house for each of Khan's wives—were arranged around a cement pad. On the pad were a Japanese motorcycle, an armored Toyota Hilux, a white Corolla, a cherry-red Mercedes—for fun, and a green Ford Ranger truck topped with a PKM machine gun. The Ford Ranger idled, ready for an instant escape, fed from a bladder of Mogas.

"*Sahib Jan!*" Maziullah called, his *kabuli* sandals finally scraping up the last of the steps to the roof. He smiled, teeth white through his well-kept and graying beard. The head of a frayed toothbrush peeked out of the pocket of his *kameez*. On his back he carried his blue AK-47, the color of lapis. Khan smiled at how the weapon had almost hypnotized the silly new American Commander at their meeting earlier in the day. The rifle did that to everyone. "How was the ride back?"

"It was good, *andiwale*."

Maziullah crouched next to Khan under a blue tarp stretched across two poles. The roof's white tile radiated warmth. "Is there tea?"

Khan had already ordered his manservant to have the *chai* waiting. *Tea, tea, and more tea,* Khan thought. *Tea with that stupid American Commander wasn't enough?* Khan pointed to the pot and two glasses at his feet. "But we must drink quickly. It's time to leave again."

"Yes, it is," Maziullah said, squatting with the blue AK-47 across his lap. He poured Khan a cup and one for himself. "But there is always time for tea."

Khan hid his impatience with his best friend by watching the city beyond his walls.

A cracked stockade of mountains encircled Tarin Kowt, an ancient city created by the Greeks, captured by the Arabs, rampaged by the Mongols, then taken over by the British, the Soviets, the Dutch, and now the Americans. The Americans wanted to leave too, in less than a year. The city—and province—would be Khan's. Not that there was much here: spare mud houses dotted the slopes and flat plain, increasing in number until they formed the close-knit city blocks around the *bazaar* at the center of Tarin Kowt.

The vendors' stalls were loaded with tomatoes, cucumbers, almonds. Sides of lamb flamed on spits, their fat dripping. A man wearing a sequined *Baluchi* cap swept the lanes between the stalls with a bundle of reeds, only stopping to answer his cell phone. Sun-bleached sedans filled the taxi pen. As usual, there were few passengers. The drivers hung out of their windows to escape the heat.

Khan snorted. He'd once been a taxi driver too, before he met Maziullah and his blue rifle. Both had transformed the simple Mir Hamza to Mir Hamza *Khan*. Now he was the richest man in Afghanistan, a target for *talibs*, gangsters, rival tribesmen, and the national government. Khan didn't pray to God anymore, except when other people were around, but every morning he uttered, "Today I fight to keep what I've earned." It was better than prayer.

To the north, near the jail that he owned, there was a billboard of Khan in his Afghan national police uniform, gold epaulets thrust forward, a noticeable jaundice tinging his skin. It read:

> ## GENERAL HAJI MIR HAMZA KHAN:
> ## THE HERO OF PEACE AND UNITY

Or that's what Maziullah told him it said. Khan couldn't read.

"What did you think of him?" Maziullah said.

Khan turned from his trance. "Who?"

"This new American Commander."

"You're the scholar, Maziullah. What did you think of him?"

Maziullah finished his tea and stood, using the blue rifle like a cane. "He seems strange."

"He's nervous," Khan said. "What do we know about saffron?" They both laughed. Past Khan's billboard, an American convoy rounded the traffic circle. Following them, trucks painted like colorful circus wagons hauled gravel for construction projects on the American base. Khan owned the trucks, the gravel, and the construction projects. Of all that he owned, nothing compared to the Security Day. Khan didn't need

Security Day only for himself or his family; he needed the weekly five hundred thousand dollars to feed, clothe, and house the 916 men that kept him in power. "He's deceiving us about Security Day, Maziullah. They have all the money in the world."

"Why does it matter, *Haji Sahib*? You're already the king of Uruzgan," Maziullah said, a quaint exaggeration that further irritated Khan. Khan had learned from the Americans that flattery distracted from progress. "That's all we ever wanted. Nothing can change that."

"We must squeeze them until the end." Khan stood and his knees cracked painfully from the hepatitis he'd contracted during the Soviet War. Already, he'd been treated twice in Mumbai and might need a third time. "Do you have the phones?" Maziullah opened his vest and revealed a row of five discreet pockets, sewn into the lining, holding cell phones. Khan was careful to avoid being listened to by the Americans. "Good," Khan said. "Get the Corolla. Let's go to Safad Khare."

Maziullah drove the Corolla fast over the Teri River Bridge and left the city. He almost hit, out of sport, two yellow dogs eating from a pile of trash. Khan laughed, loving the speed. They barreled forward through the dry Pinowa Valley, poppies picked and stems littering the fields, crossed the Teri River as it snaked back again, needing no bridge where it was ankle deep, and drove to the rusted Russian tank marking the road that turned toward Safad Khare village.

The Corolla climbed and the mud compounds of Safad Khare appeared on the crests. The road narrowed to a path. To the west of the village an almond grove spread across two hills. In the saddle between was a one-room schoolhouse that Khan had built for the boys of the village. Khan wanted a police checkpoint in Safad Khare but his tribal rival, Haji Daoud, had refused. Safad Khare was split evenly between Popalzai and Barakzai Pashtuns. The Barakzai, led by Haji Daoud, had the power to resist Khan's checkpoint for one reason: the water source was on their side of the village. If a checkpoint was built without their approval they could keep the water from the Popalzai families that were Khan's kin. Building the boys' school had been Khan's first attempt to convince Haji Daoud to approve his checkpoint. When that didn't work, Khan built a white marble, blue-domed mosque in the center of Safad Khare. No village mosque in Uruzgan could match its splendor.

The Corolla rolled past the beautiful mosque and Maziullah clicked his tongue in disgust. "All that marble wasted. The *masjid* can fit the entire village. Haji Daoud should thank you."

"Haji Daoud doesn't understand kindness," Khan said.

Maziullah parked in the almond grove, the Corolla camouflaged by the trees. A stream of elders, throwing blankets over their shoulders, entered the distant schoolhouse. A week ago, before he'd learned of the American Commander's plans, Khan had called for the *shura* to discuss the police checkpoint again. "Should I go to work immediately?" Maziullah said.

"Wait for the right moment." Khan watched for Mirwais, an important Popalzai elder and ally, among the crowd. He hadn't seen him. "Call Mirwais, make sure he is inside." Maziullah picked the red cell phone. Khan touched his wrist. "We've used that one here before. The blue one is better." Maziullah smiled at his general's caution. He called and confirmed Mirwais was waiting for them.

Weapons were forbidden in *shuras*. Khan and Maziullah left the blue AK-47 in the Corolla—unafraid of a thief taking the special rifle—and held hands as they walked up the neatly swept and water-sprinkled steps of the schoolhouse. Inside, fifteen white-bearded men reclined against overstuffed suede pillows set against the walls. They compulsively adjusted their turbans. In the center, on the floor, were silver platters heavy with *naan* and tomato and onion omelets. Cups of *chai* lined the room. Khan let go of Maziullah's hand, tore a piece of *naan*, and used it to soak up pooling oil. Everyone else began eating then.

The Barakzai elders sat—opposite the Popalzais—with Haji Daoud. His beard was black, a limitation of youth noted by Khan every time they met. Haji Daoud's bodyguard, Gran, stood behind him, his green eyes on alert for danger. Haji Daoud had become an elder two years ago, after his father and uncle were killed by a bomb that detonated under their car as they drove home. Haji Daoud claimed that The Hero of Peace and Unity had murdered them. Khan ignored the accusations but he knew that Haji Daoud would one day come for revenge. The checkpoint was essential to stop him.

After they ate the food, Mirwais spoke politely about Khan's historic generosity to the village. "He is our friend and he has called this meeting to talk with us. We should all listen." Mirwais sat down and Khan rose.

"Mirwais is a man of great hospitality. I thank him for this meal," Khan said and pressed his palm flat against his heart. He turned grave. "My spies tell me that the *talibs* will attack here soon. My spies are never wrong." He pointed at the elders. "Accept the checkpoint so my police can stop them."

Many men issued confused murmurs before a younger Popalzai elder spoke, "But the fighting season is over and the *talibs* are resting in Pakistan. They have no reason to fight."

"This is true," agreed a Barakzai. He draped the end of his white turban over his shoulder. "They never fight in the winter."

"Why here?" many of the men asked, like a chorus. "We are a peaceful village," they added, echoing each other again.

Then everyone, Popalzai and Barakzai alike, spoke at once, making it impossible to distinguish any one point. Maziullah crept toward

Mirwais. Gran watched Maziullah crawl past, prepared to kill even in a *shura* for his boss Haji Daoud. Maziullah led Mirwais outside by the hand. One by one, Khan answered each question the same way. All of his spies said the *talibs* were coming to Safad Khare. His spies had never been wrong. They must allow him to build a checkpoint.

"We can work together," Khan said to Haji Daoud, who sat picking dry skin from his bare feet. "We Popalzai and Barakzai must work together to defeat the *talibs*. They're our natural enemies."

Haji Daoud laughed. "Your people never work with anyone who isn't Popalzai."

"Lies!" two Popalzai elders yelled, leaping up. "You Barakzais are always looking for trouble with us." Khan, taller than the rest, held his hands in the air and, as if ripping a piece of paper in two, motioned for silence. The two Popalzai elders stopped but didn't sit down.

"*Sahib Jan*," Khan cooed to Haji Daoud. "It's dangerous for Barakzai elders in this village. Accept my checkpoint. For your own safety."

"We have our own Barakzai army."

"But they weren't strong enough to save your father and uncle, no?"

Haji Daoud jumped up to confront Khan but stopped when Maziullah returned with Mirwais. Gran went into action too, allowing Mirwais to pass but blocking Maziullah. Maziullah smiled and turned away. Repositioned at his pillow, Mirwais huddled with the more influential Popalzai elders. The lesser Popalzais, their beards less gray than those of their important kin, watched. Khan pretended not to notice. The influential Popalzai elders broke their conference, shifting the blankets over their shoulders.

"We want a checkpoint," Mirwais said. "We can't risk a *talib* attack here. It will bring attention from the Americans."

Haji Daoud pointed at Maziullah standing against the wall. "Did his little *shaytan* offer you the world?"

Mirwais spat on the ground.

Haji Daoud sighed. "The Barakzais could always count on their Popalzai neighbors to be reasonable, but if you want the checkpoint, we will break off into our own village. And, as always, we take our water with us." Everyone in the room began yelling. Old men with frozen knees and gnarled bones jumped up to press into the fray. It came close to blows. Gran shoved someone every direction he turned, unsure of who to hit first. Haji Daoud turned to Khan. "I don't care if you bring your best friend Hamid Karzai in here. The answer will always be no. Who were you ten years ago? A taxi driver. My grandfather was a king!" The Barakzais, Gran clearing a path, left the room. The Popalzais cursed, damning even the dust trailing the Barakzais as they went toward their side of Safad Khare.

Maziullah pressed his lips to Mir Hamza Khan's ear. "Will he ever listen, Haji Khan?"

"Yes," Khan said. "Very soon."

ZUBAIR GATHERS
THE WEAPONS

Outside Tarin Kowt City, Tarin Kot District, Uruzgan Province, Afghanistan, 13 October 2012—

They didn't know who had given the order. But they all met anyway after the last prayer, inside a copse of poplar trees, and waited for their local commander, known as Zubair, to lead them up the mountain where the weapons were hidden. Five young Pashtun men, blankets wrapped around their shoulders, water bottles hanging from their waists by cords, squatted in a half circle and looked at the ground.

They didn't question their simple missions. Moving ammunition, rifles, and rockets under the cover of darkness was the best way to eat and do their duty to their village. But it was cold and the traditional fighting season was over. The big commanders had returned to Pakistan. Who was planning a large attack when they should be resting? What trouble would it bring?

Their hushed chatter stopped when Zubair appeared inside the wood line and pointed up the nearest rocky slope. The men spread out, walked across a field of winter wheat, and pushed up the scree field skirting the mountain. Their lungs burned as the incline grew but everyone knew this was the easy climb, light as they were with only their turbans and sandals. Coming down they would suffer, encumbered by the weapons.

Going up the slope they could be killed by anyone: Americans, the Afghan Army, the Afghan Police, bandits using caves as hideouts, other *talib*s they feuded with, villagers who resented their presence. Every noise, crack, slip on a rock, baying dog, even the whiff of smoke from a cooking fire raised a stiff hand from Zubair, signaling the men to stop and listen. Halfway up, Zubair hissed the most frightening command: "Lie down."

In the valley, a motorcycle headlight bounced toward the mountain. The rider might have seen their dark silhouettes against the darker slope. If the rider was a bandit, he could radio other bandits already hiding in the mountain's caves to descend upon them. They would be surrounded instantly. The armed bandits would then force them to continue up to the buried cache and steal the weapons on their behalf. If the bandits chose to let them live, they would be punished by their *talib* commander for losing the weapons. Each had a vision of how their lives could end that night.

Down below, the rider stopped—his motorcycle reverberating through the valley—then turned and chugged away from the mountain. Zubair breathed again and ordered them forward. They sprinted one after the other over the last bit of rock to the peak, slowing only to squeeze between the boulders at the summit. Their rasping lungs reminded them that they had to earn their money. The squalling wind froze the sweat to their skin.

The weapons cache, buried under a finger of rock, was located at an intersection of mountain paths. The Pinowa Valley sat to the east and a web of donkey tracks dropped down to the west, into Chorah. From this place the men could bring the weapons anywhere in Uruzgan Province. But the orders were to bring the weapons back to the poplar trees they had started from and wait for a truck. They didn't know what type of truck, or when it would be there, but they must ensure the weapons arrived before sunrise.

The men cut the weapons out of tightly wrapped plastic and divided them among the group. They ate *naan* from their pockets, tearing into the stale bread, gulped coppery water from their bottles, and turned back down the mountain. The sun would soon rise over the Tarin Kowt Bowl.

Down, down, down, they picked their way through the rocks, fighting against the pull of gravity. Once more, they faced danger, Zubair screaming this time for his men to get down, as an American helicopter rose from the valley like a wasp. Its rotors beat overhead and they prayed to the Most Gracious and Most Merciful not to spare their lives for the sake of life but to spare them because they were so close to delivering the weapons and being paid. The helicopter floated momentarily above their heads before lifting over the mountain. It was some time before the fear left them and they could again feel the cold sweat that had soaked through their *kameez*.

Inside the poplar trees again, they stacked the rifles and rockets in a pyramid and covered everything with brush. Zubair ordered the men to wait. They wouldn't be paid until the weapons were on the truck. The men, tired and impatient, complained to themselves and zipped their prayer beads along nylon string.

As the sun washed over the mountains, an Afghan National Police truck, an American green Ford Ranger, flashed its lights across the field. The truck didn't approach and the police officers inside didn't dismount but they flashed the high beams again for a short interval. Some of the men worried—the police were their natural enemies—but Zubair knew this was the truck. He ordered them to move the weapons.

The tired men struggled across the winter wheat field with the weapons, threw the rifles and rockets in a heap near the truck and fell exhausted into the dirt. The police officers yelled at the *talib*s to pick the shit up and put it in the bed, under the tarp. The sun was almost high when the *talib*s, wrapped in their blankets, lined up to be paid, happier with each *rupee* Zubair slipped into their hands. Zubair, his job done, turned to leave.

"Where are you going?" a police officer said. He was fat, with a bushy moustache and a grease-stained blue uniform. "Get in the truck."

Zubair clicked his tongue at the order but did as he was told.

The truck drove down a thin, dusty track through Pinowa. When it stopped at a crossroad, the fat police officer told Zubair to get out and move the weapons across a freshly plowed plot and into a small, abandoned compound. He threw Zubair three Afghan Police uniforms and told him to take those too. The purpose of the uniforms was obvious, but where would it happen? And why now? Who wanted this done?

The fat police officer and the others got out of the truck, started a fire, and turned on a hand-cranked radio. They ignored Zubair as he made repeated trips back and forth to move the weapons. His purpose wasn't their concern. After he had finished, Zubair was to wait inside the compound's courtyard for three Pakistanis. The police officers left without putting out their fire.

Zubair slept in the dirt courtyard until the rusty scream of the gate woke him. He jumped to his feet as three Pakistani men entered and surrounded him. Zubair clutched his beard. The Pakistanis' *kameez* hid their human shape and only their black eyes, popping with eyeliner, gave them any familiarity. Zubair feared the chaos these foreigners would bring.

Only one spoke Pashto. He told Zubair that they were on their way to Kabul when they were called to Uruzgan. Zubair wished the Pakistanis had ignored the call, but an order was an order and he waved to the tarp with the weapons on the ground.

Glee bubbled from the Pakistanis as they drew a Russian PKM machine gun, rocket-propelled grenades with launcher, and some old American grenades. They put on the police uniforms: a blue blouse and pants. The Pashto speaker asked if there was an explosive vest or belt. They were trained in Pakistan to be bombers and hoped to fulfill the training.

Zubair's fear became disgust. Of course there was no belt because there was no glory in that. You won glory by facing your enemy. He gathered the ends of his *kameez* and walked through the compound gate without answering.

Zubair was not like these foreigners. He had the honor of a warrior.

TOOR JAN WAS YOUNG AND WITHOUT AN OCCUPATION

Safad Khare Village, Tarin Kot District, Uruzgan Province, Afghanistan, 13 October 2012—

Toor Jan held a mirror in front of his nose and, with a pair of dull scissors, trimmed his wild beard. The people in Safad Khare village teased him—called it a *talib's* beard—but everyone knew Toor Jan wasn't a *talib* even though his uncle was Mullah Sher Muhammad, the *talib* commander known as The Big One. Besides General Khan, The Big One was the *other* king of Uruzgan. Toor Jan had been teased since he was a boy. Even his nickname—Toor Jan—was a remark about his dark skin. He had been called Toor Jan for so long that no one remembered what his father had named him when was born. Toor Jan was young, without an occupation, not a *talib*, not in the government, barely considered a man in Safad Khare.

He finished trimming, admired the angle of his high cheekbones, and further turned the mirror to see his wife, Shaheen, sleeping against a pillow on the floor. Two years after her first blood, she was pregnant. Her belly swelled with their forming child.

A loud knocking came from his compound gate. Toor Jan startled and dropped the mirror. He took his rifle off its nail on the wall and looked around the room. It was small, made smaller by the wood chest—holding everything they owned—against the far wall. Shaheen turned on her back and snored. Another knock came, louder. The blankets in his brother's corner formed a human shape but there was no man among them. Toor Jan hadn't noticed it when he woke up. *That damned boy is gone again,* he thought. Toor Jan left his house and went through the courtyard toward the knocking.

It was early, the light thin, and there wasn't yet any smoke from cooking fires. The gate was unbolted, as he expected, and Toor Jan pushed the double doors open with the muzzle of the AK-47, to be safe. Gran, Haji Daoud's favorite bodyguard, stood there.

He held Toor Jan's brother, Abdul Hakim, in a chokehold. Gran looked different from most Pashtun men. His hair wasn't black, he had no beard, and his eyes were as green as the Teri River. Despite his strange appearance, Gran was powerful and a bully. Abdul Hakim broke away from Gran and stomped off, into their compound. Abdul Hakim was a full-grown man but had the intelligence of a young child. Gran claimed it was a punishment from God on Toor Jan's family for a secret sin. "You're lucky I brought him back. Next time I won't."

"I apologize for him, Gran." Toor Jan slung the rifle over his shoulder and placed his hand over his heart. "Abdul Hakim doesn't understand."

"I told you to chain him to that tree." Gran pointed to the huge and ancient almond tree in Toor Jan's courtyard. "People like that should be tied to something."

"Gran, thank you for bringing him back." Toor Jan turned to close the gate.

"Wait," Gran said. "The Americans are coming today."

"To attack?"

"No. They're bringing doctors. If any of your women are sick or pregnant bring them to the school after the middle prayer."

"*Sa yid aa,*" Toor Jan said. He went back into his house, hung his rifle on the wall, stepped over Shaheen, and went to the far corner. Abdul Hakim lay under his blanket pretending to sleep.

Toor Jan snatched the neck of his brother's loose brown shirt and drove his fist into his stomach three times. Abdul Hakim squealed. "What did I tell you about leaving? Gran might kill you if he finds you wandering again. You cannot ever, ever leave without me." Toor Jan only hit his brother to make him understand. Gran was wrong. Abdul Hakim wasn't cursed, he was unlucky. But Toor Jan had to protect him. "I'm sorry, Abdul Hakim." Toor Jan patted his knee through the blanket. "Later we will go to the *bazaar* and listen to music in the radio shop." Abdul Hakim smiled and closed his eyes.

Toor Jan laid beside his wife. "Shaheen," he called, soft. "Shaheen *Jo.*" *Jo* was the female version of *Jan* and meant sweetie, a pet name. It was the part of Toor Jan's name that he hated most. He placed his hands on her belly. "Breakfast, Shaheen." The girl turned away. He pulled her hair back, kissed her tiny earlobes.

"Toor *Janna,*" she said, making his pet name even more childish. "I feel sick."

He let his lips trail down her neck. "But we need breakfast."

"Get off me." Shaheen threw her elbow into Toor Jan's stomach. He rolled away and rocked with pain. "Toor *Janna*?" Shaheen took hold of his shoulders, the only noise he made a high squeak. "Are you okay?"

Toor Jan stopped groaning. He opened his eyes and laughed. Shaheen hit him with an open fist. "The Americans are bringing doctors to the village today. We'll go see them."

"Then I will cook now, so I have the strength to go."

"If you're sick, I'll do the women's work," Toor Jan said, getting to his feet to collect firewood for the stove. "But you eat whatever I make."

He smiled when the girl clicked her tongue at him.

DANIEL BING'S FIRST DEPLOYMENT

Multinational Base Tarin Kowt, Tarin Kot District, Uruzgan Province, Afghanistan, 13 October 2012—

From a six-seater plane flying into Tarin Kowt, Daniel Bing watched a shepherd-boy wearing a linen-colored smock and bejeweled hat trail behind a flock of sheep across the Martian desert. One word came to Dan—*biblical*. He felt like he had taken off from Little Creek, Virginia in 2012 and landed in 1212.

Two years ago, Dan had quit his Legislative Aid position with a prominent Senator in Washington, D.C. and enlisted in the Navy—at age twenty-nine—to become a SEAL. Despite being strong, athletic, driven, Dan had failed SEAL training because of a stupid accident: after a Friday night drinking with the boys, he'd made it safely to bed only to fall in his sleep from the top bunk and break his arm in three places. The Navy had retrained Dan as an interrogator and human intelligence operator and though the job wouldn't take him into the direct combat he craved, Dan took it seriously, determined to erase his embarrasing failure. But the resentment from the entire episode never left him.

Dan debarked the plane into the hell-hot air and dragged his three giant canvas bags a kilometer from the airstrip, through the main gate of

Multinational Base Tarin Kowt. He wandered down a weird maze of rusted Conex boxes, asking everyone he saw—Army soldiers, Marines, State Department civilians—for the location of the Special Purpose Unit's headquarters. No one knew what unit he was talking about.

Exhausted, he stopped and leaned against the cool shadowed wall of a Conex box. Dan wiped his brow with the back of his hand. *Fucking eh*, he thought. *I'll never find this place.* Behind him shoes scraped over the gravel. Dan straighted and turned to see a giant man in tiny running shorts and a tan synthetic T-shirt coming toward him.

"Hey, dude," Dan said. The giant man lurched forward like a car stopping short. He turned. His bottom lip was fat with tobacco. Dan was almost scared to ask him for directions. "You know where the Special Mission Unit's compound is? I just landed and I'm supposed to report there."

"You're Dan Bing?"

Dan, intimidated, could only nod.

"Why're you in uniform?" Dan looked down at his desert camouflage uniform. His last name was Velcroed to his chest. The huge man ripped it off. "My name's Beau. Officially, Warrant Officer Parker. I'm the officer in charge of the Special Mission Unit. We call it the SPU. You're gonna call me Beau." Beau Parker was a SEAL officer, a full-blooded Comanche, nearly six-and-a-half feet tall, and two hundred seventy pounds of earned muscle. He'd played college football and been in the Navy for almost twenty-five years. This was his seventh deployment to Afghanistan. Beau knew war like most people know their children's silhouettes at a distance. "We're a secret intelligence unit, brother, we don't wear uniforms. You bring any civvies at all?"

"Of course, Beau." Dan liked the informality, especially given the extreme difference in their ranks. "In my bags."

"Good," Beau said. "Follow me." They continued down a lane between the Conex boxes for a few hundred yards before turning into a cut through the HESCO barriers that led to a cipher-locked chain-link gate covered with canvas. Spools of razor wire topped the high fence. A security camera, mounted high, blinked its red light as it watched them. "This is it."

"Looks real inviting."

"You'll get used to it," Beau said. He unlocked the gate. "Let me show you around." The compound was small. Two silver Toyota 4Runners were parked in the gravel-covered yard. An American and Arkansas Razorbacks flag flew from a yardarm spiking a large cement firepit, ringed by handmade Adirondack chairs. A row of five plywood huts ran east to west like a city block and beyond their sloped roofs stood a taller cinderblock structure. "That's yours, brother," Beau said, carrying Dan's bags to the hut at the end of the row. "Should feel like home."

"Cool," Dan said. He opened the flimsy plywood door. The hut smelled like an attic and contained only a mattress on a platform and exposed wall studs. The austerity excited and scared him. "What's the plan of the day?"

"You resting to kill the jet lag."

"I'm ready to go, Beau." Dan had originally been ordered to instructor duty at the interrogator school in Virginia Beach, *the horror of horrors*. He'd schemed for deployment orders when the SPU's original Navy interrogator got sick. Dan wanted to get in on the action, not sit around in a classroom. "Let me change."

"Okay." Beau pointed past Dan's hut to the cinderblock structure. "That's the Soviet Building. Meet me inside. I'll introduce you to the team."

TOOR JAN AND SHAHEEN VISIT THE AMERICAN DOCTORS

Safad Khare Village, Tarin Kot District, Uruzgan Province, Afghanistan, 13 October 2012—

After the middle prayer, Shaheen put on her green *burkha* and walked with Toor Jan into their courtyard. Abdul Hakim sat under the almond tree. He had already asked Toor Jan three times about his promise to visit the radio shop in the *bazaar*.

"Stay right there until we come back," Toor Jan told his brother. "Then we will go listen to music."

Toor Jan adjusted his white *kameez*. He'd torn a shirt last week lugging boulders for a man who paid him to help build a wall. Before that, he'd permanently stained another shirt collecting firewood on the mountainside for a man who paid five *rupees* a cord. For a short while he had worked with a man who fixed cars; *that* white shirt turned almost black after a day of removing batteries from the engines. Each time he worked Toor Jan wore—and lost—his best shirt.

"Open up!" a voice called at his gate. It sounded Tajik. The Afghan Army Commandos that accompanied the Americans were Tajiks from the north, as foreign as any American. "We are here!" Toor Jan unshot the gate's bolt. The Tajik stood at the head of a dirt track leading down the hill to the schoolhouse. "America is here now," the Tajik said in broken Pashto. He had a thin moustache, held an American rifle, and wore a green camouflage uniform. Messy, black hair crawled out of his white undershirt toward his neck. A crooked helmet topped his head. "Doctors at school. For health."

"Go on," Toor Jan said to the Tajik, pointing at the trail. "I have a woman I'm bringing out." The Tajik soldier shouldered his rifle, leveled his helmet and walked away toward the school.

American and Afghan soldiers surrounded the area, scanning everything through the scopes of their rifles. An American fighting truck overlooked the almond grove above the school and idled loudly as Toor Jan and Shaheen went down the path to join the growing line of people.

They waited a long time. The sun was terrible. American soldiers, some handing out bottles of water, prowled the line. At the entrance to the school, the Americans waved beeping paddles over the people's clothes before ushering them inside to the doctors. It was slow work. Toor Jan asked Shaheen if she was feeling well. The girl only nodded, face hidden by mesh.

There were people Toor Jan hadn't seen in years. Dried up old men, long white beards dyed red with henna. Men with no legs, contorted hands, a cloudy eye, sometimes two. Children missing half their faces from bombs. Fat men with toothaches, farmers with ear infections. Groups of covered women. *Shaheen is strong*, he thought. *Abdul Hakim is like a child but fit. God's blessed us with health. We aren't cursed like everyone thinks.*

Halfway between Toor Jan and the school, Gran stood pointing out people in the line to an American. The American was tall with long, blond hair. Toor Jan knew they wanted information. Gran's employer,

Haji Daoud, spied for the Americans. The blond American and Gran came down the line but walked past Toor Jan. Because of his *talib* uncle, the Americans should have been interested in Toor Jan. But Toor Jan avoided trouble and *everyone* knew Toor Jan was hapless.

Toor Jan didn't know anything worth knowing.

THREE PAKISTANIS FREIGHTED
WITH SLAUGHTER

Safad Khare Village, Tarin Kot District, Uruzgan Province, Afghanistan, 13 October 2012—

The Pakistanis had a simple mission. Wear the police uniforms to get close to the Americans and Afghan soldiers in Safad Khare. Hide in plain sight. Kill as many as possible. Embrace martyrdom.

Freighted with slaughter, they walked the short distance from the abandoned compound to the village. In the distance an American armored vehicle sat on a hill. The vehicle's hydraulics popped. Below, a schoolhouse and gathering villagers. American and Afghan soldiers formed a perimeter around it all.

The three Pakistanis moved into a grove of almond trees. In the police uniforms, they aroused no suspicion. The man with the rocket-propelled grenades remained in the almond grove while the Pashto speaker and the third man, with the PKM machine gun, jumped into a muddy irrigation ditch that ran parallel to the grove.

The machine gunner opened the PKM's tray cover and snapped in a belt of bullets. His view of the scene was unobstructed. One hundred yards away, a hushed crowd waited for American doctors. Everyone in his sight should die. First the *kaffir* Americans, then the *takfir* Afghan

43

Commandos, and then the villagers receiving help from *kaffir* and *takfir*.

Outside the machine gunner's view, a man in an angelically white shirt stood beside a pregnant woman wearing a green *burkha*.

DAN MEETS HIS TEAM

Multinational Base Tarin Kowt, Tarin Kot District, Uruzgan Province, Afghanistan, 13 October 2012—

In his civvies, Dan looked like a construction worker. Hiking boots, sturdy canvas pants, the ubiquitous synthetic T-shirt and worn baseball cap. Other than being clean-shaven, he didn't look like he was in the military and that was a good start.

Inside the Soviet Building was one windowless room. A flat-screen television playing the Armed Forces Network wobbled on a makeshift stand. Maps of Uruzgan Province and its districts covered three walls. On the fourth wall, Afghan and American flags hung above a card table with metal folding chairs and laptops. An Army captain in uniform, two others in civilian clothes, and Beau hunched over the laptops. Together, they had spent a combined fifteen years in Afghanistan.

"Hey! There he is." Beau came over and put his arm around Dan. "Everyone, this guy's the rock star I keep telling you about. Now properly attired."

"Wait a minute," Dan said, pointing at the Army captain's uniform. "Secret intelligence unit, huh? This guy's blowing our cover."

The Army captain stood. He was slender and looked vaguely like Pee-wee Herman. "You're an outspoken one," he said and extended his hand.

Dan returned the handshake. "I prefer surly."

"The good captain is our liaison with the SEAL Team," Beau said. "He's the one who gets you out of trouble when you fuck up, so he looks the part of the squared-away Army officer."

"My name's Robert," the Army captain said, "but you can *always* call me Captain Cales."

"Gotcha, Captain." Dan extended his hand toward the other two.

A wiry, sharp-faced man with shaggy auburn hair and bristly mutton chops shook without standing. "Aaron. You a Team Guy?"

"No," Dan said. *Didn't you hear? I'm the moron who fell out of his bed. First time in SEAL training history a guy got taken out by a cement floor.* "Are *you* a SEAL?"

"Yeah, dummy." Aaron turned to Beau. "An FNG?"

"But this one's a good one." Beau massaged Dan's shoulders like he was a boxer. "Right, Dan?"

"I mean, I bring a lot to the table. The double threat. Collector *and* interrogator."

Aaron looked hard into Dan's eyes. "This is your first deployment?"

"Well, yeah but, I mean." Dan looked up at the pressed tin ceiling. "I've read a lot of books about Afghanistan."

"Oh Christ," Aaron said and flung himself back in his folding chair. "You look like you're old as fuck. What are you, thirty?"

"Barely. I turned thirty like a month ago," Dan said.

"And you're only an E-5. What'd you do before this?"

"I went to college, got a degree in poli-sci."

Aaron made a fart noise with his lips.

"I also—I was an advisor on foreign policy to Joe Lieberman, Senator from Connecticut."

"But were you *the* foreign policy advisor?"

"No," Dan said. He wanted to lie but Aaron seemed like the type of guy who would catch him. "One of many."

"So all you know is the shit that other people have written about." Aaron frowned. "Great."

"Doesn't matter anyway if he's a Fucking New Guy or not," the other one said. He was older—or at least looked older—short, with horn-rimmed glasses and a salt-and-pepper beard, a runner's build. He wore a button-down, plaid shirt and cargo pants. Beau introduced him as Army Brian. He was an Army reservist interrogator from New York. "We're not doing shit anyway. Fighting season's over."

"Fighting season?" Dan said.

"I thought you read a lot of books, Danny Boy," Aaron said.

"Ease up, Aaron," Captain Cales said.

"Yeah, fighting season," Army Brian said. "Taliban packs it up in late September. Commanders go to Pakistan. It's a long, chill session until April."

"I told you replacing me with a Fucking New Guy was a waste of time," Aaron said to Beau.

"I'm replacing you?" Dan asked both Aaron and Beau. "Where are you going?

"Back to doing Team Guy shit," Beau said. "And he's going to start turnover with you." He flicked Aaron's elfin ear. "Right *now*."

"Goddamn." Aaron turned—fast—in his chair toward Dan. "Listen, even if they wanted to fight in the winter it wouldn't matter. MHK owns everything, including the Taliban."

"MHK? What's MHK?" Dan said.

"It's an acronym for Mir Hamza Khan." Aaron, Beau, Captain Cales, and Army Brian all said, "*The Hero of Peace and Unity*," and laughed.

"He's the chief of police," Beau said. "In Uruzgan Province."

"Also the Mayor of Tarin Kowt City," Army Brian said.

"And CEO of the private security force that guards our base," Captain Cales said.

"They call him the Lord of the Highway," Army Brian said, leaning back and crossing his ankles. "That's some post-apocalyptic shit."

"He's a gangster and not the good kind. Nobody takes a shit in Uruzgan without permission from MHK," Aaron said. "He's *supposed* to be our ally."

Captain Cales smirked. "Oh come on, Aaron. MHK's *very* generous. He even signed off on our medical operation in Safad Khare today. That's the mark of a true friend."

"He's not." Beau shook his head. "Even if Commander Khost thinks he is."

THE DARKNESS SWIRLED DOWN BEFORE TOOR JAN'S EYES

Safad Khare Village, Tarin Kot District, Uruzgan Province, Afghanistan, 13 October 2012—

Toor Jan held his hand up to shield himself from the sun. They were almost at the school. Shaheen, bulging in her green *burkha*, trailed behind. Gran had left. Ahead, the black wands and beyond that, the doctors. Soon they would be inside.

Gunfire burped from the almond grove. Sounds like a rope snapping passed over Toor Jan. He pushed Shaheen to the ground and laid on her until a great wind picked Toor Jan up and carried him toward the school.

Tingling heat raced along his arms and ribs. A crackle of pain and the feeling of sickness. On his back in the dirt, Toor Jan raised his head into something like a cloud of smoke. But there was no smoke. Toor Jan was dying.

The smoke blew away for an instant and he could see that his best *kameez* was black with blood. *Another shirt ruined*. He couldn't find Shaheen. More shooting and the screams of women. Smoke gathered again and the darkness swirled down before Toor Jan's eyes.

A GREAT CRIME

Safad Khare Village, Tarin Kot District, Uruzgan Province, Afghanistan, 13 October 2012—

A second RPG wailed overhead. The Pakistani machine gunner jerked the trigger and released another volley at two American soldiers. He missed. Time became slow: villagers scattering, Americans diving for cover, geysers of dirt from return fire walking across the field toward him. Bullets from the American truck on the hill struck his gun's barrel. It twisted out of his hands. A final round hit the machine gunner in the chest, shearing his arm away from his body. He died instantly.

In the almond grove, the Pakistani couldn't reload the grenade launcher and he fought his equipment in despair. The American truck turned toward him. Bullets struck the trunks of the almond trees as the truck drove toward him, wheels vomiting soil behind. He continued to work. When he looked up again, the coyote tan of the truck's grill was smashing forward. Then he saw nothing else.

The Pashto speaker was frantic. His friends were dead and they'd hardly attacked. But the Pashto speaker had his faith, his mission, and if he could get close enough he might detonate his grenade like a suicide bomber. He leapt from the canal and sprinted, zagging across the field toward his enemy and the school. One by one the Americans trained their rifles on him. He felt the air pulse as their bullets passed all around.

Joy rose through the Pashto speaker, he was getting close, so close he could see an American's blue eyes. A bullet tore through the sleeve of the police uniform, grazing his arm, and he lifted the grenade to his chest. He would tackle the blue-eyed American and detonate during the collision.

Head down, he tripped in a rut of chewed-up ground just as a shot shattered his forehead. His lips pulled back around a smile of rotting teeth. The grenade rolled from his hand, spoon released, and detonated with a harmless puff. The Americans continued to fire at his body until they were sure he wasn't wearing an explosive vest.

The Afghan Commandos gathered the Pakistanis' bodies. Of the machine gunner and rocket-propelled grenade man, they found only pieces. The Pashto speaker was intact but had no phone or paper in his pockets, nothing to reveal his identity. No one, not the Americans, Commandos, nor the villagers in Safad Khare knew who was responsible. But everyone knew someone would pay.

DAN MEETS TOOR JAN

Multinational Base Tarin Kowt, Tarin Kot District, Uruzgan Province, Afghanistan, 13 October 2012—

A phone on the card table rang. Captain Cales answered with two short grunts and hung up. "Spoke too soon about the end of fighting season. The medical operation in Safad Khare was attacked, about an hour ago."

"Really?" Dan said. *Already?* "Anyone hurt?"

"None of our guys," Captain Cales said. "One wounded local national in surgery right now."

Aaron and Army Brian touched their noses and said, "Not it."

"You jaded bastards," Captain Cales said. He turned to Dan. "Beau said you wanted to get some, right?"

Dan nodded dumbly. He was too nervous to talk.

"Then get after it."

After the emergency surgery, the clinic called again and cleared Dan to talk with the local national. They didn't have any information, other than that he was a young, dark-skinned man with shrapnel wounds to his hip and a shattered arm. A SEAL had found him unconscious, about thirty yards from the school where the doctors were treating the villagers.

Dan didn't want to but asked Aaron what he should do. "How do I start?"

"Don't you know already? You're *the* double threat," Aaron said and Army Brian joined him in howling laughter.

Dan turned to leave the Soviet Building.

"Wait," Army Brian said, leaping up from his folding chair. "You need a terp."

"Yeah, dummy," Aaron said. "You need a terp. Find Qais."

"A what?" Dan said.

"You learn how to speak Pashto from your many leather-bound volumes?"

"You mean interpreter?" Dan snorted. "Yeah, I need a translator."

"Our guy is Qais," Aaron said. "He lives in the fourth hut from the firepit."

Dan dreaded knocking on the terp's door and was relieved to find Qais sitting in one of the handmade Adirondack chairs at the firepit, watching flames eat a stack of wood.

Even Qais, twenty years old, born in Kandahar but raised in Queens, New York, sensed Dan's inexperience. Qais fingered his gold necklaces, lying flat against the thick collar of his cream-colored Coogi sweater. His Timberlands were loosed and left untied. His outfit didn't make sense for the heat, the base, or for a war but Dan stared at the gold chains to avoid Qais's stare.

"You new?" Qais said.

"To here, yeah."

"You like it?"

"I don't know anything about it. I mean, I know that I don't want to stay on this base the entire time. I'm trying to get outside the wire."

"Oh yeah?" Qais said, smoothing his hand over his chinstrap beard. "I just finished three months wit' Marines in Helmand. Straight combat, bruh." He pouted his lips. "I like it here. I don't have to shit in a bucket no more."

Dan stared at Qais. "You wanna go with me to talk to this guy in the clinic, or what?"

Through the falling dusk, Qais led the way out, up a long gravel passageway between towering HESCO barriers, down a labyrinth of decomposing Conex boxes, through a hole in a cinderblock wall, and across another field of gravel to the clinic, a well-built cement structure.

The clinic had three beds. A tangle of tubes and wires ran to the nearest bed, into a dark-skinned Afghan. He moved like a larval worm, hooked up to double IV bags. Dan and Qais pulled folding chairs up to the bed. The Afghan watched them.

"He's a *talib*." Qais pointed to the Afghan's beard. The Afghan followed Qais's finger with his eyes. "Only *talibs* have beards that huge. Be careful with this guy."

Dan took a deep breath and started—with Qais translating—simply. "Hello." He discreetly took a notebook from his pocket and kept it in his lap. "How are you?"

"I'm hurt. But how are you? How's your family? Are you enjoying my country?" The Afghan rasped each phrase. "Where's my family?"

Qais shrugged at Dan. "We don't know. But we'll find out. Who were you with?"

"My wife. I pushed her down and then lost her."

"I can help find her. What's her name?"

"Nah," Qais said to Dan. He chopped his hand through the air. "Next question."

"What do you mean? Ask him."

"Nah, bruh. Don't never ask about a Pashtun man's women." He folded his arms over his chest. "You can ask about family but not specific women."

"Fine," Dan said. "What's *your* name, friend?"

"Toor Jan."

Dan scrawled *Tour Jshon* in his notebook.

Screws were sunk into Toor Jan's left forearm, attached to a metal splint. A large bandage covered his naked left hip. Blood blotted the sheets. The man tried to sit up. "I have to go home to my family."

"Lay back," Dan said. "You're too injured to leave. We'll take care of you."

Toor Jan looked down at his wounds. "Who would do this to their own family?"

Dan wrote *family member one of the attackers?*

"You put me on the helicopter?"

Delight went through Dan. "Of course. I couldn't let you die."

"Am I the only one?" Toor Jan lifted his head and looked at the two empty beds. "Did any others die?"

Dan took Toor Jan's uninjured hand. "I'm not sure. You were my only concern, Toor Jan." They held hands in silence until Toor Jan, heavy with drugs, fell asleep.

What did this guy do to his family to deserve this? Dan couldn't think of an answer that made sense.

KHOST'S GIFT TO GENERAL KHAN

Safad Khare, Tarin Kot District, Uruzgan Province, Afghanistan, 14 October 2012—

The day after the attack, General Khan invited Commander Khost to an emergency *shura* to help fix the deteriorating security situation in Safad Khare. American vehicles raced around the village. SEALs secured the irrigation canal and almond grove from which the attackers had fired. Snipers climbed to the roof of the school as a precaution. General Khan and Maziullah had joined the interpreter, Chamber, and Khost in his truck to wait for his men to set the perimeter.

General Khan wore his loose blue uniform, the epaulets removed. A Russian Makarov pistol hung from his leather belt. Colonel Maziullah had the sky-blue rifle. Khost also carried a rifle this time and had the same canvas bag with the saffron money—twenty thousand dollars—between his feet. He held it up. "I'll give this to you to distribute to the family of the wounded man." Khost passed the bag to Maziullah. "Good?"

General Khan clicked his tongue. Chamber did the same in translation. "Everyone is waiting while we talk like girls in your truck, commander. Let's meet the elders."

Signs of the attack were everywhere. The field between the almond grove and the schoolhouse had been churned to mud. A bloodied white shirt was left crumpled in the dirt. An RPG had burned a black streak on the schoolhouse wall. *This was the real deal*, Khost thought.

Inside the schoolhouse, the Popalzais took position on the left side of the room while Khost, General Khan, and Maziullah sat at the head. Khost sat on his helmet to reduce the pain of sitting on the floor. Haji Daoud and the Barakzais arrived. Gran came in last, scowling. They sat opposite the Popalzais.

Most of the elders had pocked faces and missing teeth. Even though Khost had been to many *shuras* over thirteen deployments, the wear on the locals always surprised him. *They look like they're a hundred years old.* He appraised Haji Daoud. *Not that one. Looks like a teenager.* Tea was passed to each man. After the first glass, General Khan stood to speak. Chamber translated for Khost.

"I am your protector." General Khan paused, an uneasy quiet. "But my protection has been repeatedly refused. Still, I am responsible."

"Then we finally agree on something," Haji Daoud said and worked his hands over prayer beads. Gran leaned against Haji Daoud as though he planned to use his body as a shield. "You are responsible."

"What do you mean, *Haji Sahib*?"

"I pray that God makes you to listen," Haji Daoud said and stabbed his finger into the air. "The criminal attackers wore police uniforms."

"What do you mean to say?"

Haji Daoud sneered. "Where do those police uniforms come from?"

"It is unfortunate." General Khan turned to Khost. "They're sold in the *bazaar*."

Mirwais stood. "They are sold in the *bazaar*. Anyone can buy one." The other Popalzais vocalized their agreement. "If you're saying they were the General's men, you are wrong. They wore eyeliner. I saw one of the bodies."

Even I know that only the Taliban wear eyeliner, Khost thought.

"Then why would the attack come now?" Haji Daoud said. "Fighting season's over."

Both Barakzai and Popalzai elders agreed on this point. They might defend their general from accusation but the two groups were equally upset about the attack. Some of the Popalzais even blamed the Barakzais, especially Haji Daoud, for leaving them vulnerable.

"We all want the Americans to leave, no?" General Khan said. Everyone nodded in agreement with this universal point, even Khost. Exit was the primary goal of counter-insurgency. "For the Americans to leave Uruzgan, they must secure the people from attacks." General Khan looked down at Khost, who gave him a confident nod. "This American wants to come into your village and build his own checkpoint with twenty American soldiers."

The room burst. Men came to their feet, kicked over their tea cups, and argued. The Popalzai delegation mixed with the Barakzais. Gran led the yelling, finger straight in the air as he screamed against the Americans. Khost tried to hide his surprise at General Khan's deft lie as he moved with Chamber to calm the men.

General Khan took a place against the wall with Maziullah—still carrying the blood money—and watched for nearly fifteen minutes before they all sat down again. Everyone, Popalzai and Barakzai alike, said that Khost had gone too far. Even Haji Daoud and Gran, though still visibly angry, agreed that General Khan's checkpoint was preferable. In exchange for accepting his checkpoint, General Khan would—

through his construction companies—build additional irrigation ditches so the Popalzais had more water. He would pay Barakzai leaders for the water use and provide free maintenance of both tribes' irrigation systems. *It's a textbook solution*, Khost thought. *Afghans solving Afghan problems.*

Khost was the first to exit the schoolhouse. He placed his helmet, unstrapped, on his massive head and walked to the truck with Chamber, General Khan, and Maziullah.

"Arguing and fighting, that's democracy?" General Khan said.

Khost slung his rifle across his chest. "What you did in there was brilliant, General. But please don't forget that I tried to give you something too."

"What have you given me?" General Khan said, surprised.

"The blood money." Khost turned to Maziullah, holding the bag of money. "You can use me like you did in there again but I need something in return."

General Khan turned his palms up. "What do you need?"

"Noorzai still needs to go." Khost didn't want to ask again but he'd been ordered to by the generals, who were angry that he'd been unable to strike the new Security Day deal. "He's violating human rights."

General Khan looked at Khost. He squinted, the corners of his eyes folding like a paper fan, and pressed his lips out. "I suggest that you send your men to Chorah to meet with Noorzai one last time to convince him to change. If he doesn't, I give my word I will replace him."

"We can do that. Very good, general."

Khan and Maziullah got into their own truck, leaving to attend another shura at Khan's mansion later that day. Khost admired General

Khan: How we wore his uniform. His impeccable, groomed beard. The way he ignored the blood money. Everything. General Khan was the most brilliant Afghan—*no, man*—Khost had ever met.

THE ORBIT OF MIR HAMZA KHAN

Mir Hamza Khan's mansion, Tarin Kowt City, Tarin Kot District, Uruzgan Province, Afghanistan, 14 October 2012—

Maziullah parked the truck on the cement pad in the courtyard of Mir Hamza Khan's mansion. They got out and Khan bent at the waist to stretch his aching back. "Did the American Commander say anything in English, Maziullah?"

"You saw him, *Haji Sahib*. He was silent like an idiot." Maziullah read Farsi and Pashto and spoke English. The Americans didn't know that. Maziullah held up the blood money from Khost. "Why would he give us this?"

"Because he is an idiot." Khan spit on the ground. He would provide money to the wounded man directly or to his male relatives. That was the proper way. "It's yours, Maziullah."

"General," Maziullah said. "I could never."

Khan pressed the bag into his best friend's chest. "Take it. You don't know what you might need it for."

Maziullah put the money in the footwell of the truck. Though there were more than twenty people serving as guards, servants, gardeners inside the compound, Maziullah had no fear of theft. Khan hated thieves. He'd personally killed the last man who had stolen from him.

A little boy with a mushroom of brown hair came running toward them from the nearest house, trampling a strip of flowers. "Aziz!" Khan bent down and his joint pain disappeared as he lifted his youngest son in the air. Khan kissed the boy. This was unusual for a Pashtun man but Khan loved Aziz more than he loved himself. "My boy."

Aghala, Aziz's mother, padded over, watery eyes cast down in deference to Maziullah, hands clasped behind her back. She wore a cream-colored silk dress and a transparent, rose-tinted scarf on her head. A wisp of coal dark hair peeked out. Aghala was the youngest of Khan's four wives, the daughter of a powerful Popalzai elder. He gave Aghala a world beyond her dirt village in Sarkhum Valley and, three years ago, she gave him Aziz. "It is my turn to feed you today, *Mira Jan*," Aghala said. "Please?"

"Yes, yes," Khan said, putting Aziz on his feet. "But hurry, we have our people's *shura* soon."

Aghala's house was as well-furnished as that of any of his wives, according to custom and law. Woven carpets covered the marble floors. Her sitting room had an American couch, pink to match the rugs. A Chinese television sat in a teak cabinet. Aghala hadn't seen a television, let alone a television show, until the day she came to live with Khan. Now she was obsessed with Indian and Pakistani movies. Neither Khan nor Maziullah were impressed with movies. Khan dismissed them as silly fantasy, preferring his thrills in waking life, and Maziullah was too old, too devout, and too traditional to indulge such a corrupting influence. But they sat in front of the television anyway, at Aghala's insistence, Khan taking the couch and Maziullah squatting on the floor, suspicious even of the couch's perversion.

Cardamom, cinnamon, and onion perfumed the room and Aghala brought out a platter piled high with raisin and pine nut laced saffron rice. The men, using *naan*, ate eagerly. Aghala watched, gathered their dishes when they finished, and brought their shoes to them when they had to leave. "You will be with me tonight?" Aghala said, standing at her front door, gazing at her husband as he trotted, with Maziullah, toward the mansion's *shura* room. "It's my week."

"I will see you and Aziz tonight," Khan said as he hurried on.

Weekly, Mir Hamza Khan opened his doors to the people of Uruzgan to listen to their troubles and give assistance. Though his army of guards roved the grounds like predators, these were dangerous events and there was always a chance that a bomber could sneak through and kill him. But they were necessary to maintain his rule. Khan and Maziullah changed from their police uniforms into clean and white *kameez* with black, silk turbans. Like a star in orbit, Khan sat in the exact center of his *shura* room adorned with mosaics of colored glass. When Khan nodded, Maziullah opened the tall wooden door for the gathering of people and shouldered his blue rifle.

They entered dragging unusable limbs, or crutched across the floor on makeshift canes, thrusting wads of scribbled-on paper at Khan bearing written promises from landlords or petitions to the government for compensation. Khan gave all written notes discreetly to Maziullah to read. Others with horrible coughs and weeping sores begged for attention from Khan's personal doctor as they pulled him into their infected embrace. Every single person was treated.

This went on for an hour until a boy limped inside, a tiny gray vest over his *kameez*. He walked halfway in and stopped. He had been crying. Khan went to him—recognizing the signal—picked him up and pressed his ear to the boy's lips. "The Big One says you must meet him tonight," the boy whispered. "At the usual place." The boy twisted out of Khan's arms and fainted to the ground. Several of his guards sprang into the *shura* room and rushed the boy to Khan's doctor.

"Maziullah," Khan said, making a show of rubbing his aching knee. "I'm in pain."

The people still waiting peered around each other to see the commotion inside the *shura* room. Maziullah pointed to them. "Turn the rest away?"

"Yes," Khan said, heading toward another door. "And you go home too." Maziullah hated The Big One. He wouldn't be useful at this meeting. "Is the American Commander's money still in your truck?"

"Yes, General."

"Good," Khan said. "Don't leave it behind because you think it will please me."

That night, Mir Hamza Khan covered his face with a scarf and left his mansion on his motorcycle. The moon was full and he shut his headlight off to navigate the busted roads by its light. He sped, noisy but invisible, by the people's compounds. Near his empty lot in the country, Khan turned off the motorcycle and leaned it against a skinny poplar tree. He walked the rest of the way.

The Big One stepped out of the darkness. His black *kameez* hung over his ballooning pants. He didn't wear eyeliner and his beard was trimmed short. He didn't look like a *talib*. The Big One unslung his rifle and motioned with it toward the woods.

"We can speak here," Khan said. Like all great kings, he had a supernatural sense for an ambush. "No one will see us."

"You make too much noise on that thing."

"Should I come in a full convoy? My men would enjoy that. They've been trying to find you for years."

The Big One squatted and Khan squatted too, finding a pebble to draw with in the dirt. "Even if they came with you, they could never find me," The Big One said.

Khan smiled and tossed the pebble away. *You only exist at my pleasure.*

"You embarrassed me," The Big One said.

"How did I do that, *Mullah*?"

"You said the Americans were doing an assault. Now I have to explain to the people why we attacked them for receiving medical care."

"I was lied to by the American Commander. I'm as embarrassed as you. But I've had a meeting with the elders and they'll take my checkpoint. Things will go back as they were before. For both of us."

"If God wills it," The Big One said without letting go of his anger. "But there's something else, *Haji Sahib*. My nephew was wounded in the attack. The Americans took him and he hasn't returned."

"What's his name?"

"Toor Jan, son of Haji Izatullah."

Khan needed The Big One's participation in Security Day—his *talibs* gave Khan a reason to protect the supply lines. They shared the money left after Khan had paid his army. He did whatever was necessary to keep The Big One. "I'll take care of your nephew. You'll receive the blood money."

"I'm happy that you agree."

But you'd be happier to save face, wouldn't you? "You can have a man go to Chorah. We'll give him a uniform again." Khan smiled. If the attack in Safad Khare wasn't enough, then he'd use this stupid *talib* again to keep reminding the Americans that they needed him. "The Americans are going to the District Center and I can put your man inside to shoot them."

"That's Noorzai's area." The Big One fought Noorzai often. "He will agree to that?"

"You must trust me."

"As I did the last time?" The Big One looked behind him, down the shadowed road, and back to Khan. "When will this happen?"

"We'll meet again and I'll tell you. But soon."

Khan hugged him to seal the pact. The Big One waved goodbye and Khan went away in the opposite direction, headlight on this time. As he cut through the dark, he prayed for the second time that day—*Today I fought to keep what I've earned*—and sped back to his mansion.

DAN LEARNS WHAT MAKES AN ENEMY

Multinational Base Tarin Kowt, Tarin Kot District, Uruzgan Province, Afghanistan, 15 October 2012—

Jet-lagged, Dan eventually did try to sleep but could only stare at the plywood ceiling. He lay there all night until someone pounded, hard, on the door of his hut. Sunlight speared through the palpitating door. Dan answered in his underwear.

Aaron, fully dressed, trembling from too much caffeine, frowned. "Get your shit on." He put his hand on Dan's shoulder. Aaron spoke with an Arkansas lilt, like a slack guitar string, but his hand was harder than iron. "I know you're probably real tired and all that but we got work to do. Get dressed, find your pistol and notebook, meet me at the truck."

Dan tore through his bags—for the only other civilian shirt he had packed—dressing fast but taking a long time to find a magazine for his pistol. *Get your shit together,* he thought as stress-sweat poured from his forehead. He found one, in his third bag, and ran outside.

"Sorry, Aaron," Dan said as he opened the door to the 4Runner. "I had to find rounds for my pistol."

Aaron set his sunglasses on his nose. The sky was cloudless and glassy. Dan wanted to go back for his sunglasses but didn't want to hold Aaron up any longer. "You good? Can we leave sometime today?"

Dan buckled, then unbuckled. "Wait—I need my body armor, right?"

"No, dummy. We're not going outside the wire."

Aaron ripped through the gravel out of the SPU compound, into the larger base. They turned the corner and sped down a long corridor covered with more gravel. The entire stretch, six football fields long and two wide, was graveled.

"What's with the gravel everywhere?" Dan said.

"Rain," Aaron said without looking away from the road.

"It doesn't rain in the desert."

"It *does* rain here and without the gravel we wouldn't be able to get off the FOB. It'd be a mud bath. Whoever's crushing rock is making a billion dollars." He looked at Dan. "Wish it was me." They turned again, along the airstrip. "What happened at the clinic with that guy who got blown up?"

Dan stared out of the window, hypnotized by the mountain ranges, wondering how many Taliban they hid. *Where are they?*

"Dan, pay attention."

"Sorry. It was good."

"What's the guy's name?"'

"Toor Jan."

"What's his real name?"

"Toor Jan," Dan said.

"No, that's a nickname, dummy. Toor is Pashto for black. Jan means dear. It's like calling him—" Aaron let a groan escape from his throat "—the sweetie with dark skin."

"Well shit," Dan said. "I don't know his real name."

"Really taking to this line of work, huh?"

"I'm trying." *Motherfucker.* "At least I told him that I put him on the MEDEVAC."

Aaron slapped Dan hard on the chest. "Maybe there is some hope for you. You need to go see him again and work that angle."

Dan chuckled. "The mystery man without a real name."

Aaron looked over. "Yeah, whatever, dummy."

A Cessna took off down the runway and Aaron screamed, racing alongside it down the road. The 4Runner shook like it might explode. Dan watched a tessellating crack in the windshield to keep calm. He didn't look away until they were finally beat by the ascending airplane and Aaron slowed down.

"What are we doing?"

"Really?" Aaron's blond curls fell over his sunglasses and he tossed them back. With their relaxed grooming standards, Aaron's hair had grown long. "You don't know?"

"No, I don't know."

Aaron grinned. "Why not?"

"I just got here yesterday. I don't know anything."

"We're doing a turnover meeting with Mazzy Star."

"What's that?"

"He's an Afghan Police Colonel."

"What'd you call him?"

"Mazzy Star."

"Why do you call him that?"

"We give the sources dumb code names." Aaron reached down to the cup holder, snapped open a sweating aluminum can and loudly sucked the energy drink. "He's been a waste of time so far."

"Then why do you talk to him?"

"Because he's friends with MHK."

"That's the Mir Hamza Khan guy, right? Why would his friend talk to us?"

Aaron smiled. "Because old Mazzy Star owes us. Just like your buddy Toor Jan."

"How?

"Two or so years ago a guy came up to Mazzy Star's son while he was playing and gave him a golden ball." Aaron took his hands off the steering wheel to make air quotes as he said golden ball. "Told the kid that if he broke the golden ball open with a rock, candy would come out." Aaron looked away from the road at Dan. They swerved head-on toward a truck labeled Gray-Water. Aaron righted the 4Runner at the last second. "You really think it was a golden ball?"

"I don't know. Maybe?"

"No, dummy, it was a bomb. The guy told the kid to wait until he left, the guy left, the kid hit the bomb, bomb blew up in his face." He took another gulp of his energy drink. "They tried to kill Mazzy Star's son."

The 4Runner fishtailed. Dan gripped the overhead bar. "Who tried to kill him?"

"Taliban." Aaron put the energy drink back in the cup holder and raised his hands from the wheel—accelerating the entire time—to make air quotes again. "The so-called Taliban."

"I'm kind of lost on the basics, Aaron."

Aaron unleashed a wet burp. "What basics?"

"Everything." A hot flash consumed Dan's face. "I didn't get to train with you guys. I didn't know I was coming to Tarin Kowt. I mean, I don't even know where to start."

"The enemy." Aaron drove dangerously close to the HESCO barrier wall, burlap and steel wires bulging, to avoid a convoy of oncoming, brightly painted jingle trucks. "Start with them."

"The so-called Taliban?"

"No, dummy, *the enemy*." They approached a red Conex box hidden in a culvert of tall cement T-Walls. Aaron parked the 4Runner beside the white pickup truck Qais drove. He was already inside. Aaron got out of the 4Runner. He smoothed the front of his jeans and his light blue mountaineering jacket swung open, revealing an MP5, a German submachine gun. Dan whistled. Dan became a spy to be cool. Aaron's gun was very cool. "You like that?"

Dan nodded and got out of the car, squinted in the bright sun.

"That's adorable. Keep your head in the game, dummy."

"I am," Dan said. "You never explained why Mazzy Star owes us."

"So his kid is hurt bad. I saw the pictures. Gruesome." Aaron twisted his lips. "He comes to the base, son in his arms, begs for help. Our doctors saved the kid's life. Little Abdullah. Probably big Abdullah now. Mazzy Star has come in for meetings with every intelligence collector team since."

71

"But doesn't tell us anything valuable?"

"Of course not," Aaron said. "He's torn between MHK and us. Maybe one day he'll finally spill the beans. But I don't think so. He's MHK's prince."

"I thought you said he was an Afghan Police Colonel."

"Don't take anything at face value, dummy." Aaron pointed. "See those guys?" A hundred yards away, at the main gate of the Tarin Kowt Base, five Afghans in khaki uniforms sat in the shadow of an American MRAP, their AK-47s unattended on the ground. "That's the Highway Police. They do Security Day. They're allegedly police officers. But really they're MHK and Mazzy Star's private army. Nothing here is what it looks like." Aaron opened the center console of the 4Runner, pulled out a roll of black fabric, and put it on his head. *A black beret.* "Ready?"

"The fuck is that?" Dan said, holding his laughter back.

"You'll learn, dummy," Aaron said and led Dan to the Conex box meeting room.

The meeting room smelled of cigarettes and body odor. The walls were wood-paneled, paper maps taped over them. Red carpets covered the windows. In the center, Qais and a small Afghan sat at a round table, huddled over tea. The small Afghan smiled at Aaron and Dan.

"Hello there!" Aaron said. "This is my friend I was telling you about, Colonel. He'll be meeting with you from now on."

"I hope your child recovers from his illness," Mazzy Star said through Qais. He stood and hugged Aaron. Aaron bent down and the beret almost fell off his head. "If God wills it you'll get home safely to take care of him."

"You told him you're going home?" Dan said.

"Yeah," Aaron said, backing toward the door. "My son got sick."

"What'd you say he had? So I don't fuck it up when he asks me how your kid's doing."

"Diabetes."

"Do they know what that is?"

"He seems to," Aaron said. He grabbed the door handle.

"You really got kids?"

"Yep." Aaron opened the door to leave. "Baby girl."

"Hey, what's this guy's *real* name?"

"Maziullah."

Leaning in the corner behind Maziullah was an AK-47 the color of a robin's eggshell.

"Hold on, Aaron," Dan said. "He has a gun."

Aaron laughed. "It's all good, part of his cover. He's doing liaison with us. We're the base security team. Ya good?"

"No, man. I'm really not. What do I do?"

"You improvise, dummy. We're all improvising." Aaron smiled, stepped out the door, then poked his head back in. "Ride back with Qais." He touched his black beret in salute and slammed the door shut. The 4Runner started up and drove away.

Maziullah poured tea for Dan. Qais told him to drink. It burned his tongue but he gulped it down anyway. Dan put his glass on the table and looked tensely at the rifle.

"That's a great gun, man." *Did you really just say that?* "I like it."

"Thank you," Maziullah said. He had an incessant, polite laugh. The bristles of a well-used toothbrush peeked out of his breast pocket. They were silent again, for a while.

"Where'd you get it?"

"From God." Maziullah picked it up, removed the magazine, and pulled back the bolt to show an empty chamber. He handed the shining gun over. Dan turned it, feeling the smoothness of the colored finish. He couldn't tell if it was made of precious stone or painted. It felt alive, warm as a sleeping baby.

"God gave this gun to you?"

"He gave it to an old *mujahedeen* named Abdul Wali, who killed many Russians during that war. Abdul Wali had a dream that Jibreel, peace be upon him, showed him the place in the mountains where God put this gun. He went to that place and found it buried under a rock." He motioned to the blue rifle. "Before Abdul Wali died, he gave it to me so I could use it against the enemies of Uruzgan."

"That's amazing," Dan said. *Keep him talking*, he thought. *Improvise.* "Enemies? Who are the enemies?"

"Commander Aaron didn't tell you?" Maziullah took the AK-47 from Dan. It gleamed like a diamond in the light. "This rifle is used to kill the enemies of Uruzgan but it cannot be used for anything else. If you try it will not fire. But our enemies are easy to identify."

"Who are they?"

"Our enemies are the ones who forget their promises to Uruzgan."

THE PURPOSE OF TOOR JAN'S WALLS

Safad Khare, Tarin Kot District, Uruzgan Province, Afghanistan, 17 October 2012—

Toor Jan stood alone near the main gate of the American base. The tan ambulance, Red Crescent painted over the Red Cross, chugged away behind the set of barriers. He wore a dirty *kameez* that the American doctors had given him but he still had his own pants. The same sandals too, filled with gummy blood. *Shaheen.* The skin on his neck and arms raised. *I pushed her down and felt her hard belly against mine. Then she was gone.* Toor Jan had to get off the American base and find her.

Behind shining rolls of razor wire, Australian, American, and Afghan guards controlled the terminal leading to the city. Vehicles and people waiting to enter formed two lines. Leashed dogs, led by their pulsing noses, circled the cars. Each man in line was patted down. A guard with a finch's beak nose and wiry hair on his chin approached Toor Jan. He carried a radio and wore the khaki uniform of the General's Highway Police. "What are you doing here?" The guard unclipped the radio from his shirt and pointed the antenna at Toor Jan. "Who are you?"

"Toor Jan, son of Haji Izatullah."

"Why are you wandering around?"

Toor Jan pulled up the sleeve of his borrowed *kameez*, exposing the screws and the metal rod splinting his broken arm. "The American doctors left me here. I need to get home."

"Are you from the country?"

"Yes."

"I'll show you the way." The guard wrapped his arm around Toor Jan's waist and walked him toward the gate. He reached down and fingered his pocket for money.

Toor Jan moved away. "Thank you, I see how to leave."

The guard lashed Toor Jan's back with the radio antenna, then joined a group of Highway Policemen lounging against a concrete wall.

Toor Jan reached down, his sleeve stiff with dried blood, to feel the money from The Good American. He had visited Toor Jan in the clinic again and gave him enough money for his trip home and a week's worth of food. Toor Jan thought that he might save some of the money for a midwife for Shaheen. *Because she is alive and waiting for me at home.*

The Good American had promised Toor Jan that, if he could find a way back to the American base in two weeks, a doctor would check on the splint and remove the stitches in his hip. Before leaving, The Good American mentioned that Toor Jan should call him if he learned about attacks that *talibs* might be planning. He didn't want Toor Jan to be wounded by those bastards again. The heavy roll of cash pressed against his hip stitches as Toor Jan walked and he thought of his uncle. *The Big One knows Shaheen is pregnant. Of course we would see the American doctors. Why would he do that to us?*

Limping, Toor Jan exited the base into a shadowed corridor of high concrete walls poxed with shrapnel holes. He turned sideways to avoid the cars inching through. The corridor opened into a wide lot. A herd of sheep worked, heads down, for sprouts of grass. Their boy shepherd picked through a discarded pile of American boots. Old men, about six of them, stood in a group and watched Toor Jan come into the lot. Two policemen, rifles slung, scanned the long avenue that ran past General Khan's mansion, through the city, all the way to the Teri Bridge.

Safad Khare was across the Teri Bridge, beyond the distant sand hills. Eleven kilometers. Toor Jan tested his hip. Pain burned to the bone. *I'll crawl the entire way, if I have to.* Toor Jan crouched, half-concealed by a parked dump truck. He inhaled, deeply. Strength grew inside of him. *She's alive, she's alive, she's alive.* He stepped out to walk home.

A small man stopped him.

The small man wore a perfectly black turban. A graying beard. He had a blue rifle slung across his chest. The gun and the way his beard was well-kept commanded respect. The police officers saluted, while the old men put their hands over their hearts, and the small man ignored them all for Toor Jan. "May peace be upon you. How are you? How is your family?"

"And may peace be upon you, my dear sir," Toor Jan said. He felt frightened of the small man. "I'm fine. How are you? How is your family?"

"Everything is good in my home. Are you Toor Jan? Son of Haji Izatullah?"

"I am," Toor Jan said.

The man pointed to a Toyota Hilux, its windows—except for a thin strip of the windshield—tinted black, parked at the edge of the lot. "We have a car to take you home."

Toor Jan respectfully placed his hand over his heart. "I'm sorry but I can't afford a car like that."

"There's no charge, Toor Jan."

"Who are you, my dear sir?"

"I'm Colonel Maziullah. I work for General Haji Mir Hamza Khan. Do you know him?"

"How could I not?" Down the street, in the traffic circle, the general's balding head on The Hero of Peace and Unity billboard rose above the buildings. "Why would he help me?"

"You were wounded in the attack in Safad Khare by that dog, The Big One?"

"Yes." He narrowed his eyes. "That dog almost killed me."

"Then it's our duty to care for you."

Toor Jan's heart nearly popped when he opened the door of the Hilux and discovered General Khan sitting inside. General Khan offered a limp hand to Toor Jan. He was lanky and dressed as a common man. His teeth were big, white, and straight. Like Maziullah, General Khan's face seemed to be made entirely of jaw and nose. He was unspoiled except for his eyes, tainted yellow like polluted air. "Come inside, my friend," General Khan said. "We've been expecting you. May peace be upon you. How are you? How is your family? How do you feel today?"

Toor Jan giggled, nervous. "And may peace be upon you, my dear sir. How are you? How is your family? I hope you're not bored talking with someone like me."

The General placed his hand over his heart. "You're one of my people. I'm here to fix the mistake I made by not protecting you properly."

"Do you know anything about my family? I lost my wife when I was wounded."

General Khan looked at Maziullah. He shrugged. "You don't know, Toor Jan?"

"No," he said. "It's been four days."

General Khan leaned over to his driver. "As fast as you can."

The tinted Hilux rocketed into the city. Everything, man or animal, leapt away, knowing who it carried. They reached the Teri Bridge faster than Toor Jan had ever made the trip in his life. After the tires left the buzzing concrete of the bridge and transitioned to the whispers of sandy track, Toor Jan leaned forward, eager along the approach to Safad Khare. General Khan held his hand. A traditional song warbled on the radio's tape deck.

The people of Safad Khare saw the dust from the Hilux as it crested and dipped through the hilly country. When it entered the village, they ran after the truck all the way to Toor Jan's compound, then released a collective gasp at seeing General Khan through the windshield. Toor Jan slowly got out. He parted the crowd and shuffled toward his compound. The gate was open. Abdul Hakim appeared and screamed at seeing him. It was the first time Toor Jan was happy to see the gate unlocked. "Brother!" Toor Jan said, hugging Abdul Hakim. He ran his fingers through Abdul Hakim's hair. "Where is Shaheen?" Abdul Hakim pointed to the house and Toor Jan did everything he could to stop from crying. He'd call Shaheen out after the crowd left.

General Khan left the tinted Hilux and opened the lift gate. Inside there was a month's worth of food. The people rushed to take the bags of rice and yellow jugs of cooking oil but Maziullah threatened them with his dazzling rifle. "This is for my dear friend Toor Jan," General Khan said. A palsied smile broke over Abdul Hakim's face and he carried the heavy bags of rice, three at a time, into the house. General Khan walked toward Toor Jan, arms out, and pulled him close. "I failed you, Toor Jan," General Khan said. "I hope this will make it right."

"Thank you, General."

The tinted Hilux drove away. Everyone turned toward Toor Jan. They saw the metal splint, the dried blood on the sleeve. Sitting in the tinted Hilux, a stitch in his hip had torn and blood had soaked through his borrowed *kameez*. They all ignored Toor Jan's suffering.

"We have been affected too," Mirwais, the most powerful village elder, said. His beard was as white as snow on the mountains. "We deserve some of the food too."

A group of suspicious Barakzais had also formed. They saw the tinted Hilux and knew that their enemy was inside. Toor Jan worried that he would now be their enemy too. Instead they begged like the rest.

"Toor Jan," said Haji Daoud speaking for them, "everyone here knows your uncle." Nearby, Gran held his rifle at the ready. "But what if the General found out? That would be bad for you."

I have a better beard than you, so-called elder. Toor Jan tried not to smile at the thought.

"But if you share your prize, he doesn't have to know," Haji Daoud said.

"At least don't give that food to your idiot brother," Gran said.

Toor Jan raised his hands, demanding silence with a princely air. "Do you see who my friends are? I'm an important man, now. After I recover I will show all of you my great hospitality." He yelled, "Close it up!" to Abdul Hakim, who slammed the metal doors shut on the crowd.

Shaheen stood behind the almond tree—green *burkha* on in case she was called outside—and when Toor Jan turned she fell to her knees. Toor Jan sprinted toward her, or tried to. He fell halfway. Abdul Hakim picked him up by his armpits and carried him to Shaheen.

The two looked each other over, their survival a miracle, and Shaheen lingered on the ugly metal splint in Toor Jan's arm. Toor Jan shook with gratitude to God that Shaheen hadn't been hurt. They kissed in front of Abdul Hakim.

"How did you escape?" Toor Jan asked. He looked at Abdul Hakim. Abdul Hakim looked at the ground. "You?"

Shaheen nodded.

"There was noise and I ran outside. I saw sister and took her."

Toor Jan only nodded, careful to not show too much of his approval. He didn't want Abdul Hakim to think that it would *always* be good to go outside. Shaheen hooked her tiny hand inside Toor Jan's elbow and led him toward the house. "Was that the General?"

"Yes it was," Toor Jan said as he and Abdul Hakim followed the pregnant girl inside.

"Why would he help people like us?"

Toor Jan paused. Even he was startled by the good luck. "He's our protector."

The girl thanked God and said no more.

Toor Jan's family had an enormous dinner. Spinach with potatoes and onions. Full, the three of them sat on the pillows and quietly burped. After Shaheen and Abdul Hakim drifted to sleep, Toor Jan kissed them both on their foreheads. He went outside, into the dark.

The yard had been swept as smooth as glass, making the hobbling on his ragged hip easier. The almond tree cast slivered shadows across the compound walls. Toor Jan walked along them, trailing his finger over the mud bricks to feel where they crumbled. He pushed on the gate to ensure it was locked.

The compound walls had been built by his father, Haji Izatullah, to keep things out of the house, to stop the animals and robbers and mad men from coming inside and harming the family. But the walls had another purpose that Toor Jan was beginning to understand. His family was his kingdom. Abdul Hakim's smiling and eager aping. Shaheen's growing belly and delicate clavicles showing through her dress. Their house, tiny but unconstricting. They were everything to Toor Jan. Outside, in the dark, Toor Jan thanked God for his survival and for the mud walls around his family. Those walls had been built by his father to keep things away.

In Toor Jan's time, they held everything he loved safely inside.

SECURITY DAY

Tarin Kowt City, Tarin Kowt District, Uruzgan Province, Afghanistan, 20 October 2012—

One hundred hired trucks, idling and charged engines shaking, pulling trailers, moving gravel, gray water, fuel; the Chinese and Korean haulers with exhaust pipes turned vertical against their square cabs, blowing choking fumes above the *bazaar*; all of them waiting, their line stretched through Tarin Kowt City, past Haji and Byat Hyatullah's car shop, the new *masjid*, the old *masjid,* the internet café, the fueling station with its single pump, the radio shop, Mir Hamza Khan's mansion, curled around the traffic circle, past the jail and all the way to the foot of the Teri Bridge.

In the city, behind the shadowed stalls of the *bazaar*, from deep-set doorways, under the awnings of evergreens, in kabob-shops backlit by flames, at the counter of the *naan* baker, peeking off of roofs, a thousand Uruzgani eyes watched the trucks, empty now but soon to be packed with everything they needed for life. A thousand eyes, praying for the safety of the trucks, believing in the power of Mir Hamza Khan.

All along the great line, at disciplined intervals, were armored Toyota pickups, each fitted with a machine gun. Their drivers and men—local Popalzais who had farmed dirt before this, their single qualification an oath of fealty to Mir Hamza Khan—were members of the Highway

Police. They wore the best kit the West could offer: low-profile body armor, polarized sunglasses, radios connected to headsets, even the lightweight helmets of the American Special Forces. They had night-vision devices in case weather delayed them and forced the convoy to ride after dark. These men would guide the train through the peril of Uruzgan—bombs, grenades, *talibs* like ants on a bone—to the depot in Kandahar and back again.

An American supply clerk and Colonel Maziullah, standing wobbly in the bed of a police Ford Ranger, started at the back of the line and worked their way forward, the American supply clerk with a clipboard in hand, Colonel Maziullah with his blue gun, between them a pallet as big as a stove stacked with bricks of money provided by the Americans. *Rupees*—the national *afghanis* worthless—were given out to each man in the armored Toyotas, half now and half when they returned. Colonel Maziullah, greeted as a hero, counted out the bills, the American supply clerk made his notation, and together they sped on to the next vehicle. It took nearly half an hour to finish, the thousand eyes of Tarin Kowt City forced to don scarves to shield themselves from the dust and pollution.

Colonel Maziullah then took his place at the head of the line—a colorful snake, each truck a rusted, peeling scale. The American supply clerk hopped from the bed to return to base. Colonel Maziullah lifted his blue rifle in the air, pressed a sport whistle to his lips, and blew. All down the snake, sport whistles answered his call and the rumble began.

Wheels thundering over stone and dirt, they rolled forward across the bridge, the last truck crossing the Teri nearly ten minutes after the call of the whistle, the snake slithering into the hills and mountains, watched by a thousand hungry eyes, until its tail whipped around the curving rock and was gone.

TOOR JAN DREAMED INTENSELY
OF ALL THE TINY THINGS

Multinational Base Tarin Kowt, Tarin Kot District, Uruzgan Province, Afghanistan, 27 October 2012—

Shaheen had found The Good American's money in Toor Jan's pocket while doing the wash. She put it into her dress—after Toor Jan had left to dig a ditch in exchange for twenty *rupees*—and slung his rifle over her shoulder just to know what the weight of power felt like. Abdul Hakim clapped as she strutted around. That evening, Shaheen returned the pants to Toor Jan without the money inside. After Abdul Hakim had gone to sleep, he confronted her. "Why did you steal from me, Shaheen?"

Shaheen reached into her dress and threw the money at him. "Did you tell the Americans about The Big One?"

He grabbed her face with his good arm and growled through his beard. "If you ever do that again—" Her tears dripped down his fingers. "Don't cry, Shaheen *Jo*. I didn't tell them anything."

"Then how?" She said. "How did you get that much money?"

"They gave it to me because I was wounded." He kissed the white line where her hair parted. "That's all."

"You didn't say anything to the Americans?" She pushed herself away to get a good look at him. In the dark Toor Jan's face was only eyes and beard. "The Big One will kill you if you're spying."

"He already tried to kill me." He wiped her wet eyes. "This money is for us. How else can we survive?"

"When the winter is over you can ask Muhammad Zai to end his feud. Then you can farm poppies again."

Toor Jan's compound sat on land owned by a man named Muhammad Zai. Muhammad Zai was in a long fight with a man named Islam about the borders of the property. Last year, as Toor Jan scored poppy pods, three of Islam's sons drove their truck through his field. They pointed a gun at Toor Jan and said if he planted on their property again they would kill him. Toor Jan had no hope that this would be resolved. "When the winter is over, I'll ask Muhammad Zai again."

"You can't spy for the Americans."

"I won't."

"Swear it to me."

I love this girl too much. "I'll never spy for the Americans, Shaheen."

The next morning Toor Jan woke early. He had hired a taxi in the village to drive him to the American base for his doctor's appointment. Shaheen sleepily kissed him and reminded him of his promise to not help the Americans. He told her to go back to sleep.

Though there weren't many people on the road, half a kilometer away from the American base the taxi driver demanded that Toor Jan get out and walk. "I don't want anyone to think that I go to their base."

"Look at me." Toor Jan lifted his wounded arm. "You're driving an injured man to the best hospital in Uruzgan. No one cares that it's American."

But the driver wouldn't go any farther. Toor Jan refused to pay the full amount. He tossed a few bills into the driver's lap and pulled himself out of the vehicle. The car reversed fast, nearly skidding into a shop near the road. It turned and went speeding back to Safad Khare.

The American doctors had told Toor Jan that the tan ambulance would be waiting at the gate if he returned today. There was no truck, no doctors, no one except the line of people waiting to enter. He counted on his fingers twice to make sure of the date. *Today is the day*. His splinted arm ached, he needed *the damned metal out*. Toor Jan squatted. The air was dense with the smell of fuel. A dog—yellow fur mange-burned—barked. *The Good American*. On his cell phone, Toor Jan called the number The Good American had given him. The *tajiman* named Qais answered. "Who is this?" the *tajiman* asked without courtesy.

"Toor Jan, son of Haji Izatullah, from Safad Khare."

"Yes, hello, Toor Jan. May you never be tired!"

"I'm outside your base."

"Do you have information about the *talibs*?"

"No, sir. The doctors told me to come back today but they're not here. I must go to my medical appointment."

"Okay," Qais said. "Then we'll come get you."

Ten minutes after ending their call, the *tajiman* emerged from the cement corridor behind the gate and waved. Stiff from his wounds, Toor Jan followed Qais through the gate. A line of resentful people, waiting to be patted down, watched them enter. "They don't search us?"

"When you're with us, Toor *Janna*, you're too important to be searched."

Toor Jan's stomach went a little sick with pride. Just inside the gate, The Good American sat inside an idling 4Runner. He spun a white watch around his wrist. Qais and Toor Jan got in and The Good American shifted the gear with force and accelerated away.

"It's good to see you again, Toor Jan." The Good American turned hard and Toor Jan jumped a bit when the car jolted straight again. "Do you think anyone from your village followed you to the base?"

Toor Jan laughed. "Why would they do that?"

"You never know. Maybe they don't like people visiting this base." He turned again and the truck felt like it might tip. "Aren't you worried about someone being suspicious?"

"No." Toor Jan clutched the edge of his seat with his good arm to brace himself for the next turn. "I'm only here to get this metal out of my arm."

"Of course," The Good American said. "You think you can sit with me after your appointment? We can chat about what happened to you at the school."

Toor Jan hadn't forgotten his promise to Shaheen. "I have to get home to my family."

"That's too bad," The Good American said. "I brew good *chai*." They rode on, a runway to one side and barriers to the other, until they came to another guarded gate. The *tajiman* flashed a card and two of the General's Highway Policemen waved them through. Toor Jan recognized some of the buildings. They were close to the clinic. "By the way, have you heard about any planned attacks? Maybe something like the attack that hurt you?"

"No." Toor Jan suddenly realized that The Good American could have prevented what had happened to him at the school. Would Shaheen be mad if Toor Jan told The Good American about something like that? "I'm not a man who knows about dangerous things."

"Okay, Toor Jan. I understand."

They parked in the ambulance bay of the clinic. The Good American and the *tajiman* took Toor Jan by the arms and led him inside. Qais was heavy with perfume and The Good American smelled as if he had worked outside all day.

The doctor was a woman. She asked Toor Jan to roll down his pants and The Good American became embarrassed but Qais explained that, since there were no men doctors, it wasn't forbidden. The woman doctor removed the stitches in Toor Jan's hip. The threads stung as they passed through his skin. The spot was so tender that it seemed like it might break open again but she said that feeling would be gone in a few days. It would be some time before the screws could be taken from his arm. For now, the wounds needed to be cleaned and kept covered. The woman doctor gave him a bottle of pain medicine. Toor Jan took it, nodding with humility. After the woman doctor had finished, The Good American gave him a box of bandages and ointment and they drove the 4Runner back to the main gate. The Good American parked the truck but kept the engine running.

"It's an honor for me to help you, Toor Jan."

"I will always be grateful."

"I'm sorry you got hurt, Toor Jan. This is a dangerous country."

"I hope one day it is not like this."

"I do too." The Good American reached into his pocket for a roll of *afghanis*. "This is for a taxi home. Maybe some food."

"Thank you so much." Toor Jan made sure to smile. It was enough money for six weeks of food. He would hide it better this time. Maybe he'd buy Abdul Hakim a radio. "This helps my family."

"Can I ask you something, Toor Jan?" The Good American turned in his seat. "I'm your friend, right?"

"Yes, you are. A good one." He patted the money in his pocket. *The best friend I have.*

"You told me that someone in your own family hurt you. Who was it? I'm very powerful." Qais flexed his arm as he translated. "I can make sure you have revenge."

Toor Jan shrugged. He didn't break promises to Shaheen.

The Good American let his head hang, then smiled. "Do you have a job?"

There are no jobs in Uruzgan, Good American. There's only work and work never lasts. "I can't do the kind of job you want me to do."

"No, no, of course not, Toor Jan. Since I'm new here, I need to learn about Uruzgan quick. Maybe you could teach me and I'll pay you for the lessons."

"What about the *tajiman*?"

The Good American smirked at Qais. "He's too American." Qais punched The Good American in the arm.

"But I'm not educated."

"Do you know how to be a Pashtun?"

"Of course," Toor Jan said. "It's all that I am."

"Have you ever lived anywhere other than Safad Khare?"

"No, sir."

"Then you're the ideal teacher. Think about it. Call me if you decide to do it."

Toor Jan gripped the handle of the door. "With your permission?"

"Please. Go to your family."

Toor Jan carried the box of bandages into the parking lot. Everything looked new. The mountains around his valley. The belt of green cinching the Teri River. Even the sunlight had a different quality. Toor Jan never thought he knew anything worth teaching. *But I might. And if I only tell The Good American about our land and people then I'm not breaking my promise to Shaheen. I'm not spying.*

In the taxi back to Safad Khare, Toor Jan dreamed intensely about all of the tiny things he would teach The Good American.

KHOST'S VERY PLEASANT IDEA

Multinational Base Tarin Kowt, Tarin Kot District, Uruzgan Province, Afghanistan, 01 November 2012—

Commander Khost walked into the operations center without a word. A large screen dominated the scalloped end of the amphitheater-shaped room. Khost's seat was on the highest of four tiered rows. He slumped in his chair, belly hanging, and pressed his fingertips together. Lieutenant Josh Ramsey stood at the bottom, ready to brief the staff on the movement plan for the meeting in the Chorah District Center with the police chief Noorzai. The staff turned toward Khost.

"Let's hear it, Josh." And Khost watched as though he were listening, but really he worried about how he would convince his generals to keep their price for Security Day with General Khan. *General Khan. This kid hadn't even mentioned General Khan.* Lieutenant Ramsey finished his brief and waited for Commander Khost to respond. He didn't.

"Sir? Do you have any questions?" Lieutenant Ramsey said. His uniform blouse rode up over his muscular shoulders and, aware of Khost's inspecting stare, he pulled it down. "Is there something I didn't cover?"

Khost stood. "I do have one question." He paced down the row and back again. Everyone watched, eyes locked. Khost liked their fear. "Well, a name, actually." Khost, without meaning to, snorted. "General Haji Mir Hamza Khan." He almost bowed at the flourish of the General's full name. Lieutenant Ramsey stared at Khost. "I'll say it again. *General Haji Mir Hamza Khan.*"

Lieutenant Ramsey placed his hands behind his back. His uniform blouse lifted again, revealed his pistol. "I don't understand, sir."

"I believe it, Josh. Listening to that movement plan I believe you don't understand." Khost stood iron-straight. "Here's a better way—where's General Khan in all of this?"

"In what, sir?"

"We're going to Chorah to have a come-to-Jesus meeting with Noorzai." Khost paced down the aisle again. "I suspect it won't end well, honestly. Why haven't you included General Khan or any of his police officers?"

"To do what, sir?"

"Oh, I don't know." Khost had started shaking and he turned away from the staff for a moment to calm himself. "You can always use more gun trucks in the convoy."

Lieutenant Ramsey pointed to a schematic of vehicles on the screen. Khost hadn't paid attention to it. "The Afghan Commandos. We've already worked them into the plan."

Khost shook his head. "You don't think having General Khan sit at the table with you as you talk to Noorzai about his behavior is a good idea?"

Lieutenant Ramsey, neck streaked red with the heat of his own interior monologue, glared at Khost. Everyone in the room shook their heads imperceptibly at Lieutenant Ramsey. "Khan has a lot of issues, sir."

Isaiah Khost reached for a thick binder on his chair and threw it at Lieutenant Ramsey. It hit the tile in front of him with a crack, the sound surprising everyone even as they watched it happen. "Is General Khan the most powerful person in Uruzgan?"

"Yes he is, sir."

"And are we planning to leave this province in June?" Khost paused. "Better yet, are we trying to win this war by June?"

Lieutenant Ramsey pulled his head back.

"Are you all surprised to hear me say that?"

"Yes, sir," Lieutenant Ramsey said.

"What else would we be here for?" He scanned the faces in the room. *Bunch of ticket punchers and clock watchers.* "How do we win without including the biggest player?" Khost flopped down in his chair. "Someone go get Chamber. Get Khan on the phone. Over the speakers, right now." No one moved. Lieutenant Ramsey looked at his boots. "What did I just fucking say?" An officer ran out and returned with Chamber, pulled from his bed and wearing only jeans and a yellowed wife-beater. Khost didn't look at him. He sat with his fingers pressed together and watched Lieutenant Ramsey. The entire staff, thirty officers and five enlisted, stared straight ahead not even wanting to breathe. A dial tone came up over the loud speakers and Khost pointed to Chamber. Maziullah answered and after exchanging the traditional courtesies, Chamber asked if he could put on General Khan.

"Hello, Commander," General Khan said. "This is unexpected."

Khost thrust his head forward. "Talk to him, Josh."

Lieutenant Ramsey turned his hands up. "What would you like me to say, sir?"

"Maybe ask how he's doing? How his family is doing? He lost two men during the last Security Day. The man risks his life every day to serve his people." Chamber started to translate and Khost waved him off.

General Khan breathed into the phone. "Hello? Are you there, Commander?"

"General, this is Lieutenant Ramsey." He looked at his feet. "I work with the Afghan Commandos. How are you today? How is your family?"

"They are wonderful," General Khan said, his voice brightening up. "And how are you? How is your family? Have you spoken to them lately?"

"Everyone is good." Lieutenant Ramsey kept his chin pressed against his chest and lifting only his eyes toward Khost. "I'm sure you're aware but tomorrow a couple of us are going to Chorah to meet with Noorzai and bring him back on board." General Khan said nothing and Khost implored Lieutenant Ramsey to continue with a quick motion of his hands. "What exactly do you want me to ask him, sir?"

Khost smiled. *Now you're learning, kid.* "Ask him if he wants to come to Chorah with you." Lieutenant Ramsey asked and General Khan laughed. He had many other more important things to do. Khost nodded. "Now ask him if he wants to send some of his guys along, they can ride along in those green trucks they have."

Lieutenant Ramsey breathed loudly out of his nose. "General Khan, would you want to supply a few trucks and men to come along with us?"

Khost crossed his arms over his chest and leaned back. "Say please, *Lieutenant.*"

Lieutenant Ramsey looked up and stared at Khost. His hand shook. He balled it into a fist. "*Please.*"

"Of course!" General Khan said. "But I can only spare one truck tomorrow. I hope that helps."

"That would be great, General," Khost said. "We'll be in touch later today with the details." He waved for them to hang up. Chamber and Lieutenant Ramsey put their arms behind their backs. Everyone else, filling the rows of the amphitheater, turned in their chairs to Khost. If they were made of glass he'd break them all right now. "Now, do you understand what I mean by winning, Lieutenant Ramsey?"

Lieutenant Ramsey smirked. Wiped his hand over his face. "I think what you call winning is just a very pleasant idea, sir." And he turned to leave the room.

And none of you will ruin my very pleasant idea, Khost thought as he watched the kid walk away.

MIR HAMZA KHAN TEACHES
MAZIULLAH HOW TO SURVIVE

Tarin Kowt City, Tarin Kot District, Uruzgan Province, Afghanistan, 01 November 2012—

On the way to Mir Hamza Khan's mansion for lunch, Maziullah wanted to drive through the traffic circle to see if he could spot a *talib*. The *talibs* thought they blended in but they were country people, easily recognized from city people. Maziullah wanted to laugh at them as they passed. Maziullah drove with his gun across his lap, came to the traffic circle, and zippered in with the other carts, cars, trucks, walkers and motorcycles. He opened his tinted window and looked for *talibs*. There were none. Just a boy with two goats.

Khan thought about the American Commander's strange call earlier in the day and how it made his plans easier. It was time he made his best friend understand. "There are no *talibs* in the city today."

"We'll go around the circle again to make sure?" Maziullah said.

"No," Khan said. "But I can show you a true *talib*."

"A true *talib*?" Maziullah accelerated, shooting out of the traffic circle toward Khan's mansion. "Where?"

"After we eat."

The guards opened the heavy doors as they drove into Khan's walled mansion. Behind a hedge of rose bushes, several guards were kicking a man on the ground. Their sleeves were rolled to their elbows and sweat dripped from their foreheads. The man on the ground twisted at each blow. Khan leapt from the truck before Maziullah had parked. "What's happening here?" The guards popped to stiff attention. The man on the ground curled into himself like a grub. "What are you doing?"

"He slept while on duty, general," a guard said. The others panted, looked straight ahead.

"Sleeping." Khan bent down and his back screamed. "Is that what you're supposed to do?" Dirt covered the sleeping guard's mouth and his eyes bulged. Khan slapped him across the face. "Is this what I pay you all of this money for? Why I took you from that shit village and brought you here? So a bomber can sneak into my home?" He followed each question with a slap. "So they can kill my family? So I can be killed?" Blood and slobber coated Khan's hand and he wiped it on the sleeping guard's pants. He turned to the other guards, "Continue to make him understand." Khan and Maziullah went inside to eat their meal. The beating resumed.

After their lunch, Mir Hamza Khan looked at Maziullah. "Now, we go to see a true *talib*. Give me the purple cell phone," Khan said. Maziullah was supposed to carry this cell phone in his modified vest but never use it. He followed that order faithfully. Khan dismissed Maziullah and made the call alone.

It was Friday and most people were at the mosque for prayer when Khan and Maziullah arrived near the empty lot in the country. They left the Hilux hidden in a stand of trees and patrolled down the road. Maziullah prowled ahead with his lapis AK-47 and Khan scanned the road they had walked for signs of a follower. "Where are we going?" Maziullah said. He had noticed Khan's caution. "What is this?"

"We're close, Maziullah." Khan said. He let Maziullah move a short interval ahead and then continued. "Not much further."

The Big One stepped out from the trees.

Maziullah yelled and raised the blue rifle. The Big One hadn't known Maziullah would be there, either. He'd lost many men to Maziullah. They stared at each other.

Khan stepped between them. He liked to create tension between the men who worked for him. "Let's be quick," he said and looped his long arms around them. They pushed into the trees. "Do you have a man selected?"

"We do," The Big One said. "It's all prepared."

"If you bring that man to the police checkpoint near the Chorah District Center we will get him inside."

"Where will Noorzai be?"

"I already told you that Noorzai won't stop your man."

"What's going on?" Maziullah said. He moved away from the two. "What are you talking about?"

"You don't know? Aren't you the General's best friend?" The Big One smiled. He pressed his left nostril closed, shot a wad of snot into the dirt, and turned back to Khan. "When will we do this?"

"Tomorrow," Khan said.

"Will you give him a weapon?"

"Yes."

"Then it's good, *Haji Sahib*."

They discussed the details for a few minutes more. Maziullah stared at his feet, without a word. The Big One left. Khan and Maziullah walked back toward their truck. Maziullah looked back several times but Khan, happy, pretended not to care about who might be following.

"I know we use the *talibs*, general." Maziullah looked for a reaction in Khan's face. There was none. "But I never knew you were a friend of that dog. Never."

Khan smiled. "I told you that I'd show you a real *talib*."

Maziullah spat on the ground.

"My best friend, you are a scholar but there are some things even I can teach you."

"Like what, General?"

"How to make correct business choices."

Maziullah frowned and slung his burnished rifle over his back. "I don't understand."

"The Americans must not forget that it is dangerous here. That they must pay *us* for Security Day. We will show them with The Big One's stupid *talibs*."

"But Noorzai's our good friend."

Ahead, the trail tapered and Khan stopped Maziullah. "I will provide for him."

Maziullah shrugged Khan off. "*Haji Sahib*, we've been with Noorzai since the American invasion. What's there to earn if we sacrifice our oldest friend?"

Khan looked Maziullah in the eye. "We earn our survival in this way."

DAN LEARNS THAT ONLY
THE JOB MATTERS

Multinational Base Tarin Kowt, Tarin Kot District, Uruzgan Province, Afghanistan, 01 November 2012—

The smell of shit from the sewage ponds filled the Soviet Building. The others had been there so long they couldn't smell it anymore. Dan couldn't smell anything else. "You guys don't smell that? Seriously?" Aaron and Army Brian didn't look up from their ruggedized laptops as they wrote their intelligence reports. "If I have to wait here any longer I'm gonna puke."

"You'll wait until I'm done," Aaron said.

Today was Dan's last training session before Aaron left to join Lieutenant Ramsey's SEAL platoon on the other side of the base. In the past two weeks, Aaron had turned over all his sources and educated Dan on everything he had learned working at the SPU. Dan had trained for more than a year to do this job but the two weeks with Aaron had taught him more than he'd ever learned in school.

"I mean, is there air freshener? Or maybe some spray? Can we light a candle?"

"Does this look like a college dorm?" Army Brian said. He pulled a chewed-down cigar from his pocket and clenched it in his teeth. He turned in his folding chair, leaned back with his hands behind his head, and smiled, the unlit cigar drooping from his mouth. "You're a little spoiled, aren't you, Danny boy?"

"I guess so," Dan said and touched the white G-Shock watch on his wrist, another suggestion from Aaron. Aaron wore the black beret during source meetings because the silly thing made him feel like someone else was manipulating the sources, not the *real* Aaron. The real Aaron would never wear a beret. He told Dan to do the same. Dan chose the gaudy white sports watch. "You excited to leave, Aaron?"

"Hell yeah." Aaron finished typing, hitting the last two keys hard, and stood. His machine gun was on the table. "Get over here."

Dan sat down at the laptop and looked at Aaron's gun. "I love that MP5."

"Pay attention, dummy." Aaron stood over Dan, wheeling the mouse across the screen. "You know why the system keeps rejecting your intelligence reports?"

"Obviously not, or I wouldn't have asked you." Dan elbowed Aaron and took control of the mouse.

"It's your heading format. The system is super finicky."

"Show me," Dan said.

Aaron typed into a blank report format: **Multinational Base Tarin Kowt, Tarin Kot District, Uruzgan Province, 01 November 2012—**

"What you have to do is put the exact location of whatever's being reported, starting from the smallest geographical location possible and working out to the largest. See that?"

"Yeah," Dan said, scrutinizing the format. "Why?"

"So the nerds who do the analyzing can put all the pieces together. Cross-checking, verifying. All that shit." Aaron picked up the MP5. "And that's that. You're a spy now."

"Can I hold it?" Dan said, reaching for the gun.

"You really like this thing, don't you?"

"It's very practical. More rounds than my pistol but still concealable."

"Stop playing it cool." Aaron smirked. "It looks pretty badass too, huh?"

"Yeah, of course."

"I'll give it to you."

"Can you do that?"

"Yeah, dummy. I can't take this on ops. It'll just be sitting around."

"How?"

"I officially sign it over to you, then you'll sign it back over to me when we go back home in June." He lifted the gun toward Dan, the strap chinking against the plastic. "Simple."

"Wow. Thanks so much, Aaron."

"Whatever, dummy."

Dan loosened the gun's sling and put it over his shoulder. "You're going out tomorrow, right?"

"Yeah," Aaron said. He looked around the room. The Afghan flags on the wall bubbled with the circulating air of the Chigo. "I'm pulling security for that meeting with Noorzai." He walked over to a paper map on the wall and touched Chorah District in the northeastern portion of Uruzgan. "In the District Center."

"Is it dangerous up there?"

"Nah. It's gonna be stupid easy." Aaron turned for the front door. "I'll see you later."

Dan didn't want Aaron to leave. He wasn't sure he could do it alone yet. "Hey, wait a minute," he called after Aaron and followed him out into the bright sun, to the firepit. Aaron's Arkansas Razorbacks flag waved from the yardarm above. "Hold on," Dan said, tapping Aaron's shoulder. "You got any, like, parting words of wisdom?"

"What are you talking about, dummy?"

"Is there anything else I need to know?"

Aaron looked up at his Arkansas Razorback flag and then back on Dan. "Do what you think needs to be done. No matter what."

"Okay."

"But make sure you do it so Beau doesn't get into trouble. He's looked out for all of us." He spat into the firepit's ashes. "Get the job done. Only the job matters. *Dummy.*"

Aaron walked away, disappearing behind the row of plywood huts. A breeze swirled ash with the smell of the shit ponds and snapped Aaron's flag high above Dan's head.

PART II

QASSIM

***Chorah District Center, Chorah District, Uruzgan Province,
Afghanistan, 02 November 2012—***

The Big One had chosen Qassim personally—or that's what Qassim had been told—and the *talib* commander had made every preparation for him to travel to the Chorah District Center and shoot an American. All Qassim needed to carry was a light heart prepared for death. The only condition Qassim imposed on the *talibs* was that his father would be paid when the operation was finished. Qassim's father was old and blind. He sat in a corner of their small mud hut and hadn't moved since Qassim began growing hair above his lip. The *talibs* promised that his father would be cared for and proud that his son was *shahid*, a martyr.

After curfew, Qassim heard the thin whine of a motorcycle from high on the mountain road and his heart beat fantastically. The motorcycle was coming out of the night to take him. When the rider on the green Kawasaki stopped outside, Qassim kneeled before his father and kissed his forehead. "I love you, *baba*."

"Do well, my little *zoya*."

Qassim walked out and didn't look back, afraid he might lose his courage. The rider's face was wrapped in a scarf, eyes like black lanterns. He summoned Qassim to sit behind him and grip him tight. They started like a gunshot. Qassim couldn't let go to wipe away his streaming tears as they bounced across the dead land.

The rider led them out of the valley onto a vast plateau. The shade of night passed like a panorama swarmed with *djinn*. Qassim closed his eyes, not opening them again until the rider switched the motorcycle's engine off and coasted toward a police checkpoint. Underneath the checkpoint's awning, police officers, wrapped in brown blankets, squatted around a fire. Their naked heads bobbed in the flickering light. A frail boy, not much younger than Qassim, danced around them. The scavengers watched him.

The rider nodded. Qassim shook his head. The rider pointed his chin toward the dance. Qassim refused again. *The police hate talibs. Why am I here?* The rider elbowed Qassim in the stomach. Qassim left the motorcycle and the rider held out his hand for payment. Obediently, Qassim pressed two coins—from his *talib* trainer—into the rider's palm. The rider started the engine and returned into the black night. Qassim was too scared to move.

A police officer came over. He was a small, hard man. His hair was black and his skin was the color of milk tea. He wore a moustache. "Are you hungry?"

"No."

"Thirsty?"

Qassim couldn't look at the police officer. "Where am I?"

"Close to Chorah District Center," he said. "You'll sleep here. I will come find you when we're done."

The police officer nosed Qassim onto a canvas cot inside the checkpoint. The watery shadows of the men came through the door and passed across the ceiling as they grunted and took their turns with the *chai* boy. *Not me, not ever,* Qassim thought. He looked around for a weapon, rifle, pistol, stick, or shard of glass. There was nothing. Qassim rehearsed—in his mind—what he would do if the police officers came inside to rape him. He'd keep his honor and be *shahid* in a different way than he'd intended.

In the morning, the police officer stood above Qassim. "Get up, boy." Qassim didn't move, stared straight up at the timber joists of the roof, arms crossed over his chest, holding his shoulders. "I said get up." He pulled on Qassim's wrists. Stronger than a bear, the officer lifted him out of the cot. Qassim made his body soft, heavy, loose. "What are you doing? Stand up." The police officer had a Makarov pistol on his belt. *If he tries to shame me I will grab it.* "Are you here to kill Americans or not?"

"Yes." Qassim said, awoken by those words. "But I will not be used to please any of you," he said and got to his feet, nearly a head above the police officer.

"You're not here for that, boy," the police officer told him. "Follow me."

Outside, under the leaning awning, he offered Qassim weak *chai* and *naan*, but Qassim couldn't even think of eating without feeling like vomiting. After the other police officers finished breakfast, they gathered their weapons and the police officer told Qassim to get into his police truck. The *chai* boy cleaned the mess left behind. Qassim watched him—under the *chai boys* henna-stained fingernails there was something darker, *blood and skin*—as they drove off. Qassim felt grateful to survive the night without shame.

Morning had only just entered the valley but the road to the Chorah District Center was busy. The police truck's horn blew at the wooden carts, sedans, groups of women, men broken with grisly age, all clogging the road. Qassim hid his face with his hand, yet couldn't stop watching.

He had the special knowledge that all people seek—Qassim knew how and when he would die. *They are alive but I'm free.* It was the first time in his life he had felt exceptional.

The police truck entered a high-walled and heavily guarded government building. The small, hard police officer turned to Qassim. "Stay here. Don't move."

Qassim waited for an hour in the hot cab until two other police officers, their eyes empty from smoking opium, opened the truck's door. They dragged him into the building, down a dark hall to a converted jail cell, slammed the door behind him, and threw the rough bolt. Dread welled inside of Qassim. *Why am I locked away like an animal?* He paced the cell, no bigger than a coffin. *What happens to my father?* Qassim vomited, the stream of it thin without food, on the floor. *Will I ever be a martyr?*

The bolt on the door screeched. The small, hard police officer entered, holding an AK-47 and a bundle of clothes tied with a belt. Qassim jumped to hug him, relieved to see someone familiar. The small, hard police officer undid the belt and shook out a stained blue police uniform. He noticed Qassim's dirty toenails. "*Hadith* says that there's no need to wash a *shahid*'s body. The martyr is cleaned by his own blood. You will wash Uruzgan clean today."

The Redeemer of Uruzgan, Qassim removed his vest, turban, and *kameez*, folding them neatly in the corner as if he would return for them. He tucked the large police uniform blouse into the pants and wrapped a huge leather belt around his waist. Qassim reached for the rifle but the small, hard police officer held tight. "Do you understand how to use this?"

Qassim nodded.

"You'll be on the roof. You'll talk to no one when you're up there. They're coming in the late afternoon. You must shoot the Americans that stay in the courtyard after the others are led into this building. Do you understand?"

Qassim nodded again. The small, hard police officer led him outside.

It was difficult to climb the building's wall with the baggy uniform catching on the steel ladder. Qassim hoped to make it to the top without being dragged down by the rifle hanging off of his back. Two other police officers, already on the roof, rushed to pull him up as he flung himself over the last rung, but Qassim pushed them off. After that they ignored him—except to offer fresh *chai*.

Soon, the low grinding of American trucks echoed close, their column raising dust that coated the leaves of the poplar trees. *I'll miss those leaves*, Qassim thought. The trucks stopped in front of the building and the Americans came out. Qassim's stomach heaved.

Six Americans walked into the courtyard. One moved below Qassim's perch. He was thin with blond curls that sprang out from under his helmet. His skin was the color of honey. The American spoke quietly into a radio before noticing the ladder. He climbed up and greeted the other two police officers in Pashto and shook their hands. The American turned to Qassim and put his hand over his heart. Qassim offered him a cup of *chai* and the two sipped while looking at each other.

The rest of the Americans went inside the District Center. The American standing with Qassim descended the ladder to the courtyard. He remained there for some time. Qassim waited, sweating through his uniform. He couldn't catch his breath. The American looked up at him twice, staring for a long time. Qassim gripped his rifle, wringing the sweat off his hands. Then the American bent to tie his bootlace.

Qassim raised his AK-47. The soft, exposed neck of the American bobbed in the rear sight. He was supposed to shout *Allah-u-Akbar* but forgot. Qassim pulled the trigger until the muzzle climbed into the sky and the bolt clicked dry.

The American collapsed into a spreading pool of black blood. The other Americans in the courtyard fired at Qassim. Their bullets sounded like bees. Qassim sent the empty AK-47 skidding across the rooftop and leapt onto the roof of a smaller, adjacent building. The bullets followed. *I want to live*, Qassim thought and jumped over the District Center wall into the street below. He ran hard against the fatigue and hunger in his body. He tripped several times but rolled quickly to his feet again, passing between closely packed buildings. *Where can I go?*

Ahead, the small, hard police officer appeared like a miracle, motioning wildly to an alley. Qassim ran toward him, then turned the corner. A green Ford Ranger, passenger door open, idled there. The small, hard police officer yelled at him to jump in the cab.

Qassim dove onto the bench seat. Through the open windows, the poplar leaves spread over the roofs. They turned silver in the breeze with their coating of dust. *How perfect.* The small, hard police officer walked toward the truck and removed his Makarov pistol from its holster. And as Qassim watched the leaves, happy to have a bit more life, the small, hard police officer fired into Qassim's skull, and the dark swirled down before the boy's eyes.

TOOR JAN'S MYSTERY
LOCKS TOGETHER

***Sarkhum, Tarin Kot District, Uruzgan Province, 02 November
2012—***

Toor Jan had gone to the radio shop in the *bazaar* and bought a
Chinese radio with the money from The Good American. Eager to show
Abdul Hakim that they didn't have to go all the way to the city to listen
to music anymore, he ran home and put the radio in the middle of their
room. Abdul Hakim crowded Toor Jan as he played with the dial,
clicking through the static to find the music station from Kabul. The
two brothers danced with each other. Shaheen clicked her tongue. "How
could you afford that?"

In the morning, as soon as Toor Jan woke, Shaheen asked again how
he could afford to buy the radio. He ignored her. She followed him to
the gate as he left to find work, her questions more intense, angrier. Toor
Jan dismissed her with a wave of his hand. That night, Shaheen waited
until he fell asleep and slapped him on the chest. Toor Jan woke with a
scream. She crawled up to his ear. "Who paid for that radio, Toor Jan?"

"The Good American gave me the money."

"You are spying."

"No, girl. To teach him about Uruzgan."

"Why would he need you to do that?"

"Because he's new." Toor Jan rolled away, then back to her. "He saved my life, Shaheen *Jo*. I have to help him somehow."

"Then leave us now, Toor Jan. Don't make us wait until he gets you killed." Shaheen tugged hard on her hair, thick from pregnancy. "And take your Chinese radio with you."

Toor Jan went to sleep on Abdul Hakim's side of the room after that.

The next day, Toor Jan's uncle invited him to a midday meal at his compound in Sarkhum. "They know, Toor Jan, they know," Shaheen said. Shaheen folded a blanket, unfolded it, grunted in anger, and then threw it at Abdul Hakim when he tried to hug her. "The *talibs* know you're an American spy. He's invited you so that he can kill you."

Refusing the invitation would be a great slight. He had to go. "I'll return home before the third prayer."

"You'll be returned to me," Shaheen said. "Everything except your head."

Before he left, Toor Jan hid the Chinese radio in the bottom of their wood chest. He didn't want to listen to music on it anymore.

He walked down the road to Sarkhum. It was hot and the sun burned his neck. Sweat soaked his turban but he was almost happy on the lonely road. He might come back without a head but at least he didn't have to listen to the silly complaints of a teenaged girl who didn't understand what it took to feed a family.

Every step on the road drilled through his arm and hip. He stopped twice to sit and let the pain subside. He was relieved to finally reach the gaping, mountainous draw that held The Big One's walled compound and went across the field to the house.

"Hello! It's Toor Jan. Son of your brother Haji Izatullah!" he called as he approached the walls. Toor Jan mopped away the sweat from his thick eyebrows and leaned against the bricks. He didn't dare use his cell phone this close to The Big One's house. They all knew the almost magical violence the Americans could commit using their technology. "Does anyone hear me?"

There was no answer. The double gate to the yard was unlocked. There were no guards—which was strange—but The Big One must have been hiding in plain sight, one of his more successful tactics. Toor Jan went inside. Two muddy black cows lazed under a portico of evergreen branches. Their marble-like eyes followed Toor Jan as he crossed the yard. Murmurs came from the house and Toor Jan stopped, unseen, outside the open door.

The room was filled with *talib* commanders. To a man, they wore long beards and black clothes. Their fingernails were red with henna and their eyes were exaggerated with thick eyeliner. Weapons were stacked within easy reach. *Shaheen's right. They're here to kill me.* Toor Jan pressed tight against the doorframe and watched at a sharp angle.

The *talib* commanders sat on the floor while The Big One stood at the head of the room. Their cell phones cast eerie light as they took his picture. A celebratory wreath of red and yellow flowers hung from his neck. Toor Jan had never seen his uncle like this. Alone with his family, The Big One laughed, told jokes, and secretly enjoyed forbidden Ukrainian cigarettes. The crowd of *talibs* hushed to hear The Big One speak.

"Today we did a great thing by killing an invader in Chorah."

"Commander, tell us how you arranged—" an older commander began but burped in the middle of his question. He started over, "How did you arrange this great operation?"

"We have many friends in the police force. But it was a man at the top who helped us." The Big One considered the room. "We are all trusted *andiwale*, so I'll tell you who it was. The General himself. We control him."

The *talib* commanders trilled at the revelation.

Toor Jan felt hollow. *All of them want to kill me.* Then a more dangerous thought, *Except for The Good American.* He limped away quickly, shaking his head. *I'll tell The Big One that I was sick. That I never even came.* He was sweating again. *I'll tell him I couldn't come because of my wounds.*

Someone seized his shoulder and turned him around. Two teenagers, tall and bony, with rifles—the guards missing from their posts earlier. One wore crooked eyeliner, the other an Afghan Police uniform. They looked like brothers. Behind them, in the open door, The Big One materialized, holding the ends of his unbuttoned vest and gliding toward Toor Jan. The confetti of flowers swung from his neck. Toor Jan felt like he might shit on the ground right there.

"Nephew!" They embraced, Toor Jan steadied his fearful shaking. The Big One touched the metal splint on Toor Jan's arm and squawked with concern. "Does that hurt?"

"Yes, uncle," he said, hating the word.

The Big One nodded thoughtfully. "How's your family?"

"They are good, uncle."

"And what about—" The Big One hesitated as if he didn't want to ask the question. "Have you had any police officers come to you with food? Money? Things a wounded man needs?"

"I am cared for, uncle."

The mystery locked together. The Big One had used the General for the attack at the schoolhouse. Toor Jan had been hurt and the General was forced to pay for the blood. Toor Jan was called here today by The Big One to ensure that the debt had been paid. *I'm their toy.*

"I must also care for you." The Big One disappeared into his house and returned with one thousand Pakistani *rupees*. The commanders, one after the other, filed into the yard, rifles strapped on their backs. They didn't ride motorcycles for fear of being shot by the Americans. Each one stretched, bending in half or to the side, for their walk home. The Big One and Toor Jan watched them go. "I meant for the meal to be the two of us but we had a victory this morning. Did you see what was happening inside?"

"No, uncle. I just got here."

The Big One tilted his head, trim beard scratching the flowers. "Then why were you running away?"

"I apologize, uncle." Toor Jan searched his mind for an excuse. "I walked here." He pointed to his wet turban as proof of the exertion. "But I made myself sick and I heard the voices and didn't want to intrude. I decided to walk back home."

The Big One clicked his tongue. "My wounded nephew doesn't walk in my province. Zubair, Saeed Nabi!" He clapped for the guards. "Take my nephew home."

Zubair, the one with crooked eyeliner, hesitated. The one in a police uniform, Saeed Nabi, tugged on his *kameez* sleeve. Zubair shucked his hand off. "Commander," Zubair started, "I have missions to finish tonight. Don't you think this—" he motioned to Toor Jan "—is beneath me?" Zubair had led many simple missions: digging fighting positions, retrieving weapons, enforcing the law, and just recently, emplacing mines. "I'm not a taxi driver."

Saeed Nabi took hold of Zubair and tried to walk him away. "Commander, we are sorry," Saeed Nabi said.

Zubair resisted. "Am I right, commander?" The Big One only shook his head and it was settled. Before he turned to get the car, Zubair insisted that he should leave his brother behind. "He's not one of us," Zubair said to The Big One and spat on the ground. "No matter how much he wants to be."

The Big One smiled. "Be smart, not angry, Zubair. Saeed Nabi will get you through all of the checkpoints with his uniform."

Toor Jan met the brothers outside the compound in a choking column of dust raised by their Honda Accord. A sticker of "God is the greatest" was pasted over the rear windshield. Nagma's famous album cranked loud in the tape deck. The two brothers argued about Zubair's defiance of The Big One the entire ride to Safad Khare. They didn't speak to Toor Jan once.

Before he'd even made it all the way inside the gate, Shaheen was kissing Toor Jan on his beard and nose and mouth until he fell backward and the unbalanced pregnant girl went with him. "You're here!"

"And I brought my head with me too."

"Toor *Janna*!"

He showed her the *rupees*. "For our sufferings."

"Money from your uncle is proper." She searched Toor Jan's eyes. "Money from the American isn't."

"Please, girl. Make some *chai*."

Shaheen boiled *chai* and watched Toor Jan drink it. They didn't speak. She cleaned up the glasses then laid back on the pillows, watching her husband until she dozed and began snoring softly, her mouth parted. Toor Jan took his cell phone into the yard. It was midafternoon but he didn't hear anyone from the village outside his walls. He dialed The Good American's number.

"I'm Toor Jan, son of—"

"I know who this is," Qais, The Good American's *tajiman*, said.

"Is Commander there?" Toor Jan said. He'd never used that title of respect for The Good American before. "I must tell him something."

"He's right beside me."

"Tell him I don't want to be his teacher."

"What are you talking about, Toor Jan?"

"I can protect him. Like he protected me."

"How?" the *tajiman* said.

Toor Jan watched the door for Shaheen. "I have some information."

"What do you know?"

"That an American was killed today."

"What else did you hear?"

Toor Jan expelled a long, pent-up breath. "I know who did it."

"Who?" The Good American talked as Qais translated. "Who killed him?"

"It was The Big One. He is responsible."

"*Everyone* knows that." The Good American yelled in the background. "One of our closest friends was killed in the attack, Toor Jan. We don't have time to waste with you."

"Does everyone else also know that General Khan helped him?

Qais paused. "How do you know that?"

"The Big One told me."

"He told *you*?"

"Yes," Toor Jan said. "He is my uncle."

ISAIAH KHOST HAD
LOST MEN BEFORE

***Multinational Base Tarin Kowt, Tarin Kot District,
Afghanistan, 02 November 2012—***

Isaiah Khost was in his room. Electricity—or something like it—crackled through his legs. The last time this had happened, at home, he rode his bike the ninety miles from Virginia Beach to the state capital in Richmond, ate a cheeseburger, and came back the same day. He couldn't do that here. So he did air squats—almost two hundred now—hoping to dispel the hectic energy before the video conference with the generals in Kabul.

The generals wanted to discuss the progress of his negotiations over Security Day. Again. They knew Khost had lost a man that morning. He had their condolences, they assured him of that, but Security Day must be solved. *So much for caring about your men.* There was a knock on Khost's door. Khost stopped squatting, opened the door and stared at the Master Chief. Master Chief carried a pen and notebook. "They're already on the line."

"What?" Khost said. "I thought it was supposed to happen at seventeen-thirty?"

"They want to do it now and keep it short so we can handle Aaron's ramp ceremony."

"All right, let's go." They went down the hall, through the plywood maze toward the command suite. "His family notified yet?"

"Yes, sir. About an hour ago." The Master Chief licked his lips. His grit faded. "We trained and trained for an insider attack."

"I know we did, Rick." They went through the door into the command suite. "General Khan told us things were still bad. We should've listened."

Master Chief didn't reply.

Inside the command suite on a large flat-screen television, three generals in pristine camouflage uniforms watched Khost and the Master Chief as they sat down. Their room was a replica of Khost's command suite but larger. Behind them hung a pair of crossed American and Afghan flags. Digital clocks flashed the time at American bases around the world. They sat at the same light oak-veneered oval table. None of them had papers, folders, not even a pen. They weren't taking notes or walking him through a plan. *It's a scolding*, Khost thought and sat up in his chair to take it.

"Good afternoon, Commander, Master Chief," General Casey said. He was snow-haired, wore steel-framed glasses. "First, we all want to offer our condolences again for Petty Officer Knowles." The other generals nodded, sucked in their lips. Khost thought this looked rehearsed. "If you need anything from us we're here to support."

"Thank you, sir," Commander Khost said. "I'll be sure to let you know if there's anything we need." *Like letting me do my job.* "I apologize for keeping you waiting. I was under the impression we were doing this an hour from now."

"We were, Izzy," General Branson said. He was an old friend, they'd deployed together several times. "But your issue has made it to SecNav."

The Master Chief shifted in his chair, clicked his pen, and looked at his notebook as if he were going to take minutes.

"What issue of mine would the Secretary of the Navy care about?"

General Branson chuckled. "Making a new Security Day deal with that creep Mir whatever-his-name-is."

Khost burned. "It's General Mir Hamza Khan, *sir*."

General Branson shrugged. "He's supposed to be your lackey, Izzy. Feels like he's running the show."

"How else am I supposed to win?"

They all laughed without stifling even a snicker. "Okay, okay," General Casey told the other two. "*Our* strategy is to get the hell out. Leave something reasonable in place but get out."

"Plus," General Colicchio said, speaking for the first time. He had a thick five-o'clock shadow. *You got a sweater on under that uniform, you fucking gorilla?* "The Taliban has Khan's number. As soon as we leave, he'll be the headless horseman."

"We made that deal with him a long time ago," Khost said. "We owe him what we said we would pay."

"Commander Khost," General Casey said without hiding his irritation. "Your job is to make him understand our new position. You've failed to do that so far."

Underneath the table, Khost dug his finger into his thigh. "How will we be resupplied if *General* Khan can't afford to do Security Day?"

General Branson pointed up. "The air. It'd only be for six months until you withdraw from Uruzgan."

"The population will turn against us," Khost said. "They'll blame us for the lack of food and medicine. It'll be a propaganda victory for the insurgents."

"That's why Khan will eventually take the deal. He knows his power is gone if he doesn't do Security Day and provide for his people." General Branson leaned forward. "Listen to me, Izzy, if you can't get this done you're looking down the barrel of being relieved of command. Career killer."

It was Khost's turn to laugh. His scarred face was singed red. "I'm here this time to win."

The generals were silent until General Branson finally said, "You gotta give that up, Izzy. For everyone's sake."

"Again we're sorry about Petty Officer Knowles," General Casey said. "We heard he was a good operator. Get back to that, Commander."

The screen went black without waiting for Khost to respond.

Khost and the Master Chief came out of the command suite and went straight to the operations center. "Find the shooter and we'll get General Khan to take care of him," Khost ordered the staff. "And someone get him on the line so I can brief him."

They called General Khan four times without an answer. There was no new intelligence. All they knew was that a teenager—wearing a police uniform, *from the bazaar again?*—shot Aaron Knowles and then jumped off the roof of the District Center. Disappeared into the city. Nothing else. It wasn't until after twenty-one hundred that General Khan returned their calls.

"We're sorry about your man, Commander."

"Thank you, General. What information do you have?"

"We're sending you pictures of that motherless dog of a murderer."

When Chamber translated this, all of the staff leaned toward the speaker phone.

"You have the shooter?"

"Yes. We killed him."

"He was a police officer? He was in uniform."

"Never!" General Khan said. "He was one of Mullah Sher Muhammad's men."

"Who?" Khost asked. He only knew Mullah Sher Muhammad as Objective Frostbite. "Beg your pardon, General?"

General Khan clicked his tongue. "The *talib* commander in this province."

"I see," Khost said. "What are you sending us pictures of?"

"The body. His name was Qassim. Our police chased him and killed him in the city."

In a secret section of Khost's heart, he had wanted to find this illiterate farm boy and kill him with his own hands. Lieutenant Ramsey hadn't even had the meeting with Noorzai. Immediately after the shooting stopped, they left the District Center with Aaron's body. If Khost couldn't have Qassim, he wanted Noorzai. "Bring Noorzai to me, General. This happened on his watch."

"He's gone too," General Khan said. "You were correct about starting over in Chorah."

"Oh, okay," Khost said, shocked. "I guess we'll be eagerly awaiting those pictures." After the call was disconnected, Khost turned to the room. "Well, holy shit," he said, throwing his arms in the air. The staff gripped their chairs as if they were about to be blown away by a gale. For several seconds no one said anything. "If anything good can come from this, we can be happy that he's fired Noorzai."

On the big screen in the center of the room a picture began loading of a boy in a shapeless police uniform, body splayed on the ground, an exit wound above his eye.

"It's bullshit," a short, stocky man called out from the bottom of the amphitheater. The entire room turned toward him. "MHK is lying, sir." The man's beard darkened his face. He wore a dirty and fraying baseball cap, button-down work shirt, and jeans. In a room full of people wearing military uniforms this divided him starkly from the group. "We have two sources that say MHK arranged the attack with Objective Frostbite."

The room burst open, everyone talking at the same time. The Master Chief held up his hand for silence.

"Who are you?" Khost said.

The man stood up, smoothed down the front of his pants, clasped his hands in front, then behind his back, and croaked, "Petty Officer Dan Bing, sir. I'm a source handler, sir. Down at the SPU."

"Go ahead," Khost said.

"I have two sources, one close to Frostbite, the other with MHK, and they're both telling me that Frosbite and MHK worked together to kill Aaron."

"Petty Officer Knowles."

"Petty Officer Knowles, sir."

"Who are these sources?"

Bing paused. "Can we talk about that alone, sir? I can't reveal their identities."

"Secret agent over there, huh?" the Master Chief said and everyone laughed, a release. Bing pulled his hat down over his face and stared at the ground.

The skinny, pale, and balding Lieutenant Glenn Konig, who led the intelligence analyst cell, held his hand up to be heard. Intelligence analysts were the rivals of human intelligence collectors. "We have nothing to support that," Lieutenant Konig told Khost. "In fact, everything we uncovered confirms MHK's version of events."

"Yeah, right," Bing said. "How did you guys uncover anything?"

"Signals intelligence, Petty Officer," Lieutenant Konig said. "You know, *reliable* intelligence."

Bing huffed. "You actually think MHK would talk about something like this on the phone?"

"If he was involved, we'd hear about it." Lieutenant Konig laughed. "Come on, MHK can't even read. None of them do."

"Enough," Khost said. He looked up at the digital clock on the wall. It was time. "Ramp ceremony at twenty-two hundred. Fifteen minutes to be on the airfield." Everyone cleared out of the operations center. Dan went last and Khost stared at him the entire time.

In the dark, the SEAL Team formed two lines on either side of the windy tarmac. A C-130 sat with its loading ramp open. An ambulance approached the plane and stopped. After several long moments, Warrant Officer Beau Parker, Captain Robert Cales, Sergeant Brian Chenko, and their interpreter, Qais, carried Aaron Knowles's body on a litter between the two lines. The rest stood with their arms raised in salute as the body passed.

Wrapped in an American flag, Aaron Knowles's body was placed on the plane that would carry him home, to his widow and infant daughter. Commander Khost stood at the head of the line, the last to drop his salute. He almost cried but—though it wouldn't have been shameful—he held the tears back. *Transform the hurt into aggression.* Aggression could be shaped into a plan. A good plan was all he needed to fix everything.

That night Khost turned in bed. *There's a million dollars in that safe, right outside my door. It's mine. I can spend it without the generals knowing. It's not enough money for a permanent solution but it might be enough for now.*

Khost got out of bed, dressed, and went to his office to think the plan through. It was his third night in a row without sleep.

EVERYTHING ABOUT DAN

Multinational Base Tarin Kowt, Tarin Kot District, Uruzgan Province, Afghanistan, 02 November 2012—

Beau had been showing Dan how to pack up Aaron's room to ship the belongings home to his wife and Dan couldn't stop yelling. "They all laughed at me! Khost too!"

"I know," Beau said. "Told you he was a bad egg."

"What's his deal?"

"I was in one of his platoons, a long time ago. He used to tell us that the warrior—" Beau looked up in the air to repeat a phrase he'd heard many times. "—lived by an inflexible code. So he decided to turn in a bunch of our guys for cutting their cammies into shorts so they could wear them around town."

"Really?"

"He said they'd misused government property. Warriors use resources wisely. Those guys got in trouble. A lot of it too."

"Great. Glad he's our fearless leader." Dan opened a cigar box on the plywood shelf above Aaron's bed. It was filled with loose 7.62 rounds, a shark-tooth necklace, and some poker chips. *A bunch of junk.* "You said we don't throw anything out, right?"

"Everything goes home as is," Beau said. He wore full uniform and had freshly cut hair. "Except the computer—"

"I already told you I erased his browser history."

"Hard drive too? You can't send any porn back to his wife."

"I wiped everything, Beau." Dan put the shoebox onto the pallet. The pallet would fly home with Aaron's body. *Aaron's body*, Dan thought. *How could Aaron turn into just a body?* "You ever think Maziullah would rat on MHK like that?" Maziullah had called Dan and after endless small talk he finally admitted that MHK had used The Big One to kill Aaron. Then—as if realizing what he'd done—Maziullah hung up. "For two years that guy wouldn't reveal shit to anyone and tonight he tells *me*." Dan pointed to himself. "That's huge."

"I know," Beau said. He was almost inaudible against the blow of the Chigo heater. "But Khost isn't ever going to listen to you."

"And why the fuck not?" Dan threw another box into the pallet without opening it. "Toor Jan's goddamned uncle is the leader of *all* the Taliban in Uruzgan. Toor Jan *heard* the guy say he and MHK planned to attack together. That's not good enough for Khost?"

"The guy said it himself," Beau said. "An inflexible code."

Beau had paused at a photograph of Aaron's wife and their daughter. "How many times you done this, Beau?"

"Done what?"

"Packed up someone's stuff."

"This is the fourth time," he said and handed Dan the picture. "That's Allyssa."

"You know her?"

"My wife babysits their kid when she goes to night classes. She's smart." Beau took the picture back from Dan and laid it in the pallet.

"She'll be all right, eventually."

There was a knock on the plywood door. Army Brian, shaved and in full uniform too, came inside. "You erase the porn on the computer?" he said.

"Yeah. Jesus Christ." Dan packed the rest of the framed pictures onto the pallet. "What do you think, I'm some kind of *dummy*?"

"We really have to leave, Beau," Army Brian said. Beau and Army Brian were escorting Aaron's body to the United States. They'd return in a week. "We got like five minutes."

"I'll meet you outside. Let me talk to Dan real quick."

Army Brian gave the emptying room a look and left.

Beau shook his head. "You letting this get to you?"

"Of course, Aaron is dead." Dan looked up at Beau. "We have to get MHK."

Beau frowned. "Never going to happen."

"It's wrong," Dan said. Power Bars, beef jerky, and bags of nuts were everywhere and Dan wondered if they should stay. At least they would get eaten. But he was *supposed* to send everything home—except the porn, of course. "He killed our friend."

"There are limits to what we can do here. Understand?" Beau put his hands on Dan's shoulders. "Make sure the rest of the stuff is packed neat and presentable. If you need more shrink-wrap it's in the Soviet Building."

"I'll make sure it's good to go."

"This is the most important thing you'll do on this deployment."

"I know, Beau."

Beau squeezed his shoulders and left the room. Dan went back to the pallet. A framed photograph lay on top, black and white, of Aaron's daughter Charlotte, newborn, squinting eyes, a ruffled bow on her hairless, eggshell head. She was cradled in Aaron's arms, her hands tightly clasped in front of her face. Dan cried for the first time since Aaron had died. One day Charlotte would learn that her father had been murdered. *Murdered.*

Dan wiped his face dry with his forearm. Maybe Allyssa didn't even know that Aaron had this photograph of Charlotte. *Does her no good anyway.* Dan pulled the picture from the frame and stuck it in the lining of his baseball cap. He kept the empty frame to toss in the trash.

Dan packed the rest of the room in half an hour. The last thing he laid on the funeral pallet was the black beret Aaron wore to source meetings. It was a final reminder of all that Aaron had taught Dan. That stupid beret meant everything. He hesitated at the door before stepping into the night. The room was empty. But everything inside Dan had filled with hate.

MIR HAMZA KHAN ADMIRES
THE AMERICAN WAY

The road to Kandahar City, Shah Wali Kot, Kandahar
Province, Afghanistan, 03 November 2012—

Shah Wali Kot Road came down from the mountains of high Uruzgan into the Kandahari flat. Sipping *chai* and waiting, Mir Hamza Khan and a police officer—too shy to speak to the great man—sat behind a stack of HESCO barriers at the border crossing between the two provinces. Noorzai's truck would reach them in ten minutes. Khan planned to show Noorzai his new future, just as Noorzai had done for Khan at the beginning of the American War.

Eleven years ago, Khan had parked his taxi near the traffic circle in Tarin Kowt City. The day had been slow. Khan needed one more fare to buy dinner. It was hot. He concentrated on his prayer beads—still useful to him then—to stop thinking about his misery.

Then Noorzai leaned into his open window. "The *talibs* have made some sort of great mistake, Mir Hamza," he said. Khan didn't look up. The two had known each other since they were boys. They had fought the Russians together but they'd had little reason to talk to each other since, other than to remember. "And now the Americans are coming."

Ahead, a black-turbaned *talib* religious police officer, arms behind his back, fan-belt whip limp in his right hand, patrolled the street and plotted how to enforce virtue and discourage vice. Khan didn't want trouble. He wanted cab fares. He shrugged and returned to his prayer beads.

Noorzai punched the taxi's horn. Khan jumped. The religious police officer raised his fan-belt whip, prepared to strike, until he heard a burst of giggling in the distance followed by the ping of a soccer ball. He ran off in the direction of the fun. Noorzai leaned into Khan's window again. "The radio said that the Americans are coming for revenge."

Khan found himself asking—without wanting to, "What did the *talibs* do?"

Noorzai didn't know what the *talibs* had done to the Americans. "But it's good for the Popalzais." He stood, looked around for anyone watching, and leaned back in. "We can help the Americans when they come." Khan had never been a *talib*, he avoided even giving rides to *talibs*, and he hated, more than anything, the taxes the *talibs* collected on the roads, taxes that made them rich and him poor. Noorzai knew all of this and he knew that Khan, as proven against the Russians, could fight. "Come to the mountains with me tonight. We can start a war against the *talibs*. Every man in Chorah will join us."

Khan put his prayer beads down, clicked his tongue. He started his taxi's engine. "The Americans aren't here yet. How are you sure they're coming at all?" Mir Hamza Khan left Noorzai there in the traffic circle and went home, not regretting losing another fare that day.

Then the Americans invaded. Khan saw the bearded Americans ride on horseback through the Chorah desert and immediately ran to meet Noorzai at his hiding place near the first turn of the Teri River. Noorzai had established an army of Popalzai fighters from every district in

Uruzgan and, always generous, allowed Khan to join. He even allowed him to lead the group from Tarin Kowt City. Noorzai's only condition was that Khan leave his taxi behind. Khan agreed, in conversation, but hid his taxi in his compound, prepared to desert Noorzai if the war failed and return to driving.

The first day of battle in Tarin Kowt City began with the people revolting against the *talibs*. Khan's group seized the government headquarters and drove the *talib* commanders away. After the battle, blond American soldiers clapped the skinny Popalzai fighters on their backs. For most of the Americans, it was their first firefight. They were thrilled.

That night, American soldiers and Popalzai fighters celebrated the victory together with fires and dancing in the spare courtyard of the Governor's mansion. On the second floor, in an unadorned room, American officers presented Noorzai, Khan, and the other Popalzai commanders with forbidden whiskey. The happy men passed the bottle around until it was empty. Noorzai's goofy, drunk laugh, his easy way with his men, and the trust he inspired in the Americans—in the early days, showed Khan what was possible for him to achieve.

When the *talibs* counter-attacked Tarin Kowt City with fighters in speeding pickup trucks, the Americans sent crushing waves of airplanes against them until they were blood and dust. Noorzai introduced Khan to Maziullah and in battle over the course of the next few months they all fought shoulder-to-shoulder. Khan finally submitted to his new fate after the Americans delivered three suitcases filled with one million dollars each. He used his taxi for target practice after that. And now, as Khan waited with the police officer for Noorzai at the border crossing, he thought of himself as the embodiment of the great future Noorzai had seen long ago.

A black SUV rocked down the road, its approach so fast it looked as though it might blow by the checkpoint. The police officer stepped into the road and waved. The driver braked. Khan rose from behind the HESCO barrier and walked quickly to the rear passenger door. Noorzai didn't look at Khan as he climbed inside. They sped off and left the police officer standing there.

"I'm surprised to see you here," Noorzai said, disgusted.

"These are difficult times, *akaa*." Khan said, calling Noorzai uncle as a sign of respect.

"More difficult for me than for you." Noorzai didn't wear his uniform and the great man had lost much weight since they'd last met.

Khan reached for his hand. "*Akaa*, I'm sorry."

"I don't need you to feel sorry. I feel sorry enough myself."

"It had to be this way. For all of us."

The SUV stopped as the driver squinted at a hole in the road. For several minutes all of them scrutinized the hole and—satisfied it wasn't a buried bomb—the truck continued fast toward Kandahar.

Noorzai hadn't looked at Khan yet. He spoke to the empty seat in front of him. "I did what you asked and brought the boy in. I didn't know you would use him like that."

Khan laughed to seem nervous. "Maziullah suggested the entire thing. I had to agree."

"He did not. He couldn't." Noorzai turned to Khan. "He's my best friend."

"I'm a simple fighter. You know that. How could I plan something like this?"

"Simple is true. You're only a pitiful cab driver."

And now I'm your king. "Maziullah is an educated man. He made the plan and I agreed. It was the only way to make the Americans keep their promise about Security Day."

Noorzai clicked his tongue. "And did it work?"

"They will agree," Khan said. It was his turn to feel sorry for himself. "I've convinced them that they need me."

"Tell me then, did Maziullah also plan for me to be sent away from my family and my home? To Kandahar." Noorzai said Kandahar as if he was chewing on dirt.

"You're not going to Kandahar."

Noorzai turned to the windscreen and the pale world outside of the truck. "The government has reassigned me there. I must go."

"You're not going to Kandahar." Khan pressed his finger into the air. "There is a place in the country that I have set aside for you."

Not far down the road they turned onto a path that led to a vineyard. Deep in the thick knots of vines was a large compound composed of two buildings and a tiled courtyard. It had a kitchen, a large room for the women, an eating area, and cozy bedrooms filled with rugs and pillows Khan had bought from Delhi. A noisy generator powered the house. Turrets built into the corners of the outer wall covered the single approach to the house. It was clean. A garden, dead now, would be colorful with roses come spring. Khan had built this secret home for Aghala and Aziz. The truck stopped.

"This is yours," Khan said, motioning toward the estate. "Your land extends ten hectars out. Bring your family. Maintain the vineyard. Become an old man."

Noorzai looked through the windscreen as if he didn't see the house. "You think you're not exactly like me, Mir Hamza. That you're an American, here in Uruzgan to occupy it. And you're silly to think you won't end up like me. Or worse, *inshallah*." Noorzai left the truck. He didn't turn around. He didn't look back before going inside.

"Turn around," Khan told the truck driver. "Take me home."

Calling him an American was the worst insult Noorzai could manage but Khan didn't care. Pashtuns traded their friends all the time. They came to your house at night, shot you to death, and wailed at your funeral. When the Americans betrayed their friends they promoted them or built a prison in the countryside and called it a mansion. And they never spoke to you again.

Mir Hamza Khan admired the honesty of the American way.

DAN WOULD RUN THROUGH ANYONE WHO TRIED TO STOP HIM

Multinational Base Tarin Kowt, Tarin Kot District, Uruzgan Province, Afghanistan, 07 November 2012—

That morning Dan had made a ceremony of putting on the physical objects that transformed him: MP5 across his back, the white watch, and Charlotte's picture tucked inside his hat. In the muggy meeting room, the photograph stuck to his shaved head. He liked feeling it. "Are you hot, *andiwale*?" he said to Maziullah. He'd learned the Pashto word for friend that morning. "I'm dying."

"No, I am not hot." Dan had noticed that Qais often translated Pashto to English without contractions. It was irritating. "I am angry," Qais said, for Maziullah.

Maziullah wore a scallion-colored *kameez* and spread his legs wide inside the long shirt. His customary toothbrush peeked out of its vest pocket. The blue rifle was across his lap. Maziullah sat across the round table from Qais and Dan. He hadn't looked at the tea they had poured him.

"What are you angry about?" Dan said.

Maziullah answered before Qais translated. "The General has taken Noorzai away to Kandahar." He pulled a leather pouch from his vest, pinched a wad of raw lime green snuff and tucked it into his lower lip. "To a house in the country. He will stay there forever."

Dan tugged the sleeve of Qais's red thermal shirt. Qais's cologne mixed with Maziullah's dank body odor. "It seemed like he understood the English."

"Nah, he don't know no English."

"He answered before you finished, Qais."

"Nah man. He don't know."

"Bullshit."

"Oh you know Pashto now, huh? Learned a few words this morning, now you the expert?" Qais said. "For real. I could be at the gym right now." He brushed off his black Nikes and stood. "Should I leave?"

"No, sit down, Qais. I'm just making sure."

At home in Queens, Qais worked in a bodega. He had a young wife from an arranged marriage and an infant son named Ibrahim. As a civilian interpreter, Qais made three-hundred fifty thousand dollar a year, tax free. He hadn't graduated high school but he had no criminal record, no debt, and nothing that could be used for blackmail. That made Qais the only terp with a high enough security clearance to meet sources. Qais took his seat. "Now what else we want to ask him?"

"Why did the General send Noorzai to a house in Kandahar?"

Maziullah spoke for several minutes until he was dry and finally drank his tea. "Shamed police officers always desert their posts and are never seen again. The General wants the Americans to believe that is what happened to Noorzai."

Dan frowned. "Qais, come on. That's all he said? He talked for almost five minutes straight."

"Mah God, dude! Seriously?"

"It sounded like he said a lot more than what you translated."

"Listen. These people say the same things over and over. They repeat themselves to show it's important."

"All right," Dan said. "Why does the General want us to think Noorzai left his post? Because Noorzai helped him kill an American?"

Maziullah didn't answer. He looked at the floor.

"You already told me that the General was involved. You remember that, right?"

Maziullah didn't respond.

Dan worked hard to conceal his anger. "At least tell me why the General would attack us in the first place? He's our ally."

"I already told you too much."

"But I need to know why."

"That does not mean I will tell you."

"Is something like this going to happen again, Maziullah?"

"I do not know."

"Maziullah." Dan's voice shook. "We've both lost a friend because of the General."

"Who did I lose?"

"Noorzai," Dan said. "You said he was an old friend."

"We fought the Russians together."

"Then stop playing games." Qais balked at translating the insult but

140

Dan nodded for him to continue. "You're not looking at the entire picture. How long is it until the General betrays *you*?"

Maziullah clicked his tongue.

"Look how much you've already told me. You've let the secret out." Qais matched Dan's intensity. "How long until the General hides you away too? If you help me, if you're completely truthful with me, I can help you when that time comes."

"Can you help me become a General?"

"What?" Dan turned to Qais. "You translate that right?"

Qais rolled his eyes at Dan and nodded.

"It should be General *Maziullah*, The Hero of Peace and Unity." Maziullah clutched the barrel of his blue rifle. "Because I never forget my friends."

Dan leaned back in his folding chair, it creaked under his weight. "Listen, if you want to be in charge, I can help—"

"I do not want to be in charge."

"Then what do you want, Maziullah?"

Maziullah picked up his blue rifle and checked the time on his cell phone. "I want to leave. May I have a ride to the gate?"

At the main gate, Dan pulled the 4Runner beside Maziullah's green police truck. *Don't let him slip away.* He reached for Maziullah's hand. Qais leaned in from the back seat. They whispered into his ear. "The General killed Aaron. Aaron was the American that died in Chorah."

Maziullah pulled away. "Commander Aaron? With the yellow hair? How? He was going home to his son."

"It was his last mission before he left." Dan dropped Maziullah's hand. "Commander Aaron was your friend."

"Yes he was."

"And you never forget your friends?"

"Never," Maziullah said, slightly lifting his blue rifle from his lap.

"Then prove it to me. What secrets can you tell me about the General? Things Aaron might have wanted to know but you didn't tell him. It can be something simple."

Maziullah thought for a moment. "The General is sick. He has a liver disease."

"Really?" Dan said, straightening. Qais seemed surprised too. "Is it serious?"

Maziullah grunted, as if trying to stop what he would say next. "Yes."

"How serious?" From the back seat, Qais put his hand on Maziullah's shoulders. "Deadly?"

"No doctor in Afghanistan can help him. He goes to Mumbai for treatments."

"Does he tell you when he plans to go?"

Maziullah nodded.

"Then I need to know that. Would you tell me something like that? Because you never forget your friends."

Maziullah nodded gravely. "I will find out when he is going next and tell you," he said and left the 4Runner.

Qais jumped into the front seat next to Dan. "Yo, that dude ain't never talked this much before. That's some real shit he just said, right there."

"Maybe I don't suck at this." Dan smiled and started the 4Runner. "Sorry about questioning you earlier, man. I guess I'm eager to figure this out."

142

Qais nodded. "You didn't know Aaron for long, bruh, but I get it." He looked out the window. "Aaron was a good dude."

"A great dude," Dan said and started back to the SPU. "You still want to go to the gym?"

"Yeah, buddy," Qais peeled off his thermal. Underneath he wore a white wife-beater. "Ready to go."

"Cool, I'm heading that direction anyway."

"Where you going?"

"To the headquarters building." They turned, went straight along the airfield.

Qais laughed. "Why would anyone want to go there?"

"I'm gonna find out if Maziullah's telling the truth."

Dan dropped Qais off at the gym and parked the 4Runner at the headquarters building. He went inside to find Lieutenant Konig, the intelligence officer who embarrassed him the night Aaron was killed. Konig should've been able to tell him if any other reporting corroborated what Maziullah had said about Noorzai disappearing or MHK's liver disease. That was how it was *supposed* to work: collectors gathered intelligence and analysts verified it. A partnership. But Dan knew that his hope for partnership was dead when Konig's deputy, Chief George Nunez, stood in the doorway to the intelligence analysts' office and blocked him from going inside.

"What do you need, James Bond?" Chief Nunez was cinnamon-skinned and fat. "You know you're not supposed to come in here without a uniform."

"I have a beard. Regulations don't allow you to wear a beard and be in uniform. Chief."

"You could always shave that thing, because, you know, you're in the military and all." Chief Nunez touched the end of his trimmed black moustache. It was within regulation. So was everything else, except his uniform trousers covering the laces of his tan boots.

"Don't we blouse boots when we're in uniform, Chief? We are in the military and all." Chief Nunez checked his boots and Dan scooted around him to Konig's desk. "Sir, I wanted to talk to you real quick."

"Real quick, Petty Officer Bing. Five minutes." Konig looked at his watch. "No, make that two minutes." Lieutenant Glenn Konig was tall and white as the underside of a fish. He had no fat or muscle and his skin stretched over his knobby joints. His hair was greasy. Konig often delicately gripped people at the wrist to get their attention.

"Have you guys had any reporting about Noorzai getting sent into hiding?"

Konig raised his heavy eyebrows. "Chief?" Chief Nunez had gone to his desk. "You got anything on this?"

"On what?"

Dan turned his white watch around his wrist. "Have you seen anything about Noorzai disappearing? Any reporting?"

"Uh," Chief Nunez said and clicked roughly on his mouse. "Who's Noorzai?"

Dan smashed the white watch face down on Konig's desk. "Seriously?"

"Who told you that he went into hiding?" Konig said. "Your guy that's close to MHK?"

"Yes, sir. I think MHK sent Noorzai into hiding to keep him quiet. Why would he need to keep him quiet?"

"I don't know, Petty Officer Bing. The hajis are weird."

"Or is it possible that MHK is involved, like I said the other night?"

"Okay, your two minutes is done." Konig stood from his desk.

"He set Noorzai up with some sort of deal to get him out of the way."

"Doesn't seem likely, Petty Officer Bing."

"Why not?"

"There's no signals intelligence on this. We would know."

Dan pointed at Chief Nunez. "But he doesn't even know who Noorzai is and he's supposed to be running the show. Gotta give it to MHK for being effective. Can't say the same thing about your outfit."

Chief Nunez jumped from his chair and screamed, "Out now! Get the fuck out!" He pointed Dan to the door. "Don't come in here again."

Outside, Dan kicked the tires of the 4Runner. If he had hair he would've pulled it out. *I'm the only one who gives a shit*, he thought as he drove back to the SPU. He pulled the truck into the SPU compound. Captain Cales stood in the gravel and as soon as Dan had parked, he marched toward the 4Runner. "What'd you do now?"

"I was meeting Mazzy Star." Dan almost took the white watch off, to return to normal, but he sensed another fight coming and kept it on. "Just doing my job and all, sir."

"You went to Konig's office too."

"How'd you know that?"

"He called," Captain Cales said.

"I had some information that I needed verified."

"You gotta let me handle things like that, Dan."

"You also gonna get them to care about finding out what happened to Aaron, sir?"

"We already know what happened to Aaron. He was killed by an insurgent wearing a police uniform."

"Oh Christ, you too?"

"Excuse me, Petty Officer?"

Dan started toward the Soviet Building. "Is Beau awake yet? I need Beau." Beau had returned that morning from escorting Aaron's body home. He was sleeping off the jet-lag. "Beau," Dan called down the row of huts. "Are you in your room, Beau?"

"Dan, shut up. Keep your voice down," Captain Cales said.

Beau came out of his hut, tan *Keep on Trucking* baseball cap pulled down low. He wasn't wearing a shirt. "You all right? What's going on, fellas?"

"I got in a fight with Konig and Nunez."

"A fight about what?"

"About figuring out what happened to Aaron."

Beau balled his fist. "What'd you say?"

"I wanted them to confirm my information. That's it. But it's a shit show up there."

"Dan, let me talk to Beau," Captain Cales said. Dan took a step back from between them. "Konig called and said he mouthed off. That's all, Beau. I can address it among the officers."

"They kicked me out of the building, Beau." Dan said.

Beau snarled. "I'll take care of this."

Captain Cales started, "Beau I really think—"

"Captain. Dan's my guy. Let me handle it." Beau went back into his room and came out wearing a shirt and boots. He didn't look at Dan or

Captain Cales as he walked out of the SPU as fast as it would've taken them to sprint the distance.

Captain Cales waited until Beau was gone. "That's your problem. Right there," he said. Spit filled the corners of his mouth. "There's a chain of command and you're an undercutting motherfucker." Dan smiled at him. He exhaled. "Be careful, Dan. I might wipe that smile off your face one day."

TOOR JAN'S TRAINING

Multinational Base Tarin Kowt, Tarin Kot District, Uruzgan Province, Afghanistan, 10 November 2012—

The Good American drove Toor Jan into his private compound within the big American base. Honeysuckle, white flowers drooping, climbed the cement walls. Crab grass covered the ground except where it had been worn away by the truck. The Good American and the *tajiman* led Toor Jan into a large rusted container and locked the door behind them.

Paper maps hung on the walls. Padded folding chairs were pushed under a round table. The Good American offered Toor Jan a can of strawberry Fanta and a package of Oreo cookies. There were also almonds and a huge steel pot of *chai*. The Good American poured the hot *chai* for Toor Jan. The heat and sweet-bitter of the tea calmed him but Toor Jan put his glass down after a sip. He didn't want anything else in his stomach, afraid he might throw up what was already inside. The *tajiman* had taken his cell phone away at the gate and Toor Jan nervously fingered his empty pocket.

The Good American dressed as he had before—dingy blue hat with a bill and white wristwatch—but the *tajiman* wore a bright silver chain necklace, his beard trimmed short and neat. His black sweater had no hair or lint. They were strange clothes for Afghanistan—*for spying*—but

Toor Jan was impressed by the outfit, except for Qais's jeans, which were torn in several places. Toor Jan felt sorry for those pants.

"*Sahib Jan*," he said, calling the *tajiman* dear sir. "When we see each other again I'll give you some new pants from the *bazaar*."

"What's wrong with my pants?"

Toor Jan touched the naked skin between the threads.

"The holes are on purpose, Toor Jan."

"Why would anyone want holes on purpose?"

"It's the style in America."

"The style in this country is to get new pants."

Qais and The Good American roared. Toor Jan smiled and waited for them to finish laughing.

"How are your wounds?" The Good American said. He had a notebook and pen on the table and glanced at them often. "You look better."

"My hip feels good but my arm aches." Toor Jan raised his splinted arm. "But thanks to you, I have an arm."

The Good American smiled. "I'm glad I could help, *andiwale*."

Toor Jan asked Qais directly if The Good American knew Pashto. Qais said he knew the important words.

"You want to work for me now."

"I do, Commander."

"Why? You didn't before."

Toor Jan tucked his legs beneath him. "I'm scared for my family. Everyone in Uruzgan wants to kill me."

"Your uncle?"

"Everyone."

"Who else is trying to kill you?"

"The General," Toor Jan said. "The attack in my village, when I was wounded, could not happen without him."

"Your uncle told you this?"

"No," Toor Jan said. "But I heard him tell others that they work together."

"Are you sure?" The Good American leaned forward in his seat, hovering over Toor Jan's words like a snarling dog. "You can't make things up."

"I'm sure," Toor Jan said, his mind moving fast. "This is why you need me to work for you. I go around and find out things."

"Toor Jan, this is a dangerous job." He smiled. "But maybe you're a strong man."

"I'm strong, Commander."

"So when you were wounded, what were you doing out there at that clinic? Finding out things?"

"My wife is pregnant and I wanted her to see an American doctor."

The Good American and Qais offered their hands and wished him good blessings. "You should have told us you were having a baby."

"I hope we will have a boy."

"A boy would be best. Especially one strong and smart like his father."

Toor Jan placed his hand over his heart. "By my eyes I swear this boy will be stronger than me."

The Good American flipped open his notebook. Qais told Toor Jan that The Good American would write down important parts of their conversation. Toor Jan hadn't ever seen anyone write. He was mesmerized.

"Let's start simple, Toor Jan. You walked to your uncle's house the other day?"

"*Wo.*"

"Where's his house?"

"Outside of the city."

"Where outside of the city?"

"Near the mountain."

The Good American shut his notebook, disappointing Toor Jan. He wanted to see him write. "Do you know directions?"

He looked at the dirty floor. "No, Commander."

"Yes you do. Stand up." The Good American and Qais stood too. "What way do you pray?"

Toor Jan pointed west.

"Good! That's called *shamali*. Now look at your other hand. That direction is called *janubi*. Understand?" Toor Jan nodded. The Good American then explained north and south. "An important part of our work is me teaching and you learning. But you did well, Toor Jan. You're easily trained."

Toor Jan felt his dark skin go impossibly red at the thought that one day he'd be saved by the power of his mind. They sat and The Good American put his hands behind his head. His shirt rode up and his belly fat pressed against the black band of his underwear. He had a pistol on his waist in addition to the machine gun he carried. "How close are you to your uncle?"

"I don't understand what you mean."

"How often do you see him?"

"I always see him at the Big *Eid*. But that's when everyone sees each other."

"How many other times do you see him?"

"When he calls me. I see my other uncles more often."

"Are they in the Taliban?"

"Oh no, Commander. They are farmers like my father was. One is a police colonel in Gizab."

"And he's The Big One's brother? The police colonel?"

"Yes." Toor Jan brushed off his lap and placed his feet flat on the ground. "They see each other often."

The Good American turned his big-faced white watch around his wrist. "But how does The Big One feel about him being a police officer?"

"He's fine with it."

"Why? He's a big Taliban commander."

"Our family decided that one strong son would go with the *talibs* and another strong son with the government so that either way we would be on the side that wins."

From The Good American's reaction it was clear that he was receiving training on Uruzgan. "Qais told me that you took a taxi here."

"Of course, I do not have a car. We are poor people." Toor Jan added, "But the money you give me helps my family a lot."

"Anything for you, Toor Jan."

"And anything for you, Commander."

"Can you drive a motorcycle?" The Good American reached into his back pocket and removed hundreds of *afghanis*.

"Yes," Toor Jan stammered, looking at all that money. "Everyone can."

"Go to the *bazaar* today and buy a red motorcycle. You know who Haji Hyatullah is?"

"Yes, he is famous here."

"They say that he sells weapons to the Taliban from his car shop. I want you to go there and buy a motorcycle from him with this money. If you see weapons or he mentions them, please tell me. And here." The Good American produced a yellow plastic card. "This card says you work on this base as a cleaner. I've done my research and I know the Taliban doesn't bother people doing this kind of stuff. You're going to need to keep it with you all the time so you have an excuse to meet with me."

The Good American pushed the money and card across the table to Toor Jan. Toor Jan took the money, counted it carefully. He placed it back on the table. *How am I supposed to use this?*

The Good American looked at the *tajiman*. He shrugged. "What's wrong, Toor Jan?"

"I'm not here for money. I'm here because you've cared for me and my family."

"It's my honor."

"But this isn't enough to buy a Japanese motorcycle."

"Buy another type of motorcycle."

"But, Commander, they're not good. If you want to make sure I get to our meetings on time then you should give me the money for a Japanese motorcycle."

The Good American became frustrated and stood, pulled his gray shirt down and his jeans up. He slung on his powerful machine gun, turned his white watch so that the face was on the underside of his wrist. He grabbed the money and made like it was time to go.

Toor Jan waved to the Fanta and cookies. "For my family?"

The Good American told him to take it all. The three of them got in the truck. Before The Good American started the engine, he turned to Toor Jan. "I'm new to this country and I don't know simple things like the best types of motorcycles. You'll train me as much as I train you."

I know many important things, Toor Jan thought.

"You'll buy whatever you can with this money?"

"Yes, Commander."

The Good American handed Toor Jan the *afghanis* and his cell phone and they left him at the main gate. Toor Jan entered the city for the first time as a significant man. He had a true friend and an important job. He walked toward Haji and Byat Hyatullah's car shop.

Down an alley, a child kicked a ball against the wall and Toor Jan figured out the direction the ball had been kicked, practicing what The Good American had taught him. He did this with everything he saw, all the way to the car shop. Standing outside, Toor Jan thought about how he would describe the shoddy building in case The Good American needed to know. It was south of the *bazaar*, between the new mosque and the internet cafe. Haji Hyatullah worked with his brother Byat and they sold motorcycles and cars out of a lot west of the building. He went inside. Haji Hyatullah was gone but Toor Jan asked the mean-faced, pole-thin Byat for a red motorcycle. There was much haggling and finally Toor Jan bought a red Chinese motorcycle. Byat left him immediately after taking the money.

As Toor Jan rode for Safad Khare on the motorcycle, he didn't notice the two police officers, who'd followed him all the way from the American base to Haji and Byat Hyatullah's car shop, trailing behind.

MIR HAMZA KHAN SWORE THAT NO ONE WOULD TAKE THIS AWAY

Tarin Kowt City, Tarin Kot District, Uruzgan Province, Afghanistan, 10 November 2012—

Mir Hamza Khan made sure to spend the morning at Naghma's house because she had accused him of neglecting their son—his first—Little Maziullah. "He's almost a man and he doesn't know his father anymore," she said again, as she had almost every day for the past week.

They stood across from each other in her spotless kitchen. Little Maziullah played on the carpet in the adjacent sitting room. Naghma dropped into Khan's arms. He had to brace his aching back to hold her. She peeped up at him through the drape of black hair that had fallen across her aging face. Naghma's eyes were as rich as dark earth and they stood out beautifully.

"And he'll understand why I'm never home when he is a man," Khan said. "Now stand up. I have many things to do today."

"You should spend today with us. There isn't anything that can't be done tomorrow."

"You don't know if there will be a tomorrow."

Naghma lifted her feet from the ground, straining Khan's back with her weight. She was Khan's first wife and had been with him when he was a taxi driver. She had kept their home in a shabby compound in Sarkhum. They had a joke then—every night when Khan came home and asked for food, Naghma would look up from the fire and the one pot they owned and reply, "Dirt soup or fried dirt? We had dirt soup last night. Let's have fried instead."

Naghma had always believed that Khan could run all of the police districts in Uruzgan, all of Uruzgan itself, and wasn't surprised when it finally happened. They were poor until the Americans began paying Khan for Security Day but they were always happy. Naghma liked to wear dresses from Kabul as much as the jewelry they would buy in Doha, but her greatest ache was for Khan to spend more nights with her and Little Maziullah.

Their boy was already tall and broad. At 6 years old he could read. Khan loved when Little Maziullah read stories aloud. The people said that one day he too would be a general. Khan didn't want that for Little Maziullah. Worrying every day about keeping a kingdom was a curse no one deserved.

"That's enough, Naghma," Khan said, putting her back on her feet. "You worry about this house I gave you, not my schedule."

She walked over to their son. "Go on to school." She wiped a smudge of dirt from his cheek. The boy pulled away and ran to the school room Khan had built, for all of his children—even the girls—in the compound. She turned to Khan and said, "What will Little Maziullah be when he is a man?" It was a question only rich people could ask but now it was proper for them to ask it too, *mashallah*.

"Naghma, I don't know."

"You must know something, *Mira Jan*." She threw herself into him again, gripping the mandarin collar of his uniform. He stumbled a bit and pushed her off, readjusted his blouse. She was hurt by the rejection and rolled her eyes. Khan reached for her hand.

"This boy will be lucky. He may go anywhere he wants to live. Britain or Canada. Maybe America. Anything." He kissed her perfect eyes. "Big Maziullah is already waiting. I can't spend the day here. But I'll sleep here tonight."

Naghma huffed like a dog sneezes. "You're always saying you'll be back tonight. Tonight and tonight and tonight. We shall see if The Hero of Peace and Unity, General Haji Mir Hamza Khan, returns to his wife *tonight*," Naghma said and bowed.

With Aghala, he might have slapped her until she understood the proper way to behave. But Naghma was his oldest wife and had been with him since the beginning. Khan would never shame her. He kissed her again and left.

Outside, Maziullah squatted against a courtyard wall, smiling into the sun and leaning his head back. His blue rifle blazed in the light. He wore the vest with the phones. Guards and servants rushed through the compound, conveying pots of steaming food and *chai* from one building to another. The old manservant, Azzam, moved methodically with a bucket, dipping his hand and sprinkling water onto the stony paths to clean them. Above, in the turrets and along the roof, guards made a circuitous patrol from parapet to parapet.

By my eyes, Khan thought, *no one will take this away from me.* He and Naghma had given too much for it all to disappear. He touched Maziullah's head. "I need to spend time with Naghma later," Khan said. "What must be done today?"

Maziullah remained slack, warming in the mid-morning heat. "It depends on when you plan to fly to Mumbai for your next hepatitis treatment, *Haji Sahib*. I don't want you to work too hard."

"Don't worry about that."

Maziullah shifted, picked up his rifle.

"What's wrong?"

"You know I love you, General."

"Yes."

"Then why won't you tell me your plans? Is there no more trust between us?"

The blue gun dangled from its strap toward Khan and he pushed the muzzle away. "There's trust, Maziullah. We have the trust of brothers. But here there are servants and above are the guards. We must be careful of who is around. When the time comes for me to leave, you'll be the one person I tell. That's how much I trust you."

Maziullah took Khan's hand. "Do you remember that man from Safad Khare? The one you took care of?"

"The little dark one?"

"Yes, that man. Toor Jan, son of Haji Izatullah." Khan nodded. "He was found leaving the Special Forces base. Very early this morning."

"Where is he now?"

"He's in your jail," Maziullah said. Khan paused for a long time. "You wanted everyone we found leaving the Special Forces base to be taken?"

"Yes," Khan said.

"Then what will we do with him?"

"Tell them to give him the full treatment. We'll go there but don't tell them that."

"It's done," Maziullah said and removed a phone from his vest to make the call.

TOOR JAN WAS A POOR MAN, A WEAK MAN

Tarin Kowt City Jail, Tarin Kot District, Uruzgan Province, Afghanistan, 10 November 2012—

They slammed the cell door and left Toor Jan to the gloom and the smell of shit and the clanking of chains from the other cells lining the hallways. His mouth was dry. The screws holding the metal splint to his broken arm felt hot in the bone. He sat, legs locked out straight, ankles bolted to the floor in metal brackets.

Toor Jan pulled hard and—hoping against all hopes—thought he might be able to squeeze his thin ankles out and stand. He pulled until the skin on his shins peeled away in gauzy strips. Toor Jan beat his head against the wall and closed his eyes. He could handle the *talibs* but The Good American hadn't taught him what to do if the police arrested him.

The door ripped open. Three police officers entered. Two stood on either side and stepped on his fingers so that he couldn't raise his hands. The other struck his bare feet with an electrical cord, the lash hissing down to its mark. Toor Jan screamed with each crack, so loud and constant that he stopped being able to hear himself or the grunts of the man hitting him. There was nothing else except the snap of the tool. Finally, his torturer dropped the lash and put his hands on his knees, exhausted. One of the police officers standing on Toor Jan's hands asked him, "What were you doing at the base?"

Toor Jan didn't answer. He was struck across his face. "I work there."

"You look like a dumb farmer." He leaned down, breath fresh with cigarette smoke. "What work do you do there?"

"I clean."

"That's not true."

The torturer recovered, stood up straight and cocked the lash. He struck Toor Jan twice, hard, on his neck. "Where did you get all of that money you were carrying?" The one standing on his hand asked. "How could you afford a motorcycle?"

Toor Jan didn't answer. One by one they struck him across the mouth and left, locking the cell door behind. It was as dark as death in the cell. Toor Jan was a poor man, a weak man. But didn't God love poor people? Protect the weak? What had he done to God? Who was more upright than Toor Jan, son of Haji Izatullah?

Toor Jan's throbbing head hung low. If the police didn't give him a trial they might release him and inform The Big One of the situation. There would be a trial with the *mullahs*. Toor Jan would be accused and not allowed to defend himself. The *talibs* would kill him. It always ended that way for spies. Everyone knew that. No one, police or *talib*, showed mercy to spies. The police officers tore open the door again and crowded him. They were holding the card The Good American had given him. "What is this thing?"

Toor Jan looked at it closely. In the poor light the small picture was nearly black. There was writing on the card. It was yellow. "I don't know."

"It was in your pocket," one of them said and slapped Toor Jan with an open palm. "What's this?"

"It's my identification for the base."

"No it's not." The police officer produced a red badge with a picture and writing. He pushed it toward Toor Jan so that he had to sit back to see it clearly. "*This* is identification for that base. Yours is a fake."

MIR HAMZA KHAN TIES TOOR JAN TO THE CROSS

Tarin Kowt City Jail, Tarin Kot District, Uruzgan Province, Afghanistan, 10 November 2012—

An immediate wave of human stench broke over Khan as he entered the jail with Maziullah. They walked down a long hall lined with cages. Steel barred the cells and shackles bolted the prisoners to the floor. The prison had the feeling of a wolf, taking everything it could with no scraps left behind. It had been used by many others before, as were all things in Uruzgan—first by the Pashtun king, who had built the jail; then the Afghan communists took it over, executing many innocent people in the courtyard until the Soviets occupied the building during the *jihad*. The *talibs* were the last to run the prison before Khan.

Khan and Maziullah climbed to the second floor. The prisoners—thieves, drug addicts, resistant tribal elders, *talib* bomb-makers—stared as they passed. The bomb-makers, hated by the police for their horrible weapons, had it the worst and their knuckles turned white as they clutched their shackles, fearing Khan had arrived to deliver their final punishment. Khan and Maziullah turned the corner to the section where spies were held. Police officers stood in the hallway nudging one another as they watched what was happening inside of a cell.

"What are you doing?" Khan said.

They jumped away from the door. A dry, heavy thump came from inside. A man screamed. Khan and Maziullah went into the cell. Shackles bolted Toor Jan's feet to the floor, forcing him to sit up with his legs straight ahead. His ankles bled from his struggle against the metal. The soles of his feet were swollen. The police officer beating Toor Jan wore a white American-style tank top and blue police pants that bloused into red leather boots. He held a bundle of electrical cord bound in black tape. He was panting.

"Give that to me," Khan said. The torturer handed the lash over and stood at attention. Khan struck the man in the face. He fell back, toward the wall, trying to maintain his bearing. Khan moved onto him, striking his shoulders and neck viciously. "This isn't how we treat our people." Khan handed the lash to Maziullah, who threw it and the torturer out of the room. The rest of the police officers cleared the hallway. Khan squatted over Toor Jan. The reek of his sweat was overpowering. Toor Jan's unfocused eyes rolled like a slaughtered animal's. Khan ran his hand down Toor Jan's leg to the cold burn of the shackle. He told Maziullah to find the key to release the restraints. "Toor *Janna*," Khan said. "What has happened? Why did they take you?"

Toor Jan sniveled. "I was leaving the American base."

"This must be a misunderstanding."

"It is, General." Maziullah reentered with a key and, once released, Toor Jan pulled his legs under his body. He leaned against the filth-streaked wall.

"Why were you at their base?"

"I work there."

"What do you do there?"

Toor Jan looked away. He traced a circle with his finger in the layer of grime coating the floor. "I clean."

"Toor *Janna*. You have me." Khan lifted Toor Jan's splinted arm. "You're in no condition to work."

"I like to work, Haji Khan."

Khan grabbed his hand. Toor Jan tried to take his hand away but Khan didn't let go. "Haven't I been generous?"

"You've been very kind," Toor Jan said.

Khan dropped Toor Jan's hand and stood. "Should I believe what they tell me?"

"What do they tell you?"

"That you're a spy."

Toor Jan began to cry without noise, the tears running down his long nose into his beard.

"This is a serious accusation, Toor Jan."

"I'm not a spy."

"Usually we release the spies to the *talibs*." Toor Jan's body closed in on itself as he continued to cry, shoulders meeting his knees. "And you're The Big One's nephew. He'll want to turn you into an example." Khan examined his fingernails. "They crucified the last spy."

Toor Jan looked up and snarled. "I speak to an American. I tell him nothing important. He pays me *afghanis*. That's all I do!"

"This is bad for your family."

Toor Jan threw his hands into the air. "But what can I do now, Haji Khan?"

"Who's this American?"

"Can you help me?" Toor Jan said. "If I tell you, will you let me go and keep me safe?"

"I can do anything, Toor *Janna*."

"He's a short guy with a small beard."

"What's his name?"

"I don't know. I call him Commander."

He squatted again over Toor Jan. "What does he ask about?"

"Taliban."

"What else?"

"I've seen him twice. He asks about my uncle."

"What does he ask about me?"

Toor Jan's head shot up. "He doesn't ask about you."

"Does he know that you talk to me?"

"No," Toor Jan said. "I wouldn't tell him that."

"Why not?"

"Because you're my protector."

Khan rubbed his face, pondered a thought that wasn't clear yet. "You're a good man, a good Muslim. Did you know that Holy *Qur'an* says that you should not spy?"

"No. I can't read, Haji Khan."

"I've taken care of you better than that uncle who tried to kill you. And whoever this American is." Toor Jan nodded and stared straight ahead. "And I can stop all of this. I can let you leave quietly. Keep your name protected."

"Yes?" Toor Jan said.

"But you must work for me now."

Toor Jan dropped his head to his chest. "How?"

"You'll continue to see this American. You'll continue to do what he asks but when you're done with him you will come see me and we'll discuss your meetings."

"Haji Khan, I'm not the man for this job." Toor Jan sat up. "There has to be something else I can do."

"Have you ever seen a man tied to a cross?" Khan lashed his hand around his wrist.

Toor Jan began to cry again. "Okay," he said once he had stopped. "I can tell you what we talk about."

"You must also take a picture of this man."

Toor Jan huffed. "It's impossible. I don't know how to trick people."

"Do you love your family Toor *Janna*?"

"They are the all that I love."

"Your uncle once killed a spy's entire family." Khan crouched down. Behind him, Maziullah smiled. "Do you know how to use the camera on your cell phone?"

"I do."

"You can take the picture of the American in a special way." The guards had given Maziullah everything from Toor Jan's pockets. Khan called for the cell phone and showed Toor Jan how to take a picture quickly from under his sleeve so the American wouldn't see. He ordered Toor Jan to practice the method. Toor Jan took pictures of the walls and cell door in the same way. "Enough. You're ready," Khan said. "You're a good man, Toor Jan." He turned to leave.

"Haji Khan," Toor Jan called after him. Khan stopped. "This can't work. They take my cell phone away from me when I see them."

Khan turned around. "Do you have pictures of your uncle saved on that phone?"

"Yes," Toor Jan said. "Many."

"Tell the American that you need to keep your phone so you can show him pictures of your uncle. Maybe it'll help them find The Big One and kill him. That will be good for all of us." Khan smiled. "Now I must go home to spend the rest of the day with my wife. You do the same, Toor *Janna*."

TOOR JAN FEARED GOD AND SHUNNED EVIL

Tarin Kowt City, Tarin Kot District, Uruzgan Province, Afghanistan, 10 November 2012—

The General had ordered his men to give Toor Jan his motorcycle back when he left the prison. Toor Jan went slow, afraid that in his condition—weak, hurt, hungry—he would crash and die on the long road back to Safad Khare. The *nazars*, hung from the fenders to protect him from evil, tinkled as he kept the motorcycle upright. It took a full hour to reach his compound.

The gate was open. His heart flapped in his chest. He tried to slink through, in case there was trouble inside, but the motorcycle pegs caught the metal door. Abdul Hakim sat alone under the almond tree.

"Why is the gate open?"

Abdul Hakim shrugged.

Toor Jan leaned the motorcycle against the wall. He locked the gate, stared at his brother, then dropped to his knees at the well. The water was mineral-tasting and cold pouring down his throat. He sucked the water for a long time and when he finished Abdul Hakim stood over him. "I told you to not leave it open."

"I didn't, brother."

Abdul Hakim reached for a welt on Toor Jan's neck. A painful nerve fired. Toor Jan brushed his brother's hand away, then left Abdul Hakim and went inside the house. Shaheen was sick from the baby and lying down, a slim white arm flung across her eyes. Toor Jan took off his dirty long shirt and didn't hide the damage from his beating.

"You're hurt!" She sat up. Her great belly pushed against her dress. "What happened?" Toor Jan reached inside a wooden chest for his other shirt. She walked over and touched a red stripe on his skin. She touched another and another. "They know now. They know you're a spy."

"No one knows. Some robbers on the road found me." He slipped into a gray *kameez*. Stood upright. "Shaheen *Jo?*"

"Yes?"

"Do you think it would be better if I had died as a child? You might have a better husband now."

The girl stepped back. "But who would have cared for Abdul Hakim then?"

Toor Jan left without answering.

In the courtyard, he sat against the trunk of the almond tree and pulled his knees close. Abdul Hakim appeared and sat down too, leaning against his brother. It was painful for Toor Jan but he didn't move.

"Why does God hate you?"

"God doesn't hate me."

"Then why does God always hurt you?"

"I don't know, Abdul *Jan*."

Abdul Hakim stared at the light dappling the ground through the branches.

"I must teach you how to take care of this house. In case I'm gone."

"I would like to learn, brother."

Toor Jan turned toward him. They sat so close that his beard tickled the side of Abdul Hakim's cheek. He giggled. "Listen to me!"

"I hear you, brother."

"You must lock the gate. You must always lock the gate."

"I already learned that from you."

"Then learn this: God doesn't hate me. He's never hated me. I fear God and I shun evil." Toor Jan stared at the double metal gate that sealed their compound from the world. "It's everything outside of our walls that hates me now."

ISAIAH KHOST ENDS
NEGOTIATIONS

***Tarin Kowt City, Tarin Kot District, Afghanistan, 17
November 2012—***

Isaiah Khost kneeled on the floor of his bedroom and counted out a million dollars into ten even stacks. He hadn't slept in two days and didn't want to. It had happed before—the sleeplessness—on his fifth deployment he'd gone fifty hours straight, charged by the energy of his plans. Khost lost count, interrupted by that energy, those plans, and started over. He stopped counting and looked up, sure he'd heard someone. Nothing. *I'm fucking imaging things.* Khost laughed to himself and continued.

Khost had emptied the safe of the discretionary funds, bit by bit. At night, he slipped from his room—a hooded sweatshirt pulled over his head— and went to the safe, filling the log with fake expenses, and put the money in his pocket to hide in the bottom of his collapsible laundry hamper. *The hamper*, he thought and jumped up to make sure he hadn't left any money behind. Khost turned it over and shook it out to make sure. *Nothing.*

When he had the full million, Khost called General Khan and issued a simple promise: "I have a solution for Security Day, General." General Khan sounded happy but demanded that Khost meet with him at Police

Headquarters, before breakfast. There was no other possible time to discuss Security Day. Khost agreed, eagerly. And he was even more eager now, eager to make sure he counted the money accurately and eager to finally move past the Security Day debacle.

One million. Khost had counted three times. He gathered the bills and stuffed them into his day pack. There was a knock on his bedroom door. "Give me a minute," he said. Khost slid the day pack under his bed, leapt up, and opened the door suddenly.

Master Chief startled. "Sir."

"Master Chief." Khost came out of the room and closed the door behind him. "Good workout this morning?" He placed his arm around the Master Chief's shoulders and walked toward the operations center.

"Yeah, I hit it hard with Josh Ramsey. Strong kid."

"Kid is right, I'd say." They turned a corner and continued as people pressed themselves against the walls, out of the way. "Maybe put the strong behind kid next time you describe him."

"You need to come out with us soon."

"Yeah I know." Khost hadn't worked out since he arrived in Afghanistan. He hadn't watched a movie or read a book. He'd called home twice and talked to his wife, hanging up before the kids could get on the line. "I'll start again once we get over the Security Day hump."

They passed through the doors to the operations center and the staff jumped up as Master Chief called attention on deck. Khost waved his hand for them to continue working. He went to his seat in the center of the room and sat heavily, pressing his boot soles into the ground to prevent the chair from spinning. "What's the convoy plan for meeting General Khan?"

The staff turned toward him and the Master Chief spoke, "Meeting with MHK starts in an hour. We're jocking up in twenty mikes, then we'll meet the PSD and go into the city."

"I want it lean, half the number of guys we took last time."

"Sir, that's against SOPs—"

"What'd I just say?" Khost stood. "Meet you at the trucks in twenty minutes." He left the operations center.

Twenty minutes later, Khost stood next to the convoy—day pack on his back—as they did their final communications check. He had taken his helmet off to loosen the straps, and with it finally sitting comfortably on his head, he leaned against a truck. The Master Chief had gone through the crew and talked for a long time to the Platoon Chief before coming to Khost.

"No weapon again, sir?"

"I'm armed." Khost tapped the gift knife that General Khan had given him at their first meeting. "See?"

Master Chief frowned at the day pack on Khost's shoulders. "You don't think that bag will get in the way? Not much room for it in the Vic."

Khost stuttered, a sharp noise with no words. "It's extra stuff. You know. We'll be out there for a while. Maybe some Black Hawk Down shit happens."

Master Chief squinted. "You're worried we might get surrounded but you only want to take half the number of guys and you won't carry a gun?"

A million secret dollars weighed on his back but Khost undeterred. He straightened. "Rick, tell the fucking platoon Chief to get this convoy going."

"Roger that, sir." Master Chief leaned into his radio mic. "Fire 'em up." And the engines started right away.

Commander Khost, Master Chief, and Chamber rode together through the city. Khost inhaled and exhaled loudly to control his nerves. The Master Chief saw his fear. "Sir," he said. "It's going to be as simple as telling a kid that he can't have candy every time he goes to the store."

But I'm the generous candy man.

They pulled up to Police Headquarters and went inside. General Khan stood at the top of the stairs again and invited the men into the office. He showed them to the Queen Anne chairs, now pulled up to his large desk. General Khan walked to the opposite side and stood. He wore his police uniform with a pistol and a shrunken blue patrol cap. Khost had worn the day pack into the building, ignoring Master Chief's confused look, and put it under his feet after he sat down. He patted the gift knife in the webbing of his body armor and smiled.

Colonel Maziullah, not General Khan, started the conversation. "It is good to see you," he said to Khost and Master Chief. Chamber tried to make the lifeless greeting polite in translation but Khost sensed the tone anyway.

"It's even better to see you, General and Colonel," Khost said. He waited for *chai* to be served but when the quiet came again he realized they weren't offering tea. "Is there something wrong, General?"

General Khan brought his hands behind his back and cleared his throat. "You said you have a solution for Security Day."

"I do," Khost said. Master Chief smirked, sure of what was next. Khost reached under his feet for his day pack and dropped the bag on General Khan's desk. "This is what I personally offer you. As a start."

General Khan, with some struggle, unzipped the bag and a pile of green bills spilled out. He lifted the bag, testing the weight, and his face darkened like a cloud passing across the sun.

"Izzy, what is this?" Master Chief said.

174

"Don't worry about it, Rick."

"But this is not enough," General Khan said. "I'm a rich man and I know how much this bag should weigh."

"It's a start, General."

"Commander," Master Chief got to his feet. He was looking at General Khan as he spoke to Khost. "What are you doing right now?"

"Shut your mouth, Master Chief." Chamber translated this without thinking and General Khan smiled. "General, there's more money coming. Let this be the first of my payments to you."

"Commander, like you said, we *will* solve this today. Your country has broken an agreement. I can't afford to keep Security Day without the funds. Security Day is over."

General Khan sat down in his chair and Maziullah came around the desk. They took a stack of papers from a drawer. General Khan made room by pushing the bag of money to the floor and sweeping the loose stacks to one side of his desk.

Khost froze, shocked.

"Where's that money from?" Master Chief said.

Khost didn't answer. He stared at General Khan and Maziullah.

General Khan looked up as if surprised that Khost was still there. "Did you know your man personally? The one who died in Chorah?"

General Khan had to say it twice before Chamber translated.

"What does that have to do with anything?"

Khan tucked his arms behind his back again and the shadow returned to his face. "Good luck to the rest of the Americans in Uruzgan."

Isaiah Khost gripped the top of Khan's desk. "Is this a joke?"

When Chamber translated General Khan was confused. "No one is laughing, Commander."

"What did that mean then?" Khost would have leaped across the desk if Master Chief hadn't bear-hugged him. He pounded on the desk and the stacks of money jumped. "What are you saying?"

"I'm saying it's too bad that so many of your men get hurt, so often."

Isaiah Khost brought his hand to his body armor and pulled General Khan's gift knife out with force. He raised it high above his head and drove it down through a stack of money, into Khan's desk. The stuck gift knife vibrated in the wood.

Khost left the office. General Khan ignored Master Chief as he scooped up the money and stuffed it back into the day pack. He sprinted outside after Khost. Khost's Personal Security Detachment ran to the trucks so fast that they barely shut the back hatch before they took off. Isaiah Khost screamed inside of the truck. He had removed his helmet and radio headset. Sweat gathered around his temples and beaded below his exhausted eyes. Chamber put his headphones on and ignored Khost's scene. "He fucking fooled me." He turned toward Master Chief. "That illiterate *dirt farmer* fooled me." Khost threw his helmet against the rear hatch. "We can get him now. That's what we should do. We can target him."

"You want to kill an Afghan General?"

Khost rocked in his seat. "I know but he's not what he seems. Not what he seems at all."

Master Chief picked the million dollars up from the floor of the truck. "Is this our *entire* discretionary fund?"

Khost slapped Master Chief's helmet. "If you breathe a word of this to anyone. Do you hear me, Rick?"

Master Chief put the bag back on the floor.

Khost stopped talking and watched the city teem outside. He saw everything he had missed before. Crowds packed with danger and prepared to kill anyone that wasn't them.

It was a new world that had always been there.

TOOR JAN TAKES A PICTURE OF THE GOOD AMERICAN

Multinational Base Tarin Kowt, Tarin Kot District, Uruzgan Province, Afghanistan, 19 November 2012

A wind had come out of the mountains after the *asr* prayer and raised a phantom of dust. After it started the villagers didn't leave their homes. The day's light had been robbed by the sandstorm. At night, the wind calmed to an occasional breeze and the fine powder settled into long drifts along trees, rocks, cars, motorcycles, and compound walls. The air became clear, the stars polished by the hard cold.

Toor Jan lay awake, listening to the irregular scrape of his metal gate swinging open. He left Shaheen sleeping on the floor and crossed the dark to the unlocked gate. The breeze brought it apart and shut again, in thin respiration. Toor Jan cursed his brother. A shadow flitted across the ground. It was strange, obviously alive. Toor Jan's chest tightened. He didn't move.

"Toor Jan, come outside."

Toor Jan pointed his foot in the direction of the rifle in his house but couldn't move. "Who is it?" Dirt crunched. A gun zipped against its leather strap. The rushing blue of Maziullah's rifle, bright in the darkness, came around the gate. Toor Jan breathed. "Why didn't you say who you were?"

"Because I don't want to make a lot of noise." Maziullah pulled the gate closed behind him. In the dark he seemed supernaturally powerful, like a devil that didn't need to sleep and could never die. He looked up at Toor Jan and smiled. "You're awake."

"I heard the gate."

"I was coming to rip you from your bed." He strapped his rifle across his chest and circled Toor Jan. "Do you remember what you've promised the General?"

"How could I forget?"

"Tomorrow is your next meeting with the American." He turned like a wheel around Toor Jan. "You know how to take the picture?"

"Of course I do, Colonel."

"Because we won't forget. We saved you from jail but we can send you back. Or we can tell your uncle that you're a spy. There are many possibilities."

Toor Jan looked at the ground. Maziullah raised Toor Jan's chin with his heavy paw and Toor Jan nodded to show that he understood. Maziullah disappeared into the dark. Toor Jan didn't sleep for the rest of the night.

The morning was clear. The sun cooked the road passing underneath Toor Jan's motorcycle. The engine burned between his legs. By the time he arrived at the American base, he was a slick mess. Toor Jan was nervous when he met Qais inside the tunnel. They greeted one another and the *tajiman* held his hand out for the cell phone.

"It has pictures of my uncle that I would like to give Commander. Can I keep it?"

Qais frowned. "What's happened to you? You're all beat up." His eyes followed the lines of bruises on Toor Jan's neck. "Who did this to you?"

"It's nothing."

Qais stood in front of him. "Commander will want to know what happened."

"We wrestle in the village."

"And this is what happened?"

"Yes, *Sahib Jan*."

"You shouldn't lie to us, Toor Jan."

"By my eyes I'm telling you the truth."

"For now I'll take your cell phone and we'll ask Commander what he wants." He took Toor Jan's cell phone. Toor Jan almost cried then. He didn't want to be crucified. They went through the gate and came out the other side. The Good American was sitting in his truck. Qais leaned into the window and spoke to The Good American in English while Toor Jan waited. The *tajiman* turned to Toor Jan. "Commander says he wants me to hold your cell phone until we get inside. Then you can have it."

"What the hell happened, my friend?" The Good American said turning in his seat as Toor Jan entered the truck. "Qais said you wrestled someone? Did you wrestle five guys at once?"

Toor Jan replied no, seriously, because he didn't understand the joke at first through the translation. Qais told him it was a joke. "That's funny. I only wrestled one man. Very strong."

The Good American started the truck and hurried over the bumps and holes, then skidded through the gate to their smaller compound. Inside, a chicken and a rooster fretted together through the yard, clucking and lowering their heads to the grass. Toor Jan smiled and crouched to touch the rooster. It crowed and jumped away. The men laughed at the bird.

Toor Jan stood. "Do you know how you get them to stop crowing?"

"I wish I did because that thing does it all night. I might shoot it," The Good American said, patting his machine gun.

"It's easy to get them to stop."

"How?"

"Rub Vaseline on its asshole." Toor Jan looked at the men. He turned to the rooster picking along the ground and nodded. He looked back at the men. "Works every time."

"Let's go inside," The Good American said. He put *chai* and cookies on the table. They also had slices of sweet cake on paper napkins. The Good American reached to pour the tea but Toor Jan stopped him.

"You are the Commander so I must pour for you." Toor Jan's anxious hands had steadied with the warmth of the room and the smell of sweet cake. He topped off three glasses and distributed them.

"Look at this," The Good American said. He pulled a cell phone from his pocket and handed it to Toor Jan. "That's my daughter."

She was young and smiling. Her eyes were green and her hair was brown. She played happily in a grassy yard while staring into the camera. Toor Jan's stomach dropped. The Good American had a family too. *He must truly be a good man.*

"Oh, this is good," Toor Jan said. "I said I wanted a son," he said as he handed back the phone. "But I will be happy with a girl too. I want them to be healthy most of all."

"That's what everyone wants, Toor Jan."

"Yes. Everywhere in the world we want this. But in Afghanistan it is hard to have healthy children." Toor Jan took a bite of the sweet cake and set it back down on the table. He felt like he would puke. *Why does the General need this picture?*

"When you have your child we will make sure there is a doctor to see it." The Good American smiled and opened his notebook. "Qais said you have pictures of people? Your uncle maybe?"

Toor Jan put his glass on the table and swallowed hard. In that moment he didn't want to take a picture of The Good American. *Damn the cross*. The man had a family. What if the General used the picture to find The Good American and kill him? "Yes. I will show you." He reached, his hand trembling again, for his cell phone. "I will show you my pictures."

The plastic phone was slippery in Toor Jan's sweaty hands as he scrolled to get to the camera. "I will show you my pictures." Toor Jan held the phone at his chest, the eye of the camera facing The Good American. His bearded and tanned face floated on the screen. The Good American was blurry and Toor Jan waited until the lens focused. "I will show you my pictures." The screen, The Good American's face—down to the hair on his chin—became clear. Toor Jan said, "I will show you my pictures," again. The Good American looked directly into the lens. Toor Jan pressed the button. A burst of light filled the room.

Toor Jan had forgotten to turn off the flash.

The Good American jumped across the table and Qais wrapped his arm around Toor Jan's neck. They wrestled him out of his chair. The Good American pushed Qais out of the way and lifted Toor Jan off of the ground. He said something angry in English and pinned Toor Jan hard against the wall. Qais searched his pockets. He took the cell phone and Toor Jan's prayer beads. Toor Jan didn't have anything else. The Good American slammed Toor Jan into the wall and pressed him until he couldn't breathe. He finally let go of Toor Jan but thought better of it and twisted the metal splint in Toor Jan's arm.

Toor Jan screamed.

The Good American pushed Toor Jan out of the room, kicked the rooster out of the way, and threw him into the truck. Qais drove the car to the main gate and The Good American sat next to Toor Jan with his machine gun pointed at his belly. At the main gate they skidded to a halt and threw Toor Jan from the truck, chucking the cell phone, without the SIM card, at his feet. The tires spat dust in Toor Jan's eyes as they tore away. He blinked, flushing the burning debris, and walked to the lot.

If Toor Jan could have explained the facts of his heart to men and God then they would understand. The abuse would end. But it wasn't that way for Toor Jan. In the lot outside the American base, Toor Jan sat on his red motorcycle with his scarf covering his face and cried for a long time in the hot light.

DAN WANTED TO BE A PART OF HISTORY

Multinational Base Tarin Kowt, Tarin Kot District, Uruzgan Province, Afghanistan, 23 November 2012—

Dan was so shocked by what Toor Jan had done that it took him three days to report the security breach to Captain Cales and Beau. He dragged himself from his hut early in the morning and found Captain Cales and Beau in the Soviet Building. Dan shut the door behind him without a sound, trying to be silent enough to listen undetected. Low whispers came from the main room. A chair scraped and Beau's heavy footsteps followed. They nearly collided.

"Dan! How are you, big man?" Beau shook his hand, the other wrapped like a vise around Dan's forearm. "I'm about to go to the chow hall, wanna come?" He opened the door without waiting for an answer.

"Wait a minute, Beau. I have to talk to both of you."

"I'll go grab some food and be right back."

"No, stay. I mean, I need to talk you two about something really important."

"Both of us, eh?" Captain Cales said from the main room.

"What happened?" Beau lowered his brow and nearly picked Dan up as he ushered him to Captain Cales. He pulled out a chair and put Dan into it. "You doing okay?"

"Beau, relax. Everything is good."

Captain Cales faced Dan. He folded his fingers in his lap. "What's up then?"

Dan rubbed his shaved head and looked at the pressed tin ceiling. "I got compromised." They both leaned forward. "I was meeting a source and he tried to take a picture of me with his cell phone."

"How do you know?" Beau said. "You saw him do it?"

"The flash went off." Dan exhaled. "I wrestled the phone from him and took it. Me and Qais kicked his ass off base."

"Where's the phone?" Captain Cales said.

"We threw it out with him but the SIM card is in my hut."

"Was it that Taliban fuck?" Beau said. "The one who got blown up at the school?"

"Yeah. Toor Jan." Saying his name brought anger and also something like love. "Someone did something to him. He was all beaten up when he met us. Bruises on his neck and a busted lip."

"Sounds pretty simple," Captain Cales said. He had gone back to his computer and was typing everything Dan said. "Someone got to him. Probably his uncle. They do this all the time."

"What were they going to do with the picture?" Dan said, asking both Captain Cales and Beau.

"Depends," Beau said.

"Usually, they use it to offer a reward for someone to capture or kill you." Captain Cales said. "They think you're in the CIA. It's a big prize."

"*Wonderful*," Dan said.

"You got the report, Captain?" Beau said. He stood and smoothed down his running shorts.

"Yeah, starting it right now. You going up top to tell them?"

"Yeah, I'll go put on my uniform right now."

"Hold on, hold on," Dan said. "I mean, what are we doing here? Do we *have* to say something?"

"Yes," Beau said.

"Why?"

"Because," Captain Cales said, as he typed, "if you happen to end up on Al Jazeera getting your head sawed off, it's going to make some waves. They'll want to know why."

"That's not going to happen." Dan stood up to stop Beau from walking to Commander Khost's office. "You know what Khost is going to do. Especially since they all hate me."

"You don't know that, Dan," Beau said.

"I've pissed all of them off. You actually think they'll be fair to me?"

Captain Cales stopped typing. "It's not all about *you*, Dan."

"Don't worry about a thing," Beau said and left.

Captain Cales waited until the door slammed shut before he pointed to the folding chair. Dan flopped back into it and—to show the Captain that he could still do what he wanted—put both of his feet on the card table.

Captain Cales smirked. "Listen, kid. I'm not saying I know what's going to happen but there's a good chance they shut you down."

"Then what?"

"They could put you to work in Konig and Chief Nunez's office."

"Great," Dan said rolling his eyes. "I'll get to be with *all* my friends."

"Nah." Captain Cales went back to his typing. "I won't let them."

Dan canted his head. "Wow, really?" He added, "Thank you, sir."

Captain Cales didn't look. "Because I'm going to send you home. If you can't meet sources, no one needs you. You can go do the instructor job at the interrogation school that you weaseled your way out of."

"You can't do that to me."

"I'm a fucking captain. That means I can do whatever I want to *you*." He held a hand up. "Within legal limits."

Dan puffed air out. "I haven't done anything yet. How am I going to go back and teach something I've never done in the real world?"

"What do you care? This war is over anyway. And instructor duty is good for your evaluations. You'll make rank off of that."

"I don't care about that stuff. I left a really good job back home and joined to do something important and when being a SEAL didn't work out, I wanted this job. I had to fight to come out here. I want to be a part—" He laughed, a little. "I want to be a part of history."

Captain Cales looked at Dan. "And the rest of us, the ones who have been here two or three or seven times could care less." Cales waved his hand for Dan to leave. "Go do something else and let me finish your report."

ISAIAH KHOST LOVED
THE HARSH COLD

Multinational Base Tarin Kowt, Tarin Kot District, Uruzgan Province, Afghanistan, 08 December 2012—

Isaiah Khost and the Master Chief had not spoken to each other for three weeks. It wasn't easy—they led the SEAL Team together—but it worked through an unspoken agreement that Khost's trouble sleeping caused him to miss the morning meetings and the Master Chief's obligation to visit the troops was his excuse to miss the ones in the afternoon. That way they never had to be together. During missions, when they were both required to be in the operations center, they made perfunctory conversation and the rest of the time felt each other's presence like repulsive magnetic poles.

The Master Chief had kept the bag of money—probably in his room in a safe meant for classified documents. Khost knew this because he had crept to the team's safe several times to see if the cash had been put back. Frustrated, he stared at the expense log and considered altering it to hide what he had done. But there was no hiding anymore. Khost felt like everyone could see his thoughts scrolling across his mind.

Holding a blue folder to his chest, Khost avoided eye contact as he hurried down the hall to the command suite for the weekly logistics meeting. It was an important meeting. Without a Security Day for the past three weeks their supplies were dangerously low and the airlift must begin soon. Khost stopped at the door to the command suite. It was closed and he didn't hear anyone inside. Normally, everyone arrived at the meeting before him, waiting and chatting, until the attention on deck was sounded and they popped up from their chairs.

Khost opened the door. The Master Chief sat alone, at the middle of the long table. "Master Chief."

"Sir."

Khost rolled his chair out carefully and sat the same way. "Master Chief?"

"Yes, sir?"

"Where is everyone?"

"Meeting's cancelled."

"I didn't cancel the meeting." Khost looked behind him, as if everyone would leap out from their hiding spots and yell "Surprise!" "Why are you here? It's after twelve."

The Master Chief raised his steel-colored eyebrows. The screen of the VTC flickered on.

It was Kabul. General Branson sat alone in his office. "Good afternoon, Commander Khost, Master Chief."

"Afternoon, sir," they both replied.

General Branson released a pent-up breath. "Commander Khost, I'm using this occasion to formally—" *Since when don't you call me, Izzy?* "—relieve you in place of all your duties as Commanding Officer of SEAL Team—"

Master Chief stared straight ahead, away from both Khost and General Branson.

"Who's putting you up to this?"

"—and furthermore," General Branson looked down to read from a prepared statement, "to inform you that an Inspector General investigation—"

"Is this really what you imagined for yourself all those years ago? That your job would be ruining your friends?"

"—and that an agent from the Naval Criminal Investigative Service will arrive in Tarin Kowt to conduct an audit of all discretionary fund accounts under your control. It's recommended and expected that you will cooperate fully."

"Where's that fat fuck, Colicchio? And the old Elmer Fudd, Casey? They didn't want to do this too? You draw the short straw or did you want to do this? Fucking murderer." Khost threw his pen at the screen and a rainbow of damage arced across the plasma. "Judas. You goddamned Judas."

Master Chief retrieved the pen and kept it.

"Do you have any appropriate questions at this time, Commander Khost?" General Branson said.

"Uruzgan was going to be the crown jewel of my career."

"No," Master Chief said, at last. "This was supposed to be the easy deployment. Shut down the base and turn it over to whatever government was here."

"The NCIS agents will arrive tonight. You'll answer questions to their satisfaction and then you'll be on the first plane out to the States. At which time," General Branson said, consulting his written statement again, "you will report to the Naval Special Warfare Training Detachment in Little Creek and stand by for further instruction."

"You're talking about my life," Khost said. He picked his head up and looked into the camera, at General Branson. "*This* is my life."

"Life is long," General Branson said. "This is just one part of life, Izzy."

Khost stormed out. There was no one in the hall but he could've killed anyone he saw trying to get to his room. He slammed the door behind him and tore his clothes off. Ripped the flags, maps from the wall. Fully naked, he went through each item, looked at it carefully, then tore it in half. He stopped at two photos pinned to a tack board. His wife Juliette looking over her shoulder. The beach and sun behind her. She smiled. Her hair was the color of golden syrup and the curve of her neck was beautiful. The other was of the kids when they were young, frozen in the frame as blue-eyed babies. Smiling happy, toothy grins.

He held the pictures as he dialed home on his command cell phone.

"Hello, Jay," he said when Juliette picked up the phone. The family's basset hound barked and the kids were playing. A television was on in the background.

"Izzy? Is that you?"

"Yeah, it's me." He sat on his bed, his naked thighs cold against the dirty sheets. "How are you?"

"How am I? How are *you*?" She yelled at everyone to be quiet. "What's been going on? I've been waiting and waiting for you to call."

Khost put the pictures of his family face-down on the bed. "I'm coming home."

"Really? Why?"

"I've had some problems."

"Oh no, love." She sighed. "How can they send you home? You're in charge of *everything*. Are you okay?"

"No." He flipped the pictures of his family face up, like a dealer with cards. "I'm not okay."

"I still don't get how they could remove you. You've worked for years to be in command. Who can replace you?"

"Anyone, apparently." Khost growled, to himself mostly. "I don't think I'm getting out of this one, Jay."

"Getting out of what, Izzy?" She paused. "What aren't you telling me?"

"Nothing," he said, shaking his head. He flipped their pictures face down and walked over to his gun rack. "I gotta go."

"We love you, Izzy."

Khost hung up and threw the command cell phone into the burn bag, meant for destroying classified documents. He traced his fingers along the gun rack, over the plastic and tempered metal, loving the harsh cold of his weapons. He went over to his Sig Sauer P226, the one he never carried. He checked the pistol's magazine, blew dust off the rounds, and reinserted it into the P226, chambering a bullet.

Naked and looming, he looked around the destroyed room. His unmade bed. Khost sat down on it, press checked the chamber of the P226. The dull brass glinted in the overhead light. He eased himself onto the feather pillows, on top of the pictures of his family.

Isaiah Khost put the pistol under his chin and pulled the trigger.

PART III

NAGHMA, THE QUEEN

Mir Hamza Khan's mansion, Tarin Kowt City, Tarin Kot District, Uruzgan Province, Afghanistan, 12 December 2012—

It had been five weeks since the last Security Day when the rain came. A wave of gray cloud had rushed up the palisade of mountains around Tarin Kowt City and hung there like a brass ring. It had rained for a week, the downpour so constant that Naghma, watching the rain with Little Maziullah from inside the doorway of her home, thought that the storm must be a foreign invader. It was impossible that this much water could come just from Uruzgan.

The guards stood on the parapets in slicked-down ponchos. Water sluiced from their rifle barrels and drenched their boots and each man stared, miserably, over the walls of the mansion. The mansion's courtyard had flooded. The cherry-red Mercedes—the one Naghma called her car—had sunk into the ground, tires banked with mud. Rain popped off the round, red bladder feeding Mogas to the idling green Ford Ranger. Once a month Mir Hamza would wake Naghma and Little Maziullah from their sleep and practice gathering clothes, jewelry, and the money he had hidden in a compartment in her kitchen floor, then running to the green Ford Ranger as if they needed to escape. Mir Hamza had no plan to save the other wives.

Across the courtyard, at Aghala's house, the doctor in his white lab coat appeared again. He lit a cigarette in his quivering hands and took a drag. The baby Aziz had been sick for five days. Everything he ate had turned to water. Naghma didn't know anything else. She didn't talk to the other wives except to hold court on holidays. Mir Hamza beside her, Little Maziullah at her feet, and her hands folded in her lap as those girls chattered about their wash, their sweeping, or their next trip to Canada, Britain, or some other exotic place. Mir Hamza had followed the law and provided for every woman equally—except for his love and devotion to Naghma. Every wife knew that.

The doctor, drenched now, flicked his cigarette into a puddle. He went back into Aghala's house. Naghma stroked Little Maziullah's head as he leaned into her. It was cold in the doorway, the rain glazing the transom and soaking the hem of her pale dress. Naghma hugged her son for warmth. "Are you hungry *Zullah Jan*?" It was time for the mid-day meal. She had made an almond cake, for when Mir Hamza came to sleep with her that night, but had already given Little Maziullah a slice for breakfast. She regretted it, a bit, the cake made with the last of her flour and without Security Day she didn't know when there would be more. "Let's eat."

Their wet feet nearly flew out from under them as they went across the white tile toward the kitchen and Naghma pipped—a short, controlled cry—at the two dark figures standing in front of her propane stove.

"What are you doing?" she said to Fatima and Aufia, Mir Hamza's other wives. Their black dresses and veils clung, water-soaked, making puddles on her floor. Naghma pushed Little Maziullah behind her. "Why are you inside my house?"

The girls turned to each other to decide who would answer. Aufia spoke, "We didn't want *Mira Jan* to see us." Mir Hamza was on the roof, under a tarp in his favorite spot. Since he ended Security Day, he spent most of his time on the roof. "So we came through the back."

"Of *my* house," Naghma said. She thought she might slap the girls. "This is *my* house."

"Yes," Fatima said. "But we need you." She looked at Little Maziullah. His eyes looked over his mother's shoulder. Naghma hid him from Fatima's view. "Aziz is dying and *Mir Jan* won't help us."

Leaving Little Maziullah with Fatima and Aufia, Naghma went across the courtyard through the rain—muddying her feet. Rain plucked the hoods of the cars. The red coals of the guard's cigarettes glowed in the shadow of their poncho hoods. She snagged the trail of her dress on rose bushes as she cut through the dead garden, into the mildewed smell of sickness in Aghala's house. Naghma went because she knew what Aziz meant to Mir Hamza. Those girls meant nothing to her, not really. She doubted they'd even seen a baby die, as she had seen three of her own children. The other wives were rich in a way that even with all of Mir Hamza's money Naghma would never be. She went to see for herself if the situation was truly dire.

The doctor met Naghma at the door, bowed reverentially, wet lab coat sticking to his body. He was shorter than her, dark-skinned, nose broken with veins, gray hair wild on the back of his head. He wore a moustache. "Hello," he said and waved her through the door and into the sitting area of the large open room.

Aghala sat on her American couch, black hair sweat-pasted to her forehead. Without regard for modesty, her dress hung open, almost showing her breasts. Across the room, the television murmured. A bucket of the child's diarrhea—the color of watery rice—sat on the floor. Aziz—brown hair limp, feet and hands wrinkled—hung from her lap. His eyes were sunk into his skull.

Naghma's breath left her. "Has *Mira Jan* been here?" Aghala looked up, as if surprised that Naghma would even talk to her, but didn't answer. "Has he seen this? How bad it is?"

"Twice," the doctor said. He clasped his hands behind his back. "This morning he was here. I asked him to let the trucks go so we can have medicine."

"What did he say?"

"That we wait until the Americans give up and pay him for Security Day."

Aghala brought Aziz's forehead to her lips in a kiss as if it that could heal her baby. Naghma had done the same before, to her own dead infants. Aghala looked at Naghma and said, "We cannot wait, sister."

Naghma hadn't run since she was a girl but she ran out of Aghala's house, alarming the guards, slipped in the mud and fell, got up, slipped again and continued up the stairs to the roof, to Mir Hamza. She flopped breathlessly under his tarp. Mir Hamza didn't seem to notice, squatting over an American jet-boil stove for warmth and staring out at the watery city with a distant look Naghma didn't recognize. Maziullah, standing with his blue rifle under the smallest corner of the tarp, shouted at him to help Naghma.

Mir Hamza snapped alive. "What is it?" he said and pulled her toward the flame.

Naghma ignored the delicious warmth. "We need medicine or your son will die." Down in the city a line of trucks was parked the length of the main boulevard. The drivers had shown up for Security Day five weeks ago but—without their guards—had never left. They still waited in their vehicles. "Let the trucks go."

Mir Hamza turned away from her, paced out into the rain and back. "The Americans will lose. We only have to wait." He pointed to the raining sky. "They can't bring their helicopters or planes in this weather. They're starving too. We must wait for them to call."

Naghma knew that he was so sick with rage that he was delusional—the Americans could do miracles and would always eat—and gripped Mir Hamza's beard, hard, tugging him down the steps to Aghala's house so he could see Aziz again. Maziullah followed. The guards pretended not to notice. Naghma dragged him into Aghala's house before she let him go. Mir Hamza scowled but followed her into the sitting area.

In the minutes since she had been gone, Aziz seemed to have gotten worse, his skin as thin as paper. She pointed to the doctor. "Can this be cured with medicine?" He stood in the corner, hiding, and hesitated to step forward. "Answer me. Can we cure this with medicine?"

"Yes," he said.

Mir Hamza looked at the floor, the carpet, the edge of the pink couch but not at the boy. It was too devastating. Naghma raised his chin up for him. "What is it?" he said to the doctor after chancing a glimpse of his youngest son.

"The sickness?"

"Yes. What is it?"

"Cholera."

Naghma shuddered. She was angry that Mir Hamza hadn't already asked and she was angry that the baby had the disease of the unsanitary. This should never happen in Mir Hamza's house. "Let the trucks go, *Mira Jan*," she said. Mir Hamza stood, treaded hard along the carpet, back to the doctor, past Aghala, to the television, shut it off, and came back again. "No?" He had the power to save his son. Naghma hated that he wouldn't use it. "You won't let them go?"

Mir Hamza turned to Maziullah. The small man had stayed near the door, blue rifle shouldered, watching the family. "Maziullah. Go to the

Chinese hospital." The Chinese hospital was an inferior clinic—built by the Chinese government—west of the city but it had medicine. "Take a man with you and use the Ford Ranger." Mir Hamza looked at Naghma. She nodded her head, recognizing the risk he was taking in sending Maziullah in their escape vehicle. "We'll wait here for you." Mir Hamza sat next to Aghala and stroked Aziz's bare, dry feet.

Naghma ran again, the second time since she was a girl, to her house. Fatima and Aufia sprang from the floor in the sitting room as she came inside. Little Maziullah watched without getting up.

"You talked to him?" Aufia said, both women following Naghma.

"Yes," Naghma said, flying into the kitchen. She took the box holding the almond cake meant for Mir Hamza and turned back toward the sitting room.

Aufia, feeling that the moment didn't permit fear, took Naghma's shoulders and stopped her. "Did you convince him to let the trucks go?"

"I didn't," she said. She snapped her finger at Little Maziullah. He rose slowly. Aufia let go of Naghma's shoulders and hung her head. Naghma took her hand. "He sent Maziullah to the Chinese hospital. In the escape truck."

Naghma left with Little Maziullah for Aghala's house. Mir Hamza stood as Naghma pushed Little Maziullah ahead through the door. He walked over to his first son and stopped him. "Why is he here?"

Naghma held up the cake box. "Aghala needs to eat." Across the room, Aghala picked up her head, thankful for Naghma's small mercy. "Come on, *Zullah Jan*."

Mir Hamza wouldn't let them go any further. "Why did you bring him here?"

"If he's to be as strong as you, *Mira Jan*, he needs to see what you've seen."

200

He gave way and all three went to the sitting area, Mir Hamza to the couch, Naghma and Little Maziullah on the floor below them. Naghma opened the cake box and broke off chunks for Aghala, putting them in her mouth so she didn't have to lift her hands from Aziz. Little Maziullah shrunk down, in fear, for some time. But as the vigil grew long—the doctor only leaving his corner to press the stethoscope to Aziz's bare chest, Mir Hamza rubbing Aziz's legs, Aghala's face more like a mask as time went on—Little Maziullah began to look at the dying boy and his growing strength made his mother proud. That strength couldn't save Aghala's son but it might save Naghma's later in life.

The doctor made tea and everyone drank except for Aghala and the doctor, who went back to his corner. "Maziullah isn't back," Naghma said. She put her tea glass on the ground and sat up straight. "He should be back."

"The roads are washed out," Mir Hamza said without looking at her. Before he couldn't look at Aziz, now he couldn't stop looking at Aziz. "Maziullah will return. He always returns."

"Call him, *Sahib Jan*. Find out where he is." She touched his knee and he jumped.

"No."

"Not even for this?"

"I never talk on the phone."

Though none of the others could see it, Mir Hamza still thought he needed permission to use his full power. As if it were given to him, by the people, or the Americans, or God. But Naghma knew him better than he knew himself. His power wasn't from anyone. Mir Hamza was born with it. He could say the word "go" and the trucks would leave. He controlled the *talibs*, he owned the Americans. He was a king. When he refused to release the trucks to save the boy or talk on the phone for fear

201

of the Americans, Naghma didn't feel just hate for his actions anymore. She hated *him*, Mir Hamza, her husband. She swore Little Maziullah would know how to use his power when his time came.

It was dark, a smoldering rainy dark, when Aziz gasped. Everyone stood, except Aghala, leaning down over her son's mouth. The doctor ran over. Aziz had stopped ejecting the ricey diarrhea that morning and now, emptied of water, he couldn't breathe. The doctor pressed his stethoscope on Aziz's chest and the boy sputtered again, exhaling the last of his life. Naghma hugged Little Maziullah. Mir Hamza left Aghala's house for the roof. Aghala wailed, joining the dirge of all the other mothers who have ever lived and suffered the same.

Mother and son walked through the rain and the night back to their house, careful through the slick yard. Fatima and Aufia had fallen asleep but woke as the door opened. "Get out of my house," Naghma said. She stood over them. They smelled yeasty, their clothes dried by their body heat, and they were embarrassed in front of her. "Go."

They turned to the door. She followed. Little Maziullah stood behind his mother. Before they crossed into the night, Aufia stopped. "Maziullah came back with the medicine?"

"No," Naghma said and pushed them outside. She watched them as they walked to Aghala's house. "Time to sleep, my *Zullah Jan*."

Her son flashed surprise. "I can't sleep now, mother."

"Yes, you can." She took him into his room. "Put on your night clothes." For the first time, Naghma turned around to give Little Maziullah, now Mir Hamza's only son, the privacy a man deserved to change into new clothes.

THE JUDGMENT OF
MIR HAMZA KHAN

*Mir Hamza Khan's mansion, Tarin Kowt City, Tarin Kot
District, Uruzgan Province, Afghanistan, 18 December 2012—*

Mir Hamza Khan and Maziullah squatted on the roof with the limp tarp over their heads catching the heavy rain. They watched the city. Aziz had been dead for a week.

The street leading to the *bazaar* was locked with trucks, their stranded drivers sleeping in their cabs, rolled in the carpets ripped from the floor of their vehicles for warmth. The fruit and vegetable stalls in the *bazaar* were empty and the sellers leaned against them, watching the rain. A man, walking with his son, coughed a splatter of blood into his palm. He showed it to the boy. Uruzgan had been without a Security Day for six weeks. There was no medicine or fuel. Soon all the dried goods would be consumed.

Khan leaned against Maziullah for balance and stayed there for warmth. The American jet-boil stove they had been using for fire had run out of fuel. Khan's spies on the American base reported that the American Commander had shot himself in the head and that they had no replacement yet. "Do you believe our spies?"

"I do," Maziullah said.

"Then now is the time. They're weak. They'll pay us what they promised," Khan said and wiped his nose with the back of his hand. "Call them."

Maziullah removed a yellow cell phone from the lowest pocket inside the vest and hesitated. "If the Americans can't handle their own problems why would they care about ours?"

Khan paused for a moment, not thinking but instead feeling for the answer. Maziullah was right. Khan nodded and Maziullah put the yellow cell phone back in its pocket.

A long, guttural wail came from inside the compound. It was Aghala.

Five kilometers outside of Khan's mansion, Maziullah had become stuck as he went to get the medicine that would save Aziz. The truck's wheels churned mud. He'd decided to walk the rest of the way to the Chinese hospital and beaten his companion, nearly to death, for protesting that decision. Maziullah returned to Khan's mansion soaked, cold, body spent, with medicine and a doctor—taken at the blue rifle's muzzle—but Aziz had been dead for two hours. Maziullah had never felt greater shame.

Another wail, sharper, came from Aghala's house.

"It's time for you to go home. The mourning has gone on for too long."

Maziullah looked his friend in the eye, testing for seriousness and— seeing it as hard as a mountain—took his rifle, walked across the wet roof and left. Khan stayed and rubbed his beard.

After Aziz had died, Aghala rocked the baby in her arms until her fingers were pried from the body by a guard. Khan held her, as she had the dead baby, in the shadows of her empty house. Khan's other wives brought them food but they only ate to have the energy to continue crying. After Aziz was taken for cleaning and burial, Aghala's body sputtered like a burnt lightbulb and she capitulated. She slept for a day without moving. She started crying again as soon as she woke up.

Khan lumbered down the steps, legs stiff from hepatitis. He crossed the courtyard to Aghala's house but hesitated at the door. The rain pattered on his turban. Aghala was young and there would be more children. *But would there ever be a boy as wonderful as Aziz?* Khan went inside.

Aghala was in Aziz's room. She hadn't left it since he was buried. Her eyes were chapped from crying, hair like a disturbed nest, and she wore the same black dress every day. Even her television was silent. She rocked in the corner, arms over her chest. Khan had asked her to leave three days ago but she refused and when he asked again, the next day, Aghala threw one of Aziz's toys at him. Then he ordered the room cleared of furniture, drapes, carpets, everything. It was empty like a mausoleum. The girl slept on the hard marble floor.

Khan entered the room and his bare feet echoed in the empty space. "Aghala, it's time to make dinner."

She rocked without looking at him. "Go to Naghma's house."

"I said go cook me food."

"It doesn't matter what you say. It matters what God wants."

She'd heard that from the *mullah* who had been there when Khan wrapped Aziz's body, lowered him into his shallow hole, and threw three clods of dirt on top. The same *mullah* who said that they would all be judged on the Last Day. Even Aziz. *On what? The quality of his play?* Khan didn't believe in any judgement other than his own. "In your life, it only matters what I want, Aghala."

She flashed a defiant glare. "Look at what's happened because of what *you* wanted."

"There will be more babies, Aghala."

"Maybe with the other wives but never with me again. Never with me." She sniffled, cried quietly. "I will never let you have another baby with me."

Mir Hamza Khan dragged Aghala out of the room by her wrists. She fought as she slid across the marble but he picked her up, cradled her—though it was excruciating, and dropped her onto the pink couch. Khan threw open the teak cabinet and turned on the television. "If you wish to cry do it here. Or disappear into your fantasies."

Aghala stared at the ceiling without a word.

Khan went into the courtyard, the rain driving at his face, and looked up at the walls. The guards, slick with water, watched the city outside the mansion.

"You!" Khan said, not exactly able to see the guard. "Get down here."

The guard came down a set of spiral stairs and sprinted to Khan. He saluted, nearly knocking off his limp patrol cap. It was the guard who had been beaten for sleeping on watch.

"Yes, General."

"Follow me."

Khan took the man by the collar, pushed him through the mud, the drooping garden, toward the threshold of Aghala's house. The guard resisted, pointing to his muddy boots that were forbidden inside.

"I permit it," Khan said. Aghala was stretched out on the couch. Her bare feet and ankles sent a convulsion through the guard that Khan felt through the collar. "See this man? He will be in Aziz's room." Aghala made no response and Khan shoved the man toward the room. He let go of his collar, turned him by the shoulders to the proper position outside the door. Khan looked over the guard's uniform, straightening the wrinkles and—looking the guard in the eye—clapped him on the shoulders. "She must never enter this room again. You make sure of this." The guard looked uneasy, swallowing several times, darting his eyes to the uncovered girl on the couch. Khan understood. "You will be here, even if I'm not."

"General." The man swallowed again. "Can't only a *mullah* decide that?"

"I am the only one who decides."

The guard fixed his eyes to the air ahead. Khan returned to his roof and tarp.

When Khan became the Provincial Chief of Police, the Australians flew him to their country, to show the proper respect. They took him to meetings and dinners and the great places in their big city. He wore a western suit: tie, jacket, pants, and shoes that hurt his feet. The clothing, the noise, the constant movement of people in their city was almost too much to handle. But Khan adjusted. After all, he was a king.

On the last day of his visit, the delegation took him to a zoo. Khan enjoyed it. The zoo was the only place where it was slow and quiet. He walked ahead of the others and found his way to a pit filled with green trees and thick underbrush. He was told that several Bengal tigers lived down there. From above he saw nothing. He watched the large exposed rocks, the water hole built to look like a pond, and a stand of trees that opened into a clearing. The exhibit appeared empty.

It was not until he had leaned over the railing, his strange red necktie dangling, that he saw the trails the tigers had cut as they crept through the grass that filled the broad pen. All their power was hidden under the camouflage of the plants. He watched the trail until a tiger emerged, sleek, rippling, its great head shaking water off its snout. It trotted, slow at first, and then faster to the screech of two hinges lifting a door. A zookeeper, dressed in khaki shorts and shirt, pushed a shank of raw meat through the opening. And the tiger sat like a dog before him.

If that zookeeper had encountered that animal in the wild, he would be the meal. But there, in the safety of the cages, he was the only thing that kept the tiger alive. He'd built the cage, captured the tiger, and put it inside. Who was king? Tiger or zookeeper? Khan watched the feeding for a long time until a member of the Australian delegation told him it was time to leave.

After a full week, the rain plinking the tarp had slowed, then finally stopped. As he watched Tarin Kowt City from his roof, Khan became convinced that it was the same as the Australian zoo. The city spread toward the mountains where the *talibs, stupid talibs,* hid in the caves. Between the mountain and Khan's mansion was the ugliness of the American base. *I'll let the trucks go and allow Security Day again, just to feed these animals.* All of these trapped animals. All of them in an enormous zoo.

TOOR JAN BEGGED GOD TO KEEP SHAHEEN ALIVE

Safad Khare Village, Tarin Kot District, Uruzgan Province, Afghanistan, 20 December 2012—

The rains had stopped two days ago and the ground was already dry. Toor Jan, holding an enormous knife, stood under his almond tree with Abdul Hakim. Attached to a peg in the ground, their new goat—bought with The Good American's money—wore a circle in the sandy yard. Its fat haunches swayed with each step. The meal glared at the brothers. Shaheen had been in labor for two days. Her belly was big, the skin stretched as tight as a hide, but Toor Jan could see her ribs. There was little food anywhere since the trucks had stopped coming to Tarin Kowt. Everyone, rich and poor, was desperate. Everyone needed to eat.

"Dig the hole," Toor Jan told Abdul Hakim. The boy got down on his knees and started. Toor Jan had rehearsed the prayers in his head. Though he knew the ritual, Toor Jan checked again, making sure that the goat was facing Mecca. If they were to slaughter their last animal, it would be in the way prescribed by God.

The family had added Shaheen's sister Mina to their home. Mina was young but strong. She had green eyes and light skin. She had lived in Panjwayi in Kandahar but her husband was killed by robbers on the road

General Khan was supposed to protect. She had cared for Shaheen since she arrived. Since her labor started, they sat together hidden behind a curtain that partitioned the house and waited through the pain and Shaheen's birthing groans.

Toor Jan stood over the goat, knife held at his waist. Its strange eyes, the pupil like a long slot, stared at Toor Jan from the side of its head. Abdul Hakim rubbed his hands together, waiting for his brother to slaughter. Toor Jan squeezed the knife handle. The General had stopped meeting Toor Jan after he failed to take the picture of The Good American. Without either the General or The Good American providing money, Toor Jan didn't want to kill the goat—not yet. He didn't know when there would be meat again. Toor Jan slid the knife back into the long green sheath hanging from his belt. "There's still rice." He reached down and ran his fingers lightly across the ridge of the goat's head. "We'll wait until it's gone."

"It's almost gone, brother. What do we do then?"

Toor Jan squatted and traced his fingers over the imprint of the goat's hoof. He grabbed it from the earth and squeezed the dirt in his fist. "We make sure the gate is always locked. We don't go outside except to pray at *masjid*. We protect Shaheen and Mina. And when the baby is born we thank God."

Abdul Hakim dragged his feet through dirt as he walked back into their house.

The sun was behind the compound walls by the time Mina allowed Toor Jan to cross through the curtain. She left to fill jugs with water. Shaheen reclined against a pillow pushed into the corner. Two other pillows propped her knees. Shaheen seemed to be only black hair in the dark room. Toor Jan sat down beside her. Sweat freckled her colorless forehead. The girl turned toward him, smiling. Toor Jan kissed her cracked lips. Shaheen tried to speak but her voice croaked. She smiled again.

"We're cooking rice. We found raisins to put into it." Toor Jan kissed her clammy head. "You'll eat first."

"Thank you, Toor *Janna*."

The girl turned into his arms. Her pain was real and he felt it rolling through her. She would give birth hungry. They had no doctor, no medicine. Toor Jan begged God to keep her alive.

DAN WAS HERE TO LIE

Multinational Base Tarin Kowt, Tarin Kot District, Uruzgan Province, Afghanistan, 20 December 2012—

After Khost killed himself, Captain Cales put Dan's return home on hold. A new commanding officer would be there soon, and though it took almost two weeks, Commander Russo, Khost's replacement, had finally arrived, settled in, and held his first round of meetings. He called everyone to his office. Chief Nunez and Lieutenant Konig were supposed to be there too. Before they left for the meeting Captain Cales pulled Dan aside and told him, "We're about to find out if you have nine lives."

Russo didn't use Khost's old office, nor did he sleep in his old room; instead, he converted a storage room into his work space. He had a standing desk, and more scuttlebutt said that Russo never sat down anyway, that when he slept it was up and down, like a vampire. He was a real Commanding Officer and already well-liked.

All of them could barely fit in his converted office. Commander Russo moved a few boxes to make room as everyone filed in—Captain Cales, Army Brian, then Dan. Beau stood in the doorway, impossible to squeeze inside. Chief Nunez and Lieutenant Konig were already there, waiting. Everyone wore their pistols, concealed or in hip holsters, but Dan carried Aaron's MP5 slung across his chest. He even wore the white wristwatch.

"All right, lads. My name's Mike Russo." He made a point of looking each of them in the eye as he shook their hands. "Rick told me there were some problems between the two intelligence sections." There was an alcove behind a set of bare metal shelves. The Master Chief had been standing in there with his arms crossed. "Who wants to fill me in?"

Chief Nunez looked at Konig. Konig shrugged and cut his eyes toward Captain Cales. Captain Cales looked down at his feet. Dan threw his hands up in the air. *Jesus Christ, these people.*

"Sir, it's simple," Dan said. "Age-old battle of human intelligence against technical intelligence." Captain Cales wheeled his head toward Dan. "Not that big of a deal. A difference in, uh—visions, sir."

"You must be the collectors, huh?" Commander Russo said to Dan and Army Brian. "No uniforms."

"Yes, sir," they replied together, both straightening up under the scrutiny of the Master Chief and Commander Russo. Commander Russo's jaw was as square as the Master Chief's but he had no gray in his light hair. His blue eyes were pale and soft. He was wiry, like he'd lived off the land.

"Is that accurate, Captain?" Russo said, his voice gruff but not intimidating.

"From our perspective, yes, but please, let's hear Glenn speak." Glenn was Lieutenant Konig's first name. "Glenn?"

Lieutenant Konig's pale skin glowed hot in the dim room. He thought for a moment before speaking. "We're fine, sir." He looked at Dan. "I think everyone's learning their lanes. We'll stay in them now."

"Good," Commander Russo said and clapped sharply. "I want everyone on the same page."

"But, if I can add something," Lieutenant Konig said, pointing a tentative finger. "We do have a bit of a disagreement on our host nation partners."

"Oh yeah?" Commander Russo said. "What's the problem?"

"Petty Officer Bing believes that MHK is one of the four horsemen of the apocalypse."

"I never said that," Dan said. "All I said was that we have high-level sources—"

"What he means, sir." Captain Cales cut in. "Is that MHK represents a type of corruption endemic to Uruzgan."

"No, Robert, to be fair," Lieutenant Konig said. "Petty Officer Bing believes that MHK has actively targeted our troops using Taliban proxies."

"MHK is Mir Hamza Khan?" Commander Russo said. The Master Chief nodded. "And you think that he killed our man in Chorah?"

His name was Aaron, sir. He had a baby girl. "Yes, sir."

"Do you have proof?"

"Of course he doesn't," Chief Nunez said. "Look at him. His civvies, that stupid gun. A fucking beard. He thinks he's Jason Bourne. And he can't explain why he's so confident in these sources. Buncha bullshit."

The Master Chief came over, put his arm around Chief Nunez, whispered into his ear and they left the room. Dan thought Chief Nunez was going to spit in his face as he walked past.

"Do you have proof, Petty Officer Bing?" Commander Russo said, again.

"Sir, what are we calling proof? I have a high-ranking member of the Afghan Police with direct access to MHK. I have another guy who's the nephew of Objective Frostbite. Is that good enough?"

Commander Russo pouted his lips and pressed against the wall. "So one of MHK's close guys. Are you concerned about jealousy?"

"Not at all, sir." Dan paused. "In fact, he's been working behind-the-scenes against MHK for some time." The momentum of the lie carried Dan. "We had a situation in a village called Safad Khare, where MHK wanted a checkpoint. My guy worked with the Barakzais to stop it. Commander Khost was the only reason they have one now."

Army Brian and Captain Cales looked at the floor.

"Very interesting," Lieutenant Konig said. "Why didn't you tell us those things before?"

"Sir, all due respect, no one would listen to me. I couldn't get it out."

Beau, standing behind Dan, clapped him on the back. Dan didn't know if it was in confirmation or scolding.

"Here's the deal, fellas," Commander Russo said. "This base is shutting down in four months. No if, ands, or buts. So we need our allies." They nodded their heads. "But that doesn't mean we can't clean up a little bit before we go. Find the bad guys. And work together to get it done. Understand?"

"Yes, sir."

"And if anything leads back to MHK, I'll hunt him down. But I need no-shit evidence. Otherwise we're taking a strong guy out and giving Uruzgan to the Taliban when we leave." He looked at each of them in the eye again. "Go do the damn thing."

They were silent as they left the headquarters building. Beau put on his headlamp to guide them through the night and the gravel, toward the gate, and down the maze of Conex boxes to the SPU. They went into the Soviet Building. Qais, fresh from the gym in a wife-beater and fingerless leather gloves, was waiting for them at the card tables.

"Fascinating, Dan," Captain Cales said, sitting on the edge of the card table. He was so skinny that it barely bent under his weight. "I read all your reports on Maziullah. Saw nothing about him *working behind-the-scenes*."

Beau massaged Dan's shoulders and Dan winced from the pain. "That's because I didn't put that in them. I didn't think anyone would care, Captain. Honestly."

"Honestly?" Captain Cales said.

"By the time Maziullah started telling me that—come on, Beau," Dan said, ducking out from under Beau's hands. "By the time he started talking for real everyone was already shooting me down. Kind of lost heart."

"Okay," Captain Cales said. "Swear to me that it's true. That Maziullah wants to take down MHK. If you're lying, I'll send you home the minute I find out."

"Captain," Beau said.

"Sir," Army Brian said. "We can trust Dan."

If Captain Cales could trust anyone, it was Army Brian. They'd been in Afghanistan together for eleven months, and had spent most of their time in a dangerous part of Zabul Province with the Afghan Border Police before working at the SPU.

"No, Brian, he's going to say it. Then I'm going to give him the green light to do what he wants."

I'm here to lie. The better I am at lying, the better I do my job. "I swear, sir. Send me home right now if it's not true." He looked without breaking eye contact. "Is that good enough for you?"

"I told you it would be," Captain Cales said, standing up to leave the room. "Get Maziullah back in here."

"Toor Jan too," Dan said, already turning to Qais. "I'll get him in this week."

Captain Cales stopped. "Not a good idea."

"I'm going to have to agree with him," Army Brian added.

"They're trying to get a picture of you, brother," Beau said, arms folded across his mountainous chest.

"It's just his uncle," Dan said.

"Oh *just* his uncle," Captain Cales said. "The commander of all the Taliban in Uruzgan."

Dan pulled a chair up beside Qais, put his elbows on his thighs. "Captain, I know I can control him. Toor Jan is my pet. I feed him, I water him. When he's sick I give him medicine, when he's sad I rub his belly. But he's my pet. If something happens again, I'll find a new pet."

"Absolutely not," Captain Cales said. "Too dangerous. Re-contact Maziullah. Use him to find more sources."

It was time for chow and everyone except Dan and Qais went to eat.

"Give me the cell phone," Dan said. "We'll be quick." He scrolled to find the number he wanted and handed the cell phone back to Qais. "Call Maziullah."

"That's not Maziullah's number."

"Yes it is."

"No it's not," Qais said, showing Dan the screen. "It's Toor Jan's."

"Call the fucking number."

"The Captain said you can't talk to him."

"Call the number, Qais," Dan said. "Or you can go back to eight-fifty with no bathroom breaks at the bodega. Rent's getting real high in

Queens too. And we gotta make sure little Ibrahim's staying fresh in the newest Jordan's, right?"

Qais dialed. Toor Jan said hello. "What do you want me to say to this guy, Dan?"

Dan smiled. "Tell him we've missed him."

TOOR JAN AND THE PULL OF HUNGER

Tarin Kowt City, Tarin Kot District, Uruzgan Province, Afghanistan, 22 December 2012—

Toor Jan sat anxiously with Abdul Hakim inside the house. The curtain had been torn down. Both women were in the yard, Shaheen straining to force out the painful girth of the baby. For hours, Shaheen had squatted and groaned. Vaporous steam rose off her back. Her low moans and cries waned until—the bone white gleam of the moon illuminating the courtyard—Mina pulled the baby from her and whispered, "*La'illa Allah, Muhammad rasul Allah.*" Mina wrapped the bloody baby in a blanket, cut the cord, and went into the house, passing the two brothers as they rushed outside.

"*Alhamdulillah,*" Toor Jan cried. Abdul Hakim danced in the courtyard with the family's AK-47. He smiled innocently at Toor Jan before firing the rifle wildly over their heads. The tracers skipped through the air like angry bits of broken stars. Toor Jan snatched the rifle from his brother and picked up Shaheen who'd been laying near the goat. He carried her into the house. The family, exhausted from the ordeal, fell into sleep.

At dawn Toor Jan wrapped his head delicately with his black turban. He drew a crackling fire out of the woodstove and warmed bread. He wanted to help before he left to meet The Good American. "Toor *Janna?*" Shaheen said, her face peeking out from the blankets.

"Yes, Shaheen *Jo?*"

"The baby." She lifted the baby to Toor Jan. The boy's face, like a rabbit's, was split from nose to lip.

"What's wrong with his mouth?"

"I don't know," she said. "Can it be fixed?"

"Of course it can." Toor Jan felt the pull of hunger from everyone in his house. And now they needed a doctor. He put the baby on Shaheen's chest and pulled the blanket up so that they were sealed in their own heat. "I have to go."

"Where are you going?"

"To find food and a doctor."

Toor Jan went to the other end of the room. "Abdul Hakim."

A groan issued from the pile.

"Make sure nothing happens to this house."

Abdul Hakim groaned again.

Toor Jan kicked Abdul Hakim. "Do you hear me?"

"I hear you, brother."

Toor Jan left the house. The goat, still fearful of being slaughtered, ran behind the almond tree. Toor Jan walked carefully across the yard, his cell phone hidden in his right shoe. The Good American had ordered him to leave the cell phone at home but Toor Jan thought he might need it. It wasn't the only thing he needed. He felt his pocket for prayer beads and asked God to protect him from the Evil Eye, the bombs, the police and the army, the Americans and *talibs*. Toor Jan swung onto his Chinese motorcycle and the blue *nazars* on the fenders tinkled. He was glad to have those too.

"Toor Jan," Mina said, standing behind him, shivering in her blanket. "Tell the doctor that the baby has an infection in his eye too. Get medicine."

Out of the valley and across the great dust plain, Toor Jan rode for twenty cold, brutal minutes along the river. The path twined through the shallow water, empty fields, and squat mud-brick houses. He sped past the rusted Russian tank but slowed at the turn where three men stood in the road. They wore black turbans and big beards. A dog, attracted to their fire, circled their makeshift checkpoint. All three men had weapons. Toor Jan stopped.

"Turn that off," one of the men said. He held an ICOM radio in one hand and an AK-47 in the other. He was the leader. The two other men had Enfield rifles and bandoliers of ammunition strapped across their chests.

Toor Jan stood and balanced the hot motorcycle between his thighs. "My friends, I don't want any trouble. I'm a poor man with nothing to give robbers."

"We're not robbers. We are *mujahedeen*." The leader seized the handle bars. "Lift your shirt. Where's your cell phone?"

"I don't have one," he said and pushed his right foot deep into the dust.

The leader reached into Toor Jan's pockets. "Do you know where you are?"

"Of course," Toor Jan said, pointing beyond the yellow mounds. "I live in Safad Khare."

The leader took the prayer beads in Toor Jan's pockets. "No money? How will you pay the toll?" The other two raised their rifles at Toor Jan. "This is The Big One's road."

"That's my uncle," Toor Jan said. "You work for him! This is good!"

"Mullah Sher Muhammad is your uncle?"

"Yes. I'm Toor Jan, son of Haji Izatullah."

The three men slung their rifles and huddled together near their fire. The skinny yellow dog sniffed at their feet. After a moment the leader walked toward Toor Jan. He was like a *djinn* with his flowing clothes and black eyes burning behind his beard. The dog followed.

"Mullah Sher Muhammad?"

"Yes."

The leader spoke into his ICOM, "Commander Zubair, we got a guy here. He says he knows The Big One."

The radio warmed to life and through the white noise Zubair's voice cracked, "What's his name?"

Toor Jan repeated his name, his father's name.

Zubair responded, "Does he have metal attached to his arm?"

Toor Jan rolled his sleeve and showed the leader the edge of the splint and screws.

"Yes, Commander Zubair."

"I know him. Let that one go, now. Don't bother him again."

The leader leered at Toor Jan. "You heard what he said."

Down the dirt hill faster and faster, Toor Jan spread his legs wide as the elation streamed off his back. The motorcycle wobbled on the chewed road and, with a sprint of his heart, Toor Jan jammed his feet onto the pegs and hugged the handle bars to regain control. The sun came up from behind the mountains and warmed him as he went.

At the Teri Bridge, cars and trucks were backed up in a long line. Two green police Humvees with Russian DShK machine guns choked the road on the city side of the bridge. Everyone was being questioned and searched. In an hour The Good American would be waiting for Toor Jan in the city. If the line didn't move fast, he would miss his fresh chance with The Good American. Twenty, thirty, and then forty minutes passed before Toor Jan crossed the bridge. He walked his motorcycle forward to a fat police officer. His uniform's buttons stressed around his belly. The leather of his gun belt was worn from the constant rubbing of weight. Grease stains splotched camouflage-like down the front of his pants. He twisted one end of his moustache and watched Toor Jan.

Toor Jan mopped his wet brow with his hand.

"Stop," the fat officer said. "Lay that motorcycle right there."

He drew his pistol, scanning Toor Jan's body. The crowd backed away and other police officers took cover. The two Humvees swung their machine gun barrels down. The fat officer came forward, with some bravery, and searched Toor Jan. He had been trained by American police officers from New York City and his palm invaded all of Toor Jan's crevices. The fat officer found nothing. "Why are you sweating like that?"

"It's hot," Toor Jan said.

"I saw you sweating and your *talib* beard and thought you were a bomber."

"I'm not a bomber," Toor Jan said, shaking his head.

"You look like a bomber." The fat officer holstered his pistol. "Bombers sweat because they're nervous."

"I'm sweating from the sun."

"We haven't had a bomber in two years—" He spat into the dirt at the thought of bombers. "Because we have Mir Hamza Khan." The fat officer motioned through the haze of the city toward the billboard of General Khan. "But there's rumors that bombers are coming. Have you heard of any?"

"No," Toor Jan said. "I don't know about things like that."

"Go on then. There are Americans at the *bazaar* searching people too. Turn at the jail and go around them."

"Thank you," Toor Jan said. He bore down and pushed the motorcycle hard to meet The Good American on time.

At the *bazaar*, Toor Jan slowed to a halt at a vegetable stall, freshly filled now that the General had run a Security Day again. He leaned his motorcycle against a post. Across the street, Americans were searching traffic and people. Their vehicles idled nearby. Qais stood with the Americans. Toor Jan walked toward him, as he'd been instructed to do the previous night over the phone.

"Stay there!" Qais said. "Good. Lift your shirt. Keep it up. That's it. Turn around. All the way around. Okay. Stay there. Don't move. Why are you in the city today?"

"I'm going to the *bazaar* to get food for my family," Toor Jan said, repeating the code The Good American had taught him so they knew Toor Jan hadn't been followed.

"You can't leave your motorcycle there like that," Qais said and handcuffed Toor Jan like he had been arrested. He led him to a truck in their parked convoy. Qais even smacked the back of his head to make it convincing to anyone watching. "Get inside."

The rear hatch of the vehicle unlocked with a hiss. The Good American sat on a canvas bench, wearing a loose shirt and sturdy pants. His boots were untied. He wore his gray American hat with a bill. His machine gun was in his lap. Toor Jan sat opposite and Qais on the floor between them.

Toor Jan didn't think he would be filled with so much awe. "Hello, Commander. I have missed you."

"I missed you too, Toor Jan."

"I am sorry I was almost late. I was stopped twice."

"Who stopped you?"

"The police and some *talibs*."

"Why?"

"The *talibs* wanted money so I told them who my uncle was."

The Good American laughed.

"The police were looking for bombers. I was nervous and sweating so they thought I was a bomber."

"Do you know anything about suicide bombers?"

"Nothing," Toor Jan said. "But I am sure my uncle has them hidden somewhere."

"Where?"

"I don't know. I will find out for you, Commander."

The Good American took off his hat and a glossy picture flashed from the liner. He rubbed his shaved head. Qais stood, stooping in the tight vehicle, and shook out his legs. He sat next to Toor Jan on the canvas bench.

"We've had some trouble in the past."

"Yes we have, Commander."

"I don't mind that you took that picture. I know your life is tough." The Good American took his hand. "But I need to know who wanted it."

"Who wanted the picture?" Toor Jan didn't know what God willed for him. It had always been the thing he didn't expect. From now on he needed to be prepared for anything and he knew there was some value in protecting the General. "My uncle, of course."

"Of course," The Good American said, looking relieved. He pulled his cell phone from his pocket. "And he'll want that picture you tried to take? That'll keep you out of trouble and able to come to the base and meet with me?"

"Yes." Toor Jan said, going along. "But how, Commander?"

"Like this," he said and turned his cell phone toward Toor Jan. A thin man with blond, curly hair and a sharp nose stared ahead. "I'll send this to your phone and you give this to your uncle. Tell him it's me."

"But it's not you."

"I know. Just say it is."

Toor Jan was intrigued. "Who is it?"

"A friend of mine. But from now on it's me." The Good American leaned forward. "You left your phone at home like I told you?"

Toor Jan pressed his heel into his cell phone in his shoe. "Yes, Commander."

"Perfect," The Good American said. He seemed to relax even more. "I'll Bluetooth this picture to you. You'll see it when you get home." The Good American Bluetoothed the picture and put his cell phone away. "I have a new plan for you, *andiwale.*"

Toor Jan nodded.

"We need to find the people who give your uncle weapons. Your uncle's men can't attack without weapons."

"This is a good idea, Commander."

"You remember Haji Hyatullah?" He pointed out the porthole at Toor Jan's red Chinese motorcycle leaned against the pole near the vegetable stall.

"How could I forget? You changed my life with that motorcycle."

"What do you know about Haji Hyatullah?"

"That he's the General's man."

The Good American straightened. "How?"

"The General calls Haji Hyatullah his uncle."

"So they're related?" The Good American looked at Qais. "Right?"

"No, Haji Hyatullah is very important to the General. So the General calls Haji Hyatullah uncle."

"Because they sell weapons together?"

"Yes."

"How do you know this, Toor Jan?"

"Everyone knows."

The Good American looked at his white watch. "We have to go. Can you meet me next Tuesday at eleven-thirty? At the base?"

"*Wo*," Toor Jan said. He smiled. "I had my son, Commander."

"Congratulations," The Good American said. He shook Toor Jan's hand.

"But there is something wrong with his lip. And his eyes are infected. We need a doctor."

"Go to the Chinese hospital." The people said that a man who went to the Chinese hospital complaining of elbow pain would leave with an amputated arm. It wasn't a good place. "They'll take you for free."

"My son's lip is torn in the middle," Toor Jan said. "Only your doctors can fix that."

The Good American stared at Toor Jan. "I can get you a doctor. But you must earn back my trust. Find out more about Haji Hyatullah and there'll be more trust."

"What do you need to know, Commander?"

The Good American inhaled sharply. "What does he look like?"

"He has many skin tags."

"No, Toor Jan, I need more."

"Like a picture?"

"Yes," The Good American said. "Like a picture. We all know you can take a picture."

Toor Jan looked at the floor in shame.

"You do that and I'll get you a doctor for your son. And your arm." He touched the hardware still splinted into Toor Jan's arm. "Now go and do work."

Toor Jan drove fast—the motorcycle's engine making a dying sound—to the heavily guarded gate of the National Police Headquarters. The police officers there wore crisp uniforms, pressed and unstained. The AK-47s slung on their backs were clean and greased shiny. They stood behind a pike and stopped Toor Jan. "What do you need?"

"I'm here to see the General."

The men laughed at him. "Go away!"

"Call him." He got off his motorcycle and walked it toward their pike. "He knows me."

"Toor *Janna*," a soft voice called. The General stepped from the shadow of an open door. The guards popped to attention. "Come here, my friend."

They sat at his huge desk. The wall behind the General was filled with framed pictures. The General shaking hands with American commanders. Addressing police officers in formation. On operations. Wherever there was room there was a photograph.

"Why are you here?" the General said.

"I finally have a photograph of the American."

The General sat up. "Yes?"

"Right here," Toor Jan said, giving him the cell phone from his right shoe.

General Khan looked it over and handed it back. He pressed his hands together in front of his pursed lips. "How did you do it?"

"As you taught me, *Haji Sahib*, but without the flash."

He leaned back. "Why did the American take you back?"

"He needs to kill my uncle."

The General walked around the desk and sat in front of Toor Jan. He wore a white *kameez*, black vest, and a black silk turban. "And they don't suspect us?"

"Why would they? You're their ally, *Haji Sahib*."

"Your uncle is their enemy, he's my enemy, and he's your enemy. We'll help the Americans get him." He clasped his hands behind his back. "If there's anything else I can do, tell me."

"I didn't want to say this." Toor Jan looked at the green carpet. "We had a baby last night."

"Toor *Janna*! What is the sex?"

"A boy."

"Oh a boy!" The General said, picking Toor Jan up and sweeping him into a hug. "A boy, a boy, a boy." He put Toor Jan back down in the chair. "You take care of that boy."

"I am. But there's an issue."

"What is it?"

Begging to survive shamed Toor Jan. But The Good American was no help.

"Toor *Janna*?"

"He's sick. We need medicine."

"How? It's too early. How can a beautiful baby boy be sick so soon?" The General walked around to the other side of the desk and leaned on it to steady himself. He stared into empty space. "He can't be sick."

He didn't want to say anything about the lips, yet. "It's an infection, in his eye."

The General choked back some words, looked away from Toor Jan. "No one will be sick anymore. Security Day is back. I will cure everyone."

"Then you can help?"

"It's done, Toor Jan."

"Thank you, *Sahib Jan.*"

As the General stared at the top of his desk, Toor Jan noticed a small photograph tacked to the wall with a penny nail. Three men, arms around each other, stood in a field of red poppies. Toor Jan tensed hard to arrest his nerves and pointed to it. "Is that your *akaa* Haji Hyatullah? The one who sells cars in the *bazaar*?"

The General removed the picture. "It is. We're at a wedding."

"I knew him when I was young. I miss him." It was a Pashtun custom to give what was asked for, directly or indirectly. The General handed the photograph to Toor Jan. "No, I can't." Toor Jan pushed it away but he knew the General wouldn't take it back. "Please, no."

"It's yours," the General said. His eyes seemed to be looking for a form that wasn't there. "I'm sorry for ending Security Day. So many have suffered." He pointed his finger in the air. "I will send you home with the medicine and food too, for your new son."

Toor Jan left and walked alone down the carpeted hall, around the pike, to his motorcycle. He studied the worn photograph. The General glowing with power. Maziullah, fearless and confident with his blue gun. And Haji Hyatullah. A handsome face with everything in its proper place. It wasn't fair that they lived without deformity. He said *mashallah* and removed his right shoe to slip the photo inside. He came outside and a wood crate filled with a bottle of pink medicine and sack of rice had already been fastened to his motorcycle.

Home before early afternoon, Toor Jan walked his motorcycle through the gate and leaned it against the wall. Mina and Abdul Hakim waited in the courtyard. He motioned to the wood crate. "Medicine and food." Mina unfastened the load and hurried into the house. Toor Jan wiped the dust from his face. He looked at Abdul Hakim. "Did you do what I told you?"

"What did you tell me?"

"To make sure nothing happened to this house."

"I did, brother. What did you do all day?"

"I made sure nothing happened to this house or any of the people in it."

MIR HAMZA KHAN AND THE LITTLE TALIBS

Multinational Base Tarin Kowt, Tarin Kot District, Uruzgan Province, Afghanistan, 23 December 2012—

The new American Commander had called Mir Hamza Khan to ask if he could come to the American base for an introduction. When Khan asked what had happened to the old American Commander he said Khost left to take care of his family in America. Khan laughed without explaining himself.

The meeting was in the American's *shura* room. They used it for their Christian church, the wooden cross pushed into a corner and covered with a sheet, but now there were red suede pillows, expensive carpets, a long table with bread and tea and food. A large picture of Hamid Karzai was on the wall, the President of Afghanistan looking sternly at something outside of the frame. Karzai was a personal friend of Khan's. It was nice to have a friend among the American tigers.

Khan and Maziullah entered the room and were met by a large entourage of American officers and the new American Commander. He was tall and strong. His eyes were blue like mountain streams. He greeted Khan in the proper Islamic way, in Pashto without help from his *tajiman*. The new American Commander put his hand across Khan's back and pulled him toward platters of silky omelets and rice flecked with golden raisins and ribbons of fried onions. The group ate heaps of the delicious food, mopping the excess with scraps of *naan*.

Several local workers came into the room and took away the empty dishes. Two big steel pots of *chai* were left behind and they passed full glasses as the new American Commander, sitting cross-legged and facing Khan, started, "General, we're happy to have you here with us." He smiled. "I wanted to meet you and sit for a meal."

"Your hospitality is that of a great friend and I invite you to join me to eat at my home in the future."

The new American Commander said something in English to the crowd that caused them to laugh but the *tajiman* didn't translate. Maziullah frowned. The new American Commander's mood changed. "I'm sorry about your son."

Khan wrapped both hands around his *chai* glass to hold them still.

"General, if you need a doctor in the future all you have to do is ask and it'll happen."

Khan stared at him, his eyes black and empty.

"You can even call me directly. One will come, right away. Such a simple disease could easily have been—"

"Enough." Khan said, holding up his hand. "Your old commander could have helped by paying me what was promised. Then we would have had Security Day and my son would have had medicine."

"All due respect—" The new American Commander removed the glass from his knee and placed it onto the carpet. "You made Security Day complicated for us."

"Have you been here before?"

"Seven times, General."

233

"Then you know how complicated things can be."

"I know we've had a good meal and that we'll meet again." He got to his feet in one fluid motion. "And soon."

Khan stood slowly, through his pain. "We will meet again."

Maziullah brought the truck around and they left the American base. Khan didn't speak until they were almost at the traffic circle. "What did he say in English?"

"When, *Haji Sahib*?"

"You know when. When those sons of dogs laughed at me."

Maziullah shrank into his seat. "He said he would like to eat at your home if he didn't think he'd get shot in the back."

Khan punched the dashboard until it broke into pieces. "Things will never go back to what they were before, Maziullah."

Maziullah turned into the police headquarters, parked and shut off the vehicle. The engine popped as it settled. "The *talibs* will win after the Americans leave," Maziullah said. He breathed, deep. "But they don't have to win in Uruzgan."

"What do you mean?"

"Can we keep The Big One without Security Day?"

"No, he'll turn on us too."

"Yes," Maziullah whispered. He cleared his throat. "But he must have enemies."

A young officer came to their tinted window and knocked. Khan opened the door halfway and told the young officer to go fuck his mother. "But who?"

"The little *talibs*. His young local commanders. We cut The Big One out. We don't say anything other than that the American contract has been lost. Then we meet with the Little Ones. You wear your best *kameez*. You take them to your mosque in the mansion and pray. You tell them about your time at the *hajj*. When they believe in your religion, you offer them a taste of whatever business we have left. You also offer them the ability to operate with your assistance. Don't you think they have bombers?"

"They always have bombers."

"Then we tell them we'll keep their bombers safe until the time is right." Maziullah sat back confidently. "All the while you control them until a time of your choosing."

Maziullah was right. Mir Hamza Khan needed those little *talibs* if they wanted to survive.

ZUBAIR, HAJI HYATULLAH, AND THE ENGINEER

Kotwal Village, Tarin Kot District, Uruzgan Province, Afghanistan, 26 December 2012—

The women began trilling when the compound gates burst apart and the men carried his dismembered body into the courtyard. Their wailing was like the scream of wounded dogs, those who suffered boils, *djinn* raised from smokeless fire, and infants fresh from the womb. The morning was warm and clear and their voices carried into the mountains, heard even by the monsters roaming up there from gorge to twisting gorge.

Zubair and his father came into their courtyard but didn't understand what had happened. Then they saw the pooled blood. "What is that?" the father said.

"The Americans have killed your youngest son."

The father sank onto his clicking knees. "How?"

"He was standing on the road with his motorcycle as their convoy passed. They shot him to pieces."

"But Saeed Nabi is my good boy." The father cried without embarrassment. "Why would they kill him? He was a police officer."

Water and a white sheet were brought to the pulp of Saeed Nabi's body but the washing and preparation were useless on what was left of him. Some of the men who had carried his body went to find the *mullah* of Kotwal. Zubair watched. Rage surged through his sturdy soul. He released a long mourning cry that could be heard through the entire village.

Haji Hyatullah, the man who sold cars in the *bazaar*, heard Zubair's scream from inside his own compound. His brother Byat, stick-thin, eyes the shape of an almond, heard it too.

"That's Zubair," Byat said to Haji Hyatullah. Both men felt a special connection to Zubair and Saeed Nabi, both pairs of brothers were close and lived almost like they were one person. "I'll stay with the women. You go."

Haji Hyatullah rose from the floor in the long room of his huge stone house and glided through the courtyard, seeming to pass through his gates without opening them, into the field toward the Zubair's cry. He carried a string of wooden prayer beads.

"Is something wrong, my best *andiwale*?" Haji Hyatullah called over the walls of Zubair's father's compound. The bolt stirred, the gates came open, and the full gruesome scene appeared. Haji Hyatullah put his hands to his mouth and inhaled the shock. He thumbed the prayer beads fast in his hand. "This is Saeed Nabi?"

"My best boy," the father said as he lay beside the wrapped pieces of Saeed Nabi. He looked at Zubair. "What have you done?" The father pulled himself up and walked to Zubair. "*Zoya*? What have you done?"

Zubair shrugged. "I didn't want to do my missions last night."

"Yes?"

"So I gave him my wire and remotes."

"Yes?"

"He took my yellow jugs. He wanted to. He was upset I didn't want to do my missions." Zubair snorted like he might cry. He stared at the pile of his brother and his wrath glowed. "I told him I was done with the *mujahedeen*. I get no credit for my work." He aggressively charged his old father. "Nothing! They praise The Big One. But he never fights. I fight. I didn't want him to take the mines. I didn't think he would. He must have been putting them in the ground when the Americans spotted him."

"My good boy," the father said and fell again.

Haji Hyatullah loved Zubair and Saeed Nabi. He loved their old father. Some of his women were married to their people. He must help avenge the family. "Are there any more bombs we can use against the Americans?" Haji Hyatullah said.

Zubair sobbed. "He took the last of them."

"Then I must go to The Engineer," Haji Hyatullah said. "We must get the best." At night, Zubair was the most dangerous man in the valley. And he would be again. But first he must let Haji Hyatullah work. "I'll return tonight with a bomb from The Engineer."

Haji Hyatullah squeezed into an orange Toyota Corolla. It was one of the many cars from his car shop and he switched his vehicles often because he feared the Americans. The Engineer lived in a difficult section of Dorafshan and it took Haji Hyatullah an entire afternoon of labored driving to reach his compound. He parked in a *wadi* some distance from The Engineer's compound and walked the rest of the way.

At the gate of The Engineer's compound Haji Hyatullah leaned in and listened. A tarp was being dragged and heavy things thudded on the ground. Goats bleated regularly and their hooves clicked. There were no human sounds. Haji Hyatullah tapped at the stamped sheet metal door with two fingers circled in prayer beads. The movement stopped.

The Engineer called out, "Who is there?"

"It's the one who sells cars in the city. The one who hid you when you were a *muhjahid* and the old *talibs* hunted you. The one who visited you in *talib* prison. The one who supplied you weapons when the Americans came to drive the *talibs* away." He stopped then added, "The one who's never left your trust."

The double gate opened and The Engineer stood with his arms spread wide. He limped on his shrunken foot toward Haji Hyatullah and—with his two burly arms—pulled him close. The Engineer was so large that Haji Hyatullah couldn't meet his hands around the man's back. In the courtyard, several boys were cleaning up the day's work. The Engineer wiped his sweating curls and smiled. "Boys! Bring *Haji Sahib* tea." The boys flew off into the house and fetched *chai* and dried blackberries. The two men sat cross-legged under a poplar tree, its slanting shadows cooling the heat of day. The Engineer gulped down several glasses of tea and rubbed his shrunken foot, regarding his friend happily before he spoke. He looked at Haji Hyatullah and smiled again. "What brings you here?"

Haji Hyatullah began to weep. "They've killed Saeed Nabi!" The Engineer cradled the crying man in his large arms and listened to the story. Haji Hyatullah ended it with, "There must be revenge. I must bring a powerful bomb back for Zubair."

The Engineer took a deep breath, as though the air was pulled into his whole being by a bellow. He agreed to the work. The two men had been friends for years and some of his women were married to Haji Hyatullah's people. Haji Hyatullah had kept him and fed him during the bad years. He would build a perfect bomb for his old friend.

"Boys! Everything must come back out! All of it!" The Engineer pulled his sleeves to his elbows and rolled them tight before limping over to the awning covering his work space. The boys spread the gruesome agents at his feet. Blue tarps layered with a paste of dried ammonium nitrate. Five yellow cooking oil jugs. Diesel fuel. A mottle of insulated wires. One remote, miniature, plastic and black, placed ceremoniously on the earth. The boys carried several batteries from the compound before The Engineer picked his favorite.

Before The Engineer was ready to work, he lowered himself to his knees and pressed his hands into the dirt. He raised his hands to his face, smelled the dust and clapped it off, sending it floating through the sun's beams.

Haji Hyatullah watched the particles in the light. It didn't seem that the circle of friendship and revenge would ever be broken but maybe in another life, another universe, or in one of the heavens things could be let alone and there would be peace. But here and now there was only heat and the scrabble of mountains and the necessity of revenge that kicked dust into the streaming light of the sun.

The crippled Engineer finished the deadly parcel, wrapping it in clear tape and laying it at Haji Hyatullah's feet. Haji Hyatullah thanked him sincerely and cradled the bomb to his rusting car. He pulled away from The Engineer's compound and crawled over every bump and crease in the road that led to Kotwal. In his trunk he bore the gift of fire and blood that would be placed in the earth and used when God willed it. He didn't want it to explode before its time.

In Kotwal, Haji Hyatullah laid the tightly packed menace at Zubair's feet. If Zubair hadn't known that God was wise, compassionate, and merciful he would think that this bomb was created by God uttering "be" and making it so. To honor The Engineer's work, Zubair officially swore his revenge.

The next evening an Afghan Commando convoy passed down the bumpy path through Zubair's valley, stopping frequently to scan the way ahead for buried danger. Only the faint breath of swaying grass disturbed the countryside. Confident, the convoy turned toward Tarin Kowt City where the earth erupted beneath a truck, twisting the metal of the frame and the men in a murderous way, all of it disappearing into soil, scorching fire, and clotted blood.

MIR HAMZA KHAN NEEDED THOSE TERRIFYING WEAPONS

Mir Hamza Khan's mansion, Tarin Kowt City, Tarin Kot District, Uruzgan Province, Afghanistan, 28 December 2013—

Aghala was completely naked. Her black hair swung down her back, long legs stretched across the mattress. She cupped her full breasts with her hands. But Mir Hamza Khan, after he had passed the guard—still in the hallway preventing anyone from entering Aziz's old room—and entered Aghala's room, noticed none of it. Aghala's hair on her bare skin, the color of night against the color of sand, made Khan think only of Uruzgan and how he must control it. He got into their European bed without a word.

Aghala's anger had left and now she became obsessed with replacing Aziz. She even refused to travel with Khan's other wives on an upcoming trip to Canada, for shopping in Montreal and Toronto, just to have an extra week with Khan. "Do you see me, *Mira Jan*?"

"I see you," he said, turning away. "I must be awake early tomorrow."

She crawled up to him, her hand sliding down his belly to the tangle of hair. He took her hand away. "You refuse again?" she said.

"I told you go to Canada with the other women and get the medicine that prevents children. Then I won't refuse."

Aghala was done crying, she had cried enough for a lifetime. But she was set and determined. She also had rights. "I don't want you to sleep here tonight."

He turned over suddenly. "What? It's your week."

"*Qur'an* says that there must be equity between the wives." She spoke without facing him. "If you give them babies but refuse me, that's not equal."

"I have important business tomorrow morning, girl. I have to sleep well."

"Then let's make a baby."

Khan bolted upright. His skin flushed. The empty room down the hall echoed with Aziz's laughter whenever he passed and he hated it. "Never. Never, never, never. Little Maziullah is my last son. His survival is my focus." He jumped out of bed, ripped the sheet off Aghala, and went to his spot, under the tarp, up on the roof.

Khan slept fitfully, the sheet nothing against the cold, his hepatitis-inflamed body locking at the joints, and woke with the rising sun and the cocks crowing through the streets of Tarin Kowt. He forced himself, despite screeching knees and ankles, to go down into the compound and prepare for the young *talib* commanders who would be coming for a meeting in an hour.

Mir Hamza Khan had timed the arrival of the young *talibs* to the *azan* so they would hear the call to prayer as the great steel doors opened. Khan walked slowly, contemplatively, toward their truck as it pulled inside. His *kameez* was holy white, he wore a prayer cap, and he carried prayer beads. Khan greeted the young *talibs* as Muslim brothers.

They were a bunch of poor filthy children. Not commanders to respect. *Children* and nothing more. Their clothes had deteriorated to

243

threads and their feet were powdered with fine dust from walking in sandals. There were six of them, one from every district in Uruzgan, and each had their own ambitions to rule the province. But they hadn't fought the Russians or lived through *mujahedeen* times. They had barely fought the Americans. They were the runts that Khan would have shot through the head when he cleared their villages with his police officers.

He ushered the children to the water for ablution. They rolled up their sleeves and pants legs, removed their shoes, and scrubbed themselves under the icy water of the spigot. Finished, they entered the *masjid* and prayed. After the prayer, Khan faked enthusiasm:

"*Takbir!*"

"*Allah-u-Akbar!*"

"*Takbir!*"

"*Allah-u-Akbar!*"

Khan moved everyone to his *shura* room and called for food. They ate like animals. They took handful after handful of rice, scooping it with *naan*. The hunched manservant, Azzam, came to take the scraps away but the young *talibs* wouldn't let him and soaked the oil up with the bread until there was nothing left.

Finally done, they leaned back, waiting for Khan to speak.

"My brothers, it's nice to meet good Muslims willing to resist the rule of infidels."

They picked their teeth and waited for him to continue.

"I know you were surprised to be invited here."

They nodded in agreement but were unimpressed.

"I've changed greatly since I did the *hajj*. God wills a *mujahedeen* victory and I've been on the wrong side of this battle for many years."

The children continued to pick their teeth, disbelieving Khan's confession.

"Yet, because of my mistakes, I'm in a special position to offer assistance."

They frowned at Mir Hamza Khan. It seemed that breakfast was all that would result from this meeting.

"I want to help young fighters like you, so when the government falls you will remember me as a friend."

They stared blankly at Khan but he held his silence until it forced one of them to speak.

"What do we get?" said the child commander from Chorah District.

"Assistance in operations. Your men will pass through the checkpoints without being stopped. My police trucks can transport weapons. I have houses in the city to keep your bombers."

The commander of Tarin Kot District, the one called Zubair—his brother had been one of Khan's police officers until the Americans mistook him for a *talib* and killed him—cleared meaty strings from his yellowed teeth and said, "We don't need those things."

"But you need this." Khan left the room and returned with a green canvas sack. He opened it and poured millions of *rupees* onto the floor.

The children reached to snatch the money. Soon they were swiping at each other.

Khan laughed. "There's plenty for each of you. And more to come."

The children stopped fighting and looked at Khan. Then they smiled as he had never seen them smile before. "What about The Big One?" the Deh Rawud commander said.

"He's from the old world. He spends his time in Pakistan. He doesn't visit his fighters. How many times have you seen him with your own eyes?"

The six child commanders shrugged.

"And you're his commanders. A leader must see his men. When the government falls you'll be in charge. The ones who remained in this country and fought. The Pakistani commanders will roast on the ends of our spits."

Khan brought out six empty bags to split the money between them, all the while brokering an agreement that their fighters wouldn't show aggression toward his police officers anymore. The children also agreed, without resistance, to let Khan keep their bombers. Khan needed to possess those terrifying weapons and use them when he decided, to destroy what he chose.

That night he was on the roof again. It was cold and damp. But he couldn't go back to Aghala's house and that meant he would spend another five days out in the open until it was Fatima's week. His throat hurt from pretending he believed in the religion. Below, the zoo spread around his compound, an unfit place for Aghala to bring a new and innocent boy into.

DAN AND ISKANDAR

Multinational Base Tarin Kowt, Tarin Kot District, Uruzgan Province, Afghanistan, 02 January 2013—

Dan held up Toor Jan's photograph of Haji Hyatullah. "How the hell did you get this picture?"

"It was easy, Commander," Toor Jan said.

"You're a smart man," Dan said. "But how?"

"I was at his house. Some of my people are married to his people. He gave this picture to me." Toor Jan brought his knees to his chest in the chair. "It's our tradition to give what is asked."

Dan recognized Mazzy Star, carrying his blue gun, and MHK. MHK had the look of an arrogant gangster posing for his first mug shot. They had their arms around a third man with several skin tags on his forehead. Dan put the photograph back on the table. "Tell me who these men are."

"These ones I do not know but the man in the middle is Haji Hyatullah."

"You're sure?" Dan said. He pointed to MHK. "Not even the one right there?"

"No, neither one."

"Wait a minute, Toor Jan. Didn't you say that Haji Hyatullah was General Khan's uncle?"

"Yes," Toor Jan said, looking at his fingernails.

"Don't you know what the General looks like?"

"I've seen him in the traffic circle."

"And he's not in this?" Dan tapped the picture hard. "He's not one of these men?"

Qais tugged on Dan's sleeve. "It's weird, bruh, but sometimes these dudes can't recognize people in a picture." He rubbed his chin strap beard in thought. "Like they don't know how to understand a picture."

"He's not stupid, Qais," Dan said, turning back to Toor Jan.

"Nah, man. That's not what I'm sayin'. They ain't seen enough pictures to really get it. That's all." Qais sat back, crossed his arms over his chest, then sprang forward again. "It's not like he lyin'. He just don't know."

Dan didn't believe Qais, didn't really understand why Toor Jan claimed that he couldn't recognize a picture of the most famous man in Uruzgan, but he'd already pissed Qais off enough that he didn't want to push it. He opened his notebook to begin writing. "Fine. Where was this picture taken, Toor Jan?

"In Kotwal village."

"Where is that?"

"It's across from the first bend in the Teri." Toor Jan held his hand in front of his face, as if his palm were the map. "Near the start of Pinowa valley."

"Remember the directions I taught you, Toor Jan?"

"I *know*," Toor Jan said. "You know the start of Pinowa," he said to Qais. "Right?"

Qais shook his head.

"Is it north of here? West? What is it near?" Dan said.

Toor Jan grumbled. "It's on the river." He looked around the meeting room, as if seeing it in his mind. "You know where it is—near the plain where we killed Iskandar's men. You know that place? Right where we ambushed many of Iskandar's men."

"Iskandar?" Dan wrote the name down. He'd check the reports for a Taliban commander with that name later. "You said Iskandar, right?"

"Yes. That's right. Iskandar." Toor Jan exhaled. "I'll find out the directions for next time."

"Is that where Haji Hyatullah keeps the weapons? In Kotwal village?"

"The people say he does not have weapons at home. Most of them are in his car shop. The rest are at Doctor Baki's house."

"Who?" Dan had never heard of Doctor Baki. He wrote that name down too. "Repeat his name."

"Doctor Baki."

"And who's that?"

"He is a doctor who lives in the city."

"Where in the city?"

"I am not sure where but I know he is next to a police checkpoint. The police give him the weapons they take on raids and he gives them to Haji Hyatullah to sell."

"How do you know this?"

"Everybody knows this, Commander." Toor Jan paused. "I can find his house." He looked at Dan and then at Qais. "It will be easy."

"How will you do that?"

"My son needs a good doctor. We don't have good doctors in the country. I can ask around the city and someone will show me his house."

"Could you go inside?"

"Oh yes," Toor Jan said.

This was dangerous. If Doctor Baki was who Toor Jan said he was, then even suspicion would be enough to get Toor Jan killed. But—for all they knew—Toor Jan was working for someone trying to kill Dan anyway. If he was willing to work, Dan would let him.

"Go ahead and do it, Toor Jan. If you pull it off, it'll help your case with our doctors."

"Yes, Commander."

Dan closed his notebook and pulled a hundred *afghanis* from his pocket. "Time's up, Toor Jan."

Toor Jan reached for the money and Qais slapped his hand. He took it and didn't give it to Toor Jan until they were at the gate.

Back at the SPU, Dan parked the truck and ran into the Soviet Building, the MP5 swinging on his back. He'd keep the picture of Haji Hyatullah, putting it in his hat beside baby Charlotte, until he could confirm it, but right now he needed Captain Cales to help with Dr. Baki. He ripped open the door. The television was blaring. Captain Cales and Army Brian were sitting on the couch watching a college football Bowl game.

"Gentlemen," Dan said, opening his notebook. "You busy?"

The two grunted. Dan turned off the television.

"Come on," Army Brian said. His feet were up on a table and coffee steamed from a paper cup beside him. "I'm trying to relax."

"There *is* a war going on. You know that?" Dan flipped to the pages from the meeting. "Captain?"

"Petty Officer Bing." He put his feet up, beside Army Brian's, and folded his hands behind his head. "How was your meeting with the great and powerful Maziullah?"

"It was very good. Ever heard of Doctor Baki?"

Captain Cales smirked. "Yep."

"What about him?"

"He's all over reporting. A weapons guy."

"A weapons guy who helps Haji Hyatullah."

"That's what they say."

"And Haji Hyatullah helps MHK."

"Allegedly, at least."

Army Brian shot to his feet and turned on the television. "I'm trying to watch the game, Dan. Where're you going with this?"

"Why have we never gone after him?"

"Because." Captain Cales stood and went to his computer. Dan followed and Army Brian cheered, the football game unobstructed. "We've never known where he lives. Why?"

"Maziullah will tell us where his house is."

"Interesting," Captain Cales said, typing into the intelligence reports search engine. Twenty-three reports came back on Doctor Baki. "We already got enough on him to launch an operation."

"Operation? *Very* interesting," Army Brian said, coming over. "Time for a good old-fashioned interrogation?"

"Absolutely," Captain Cales said. "If they bring him back alive."

"He must come back alive," Dan said. "We need him to give up MHK."

"Don't get too excited, Dan," Captain Cales said. "I want you both to get read up on Doctor Baki right now. I'll talk to Beau and we'll talk to Russo to work it into the operations. *If* Maziullah can find where he lives." Army Brian and Dan went to their computers. "Brian, you got lead interrogator."

"*What?*" Dan said.

"What's wrong?" Captain Cales said, leaning in close to his screen.

"This is my fucking operation. I'm interrogating."

"Oh really?" Captain Cales said. "Brian, how many detainees have you interrogated?"

"Fifty-five, lifetime." Army Brian took a wet chewed cigar from his pocket and put it into his mouth. "What's your count, Danny boy?"

"I'm the one who's finding the bastard."

"You are," Captain Cales said, holding his ubiquitous folder. "But we don't do Abu Ghraib around here so you're going to play your part, support Brian, observe a professional at work, and learn something before you do the real thing."

"This ain't school, buddy," Army Brian added.

Dan shook his head. "Okay, fine. One more thing, have you heard of a Taliban commander named Iskandar?"

"Iskandar." Captain Cales said. Army Brian laughed.

"Yeah, Maziullah said that Haji Hyatullah's village is near where they killed Iskandar's men but I've never heard of him."

"Yes you have," Captain Cales said.

"No, sir. I have not."

"You have, Dan." Army Brian said, the cigar clenched in his teeth. "Iskandar is Pashto for Alexander. As in Alexander *the Great*." He thrust his hand liked he was holding an ancient sword. "According to your dear friend Maziullah, Haji Hyatullah's house is near one of Alexander the Great's battle sites." He smiled. "How 'bout that shit, huh?"

Toor Jan said a few months were only like yesterday. In Uruzgan, so were a few thousand years.

TOOR JAN LOOKED LIKE ONE OF THOSE TALIBS

Tarin Kowt City, Tarin Kot District, Uruzgan Province, Afghanistan, 02 January 2013—

Toor Jan, a scarf tied across his nose, took his motorcycle to the best fruit stand in Tarin Kowt City owned by a man named Abdul—known to everyone as Abdul Fruit. Abdul Fruit was a slight man, middle-aged. He wore a black leather coat over a steel-colored *kameez*. A glittered *Baluchi* cap sat off-center on his head. Though renowned for his wares, Abdul Fruit was even more famous for knowing all the gossip in the city.

Abdul Fruit packed dried berries into green plastic bags and passed them to waiting men. He took money and returned change. He stopped counting a few *rupees* when he noticed Toor Jan. Toor Jan pulled the scarf down below his chin and held up a fist of dried unshelled almonds. "Pass those to me," Abdul Fruit said and packed the nuts in a small bag. He shot his free hand toward Toor Jan for money. "Right here."

Toor Jan counted a few bills and passed them, greasy with sweat, to Abdul Fruit.

"Ah, *Afghanis*. Do you work at the foreigner's base?"

Toor Jan looked at the men waiting behind him and back to Abdul Fruit. "Never."

Abdul Fruit passed the bag of almonds to Toor Jan. "Go on, go. I have more customers."

"Wait." Toor Jan pulled the scarf to his face again. "I need something else."

"What is it?"

"I'd like to know—" The voices of people as they walked along the road mixed with the creaking wheels of carts drawn by donkeys. Still, Toor Jan lowered his voice, "—where can I find Doctor Baki?"

Abdul Fruit looked Toor Jan over closely. Toor Jan knew he looked like one of those *talibs* that the city-people hated. He tried to show no fear. "You need a pistol?"

"No! We need a doctor for our baby. There's no one good in the country."

Abdul Fruit pointed. "Doctor Baki is that way past the traffic circle. There's a cell phone tower in his compound and a police checkpoint across the street. Walk that way and you'll see it.'"

Toor Jan turned to walk past the traffic circle. *But will I be invited inside?* Once inside the compound he could memorize the entire layout. That kind of risk was what The Good American required to help Toor Jan get a real doctor to fix Ibrahim's lips. Toor Jan crossed three streets before he looked up again. A cell phone tower, painted red and white, spiked up from inside the walls of a compound. Across the street from the compound, sandbags were heaped high and topped with a machine gun. A belt of ammunition swung in the cold breeze. Several police officers sat around a radio. The police officers laughed at whatever was playing.

Toor Jan lowered his scarf and went to the compound's gate. Children were playing inside. He knocked softly. They yelled and ran away. Toor Jan looked back at the police officers. They ignored him and everything else. He knocked again.

"I'm coming!" a man called from the other side. The children followed, their feet pattering, to the gate. "Who is it?"

Toor Jan said through the door, "My name is Juma Gul. I'm from Sarkhum. I need to find a doctor for my baby." The man cracked open the gate and stuck his long nose through. He wore a pair of wire-framed glasses. *The left lens is cracked*, Toor Jan thought as he memorized the face. "Are you Doctor Baki?"

"Who are you again?"

"Juma Gul from Sarkhum." Toor Jan glanced over at the police officers. They were now drinking tea. Their guns hung loosely from their backs. "Please, sir. My baby has a problem with his lips." Toor Jan turned his hands out, as he would when he prayed. "You are Doctor Baki? Some of the people told me to come here."

The man opened the door further and pushed his bony shoulders through. His neck was long and covered in flat brown moles. "This problem with the lips is like this?" The man traced his henna dyed finger from the bottom of his nose through his upper lip.

"Yes. Are you Doctor Baki?"

"Yes. I'm Doctor Baki. How old is your baby?"

"He's a few weeks old. I'm not sure exactly."

"He's too young to have an operation now but I'll take care of your baby." Doctor Baki stepped back and shut the gate hard against Toor Jan. "Bring the child in two months," he added behind the closed door.

Toor Jan turned away, back to his motorcycle. He rode fast to make it home before the sun went down.

Toor Jan jumped off and walked his motorcycle over the last hill into Safad Khare. The bike was light and easy to push. He had started doing this so the people didn't hear him returning from his meetings with The Good American. He crested the hill and the mud houses spread across the flat below. Gray cooking smoke twisted from the compounds. In the distance, two men were at his gate. A smaller man stood over a larger one and kicked the larger one in his side. It was Gran and Abdul Hakim. Toor Jan threw down his motorcycle and ran toward them.

"What are you doing?"

"Your retarded brother escaped again." Gran held Abdul Hakim down. Abdul Hakim was crying. "I told you to tie him up."

Toor Jan grabbed Gran's face and squeezed. Gran's eyes bulged from his skull. Toor Jan wanted to drive his thumbs into Gran's eyes but knew that if he did, then Haji Daoud and all of the Barakzais would swear revenge. Toor Jan let go. He picked Abdul Hakim up and they went together through the open gate to the almond tree.

"I wanted to be outside," Abdul Hakim said between sobs. Bruises were already showing on his neck and face. "That's all I wanted."

"I know, brother. But that's impossible."

Gran watched them through the open gate. His face was red from Toor Jan's squeezing. He wasn't armed but looked ready for a fight. Toor Jan let go of Abdul Hakim and walked out to get his motorcycle— eyes on Gran the entire time. He slammed the gate shut behind him. "Keep the gate closed," he said to Abdul Hakim. "Or next time you go outside Gran might kill you."

Toor Jan left Abdul Hakim to call The Good American and tell him that he had found Doctor Baki.

DAN GETS INTO THE WAR

Multinational Base Tarin Kowt, Tarin Kot District, Uruzgan Province, Afghanistan, 08 January 2013—

Maziullah stuffed a plug of lime-green *naswar* into his lower lip. Dan offered him a paper cup but he waved it away and walked outside of the meeting room to spit. They didn't talk for a while, waiting for the settling effect of the tobacco. Dan and Qais leaned forward when Maziullah indicated that he was ready. They were irritated with him. He hadn't yet told them when MHK was going to Mumbai for his hepatitis treatment.

"The General has changed since his son died." Maziullah stood, went to the door, opened it, and spat outside again. He turned to Qais and Dan, "As if no one but him has ever suffered."

"What about Commander Aaron's son, Maziullah?"

"What do you mean?"

"You were supposed to tell me when he's going to Mumbai." Commander Russo had asked Dan specifically to find out MHK's plans. "Can you do that?"

"No, not now." Maziullah said and brushed tobacco flakes from his lap. "He has been hiding it from me."

"Why?" Dan said. "Does he know you talk to us?"

Maziullah looked down. "No. He is still my best friend but he's changed."

"But as soon as you know when he is leaving, we will know?"

Maziullah pulled himself into the blue rifle's sling and smoothed his long pastel purple shirt. "I must go, my friend."

They went into the yard where their silver 4Runner sat in the mud. It had rained again. The stone walls were glazed with water. Dan opened the driver's-side door and stopped. "You ever look into Doctor Baki?"

"Yes," Maziullah said. "He is nobody." Maziullah removed his toothbrush from the breast pocket of his *kameez* and brushed, checking his reflection in the window for any *naswar* between his teeth. "You do not have to worry about Doctor Baki."

"Are you sure?" Dan stomped mud from his boots on the running board. "I've heard a lot of bad things."

"He is not involved in anything," Maziullah said. He looked Dan in the eye. "As soon as I know when the General is leaving for Mumbai, I will call you."

"Thank you, *andiwale*," Dan said.

They pulled out of the SPU and slalomed through the mud to drop Maziullah off at the main gate. On the way back, Qais was silent. He still wasn't happy with Dan.

"Qais."

"What, man."

"You mad?"

"Nah, man."

"Then what's the problem?" The windshield wipers stopped working. They both leaned forward to see through the sheet of water.

"You know I'm just trying to do my job."

"Some job, bruh." Qais pointed ahead at the taillights of a cement truck. "Look out."

"I see it," Dan said, moving around the stalled truck. The 4Runner's tires whizzed through the mud. "What's that supposed to mean?"

"It means that these dudes is playin' you. Toor Jan's not a good dude. He has bad relatives."

"No shit," Dan said. The windshield wipers flipped back on. "But I control him."

"Yeah, maybe. But I ain't tryin' to get fired neither."

"They tried to fire me a month ago. I'm still kicking."

"That don't make me feel better."

"Don't worry about it," Dan said. "No one's going to find out we're talking to Toor Jan."

"Then how 'bout Maziullah? Look at that dude. He straight up lied about Doctor Baki. That's because he don't want to mess with the good thing he got goin'. See, these dudes will play everyone they can. Tell you what you want to hear if it benefits them, lie about anything else. Maziullah got somethin' going to Doctor Baki, I'm tellin' you, bruh."

They came onto the gravel road and Dan pushed the speed. "Doesn't matter. We're going to get Doctor Baki tonight, anyway."

"I been 'round long enough." Qais said, sitting back and crossing his arms. "I know how this goes."

Dan pulled into the SPU. "How's it going to go?"

Qais balled his fists, shook them, and spread his fingers. "*Kaboom.*"

That night—the ground wet but the sky clear and cold—Dan, Army Brian, and Qais got into the 4Runner, surged out of the SPU and onto the lane that ran along the airfield. The truck rocked on its chassis. Army Brian turned off the headlights for a moment. Complete darkness closed over them with the finality of drowning. There was no night in the world like night in Uruzgan. They went on to the guard house at the entrance of the Commandos' compound on the north side of the base. An Afghan Commando, wearing an old American uniform, stepped into the road. He raised his hand to stop the 4Runner and the baggy uniform hung from his arm.

At some forgotten warehouse in middle America there were stacks of these uniforms. They were cheap and—out of service for the American military—sold to the Afghans. Like little brothers, they wore the Americans' old clothes. Somewhere, someone was making a lot of money from the deal.

Qais spoke to the guard and he waved them inside.

The Afghan Commando compound consisted of ten huge, tan Quonset huts arrayed around a gravel-covered parade ground. Each hut had a patch of garden. Two peacocks walked around, their plumage furled. A small radio tower was anchored by nylon cords to the edge of the parade ground. From the closest Quonset hut, a man screamed clipped phrases, broken by the sizzle of static. He was the Commandos' radio man, talking to the troops as they assaulted Doctor Baki's compound. Captain Cales was already waiting on the parade ground, holding the hand of an Afghan with a heavy moustache. The Afghan was built like an American high school wrestler. He wore a gray Puma track suit, the relaxation uniform of the Commandos.

Army Brian turned off the truck and sprinted to Captain Cales. Dan gathered six cans of iced coffee, balancing a notebook and digital camera on top, and chased after Army Brian. Qais glumly followed.

"*Chi tor hasti, dostaman*?" Army Brian said in Farsi to the small man holding Captain Cales's hand. "How are you, friend?"

"You got a new boyfriend?" Dan said to Captain Cales.

"Dan, this is Charlie," Captain Cales said. "He's the Intelligence First Sergeant."

Dan took Charlie's hand. Every other Afghan gave a wilted handshake—it was cultural—but Charlie's firm hand impressed him. "You excited?" Dan said.

Charlie nodded enthusiastically. "*Khob, khob, khob.*"

"All right guys, here's the deal," Captain Cales said. "They got Doctor Baki. It just came over the radio. But he's the Commandos' prisoner. Not ours." He let go of Charlie's hand. "Part of the withdrawal plan is having the Afghans take the lead. So you get tonight to conduct an interrogation before we turn him over."

"How are we supposed to do anything with that?" Dan said.

"It's how the agreement works. They're *allowing* us to interrogate this guy. For them he's just another mouth to feed so they want him in Bagram prison as soon as possible."

"That's stupid," Dan said. Good interrogations required time, rapport, a relationship. It was already midnight and they'd only have until the sun came up to get something done. "Tell them to give us more time."

"Stop, Dan," Army Brian said, holding up his hand. "I'll do what I can." He turned to the Captain. "What do you want me to go for then?"

"They said they found weapons in his compound—"

"Good," Dan interrupted. "Connections to Haji Hyatullah and Mir Hamza Khan. That's what we need to focus on."

Captain Cales rolled his eyes. "Whatever you can get, Brian. Charlie will interrogate him too, tomorrow after you're done."

Charlie raised his hand above his head and brought it down like a cracking whip. Army Brian and Dan laughed.

"I didn't see him do that," Captain Cales said, "if anyone in a court of law asks."

An hour later, fifteen tan Humvees, one after another, pulled onto the parade ground. Commandos stood in their turrets with their PKM's at high port, to avoid sweeping each other. No other Afghan Army unit was disciplined enough to do that. The rumbling trucks filed onto the parade ground. Then everything went quiet again as the trucks turned off at the same time. The men dismounted and got into formation.

Two Afghan Commandos crunched through the gravel toward Army Brian, Dan, and Qais. Between them was a hooded man with his hands bound behind his back. A door to a Quonset hut opened and Charlie darted out, taking the prisoner inside.

Charlie had set up a make-shift interrogation booth in a room where the Afghan Commandos held classes. Desks and benches long enough to seat six men were crammed against the chalkboard wall. Four unbalanced chairs—three arranged to face the last one—were left in the empty middle. Seven AK-47s, one PKM machine gun, a sniper rifle, and a nine-volt battery, all found in Doctor Baki's compound, sat on a tarp on the floor.

Army Brian asked Charlie to bring in a lamp and he faced Doctor Baki into the bright light. He told Qais to pull his chair beside Doctor Baki and mirror the speed and intensity of his speech. Army Brian sat so close to Doctor Baki that his knee touched the hem of Doctor Baki's long shirt. Dan sat in the last chair with the MP5 and digital camera in his lap. Captain Cales came into the room, near the door, and watched.

Army Brian took the hood off Doctor Baki. He wore wire-frame glasses. A lens was cracked. Blackheads peppered the tip of his hooked nose. His beard was thin. Most Pashtuns took pride in their beards as a symbol of manhood. They brushed and oiled them. Doctor Baki's was knotted around itself.

Army Brian asked Dan to remove the cuffs and told Doctor Baki to remove his shirt. He was gaunt and his shoulders showed through his skin at sharp points. A large bruise covered his back. "Let's go Danny boy, time to get into the war." Army Brian turned Doctor Baki around. "Take a picture of that bruise with the time on your watch clearly visible in the frame."

Dan took the picture twice, the time on the white wristwatch difficult to make out in the first shot. Qais gave Doctor Baki back his shirt.

"Captain Cales, you're our witness," Army Brian said. Captain Cales nodded. "When we're done with the interrogation, we'll do it again so we have proof that we didn't cause that bruise."

Army Brian looked at Doctor Baki for a long time. He nodded, nearly imperceptibly, then reached into his pocket for a fresh cigar. It took a few minutes to cut the end off to his satisfaction, fire up the tip, and draw until it glowed hell red. Army Brian savored the taste, tilted his head and exhaled the floral smoke into the air. It hung over their heads.

"What's going to happen next?" Army Brian said to Doctor Baki

Doctor Baki started to reply to Qais.

Army Brian snapped his finger beside Doctor Baki's ear. "You only talk to me and you only look at me. That's how it works around here."

Doctor Baki turned but didn't look Army Brian in the eye.

"I'm here to understand what happened at your house so we can figure out what's next."

"What do you mean next?" Doctor Baki's voice was high and pitchy.

"There were weapons on your property." Doctor Baki looked away and Army Brian snapped his fingers. He jerked his head up. "Right?"

"That is what *you* say."

"See them?" Army Brian pointed out of the window at the Afghan Commandos on the parade ground. They were unloading and cleaning their trucks from the operation. "They found a pile of guns at your house. And a battery! Don't forget the battery. They're ready to send you away to Bagram."

"Send me to Bagram?"

"To the big prison up there."

"For what?" Doctor Baki's voice spiked again.

"For giving weapons to the Taliban."

Doctor Baki smiled. "*Talibs?* We are not with the *talibs*. We are with the General." He clicked his tongue. "We do not have weapons."

"You're a doctor?"

"Yes."

"So you're educated?"

"That is how I became a doctor."

"So you're smart?"

"Yes, I am smart."

"I don't know what happened. I wasn't there. But there's a pile of guns. And that freaking battery. The Commandos said they took them from your house." He puffed from the cigar and released a column of smoke. "If you don't have weapons, whose could they be?"

Doctor Baki said nothing.

"My job is to understand your story so we don't accidentally send an innocent man to prison for a long time."

"Prison? For a long time? For what?"

"You have a family?"

"Yes."

"Do they know where you are?"

He shook his head.

"Children?"

"Two sons."

"I have a son as well!" Army Brian pulled out his wallet and removed a laminated photograph of a brown-haired, seven-year-old boy that he had found on the internet. Doctor Baki looked at the picture with little interest. "I'm far from him now."

"You Americans have come a long way to be in my country."

"At least he knows where I am."

"Yes," he said crossing his legs and shrugging. "That's a nice thing."

The Commandos had turned over everything from Doctor Baki's pockets. A few *rupees*, prayer beads, and a tin of *naswar* with nothing more than a pinch left. It smelled of slaked lime. Army Brian had it in his pocket and offered it to Doctor Baki. He took the powder and jammed it between his cheek and gums. "When do you think you'll talk to your sons again?" Army Brian said, snapping the tobacco tin shut. "Maybe never again?"

"You decide that."

"That's not entirely true. *If* you tell me about the guns we can figure out a way to get you home to your sons. Who did you get the guns from?"

"I don't know anything about guns." He spat a dark stream of tobacco onto the floor.

"Can I ask you a question?"

He nodded.

"Does a man choose what happens to him or is everything planned before he is born?"

"God wills all things."

"Did God will that tobacco into your mouth?" Army Brian stood and paced in front of Doctor Baki. Qais mirrored, behind. "Or did *you* stuff it into your mouth?"

"I put it into my mouth."

"You chose to put it into your mouth?"

"Yes."

"So you choose to do things? Not everything is forced by *Allah*?"

"I choose *some* things."

"Why do you choose to go to jail and be away from your boys?"

"I don't choose that."

"*But you are choosing that*," Army Brian said. "These Tajik Commandos don't care about Pashtuns. They want to send you to the prison in Bagram. They would send all Pashtuns out of the country if they could. Look how easy you're making it for them. They have *your* guns. And *your* battery. Oh, the battery, my friend. The one used for making bombs. You know how they feel about people who make bombs. You're lucky they didn't execute you in your own house, in front of your sons."

Doctor Baki clicked his tongue. "But I don't make bombs."

"No you don't do anything. Except *choose* to get taken from your boys." He stopped pacing and turned, his voice softening. "What are your boys' names?"

"Musa and Yusef." He spat another belt of tobacco across the floor. "They are five and eight."

"My boy's name is Jake. In another life they might have been friends." He sat down and Qais did too. "There's a police checkpoint across the street from your house?"

"Yes."

"At what age do they take their *chai* boys?"

Doctor Baki's hands began to tremble. He jutted out his lip.

"Soon Musa and Yusef will be the right age," Army Brian said.

"They won't take them."

"Will Musa and Yusef be good *chai* boys? Can they dance?"

Doctor Baki turned from Army Brian.

Army Brian crouched down so Doctor Baki could see him. "Of course they can dance. And they've brewed tea too. Right?"

Doctor Baki looked up at the ceiling. Army Brian stood in front of him.

"But how good are they at sucking cock? Can they suck four cocks a night? Four police officers is a slow night. When they get better more will come. Right, Doctor?"

"I don't know." His face was colorless. "Stop saying these things."

Army Brian put his cigar to his lips and drew. "You know how cops are. What are they supposed to do? Fuck their ugly wives' pussies?" He blew smoke at Doctor Baki. "Those cops saw you get arrested tonight. They've probably already walked over to your compound and leaned their ear to the cold metal gate to listen for noise." He pushed his ear against his hand.

"That hasn't happened. The General won't allow it."

"The General cares about money, especially the money from those weapons you got confiscated tonight. If he has to let your sons become fuck toys to teach you a lesson, he'll do it. We both know that."

"You are a dog."

"Those cops are listening to your boys in the courtyard without your manly footsteps following, right now, as we speak. Your wife whispering harshly for the boys to be quiet. Who will stop them from ramming your gate? Can two small boys resist a group of men?"

Doctor Baki made a sound like a dry heave.

"Maybe there won't even be a fight. Maybe they'll lead them by the hand from your house. Promise them candy. Let them listen to the radio. And when it's dark," Army Brian began to whisper and Qais did too, "when the city is quiet and the air is icy, they'll slip your boys' shirts over their heads, admire their small bodies. And, after they've danced a bit, they'll teach Musa and Yusef to suck their hard cocks."

Doctor Baki's body shook.

"Doctor, doctor please," Army Brian said, tutting. "Please. I understand your fear." He reached for his hand. "Remember what we said about choices? Choose to help me save your boys." Army Brian pointed to the nine-volt battery on the tarp. Dan gave it to him. "This. This is what those Tajik Commandos' hate the most. If you can tell me who gave it to you, I can convince them to arrest the person who has got you into this situation instead. Tell me his name. He's who I want. Not you. Where did this IED battery come from?"

Doctor Baki exhaled abruptly and crossed his legs. His sandal hung, bouncing, from his shaking foot. "A man we call The Engineer."

"The Engineer?" Army Brian stood. Dan wrote it in his notebook. "What's his real name?"

"I don't know."

"And what about these guns? Where did you get them from?"

"I don't have any guns," Doctor Baki said.

"Those ones right there." Army Brian waved his hand over the weapons. "On the floor."

"I do not see any guns."

Army Brian picked up his empty chair and threw it across the room.

They continued like this for hours, taking several breaks, drinking all the iced coffee, until the sun showed pink through the snowy mountains and Army Brian's cigar was a nub. Doctor Baki was tired and his lids drooped but he wouldn't admit to even the existence of the weapons on the floor because it would give up MHK.

Charlie entered and told them to stop the interrogation. The Afghan Commandos were starting their day and were required to allow Doctor Baki four hours of sleep before their own interrogation. Dan took a second picture of the bruise and Army Brian, Qais, Captain Cales, and Dan filed out into the 4Runner. The rising sun gave them a slight bump of energy. And Dan, as always, was angry. "He didn't fucking break."

"This ain't school, Danny boy," Army Brian said. He was driving and looking at Dan from the rearview mirror. "It's almost always like that."

"Think about all the trauma anyone we interrogate has been through," Captain Cales said. "They're not susceptible to a lot of our interrogation techniques. We can't describe things that are *more* horrible than what they've already been through."

They passed along the airfield and the mountains almost looked inviting in the new light. Army Brian flipped down the visor to shield his eyes as he drove.

"Same in Helmand," Qais said. "They seen it all."

"We didn't get shit," Dan said.

"Sure you did." Captain Cales tapped Dan's notebook. "All right there."

"What? What'd we get?"

"Who's The Engineer?"

Dan looked at Army Brian in the rearview mirror. He shrugged. "I don't know who The Engineer is, Captain."

"Then go find out."

And they all yelled *dummy*, even Dan, punctuating Captain Cales's order, as they pulled into the SPU to get some sleep.

TOOR JAN'S HONOR

Safad Khare, Tarin Kot District, Uruzgan Province, Afghanistan, 12 January 2013—

Shaheen tied Ibrahim into a tight papoose and put him on her back as she swept the yard. Her hair wasn't covered and swung almost to her waist. Ibrahim's face peeked above his mother's shoulders. The two passed Toor Jan, sitting under the almond tree, without a look. Inside the house, Mina sung along to a song on the radio and rhythmically worked a knife. Toor Jan loved the sound of wet, chopped vegetables frying in a pool of hissing oil.

Abdul Hakim stood in front of Toor Jan with a short axe. He had finished splitting a pile of fire wood. "You did good work, brother," Toor Jan said. "Now bring me the axe." Abdul Hakim trotted over, the axe across his back. With his last exaggerated steps, he offered it to Toor Jan by the head. "Stay with me." Toor Jan held Abdul Hakim's hand.

Shaheen kept sweeping. Ibrahim ground his naked gums and his harelip opened and closed. Abdul Hakim watched the baby. "How did Ibrahim make God mad?"

"I told you before that he didn't. Sometimes things happen to people."

"But things can't just happen, brother." Abdul Hakim had been obsessed with the boy since his birth. He touched the baby's lips so often that Shaheen wouldn't allow him to hold his nephew anymore. "God makes all things possible."

"God makes all things possible but he doesn't make all things." Toor Jan squeezed his brother's hand. "Stop worrying yourself."

"What did I do to make God mad?"

"Nothing." Toor Jan squeezed Abdul Hakim's hand harder. "Let it go, brother."

"But God controls who's born and who dies. He controls the sun and the moon. He controls everything. He gives good people rewards and punishes the bad people. Right?"

"Yes, you're right."

"Then *Baba* did something wrong. I'm his punishment."

Toor Jan dropped Abdul Hakim's hand. "Why would you say that?"

"People say I'm stupid because father was sinful. And now the baby is strange. You must be sinful too, brother."

"I'm not," Toor Jan said.

"It must be." Abdul Hakim smiled. "God is punishing you for sins." He repeated himself under his breath.

"Enough!" Toor Jan grabbed Abdul Hakim's face. "It's nothing! These things happen for no reason! None!"

Abdul Hakim squirmed like a muzzled dog. "I'm sorry, Toor *Janna*. I only want to understand things."

"Go get ready to eat," Toor Jan told him. Abdul Hakim went inside. Shaheen had been watching but when Toor Jan looked over she returned to her sweeping.

Mina finished cooking, a real feast, and the family hunched around a single platter and ate. Tired and full, they passed Ibrahim between them while Abdul Hakim glared at them from the corner.

"They grow fast," Toor Jan said, cradling Ibrahim's head. "But he doesn't smile."

"This takes time, *laalaa*," Mina said. She pulled her wheat-colored hair over her shoulder and brushed it with her fingers. "He grows because we eat well now."

"We eat well because my husband works hard. This new job is a blessing from God."

Toor Jan had told the women that he was working for a man in the *bazaar* selling car batteries. The women pouted their lips, impressed. Toor Jan spent his days riding through Pinowa, Tarin Kowt, Dorafshan, and Sarkhum looking for bad people to report to The Good American. It excited him to have somewhere to be when he awoke in the morning.

"Get over here, brother," Toor Jan said. Shaheen shot a look of concern. "Come see the baby." Abdul Hakim pulled the blanket over his head and ignored them.

"What's wrong with him?" Shaheen said.

"He thinks this thing with Ibrahim's face is a punishment," Toor Jan said, passing the baby to Shaheen. "I have to prepare for work tomorrow," he said and left the room.

Toor Jan checked to see if he had enough *Roshan* minutes on his cell phone. He inserted a Micro SD card and reviewed the memory. The card was empty. The Good American didn't like Toor Jan using phones but he might need it to take pictures. Pictures were always worth more money. Toor Jan took a plastic bottle outside to the water well. He dunked the bottle, waited for two glugs, and put on the cap. His motorcycle was leaning against the almond tree and he checked the gas, the chain, squeezed the clutch and brake. He ran his hands along the wires, feeling for cuts in the lines. He found none.

Toor Jan had proved he was good at his job by stealing the picture of Haji Hyatullah from the General without detection and easily finding Doctor Baki. He was becoming a powerful man. His troubles weren't from commiting sin, or doubting God, or having a cursed family. Troubles came for men who believed they were too weak to defend themselves.

He returned inside. Ibrahim was sleeping on his back, legs and arms stretched out. Mina and Shaheen curled on the floor. The blanket still wrapped Abdul Hakim. Toor Jan undressed and laid beside his wife. The air was cool and dark. He welcomed sleep. He needed good rest for tomorrow.

Near midnight, Mina screamed.

Shaheen, the humid rush of her breath on his face, shook his shoulders. "*Toor Janna!*" She stood. "Get up!"

Mina cried again.

Toor Jan leapt from his back, into the yard. He was blind without the moon but he moved toward Mina's cries. He found her, a shapeless form, kneeling at the gate. The open gate thudded against something on the ground. A body.

"Is that the goat?" He touched the body, the unsteady rise of lungs under a shirt. "Please, God, no."

It was Abdul Hakim.

Toor Jan pulled him into the yard. He slammed the gate's bolt home so that all of Safad Khare could hear. They flipped Abdul Hakim over to his back but couldn't see his face. Shaheen stood over Toor Jan. He told her to find his cellphone. She ran, fast. Ibrahim droned inside the house.

Shaheen returned and passed Toor Jan the cellphone. He turned on the camera light.

Abdul Hakim's face was nearly destroyed. Blood covered it like a horrible paint. His skin looked like it might erupt from the pressure. His eyes, out of his dreadful skull, searched for Toor Jan. Abdul Hakim tried to talk but spat blood. It spilled down the sides of his mouth, pooling on the ground below his head.

Toor Jan turned the boy's head. "Tell me what happened."

All Abdul Hakim could do was cry.

"Please, brother. Who did this to you?"

Abdul Hakim pulled Toor Jan close to be heard. "I went to Gran's house and I told him to come out. He came out and I told him what you said to me today. That God didn't curse us. God doesn't control the things that happened on earth." He spat blood again and Mina wiped it away with the corner of her scarf. "He took me to the canal and threw rocks at me until I didn't move. After he left I crawled through the woods to our gate."

Toor Jan took his brother into the house. The women followed. Toor Jan put Abdul Hakim on his own pillow, the best in the house, and told Mina to fetch water. She returned with a bucket and began cleaning Abdul Hakim. He cried as she dabbed at his wounds.

Shaheen went to the nail on the wall where the AK-47 hung. She lifted the rifle toward her husband. He didn't take it. "Here's what you need." She pressed it against his chest. "Take the gun."

"No."

"You can't?"

"I'll be killed if I do." He took a step toward the door and Shaheen grabbed his shirt. "What?"

"You must do it."

"Then what happens to you? And the baby? Who will care for you? My brother?" Toor Jan threw her hand off. "I have to sleep. I have work tomorrow."

Toor Jan went to sleep, trying to ignore his brother's pain.

After he had found where Doctor Baki lived, The Good American rewarded Toor Jan by taking him to the American clinic again and demanding they remove the metal splint from his arm. He yelled at the doctors and they submitted to him. Toor Jan was finally free of the painful contraption. Toor Jan, in gratitude, had demanded more work. The Good American asked about a man called The Engineer. He built bombs and had a mangled foot.

"His name is Sadiq Ustaz," Toor Jan said. "I know about him through my uncle."

The Good American ordered Toor Jan to find Sadiq Ustaz and paid him more money than ever before. He said that he was trying to arrange a doctor for Ibrahim. He complimented Toor Jan on his intelligence and his hard work.

Toor Jan woke early. He went over to Abdul Hakim. The boy was broken, unrecognizable. Tears filled Toor Jan's eyes. He turned and left the house to find Sadiq Ustaz.

Toor Jan went through the hills wearing black American sunglasses that he had found on the road and a knitted black cap. It was warmer on the valley floor but the wind blew frigid off the river. Toor Jan pulled himself close to the handlebars, toward the heat of the engine. He memorized the features in the earth and quizzed himself throughout the trek on what he had last seen so that he could show The Good American the way to Sadiq Ustaz's house on a map.

Toor Jan crossed the Teri Bridge and turned north into the Dorafshan Valley, toward Chorah. The sun heated his left side but the right side, in the dark shadow of the mountains, was frozen and stiff. Close to the area where he thought Sadiq Ustaz lived, he stopped two men standing in the middle of a field.

"Peace be upon you! How are you today?" The men didn't move toward the road and Toor Jan had to yell into the wind. "Can you hear me?"

"We hear you. What do you need?"

"I'm looking for Sadiq Ustaz. Do you know where I can find him?"

Toor Jan spat on the road and when he looked up again the two men had stooped down. They stood, with rifles, and stalked toward Toor Jan.

"Brothers! I'm sent by an important man!" He threw his hands in the air and shook his head. The motorcycle teetered between his legs. "I mean no harm. I'm here to talk to him."

The two men closed the distance, their guns raised at Toor Jan. "Who sent you?"

"An important commander in this area."

"Who?" They surrounded him. They were young, barely men, with faint whiskers over their lips. Each wore a light green *kameez* and brown blanket. Their heads were uncovered. With guns they seemed much more frightening than they were. Toor Jan imagined them running after a soccer ball and that thought gave him courage. "Who do you come from?"

"The Big One sent me to find Sadiq Ustaz."

The two man-boys looked at each other without lowering their guns.

"He's my uncle. You can ask Sadiq Ustaz all of this. He knows that The Big One is my uncle."

One of the man-boys lowered his rifle and took a red phone from his pocket. He dialed and held the phone to his ear while staring at Toor Jan. The other man-boy flicked his safety off, ready to shoot.

"I have a man here who says his uncle is The Big One." The man-boy asked Toor Jan his name. "He is Toor Jan, son of Haji Izatullah, from Safad Khare. Yes, okay. Good."

With each passing moment the other man-boy edged his rifle toward Toor Jan's face. By the end of the phone call the muzzle was an inch from Toor Jan's forehead.

"The Engineer says you can see him." The man-boys nodded toward the path that led to the compound. "Keep going that way."

Sadiq Ustaz stood at the gate, his massive head held high between his broad shoulders. His long shirt was open in the front and the hair from his huge beard mixed with the shag on his chest. The legs of his pants were rolled up his thick calves. He smiled at Toor Jan as he approached. Toor Jan returned the smile. "Peace be upon you!" Toor Jan said, yelling over the sound of the engine. "How are you?"

"And peace be upon you! We are good. You?"

"Very good, thank you, *Sadiq Janna*!"

Toor Jan rested his motorcycle against the compound wall, and hugged the enormous man. Sadiq Ustaz's huge paws clapped him so hard that it hurt even through the thickness of his coat, sweater, and long shirt. They took each other in for a few minutes before Sadiq Ustaz stepped back on his shrunken foot.

Toor Jan tried to memorize everything about Sadiq Ustaz: body-type, height, age, and the length of his beard. A large liver spot on the left side of his neck. Two buildings rose above the compound walls and there wasn't anything to prevent a man from climbing over them. The gate was yellow and appeared reinforced. There was a gun port on either side.

"You're here for me?"

"Yes, sent by my uncle, The Big One."

"You work for him now?" Sadiq Ustaz pulled the sleeves of his long shirt up to his elbows. "Since when?"

"The Big One is interested in your services."

"He's never been interested in sending a messenger to me before." He stepped closer to Toor Jan and sniffed. "You still live in the country?"

"Yes I do."

"I can smell the cow shit."

Toor Jan remained steady. "Are you interested in work or not?"

"I have a family." Sadiq Ustaz stared into his eyes. "I'm always interested in work."

"Good." Toor Jan started to turn. "We'll call."

Sadiq Ustaz snatched Toor Jan's wrist. "I remember you from long ago. Your skin is less dark now than it was then." Toor Jan looked up. Sadiq Ustaz stood nearly half a meter above him. "But you look more scared than ever." Sadiq Ustaz laughed deeply from the bellows.

Toor Jan leaped on his motorcycle and went to the city.

In the city he bought bandages and ointments to clean Abdul Hakim. His cell phone, in his pocket, buzzed against his leg. He ducked into a trash-strewn alley and answered.

"Hello, Commander."

"Are you okay, Toor Jan? You're whispering."

"I'm in the city." He looked around. A black cat sat upright at the end of the alley. "I found Sadiq Ustaz."

"Yeah? Where?"

"I can come show you on your map."

"Do you know what he looks like?"

"I was at his house this morning." Toor Jan came out of the alley and went to where he left his motorcycle. He strapped the medical supplies to the crate. "We need to meet."

"Yes we do. In two days. Can you do that?"

Toor Jan swung his leg over his motorcycle. The noon sun scattered most of the people from the *bazaar*. "I will be there."

"Good," he said and hung up.

Shaheen was in the yard when he came home. She was without the baby. Her arms were crossed. "You don't sell batteries in the city," she said. "I knew when you came home with the motorcycle, the day you said robbers on the road had beaten you."

Toor Jan peeled the knitted cap away, its imprint sweated into his hair, and took off the black sunglasses. He turned to her. "We eat now?"

"Yes," she said. It was the first time she had ever looked disgusted by her husband. "But what about our honor?"

"Honor is for men to worry about." He handed her the bandages and ointment and walked away to their outhouse to release the piss he'd held since leaving Sadiq Ustaz's compound.

MIR HAMZA KHAN'S FINAL PLAN

Mir Hamza Khan's mansion, Tarin Kot District, Uruzgan Province, Afghanistan, 14 January 2013—

Mir Hamza Khan had already won over the little *talib* commanders and he knew, clearly, what must happen next. First, embarrass the new American Commander. Remind him of the power of Khan's network to make him vulnerable to suggestion. They were in his compound and Khan was taking him and his *tajiman* around for a tour.

"Commander, come over here," Khan placed his hand on the small of the *tajiman*'s back and pushed him toward a wet bed of turned earth bordering Fatima's house. "Have you seen the roses in Uruzgan?"

"I have, in the spring, of course." The new American Commander said, his hands on his hips. "Is this a rose bed?"

"Yes, it is. Prepared for planting." Khan put his arms around each of them. His shoulders burned with pain. "I love roses. I love beauty. I believe in beauty."

"You seem happy today, General," the new American Commander said, regarding the patch of dirt. "I like to see you in a good mood."

Khan smiled. "Yes, I am." He turned to the new American Commander. "I was rash when we first met. I apologize. I was mourning my son."

"I understand. I should have been more sensitive."

"No, please don't say that. I know how you felt. We were feeling the same way."

"We were?"

"Yes," Khan said. He took the new American Commander's hand. "You were also mourning."

The new American Commander turned his head like a confused dog.

"The old American Commander." Khan raised his eyebrows. "You were mourning him."

The new American Commander squinted, looked at his interpreter to check if he understood. It was translated correctly.

"Suicide is forbidden in our *din*. But I understand the pressure he was under." Khan looked the new American Commander in the eye. "But please don't hide that type of thing from me. Hiding hurts our friendship."

The new American Commander waved toward the *shura* room on the other side of the compound. "Shall we?"

The new American Commander had come with only a three-man security detail and his deputy, the one with the blue eyes and gray hair who had worked for the old American Commander. Except for his guards in the towers, Khan was completely alone. Maziullah was too sick to work today. *Chai* was served and the new American Commander drank two glasses.

The second step of the plan was to stop the Americans from disrupting his businesses.

"You sent a man named Amir Baki to prison in Bagram on false charges. He is an important man around here. An important doctor."

Khan took a sip of his own tea. "I want him returned home."

"No, General. The Afghan Commandos executed a raid on a suspected arms dealer, found weapons, obtained a confession during interrogation, and sent him to Bagram to be prosecuted through proper legal channels."

To Khan, the capital Kabul, where Bagram prison was located, was as far away as the moon. He didn't respect the authority of the Afghan Commandos to arrest anyone in his province and they had obtained a confession because they had beaten Doctor Baki with a length of electrical cord during their interrogation. "He is none of those things. Do you not think I would know? I know that your old commander put a pistol to his head and pulled the trigger, though you tried to hide it."

The four other Americans shifted uncomfortably after hearing the translation. The deputy looked like he might puke.

"General, I understand you have your opinions. But your fight isn't with me. It's with your countrymen. It was their mission."

Khan giggled. Those Tajiks weren't his countrymen. "Can I tell you more secrets?"

The new American Commander swallowed. "What?"

"Doctor Baki did store weapons. For my men. From legal raids against the *talibs*. That's a big secret." Khan finished his *chai* and waved his manservant, Azzam, over to refill everyone's glass. "But he stored them until we could dispose of them properly."

"That's illegal, General. A civilian storing machine guns and sniper rifles is illegal."

"Not if *I* allow it."

They stared at each other.

"Is this the urgent matter you called me here to discuss?"

The last part of Khan's plan was the easiest: set the Americans against his tribal enemies. "My spies say that there have been several meetings between Haji Daoud and The Big One, Mullah Sher Muhammad. Do you know them?"

"I do."

"They are planning to bring bombers onto your base."

"Okay," the new American Commander said.

Khan knew if the Americans were interested in information they pulled notebooks from their pockets and wrote down what was said. No one moved. "Would you like to know when they plan to do this?"

"Yeah, sure."

"Two weeks from now there will be bombers and car bombs on your base. I recommend that we conduct an operation against these men and their people."

"I will think about it." The new American Commander finished the last of his tea and looked at his men. "I must return to my base, General."

"Have you forgotten our agreements, Commander?"

"What agreements?" he said as he stood. The others gathered their guns, helmets, and armor.

Khan remained sitting. "The agreement that we share intelligence."

"I am bound to it."

"Then what will you do about this information? It is good information. You know now that my spies get good information. They found out about the old American Commander killing himself."

"I'll ask my people what they think."

"And then we will do an operation? If not, I will do it on my own."

The new American Commander looked down at Khan and smirked, the same smirk he had when he'd made the joke in English, at their first meeting, about Khan shooting him in the back. He offered his hand to help Khan to his feet, but Khan dismissed the gesture and stood, rising through the hepatitis pain.

"We will talk more about an operation when you come back from your treatment in Mumbai."

"Mumbai."

"You're not going in a week?"

"I am."

"I thought so."

The American trucks were already running when they came into the courtyard and the power of the engines rattled the metal doors of the compound. They pulled away for the short drive to their base and exhaust filled the yard long after they were gone.

Khan went to Naghma's house. Little Maziullah sat on a pillow and read from a book. He read as well as the man he was named after. His lips moved as he silently sounded each word out, his eyes racing along the lines. Little Maziullah read, his father watching, until Naghma called them to eat. As Colonel Maziullah's namesake bounced away toward the food, Khan thought about what he would rename him. He was the only son he had left, he loved him more than he loved himself, but it couldn't go on like this. Not his son's name, not the shared businesses, not even the friendship.

The Americans weren't supposed to know that Khan had hepatitis. And no one but the man his only son was named for knew that Khan was going to Mumbai for treatment in a week. Khan hadn't even ordered the plane yet.

Maziullah was spying for the Americans.

PART IV

THE ENGINEER KEPT
A STRANGE HOUSE

Dorafshan Valley, Tarin Kot District, Uruzgan Province, Afghanistan, 25 January 2013—

The Engineer laughed, a deep roar. He was handcuffed, jammed into the corner of his courtyard. The Americans and Afghans had entered the large room of his house.

"There's nothing to find," he said. An American shoved him into the wall and told him to shut up.

Inside the room, ten clean and manicured boys, all under the age of fifteen, sat serenely in two rows. The boys wore brown leather coats lined with gray fur. The Americans let the Commandos lead, their rifles swinging wildly as they screamed at the boys to lay down.

"Down now!" The leader of the Commandos said. He was short and lean. He had a big moustache. The Americans called him Charlie. "Now!" Charlie yelled again. The ten boys, as if synchronized, fell to the floor from where they sat in the rows. Charlie went back outside to The Engineer.

He pressed his face toward the enormous man. "What's your name?"

"You're too small," The Engineer replied and laughed again. The Engineer was bizarre, unlike any man Charlie had ever seen. "My name is Sadiq Tarzi."

"You lie. Your name is Sadiq, The Engineer." Charlie slapped him across the face. The Engineer's head didn't move. They had found The Engineer outside of his compound, pressed like a wax seal against the horizon. He'd had a shovel and an empty burlap sack. Charlie thought he'd been burying a booby trap but there was nothing in the hole or near it. They restrained him without resistance, using two plastic pairs of handcuffs to hold his giant arms behind his back. "What were you doing outside with that shovel?"

The Engineer said, "Farming." And flared the nostrils of his thick bull nose.

Charlie left The Engineer and went back into the large room. The ten boys remained on the ground, motionless. They didn't cry or tremble as most children would. Charlie asked the American medic to shine his pen light into every child's eyes to see if the pupils were dilated. He thought they had been drugged. After their black pupils contracted normally, they were moved to the courtyard.

"Commander," an Afghan yelled for Charlie. He was in the next room. "You need to come in here." Charlie hurried into the room. Standing against the walls were five women in *burkhas*. The dark robes hid their bodies, the black mesh hid their faces. They were refusing to lay on the ground.

"Get down, get down!" the men screamed. Charlie joined them. The women didn't move. Everyone was hesitant to go forward—the taboo of violating a woman too great—but Charlie had had enough and feared that the danger was growing. He charged and threw one of the women down. A rifle, wrapped in a towel, fell on the floor. The four others were put down fast. All of them had been sitting on AK-74s.

AK-74s were expensive weapons carried by *talib* commanders. On this deployment, the Americans had found only a single AK-74 in a cache belonging to The Big One.

The Engineer had five AK-74s.

A woman grunted during the scuffle and an American—following his intuition—raised the *burkha* from her face. A serene and fleshy-lipped teenage boy smiled at him. He wore a white *kameez*. When they removed the rest of the *burkhas* they found that all were hiding boys over the age of fifteen.

The Engineer kept a strange house.

The Engineer's courtyard was heavy with the smell of ammonia. It could have been urine or the lingering presence of an essential component for making bombs. The boys in the brown coats were examined again and their nail beds held smatterings of silvery glitter. Aluminum dust was a common accelerant used by bomb makers. The Americans and Afghans tore through the house with kits to detect trace chemicals and metal detectors to look for explosives. They found nothing.

It was Charlie who, moving one of the shivering boys from one spot to another, felt a hard lump in the child's jacket. He removed the coat, tore out the lining, and found three remotes used to initiate IEDs. Charlie ordered his men to tear every jacket apart. They found thirty individual remotes.

He waved the detonator in front of The Engineer as the helicopter landed to take them away. "You're one of those cowards?" Charlie yelled. The Engineer laughed, the sound easily heard even with the rotors of the helicopter. Charlie stomped on The Engineer's deformed foot. The Engineer bent over at his waist and hissed. He stood up and towered over Charlie. "Get him on the helicopter."

An American and an Afghan led the giant man through the dark toward the helicopter. They left the children, all of them, behind.

THE ILLUSION OF DAN

Army Brian burst through the door to Dan's hut. A fresh cigar was in his shirt pocket. He had the camera. "We got him. He's in the Commando compound."

"Already? That fast?"

"Yes," Army Brian said. "And he's *huge*."

Dan tapped his white wristwatch, took his baseball cap off its hook, checked the liner for the photographs of baby Charlotte and Haji Hyatullah, and put it back on his head. He and Army Brian left in the 4Runner.

At the Commando compound, in the converted classroom, Army Brian and Captain Cales kept guard behind Sadiq Ustaz's burly shoulders. He was so big they couldn't get his hands behind his back, so they were cuffed in front. Dan sat in front of Sadiq Ustaz with Qais at his side. Dan tapped his boot on the floor—an agitated beat—beside the husk of Sadiq Ustaz's shrunken foot.

"Really? You were farming?"

"I was digging holes for planting."

"Who farms in the middle of the night, Sadiq Ustaz?"

"I am fighting with my neighbor over water. I have to draw it when he is sleeping. Don't call me Sadiq Ustaz, I am not an *ustaz*. My name is Sadiq Tarzi." In Pashto, an *ustaz* is a man who has mastery over some sort of skill or knowledge, such as engineering. Sadiq Ustaz had given his name as Sadiq Tarzi, to hide his trade. "I am not the one you are looking for," he said. Gusts of breath pulsed from his aquiline nose. "I am Sadiq Tarzi, a farmer. Never an *ustaz*."

"You like teenaged boys?"

"What?" Sadiq Ustaz said.

"Never mind. Let's focus on the problem." Dan looked down at his notebook. "They said you laughed at them. A giant laugh from the corner of the compound."

"I did," Sadiq Ustaz said and laughed, a roar that unnerved Dan. "They were wasting their time."

"You sure about that?" Dan said. "Doesn't seem like it to me." Before the interrogation, Charlie had personally given Dan the remote detonators, individually wrapped in plastic freezer bags. Dan had arranged each neatly on the floor at his feet. For Sadiq Ustaz this interrogation would come down to simple math. "Five years, ten years, fifteen years," Dan said, pointing at each detonator. "That's twenty and then there's twenty-five. You understand?"

"No," Sadiq Ustaz said.

"Each detonator is five years. There's thirty here. Can you do math?"

"I never went to school."

"I don't believe that, Sadiq *Ustaz*. You're The Engineer. You measure ratios of ammonia to nitrate, Sadiq *Ustaz*. Right, Sadiq *Ustaz*?"

"Stop calling me that."

"I'll do the math for you. Five multiplied by thirty. That's fifty-five years."

Qais stopped translating and looked at Dan. "Yo, that math ain't right."

"I know," Dan said to Qais. "He's not going to get the concept of one hundred fifty years in jail. Just say what I said."

Qais told Sadiq Ustaz those detonators were fifty-five years.

"Fifty-five years of what?"

"Jail. You're going to jail for fifty-five years."

"Fifty-five years? But that's my whole life."

"It sure is. You have enemies?"

"No. Everyone in Afghanistan is friends."

"Really? You been outside lately?" Dan smiled. "Why would you need five AK-74s if everyone is your friend?"

Sadiq Ustaz shrugged.

"Each one of those guns adds another year to your sentence. Look man, you're going to die in prison." Dan looked at Sadiq Ustaz for a moment. "Unless you tell me where you got the detonators."

"What detonators?"

"Shut the fuck up—are you serious? The ones on the floor." Dan pointed at them. "Those detonators."

"I don't know." He shrugged again. "They're yours. I never saw them before."

"Never?"

"No. I don't even know what they do." He crossed his legs and leaned back, relaxed. From behind Sadiq Ustaz, Army Brian pointed to the door.

"I'll be back. Sadiq *Ustaz*."

They went outside to the parade ground. Army Brian put his hand on Dan's shoulder, squeezing twice. "You're doing good, man."

"Are you kidding me? He could say all night that we planted the detonators. What can I do about that?"

"I know. It's tough. And he's a high roller so he's not going to rat out anyone else."

"I want him to talk about Haji Hyatullah."

"Yeah? Then what?" They stood under a flood light. Two Afghan Commandos came over. They motioned, offering cigarettes. Dan declined and the Commandos walked away. "What happens then?"

"We get Haji Hyatullah."

"Yeah? What happens when you get Haji Hyatullah?"

"We link all this shit to MHK. Then Commander Russo goes after him. Like he said he would."

"MHK isn't going anywhere. Not in this country. Not in 2013." Army Brian chuckled. A helicopter rose from the airfield and began making long, noisy circles around the base. A tube of light from its nose scanned the ground. "We invented Mir Hamza Khan." Dan turned to go back inside. "No—hold on," Army Brian said and caught his shoulder. "I got an idea."

"What is it?"

"Tell him you'll arrest his boys. If the detonators aren't his then they must be the boys' because that's who we found them with."

"You think so?" Dan said.

"What's your interrogation count again?"

Dan rolled his eyes.

Army Brian smiled. "Maybe give it whirl?"

Sadiq Ustaz sat up, as if he'd inflated himself, when they came back inside.

"So the detonators aren't yours?" Dan said to The Engineer.

"No."

"Then, unfortunately, we're going to have to go back to the compound."

"Yes, please, take me back."

"No problem, Sadiq *Ustaz*."

He lifted his hands for them to cut the flex cuffs off. "Let me out of these—"

"Shut up. I'm trying to explain. We'll take you back to your house but we gotta arrest the kids and send them to Bagram. They *were* the ones with the detonators. Must be theirs." Dan looked at Qais and said, "This was easier than I thought."

Qais translated that too.

"You'll arrest the boys?" Dan made a show of packing each of the detonators into a plastic tub. He went on as though he didn't hear Sadiq Ustaz. "I asked if you are going to arrest the boys, *Sahib*."

"Uh, yeah," Dan said and looked at Sadiq Ustaz. "Gotta get whoever's responsible for this mess."

Sadiq Ustaz exhaled through his nose. He looked at Qais. Qais shrugged and chewed on his fingernails. "Then they're mine. Those things are mine."

Dan snapped his head up. "What's yours?"

"Those things you call detonators belong to me."

Sadiq Ustaz didn't say anything else. He pressed his inked thumb on a confession sheet to confirm that he was admitting guilt. They took a picture of the process to submit as evidence in an Afghan court, vital to convicting him at trial. But he said nothing else for the next two hours as Dan railed at him. He said he didn't know Haji Hyatullah and that he'd never heard of a man named Mir Hamza Khan.

After Dan had finished, he found Charlie on the parade ground and told him, through Captain Cales, "He's tough, my friend."

Charlie rubbed his hands together. "Yes, but I think he will talk to me."

They left the Commando compound in the 4Runner. Above, more helicopters circled with their searchlights on. One followed their truck until they entered the SPU. Qais and Army Brian left and Dan and Captain Cales went into the Soviet Building. Beau peeked around the corner, the phone to his ear. "There you are. Brian and Qais with you?"

"They went to their rooms," Dan said.

Beau clapped Dan on the back and turned to Captain Cales. "The thing's happening."

Captain Cales pointed to the ceiling. "The helicopters?"

"Yes, sir," Beau said and smiled.

"What's going on?" Dan said. *Did someone else get killed?* "Tell me."

"Reporting indicates suicide bombers and vehicle IEDs are on the base right now," Beau said and wrapped his arm around Captain Cales.

"Really?" Tightness rose in Dan's chest. He had to call Toor Jan. "I'll call Maziullah right now and see what he knows."

"Don't call anyone, Dan."

"What do you mean? He might know where they are."

"No, he doesn't," Captain Cales said. "Trust me."

"How do you know?"

The Captain rubbed his baby chin. "It's Gran. He works for us. We told him to find car bombs. So we can understand the network. The Australians are reporting this from their sources. They don't know we're behind it."

Dan clicked his tongue like an Afghan. "I need to know about things like this."

"You don't need to know about everything."

"I work here. I'm on this fucking team."

"Sir."

"Yes, you're right. *Sir.*" Dan clicked his tongue again. "You're welcome for that confession from Sadiq Ustaz. Nailing an IED maker's gonna make the SPU look real good."

Dan went to his hut. He didn't turn on the light. Helicopter blades beat overhead. They announced on the speakers Dress State Four which meant that even if Dan only needed to take a piss, he'd have to wear a helmet, body armor, and carry an M4 rifle. Dress State Four would continue for as long as they thought there was a threat. But Dan had enough water bottles to piss in and trail mix to eat for a week. *I won't ever leave this fucking hut again. I don't need them. Any of them.*

A good spy relied on illusion. Captain Cales and Beau were good spies. The entire base was locked down, protecting itself from their illusion of bombers. Dan wasn't a good spy. He didn't break Sadiq Ustaz, they weren't any closer to getting MHK, and his officers didn't trust him. Dan took his hat off and looked at the picture of Charlotte. *What would Aaron think about me now?*

TOOR JAN'S REVENGE

Safad Khare, Tarin Kot District, Uruzgan Province, Afghanistan, 31 January 2013—

Shaheen asked for revenge again and Toor Jan refused. She swung at him but he slipped the punch and she fell. He picked her up and they walked to the well and sat on the edge. Beside them was a bucket filled with Abdul Hakim's bloody rags.

"Do you see how your brother suffers?" she said. "He's broken."

"I know," Toor Jan said. He swallowed. "This wouldn't have happened if he had understood what I said."

"But you have to do something." The bright moonlight carved Shaheen's face out of the dark. "What will you do?"

"Nothing."

The girl left. Her figure blotted out the light of the door, then vanished. Toor Jan sat a moment longer before retrieving his bag, packed earlier, from the crate on his motorcycle. He'd prepared for this operation without being discovered—even by Shaheen—and he prayed to God that no one would discover him now. He climbed over the wall to avoid the noise of the gate.

Toor Jan's shadow was invisible in the dark woods. He laid on his belly by the irrigation canal, across from Gran's compound. His heart shrank with fear. The last light in Gran's compound was put out, the smoke thinned, but Toor Jan waited until the stony moon rose above his head. He walked tenderly, careful not to disturb what was in the bag across his shoulder, and came out of the wood line to the road that ran along Gran's compound. He squatted and scanned both directions.

A wandering dog padded up. It held its muzzle at high port and the leather patch of its nose worked the air. The dog stopped for a moment—Toor Jan didn't move for fear that it would bark—and then trotted down to the irrigation canal for a long drink. Toor Jan waited, never taking his eyes from Gran's gate. The dog splashed across the canal, up into the trees on the other side, and was gone. Toor Jan crawled low across the road.

At Gran's gate, he scanned the dark again. *Nothing*. Toor Jan took off his bag, placed it beside him, and pulled out what he had been so careful to keep silent: a tin can he had filled with rocks. Toor Jan had tested it yesterday in an empty field far from Safad Khare, careful to make sure that it was as quiet as the night, and he learned it took many more rocks than he had assumed to make enough noise. Toor Jan held the heavy can in his hand and paused. *Praise be to the most Blessed, the most Merciful.* Toor Jan heaved the can. The can and its rocks rattled inside compound, the loudest thing in the night for miles around.

Toor Jan waited, afraid for a moment that nothing would happen but soon he heard the voices of Gran's children, near where the can had landed. Then he heard Gran.

"Get inside."

The children ran away and Gran crunched toward his gate. The gate swung open and the long wood barrel of an Enfield rifle emerged, sliding out inch-by-inch. Gran's slender finger, on the trigger, glided into view.

Toor Jan ran at the barrel and spun it out of Gran's hands. The gun clattered away.

Toor Jan leaped onto Gran and stretched a piece of Abdul Hakim's bloody rag across his face, working it into his mouth like a bridle, fighting to pull Gran into the woods and down to the irrigation canal. Toor Jan struggled and his muscles screamed and he couldn't catch his breath as they went through the loose dirt, to the wood line. All the time, Toor Jan forced the rag deeper into Gran's mouth.

Steam billowed off the two fighting men. They neared the woods and the bank of the canal. Toor Jan slipped. They tumbled together, twisting down. Toor Jan held tight to his brother's rag. They stopped rolling and Toor Jan pulled hard. Gran's cheeks tore. His molars, dry and hard, cut Toor Jan's finger. He drove Gran's head into the ground and mounted his neck with his knee, slamming it there again and again to end Gran's squirming.

The blackness of the night spread and filled Toor Jan's eyes and body with blindness that lifted only after Gran's neck broke. Toor Jan went up through the woods and to the road, found Gran's Enfield rifle, and buried it under a rock. The gates to Gran's compound were hanging open but there were no people or voices. Toor Jan ran to his compound.

He came inside. It stank of Abdul Hakim and sleeping bodies. Toor Jan removed his clothes and laid down beside Shaheen. He kissed her forehead. She stirred. He kissed her again. He lay on his back. It was finally done. His hip and arm, healed but forever tender, ached with the exertion. The man who didn't know his real name, or his birthday, the man who was denied a livelihood, mocked his entire life, the man who was less than a man, had fulfilled his duty for his family. Toor Jan closed his eyes. He waited for sleep.

His eyes shot open. *The bag.* Toor Jan had left it outside of Gran's compound.

The sun had almost risen when trucks roared outside the walls of his compound and halted. Toor Jan stood in his yard, unable to sleep the entire night. The baby screamed and Shaheen and Mina sat up from where they had slept. Abdul Hakim groaned. Toor Jan didn't look back. If outside the gate were Haji Daoud and the Barakzais to get revenge for Gran, he would face the consequences. Rifles charged and trucks revved. Toor Jan held his breath and opened the gate.

"Hello, Toor Jan," the General said and smiled. Behind him, platoons of police officers milled, their pants legs wet with mud. The fenders of their trucks dripped with water. Maziullah haunted the scene with his blue rifle. The General pointed to the ground, beyond where Toor Jan could see. He went outside. Gran lay there, waxy and dark. Scarlet blood lined his torn cheeks. "Where's this dog's friend?"

"Which friend, General?"

"Haji Daoud." He walked Toor Jan away from Gran's body. "When was the last time you saw him?"

"This one?" Toor Jan said, pointing at Gran's corpse.

"Haji Daoud."

"It's been a very long time, General."

The General smiled at Toor Jan again. He looked at Gran's body and at Toor Jan, drawing an eternal tether between them with a quick flick of his eyes. "I see we're still friends, Toor Jan." Maziullah trotted up and dropped Toor Jan's bag at his feet. "Your phone is in there."

The General left. The mass of police officers swept toward the Barakzai side of the village. White bulldozers followed behind. After they were gone, Toor Jan called to Shaheen, "Cover yourself and come here." The girl came out but she didn't speak. "Do you see?"

"I see."

"And?"

"Who is it?"

Toor Jan led her around to see Gran's broken face. "See?"

"They never look like they do when they're alive."

"It's Gran. This is finished." The girl reached from under the *burkha* and slipped her hand inside of Toor Jan's. He took his bag and they turned together to go into the compound.

Inside, the women joked with each other. The baby rocked in his mother's arms. Ibrahim reached his hands in the air, spread them in front of his split face, and brought them to his mouth. The baby did this many times before Toor Jan noticed Abdul Hakim. Abdul Hakim could sit up now and the swelling of his eyes had gone down enough that he could see. He was watching. Abdul Hakim was staring at the baby.

"Abdul Hakim." Toor Jan snapped his fingers. "Stop. Leave the baby alone."

But Abdul Hakim would not look away.

MIR HAMZA KHAN'S TWO
SIMILAR WEAPONS

*Safad Khare, Tarin Kot District, Uruzgan Province,
Afghanistan, 01 February 2013—*

Someone said the man had a gun so the police officers chased him through a goat's pen between two compounds, out into an open grassy area, and toward a stand of poplar trees that grew along the irrigation canal. The man jumped into the canal and scrambled up the opposite bank. He ran like a dog on his hands and feet. The police officers watched from the opposite side.

Mir Hamza Khan fired first. Then, the rest. Branches and leaves sheared from the trees. Spouts of dirt erupted from the bank as the bullets followed the man. He was hit twice in the back, then again in the neck. The man rolled down the bank—spinning like a toy—and sank into a bench of mud. His face was covered with the black paste. Khan leaped across and shot the man with his Makarov pistol, twice, in the head. The police officers continued their operation.

Bulldozers rolled through the irrigation canal. Water pooled against the newly moved earth. The bulldozers plowed until no water flowed to the Barakzais of Safad Khare. Two red excavators moved the dirt from the destroyed canal into HESCO barriers. A forklift stacked one HESCO on top of another, creating the fortressed outline of a second police checkpoint in the village. A platoon of police officers guarded the work. Half-finished, they raised the Afghan flag and erected a picture of Khan. He was gesturing sternly. Underneath it read:

> ## GENERAL HAJI MIR HAMZA KHAN: THE HERO OF PEACE AND UNITY

Maziullah stood under the picture and yelled into a megaphone. "Where's the criminal Haji Daoud? Who's hiding him? This criminal threatens the peace of Uruzgan!"

The Barakzai side of Safad Khare was built on a sunken flat of loam. Khan's white schoolhouse, the site of the autumn attack, was due east. Beyond, almond groves feathered hills that swelled into mountains. There were good fields of freshly turned earth. Goat bells chinked far off but there was no sign of humans.

"Barakzai people! Don't suffer for this criminal! Where's Haji Daoud? Barakzai people! Don't aid the criminals of Uruzgan! Where's Haji Daoud? Where is his friend Mullah Sher Muhammad?"

The Popalzai people lived west of Khan's schoolhouse, where the mountains rose into a sudden, sheer wall. The ground was rocky, torn. A wandering brindle dog barked. Every cooking fire had been put out at the sound of Khan's trucks. Usually during a sweep, young men would ride away, in all directions, on motorcycles. But Safad Khare had no *talibs*. Not on the Popalzai or the Barakzai side. There were no men who needed to run away. This made everyone more frightened.

"Haji Daoud, we have a message for you. Your criminal deputy is dead. Gran is dead. Don't let the same fate happen to you."

Khan was pleased that Toor Jan had killed Gran, whatever his reasons. Especially since the new American Commander had refused to help him capture Gran and Haji Daoud. Maziullah took the megaphone away from his face and unslung his blue AK-47. Khan motioned for him. "Get on the radio and tell them to begin sweeping."

Maziullah made the call and three green Ford Rangerss sped into the Barakzai area. Khan's police officers, packed into the open beds, leaped out. They entered and exited the compounds without order, like a riot instead of an army.

"Maziullah," Khan said. "Tell them to search like they were taught by the Americans."

Khan's men were mustered again at the trucks. They formed a line and moved in a wave through the Barakzai side of Safad Khare. Khan and Maziullah followed. The two went inside a house occupied by an old man and a woman in a *burkha*. The old man was arguing with two police officers.

"We have nothing here, we're farmers," the old man said, voice already hoarse. The police officers tied him up and threw him outside. They went back into the house and turned over several wooden chests. The woman stood by as they tore the family's blankets and stepped on her pillows with their muddy boots.

Khan and Maziullah watched from the doorframe.

The two police officers threw the cooking pots, stacked in the corner of the room, out of a window without paying attention to the woman. She took her hands out of her dress and threw a Russian grenade at the police officers.

Maziullah jumped on Khan.

After the flash, the noise, the concussion that ripped the breath from their lungs, Maziullah rolled off of Khan. They crawled through hay and rocks, back inside the house. The walls of the room were scorched and covered with the blood and pulp of the two police officers. The woman had been thrown against the opposite wall. Her *burkha* was torn from her body. Blood spread around her. Khan pulled himself up by the doorframe.

"Tell them to bring the bulldozer to me."

The machine came clinking through the muddy tracks to the house. Other police officers had come and removed the torn bodies. They put the tied-up old man back inside. Khan pointed to the compound and the bulldozer went to work. The heavy blade scraped the earth and pushed the mud bricks aside until there was nothing, not even the old man. Khan walked through the village and picked out every house that insulted him with its build, color, or arrangement and called the bulldozer over to destroy it.

The people who had lived in the destroyed houses gathered among the poplar trees along the irrigation canal. They had the look of stupid animals forced away from their cages. A few Barakzai men, those not in the trees, took one or two shots at Khan and his men before dropping their weapons and running away. Maziullah went after them with his gun and returned dragging shooter after shooter behind him. He killed four Barakzai men that way.

The police officers gathered whatever weapons they found and packed them up to sell to Haji Hyatullah. They completed the checkpoint. Finished, they drove away fast, fearing that the *talibs* had already buried bombs on their return route.

Inside a speeding vehicle, Maziullah's rifle nearly spun onto Khan's lap. "That was a great thing you did today, Maziullah. With the grenade."

"I would do anything for you, General."

"I know."

"Anything."

"Because I'm like your rifle?"

Maziullah looked at him.

"You could say that your rifle is like any other but we know that isn't true. The color, the finish. Your rifle is special. Just like me. We are two similar weapons."

Maziullah squeezed the blue rifle.

"I can buy one thousand rifles. But none would be like yours."

Maziullah went to take Khan's hand. He refused.

"I can also buy one thousand Maziullahs. Never forget that. But there is no one alive who is like me."

DAN'S BROTHERS

Multinational Base Tarin Kowt, Tarin Kot District, Uruzgan Province, Afghanistan, 02 February 2013—

The SPU didn't acknowledge it but Charlie had beaten Sadiq Ustaz with a braided, ten-inch electrical cord wrapped in tape. It was a devastating weapon. No man, no matter how big—or previously abused—could withstand that interrogation approach. Sadiq Ustaz confessed to Charlie that he had made a bomb and given it to Haji Hyatullah to take to a Taliban commander named Zubair. That bomb had killed an Afghan Commando riding in a convoy through Dorafshan valley in late December. Sadiq Ustaz even told Charlie where Zubair lived.

The mission against Zubair was given the green light and Charlie was leading the Commandos himself. He hated bomb-makers but he hated their emplacers even more. The helicopters had lifted away five minutes ago to attack the compound where Zubair and his father lived. Charlie, the Commandos, and the SEALs would either kill Zubair or come back with him alive. If they took Zubair prisoner, Dan would conduct the interrogation.

Dan was preparing in his hut. He had two files—that shouldn't have been removed from the Soviet Building—and the notes that Captain Cales had transcribed from Charlie's debrief.

Dan checked his watch. He put on his hat—pictures of Charlotte and Haji Hyatullah still in the liner.Hadgdfg It was time to go. Dan and Beau had planned to watch the mission for Zubair on the live feed in the operations center. Beau came around the corner of his hut just as Dan stepped outside.

"Dan the man," Beau said without stopping his momentum toward the gate of the SPU. They both charged out of the SPU, through the maze of Conex boxes and toward the headquarters building. "Fired up about tonight?"

"Yeah," Dan said. "Let's go burn it down."

They entered the headquarters building, walked down a long hallway, past Commander Khost's empty room, into the operations center. Every seat was filled, in every row. Computer screens flashed with information. Each head bent down to the work.

The weatherman, a bald, thick-necked Chief, updated a screen with the moon illumination and temperature. It was two degrees Celsius in Kotwal. Moonlight was at sixty-five percent.

Lieutenant Konig, on his own screen, had a picture of Zubair—taken the last time he'd been captured by American forces—and his height: 5'2"; weight: 131 lbs.; suspected activity: weapons facilitator. Lieutenant Konig watched Dan and Beau enter. He didn't wave.

The communications officer, a young, dark-haired female with a pixie haircut and high cheekbones monitored the radios and the live feed. She directed the drone's camera to the area where Zubair's compound was located. A dark grainy blotch appeared on the screen.

"Sir," she said to Commander Russo. "That's Objective Zoloft's compound." Objective Zoloft was the codename for Zubair. "And the helos have landed."

"Thank you, Lieutenant Dolan." Commander Russo rolled chairs over for Beau and Dan. "Pop a squat, boys." Beau fell heavily into his, the joints in the chair crying out, and leaned back with his hands behind his head. Dan lowered himself down slowly. "You two good?"

"Great, skipper," Beau said. He pointed to a bag of chocolate-covered almonds on Commander Russo's desk. "Don't hold out on us."

"Go for it," Commander Russo said. He turned back to the screen. Lieutenant Dolan told the room that the Commandos and SEALs were patrolling, three kilometers to Zubair's compound. The temperature was still two degrees Celsius. "This Zoloft's a real motherfucker, huh?"

"The worst," Dan said, taking a few almonds from Beau. "Not as bad as Haji Hyatullah, though."

"And MHK is Satan himself." Commander Russo turned from the screen and motioned for the bag of chocolate almonds. "I know how you feel, Dan."

Dan turned back to the screen. The drone had zoomed into Zubair's compound. A sharp, dark square inside of nothing. He felt nothing but hunger for Zubair sitting in front of him and confessing his ties to Haji Hyatullah. And if Dan couldn't break Zubair, at least they had Charlie and his whip on their side.

Commander Russo stood. "Coffee, you two?"

"Sure," Beau said.

"Yes, sir." Dan said, eyes locked on the live feed. "Lots of cream." He looked back at Commander Russo and smiled. "Just kidding, sir."

"Cordon is set," Lieutenant Dolan called out. She had been standing, headset on, staring at both the live feed and her computer. "See them?"

On the screen a string of luminous dots—men in the drone's night vision—looped around the sharp, dark square of Zubair's compound.

The dots held for a moment. Commander Russo put a paper cup of coffee in front of Dan. He sipped it, choking a bit on the hot liquid. Other than the temperature, it was perfect. A few of the luminous dots broke away from their circle and moved in single file toward the compound.

"Zoom in, please?" Commander Russo said to Dolan. She bent over her computer and on the screen they could see a close-up. The men lined up along the wall with the gate into the compound. The courtyard was empty, except for what looked like a dash—probably Zubair's motorcycle. "Let me know when they call in the assault."

"Yes, sir," Dolan said.

Beau watched the screen, legs on the desk in front of him. His pants were baggy but his quads, earned from years of hard work and combat, showed through. Beau popped an almond into his mouth. Dan laughed, loud. Commander Russo and Beau looked at him.

"Sorry," he said. Dan's hands shook. He was nervous, like he was the one lining up to go into a dangerous man's house. *Why?* It was seventy-two degrees in the operations center, in Dorafshan the temperature had dropped to one degree Celsius. Dan's perfect coffee had cooled. *I'm eating candy, for fuck's sake.* His legs were sore from barbell squatting that morning, not from patrolling over fields and rocks and canals. He'd never be like Beau, never be a SEAL, never see combat. *But I can be whatever it is that I am.*

On the screen a bright dot charged out of the sharp, dark square and toward the gate. The Commandos, a perfect row of light, still waited on the other side.

"Assaulting," Dolan said. The row of light entered the gate and collided with the charging dot. "Troops in contact." The line of Commandos spilled back and the charging dot ran through them and into the larger black. It disappeared into a copse of trees along a hillside. "There's a squirter from the compound. You see him, sir?"

"Yep," Commander Russo stood. The staff watched intensely. "They talking to air?"

"Yes, sir," Dolan said. "AC-130's on station. JTAC's coordinating fires."

A man from the line of Commandos had remained inside Zubair's compound after the others flooded out. The Commandos re-entered, cleared the area and surrounded the man who had remained inside. He wasn't moving. "We have one wounded."

"Who?"

"Wait one, sir." In the trees, the squirter struggled up the hill. He slowed as the climb steepened and even slipped backwards a few meters before getting up again. A bloom of light appeared low on the screen and then another. It was the AC-130 firing at the man. The explosions walked up, chasing the squirter faster and closer until a flash washed out the screen. When it came back the squirter was gone. "Squirter is down," Dolan said. The room cheered.

That was our goddamned guy, Dan thought. He kicked the desk in front of him.

"Our wounded man is KIA," Dolan said. The room became quiet. The camera on the drone turned back to Zubair's compound. The men circled their dead brother. "It's an Afghan Commando." Lieutenant Dolan pressed her headset closer to her ears. She struggled with the name. "Chaman or Chymin? I'm not sure, sir. Sounds like they're saying Chaman. Chaman-gul."

Dan looked over and Beau shrugged. They didn't recognize the name. Commander Russo sat and then stood just as fast. "I want to know if that squirter was Objective Zoloft." He turned toward Lieutenant Konig and pointed to his slide with Zubair's picture. "They got that with them?"

"I made sure myself," Konig said.

"Lieutenant Dolan. Get confirmation."

Two pairs of dots ran out of the compound and toward the copse of trees on the hillside. They didn't struggle as they went up. Each hopped through the damage of the bombs toward the spot where the squirter disappeared. If there was anything of his face left, they would know if it was Zubair and Dan would know if their link to Haji Hyatullah and MHK was gone. He ground his teeth together and waited for the answer.

"Objective Zoloft is KIA," Dolan said and smiled. Another cheer rose up through the operations center. Dan shot up out of his chair and ran back to the SPU.

In the SPU, Captain Cales and Army Brian had started a fire in the pit and were warming themselves in front of it. Dan walked by, kicked the wall of his hut, turned around. "They fucking killed our guy," Dan said. The flames twisted high as they fed on the wood. "I can't believe it."

"I know. I was watching the feed in the Soviet Building." Captain Cales looked at the fire. "It's war."

The SPU gate squeaked open. Beau came out of the darkness toward Dan and put his arm around him. Army Brian pulled out cigars and gave one to Beau. They lit them in the fire. No one spoke for a long time.

"This really sucks," Beau said, the cigar sizzling. "Are you all right, Dan?"

Dan put his hands out toward the fire. "Yeah. Shit happens."

"Are you sure?" Captain Cales said.

"Yeah, I'm sure," Dan said, rubbing his hands over the fire. The helicopters with the SEALs and Commandos returned to the Tarin Kowt Bowl, rotors thundering as they landed, then everything went quiet again. "What'd they say the dead Commando's name was again?" Dan said.

Captain Cales dropped his head. "Chaman-gul."

Dan shrugged. "Any idea who that is?"

"Dan," Army Brian said and looked up from the fire. "Chaman-gul is Charlie."

At two that morning, the C-130's ramp opened onto the airfield's smooth white concrete. Afghan Commandos—light-skinned and narrow-eyed Hazarans and heavily built, ruddy Tajiks—stood in two flanking rows. They all held the same picture of Charlie. He was smiling, in camouflage fatigues and a red beret, standing with two other plainly dressed Afghans. *His brothers.* Their arms were linked.

Captain Cales, Beau, Army Brian, and Dan found a place at the end of the Afghan Commandos long line. Captain Cales bent to Dan's ear. "I thought you might want to know that Haji Daoud ran away to Kabul and we haven't heard from Gran." He pulled away and stared straight ahead. "Maybe Maziullah knows something."

The headlights of the ambulance appeared from the outer dark and parked at the end of the line of men. Adorned with bright red flowers and sacks of rice, a stretcher carrying Charlie's body was removed by four Afghan Commandos. They carried it between the rows of raised salutes. Their hard, aged faces were wet with tears as they moved toward the open plane.

If Dan had ever interrogated Zubair maybe he would've learned the reason he had joined the Taliban. Money for a sick family member, adventure, or maybe the best bad choice for the smartest boy in the village. Dan had chosen to join the Navy, chose to go to SEAL training. He didn't choose to fail training but the way he worked hard and aggressively as an interrogator afterward was a choice. He would die by his choices if he had to. Like Zubair choosing to run into the hills to escape. Like Charlie choosing to push through a closed gate into a dangerous compound. They were brothers in choice. The war had killed two men today. Dan saluted them as the stretcher passed. They were both his brothers.

TOOR JAN TURNS ABDUL HAKIM INTO AN ANIMAL

Safad Khare Village, Tarin Kot District, Uruzgan Province, Afghanistan, 05 February 2013—

Abdul Hakim snatched Ibrahim from his crib and forced the boy's head into his shoulder. He moved outside, through a thin slice of moonlight, beneath the dismal almond tree to the well. Water dripped, the sound light and sharp. Abdul Hakim stood at the ledge and looked down. Darkness. He lifted Ibrahim up and dropped him in the water. The baby screamed, then turned face-down in the freezing pool.

Toor Jan ran outside. "Where's Ibrahim?" Toor Jan seized Abdul Hakim's shoulders and shook him. Abdul Hakim went limp. "Where's the baby? Abdul Hakim?"

Abdul Hakim said nothing.

Ibrahim splashed in the water, his back an exposed, fleshy dune. The two women came out brandishing the light from Toor Jan's cell phone and all at once they saw the baby. Toor Jan pulled him out, the cries fresh and loud, and handed the dripping child over to Shaheen. Shaheen and Mina turned toward the house, but Toor Jan overtook them, roughly, and went inside. He returned to the yard with a length of hemp rope.

Abdul Hakim had collapsed on the ground and Toor Jan dragged him to the almond tree. He wrapped Abdul Hakim's ankle with the rope, three times, and made a knot the boy couldn't undo. He circled the trunk and tied it off. Four feet of leash lay on the ground. He walked back into the house. The women stared at him in horror.

"He stays there," Toor Jan said. "Otherwise none of us are safe." He sat down for a moment, then rose again and found a threadbare blanket. Toor Jan went outside and threw it at his brother. "There is no curse."

In the morning, he walked past Abdul Hakim. The boy stared at him, eyes and face swollen, as Toor Jan, dressed in sunglasses and wool cap, kicked his motorcycle alive and left for the city. Toor Jan crossed the Teri Bridge without meeting anyone along the way. In the *bazaar*, shoppers flooded the stalls. Toor Jan was jealous of their simple lives. He got off his motorcycle and walked it through the crowd.

Hunger ached through Toor Jan. He went to Abdul Fruit's stand and asked for a bag of almonds. Abdul Fruit wore a leather jacket, collar upturned. A *pakol*, rare for Pashtuns in Uruzgan, rolled over his ears. "I remember you," Abdul Fruit said. He filled a green plastic bag with almonds in the shell. The other stalls were packed, people reaching over people, but Abdul Fruit's was empty. The late winter produce was bad. "Did you find the pistol you were looking for?"

"I found it," Toor Jan said.

"Doctor Baki was arrested that same week."

Toor Jan didn't haggle and handed over *afghanis* with one hand, taking the almonds with the other. He stood there for a moment. "I need more."

"Of what?"

"Weapons. Does Haji Hyatullah still keep them at his car shop?"

Abdul Fruit snatched the American sunglasses from Toor Jan's face.

"Hey!"

"You pay in worthless *afghanis*. You drive an expensive motorcycle. You wear their stuff." Abdul Fruit crushed the sunglasses in his hands. "You ask strange questions. Are you helping the invaders?"

Toor Jan almost climbed the stall to beat Abdul Fruit to death. He knew he could do it. But he decided to be calm. Use the power of his mind. "I don't ask for myself," Toor Jan said. He bit into a brittle shell, spit away the pieces, and sucked out a buttery almond. "Maybe you don't know who my uncle is."

Abdul Fruit regarded him. "Who's your uncle?"

"Mullah Sher Muhammad."

"The Big One?"

Toor Jan tossed the spent almond shell at Abdul Fruit. "You should know who you're speaking to before you choose to be disrespectful."

He mounted his motorcycle and drove away. If Abdul Fruit wouldn't help, there was one man in Uruzgan who owed Toor Jan *and* knew Haji Hyatullah. The General. Toor Jan raced toward the Provincial Police Headquarters.

Toor Jan hid his motorcycle in an alley. If it was stolen, so be it. He'd return to walking as he always had. Toor Jan pressed himself as flat as a blade against the wall. Around the corner, the wood pike of the guard house moaned as it lifted. Uzbeki cigarette smoke wafted over. A voice on their radio claimed the Barakzais of Tarin Kot were staging attacks on Popalzais through the district.

He called the General's phone. No answer. Toor Jan took the knit cap off his head and replaced it with a *Baluchi* cap from his pocket. He walked to the guard house.

"Peace be upon you."

"And peace be upon you. Are you here for the General again?" It was the same guard from last time.

"I am," he said and added, boldly, "Tell him Toor Jan has arrived."

The guard, his boots freshly blackened, dropped his chin to his chest in deference. He went into the shack to the communications radio. Two other guards discussed what they would do if an angry mob of Barakzais came to the headquarters. One said he'd kill them all and the other said he couldn't hit a wall with his rifle. The other guard returned shortly. "The General isn't here, today."

"Where is he?"

"I can't tell you that," the guard said. "Perhaps call him."

"I tried." Toor Jan looked up the face of the building, the windows as narrow as jail cells. "What about Colonel Maziullah?"

"He's in the courtyard training new officers," the guard said, pointing. "Please go in."

Toor Jan remained in the portico as Maziullah spoke to the formation. They didn't even have uniforms yet but they had fear of Maziullah. It was well-founded. "Thirty minutes for lunch begins," Maziullah said looking over the rows. "Now." The recruits scattered.

Toor Jan stepped into the open. "Hello, Colonel."

"Why are you here?" Maziullah said, looked around, and brought Toor Jan back into the shadowed portico. "Do you have information about your uncle?"

"No," Toor Jan said. He stared at the blue gun on Maziullah's chest and felt hypnotized. "I need help from you and the General."

"We can't help you." Maziullah stepped away from Toor Jan. "Go home."

"I did a very important job for you."

"What was that?"

Toor Jan closed the distance, his *kameez* swooshing, and whispered, "You know who I killed."

"We never asked for that," Maziullah said. "But it was useful."

"The entire Barakzai tribe is after me now. I need weapons."

"Go to the usual people."

"No," Toor Jan said. He whispered again, "I need a machine gun. For my roof. They all want to kill me."

Maziullah hooked a plug of *naswar* from his mouth and threw it on the ground. He wiped his hands on his blue trousers. "Who do you want to go to?"

"Haji Hyatullah."

"What do you know about him?"

"That he can give me what I need." Toor Jan balled his fists. "Like I gave you and the General what you needed."

Maziullah looked over Toor Jan, or maybe into him. Did he see the truth? Fresh sweat broke out in Toor Jan's armpits. "Don't bother with his car shop, there's no machine guns there," Maziullah said. "Go to his house."

"I don't know where he lives."

"The police checkpoint in Kotwal, his house is directly behind it. Past two walls and a field. Tell him the Colonel is happy with his work. Say it exactly like that. It's the signal."

Toor Jan said nothing and swirled around, ran to his motorcycle.

"You must fix my son now," he yelled through the phone at The Good American's *tajiman*. He was riding to Kotwal. "I'll bring you to Haji Hyatullah's house."

"Are you on your motorcycle? We can barely hear you."

"I'm on a mission for you."

"Where?"

"Going to his house in Kotwal."

"Are you sure?"

"I haven't failed a mission yet." He swerved to miss a hole in the road and nearly dumped the bike. "I'm good at this."

"Stay by your phone. We'll call you."

"Fix my son," Toor Jan screamed.

The Good American's *tajiman* hung up.

Toor Jan found the police checkpoint in Kotwal. It had the same look as all of the others; brown, irregular, lumpy like an old cake. He laid his motorcycle behind one of the walls, climbed it, came to another wall—just like Maziullah said—along the field with the house. It was large, two buildings stretched inside a long rectangle of compound wall. A child laughed, inside.

Toor Jan put his foot on the second wall to climb up but stopped. *I can't. Abdul Fruit noticed me.* How long before everyone realized that whoever Toor Jan encountered was captured or killed by the Americans? Maziullah had said, clearly, that machine guns weren't kept at the car shop. Machine guns were in Haji Hyatullah's house. *I don't have to go inside. But I'll tell The Good American that I did.*

Toor Jan thought of a few lies, like he had seen a bomb in the courtyard, and a mine near where Haji Hyatullah kept his animals and other things about the insides of the house. *When have I been wrong before? The Good American will get what he wants and my baby will be fixed. I'll save my family.* Toor Jan repeated the lies to himself as he rode home.

Abdul Hakim, on his leash, was laying under the tree when Toor Jan came into his compound. Toor Jan didn't look at his brother. Inside, the women stood around the baby. They didn't look at Toor Jan either.

"Shaheen."

"What?"

"This baby will be fixed. Soon."

DAN'S REVENGE

Multinational Base Tarin Kowt, Tarin Kot District, Uruzgan Province, Afghanistan, 05 February 2013—

Commander Russo had called the SPU for a targeting meeting that afternoon. He wanted blood for Charlie. There wasn't much time left on the deployment but he was going to send a goddamned message to the enemy before he left: don't fuck with our allies. He said that, to open the meeting, and added: "Charlie died for us."

Commander Russo sat at the head of the table. The Master Chief sat opposite. Dan, Beau, Army Brian, and Captain Cales sat on one side, Lieutenant Konig and Chief Nunez on the other.

"No low-hanging fruit," the Master Chief added. "We can do that any day of the week. We want someone who matters. Even if it causes political waves."

Captain Cales tapped his pen against his notebook and Lieutenant Konig picked his fingernails. Beau folded his arms over his chest, muscle bulging. "Tell them, Dan," Beau said.

"We know where Haji Hyatullah is."

Commander Russo leaned forward. "What's the Objective Name?"

"Objective Final Blade."

"Well, there's a problem with that," Lieutenant Konig said. "He's MHK's blood relative. We're already getting reports that the Barakzais are rebelling everywhere. You want to fuck with our *other* allies?"

"There's more to it than that," Beau said to Lieutenant Konig. "Hear him out."

"First, he's not MHK's *blood* relative," Dan said. "He calls him uncle out of respect. We have a source very high up who's willing to give Final Blade up."

Chief Nunez snickered. "This shit again?"

Commander Russo held his hand up. "Go on, Bing."

"That's it, sir. He found the house of the biggest weapons dealer in Tarin Kowt. Maybe Uruzgan."

The Master Chief looked at Commander Russo.

Commander Russo canted his head. "How sure are you of the weapons?"

"Positive, sir. As sure as anything," Dan flipped open his notebook and read what Toor Jan said he had seen in Haji Hyatullah's compound. Batteries, accelerant, rocket-propelled grenades. Even a mine that could destroy a tank hidden in an animal pen. "This is the same guy who got us Doctor Baki and Sadiq Ustaz."

"Master Chief?" Commander Russo said.

The Master Chief spit dip into a plastic bottle. A bit dribbled over his lip. He rubbed his short, gray hair. "Final Blade will make an impact."

"It's suicide if it goes wrong," Lieutenant Konig added.

"We're fine," Dan said. "There will be weapons there. This guy always comes through."

Commander Russo leaned back. A brittle quiet fixed the room.

"Tell him, Dan," Army Brian finally said. He pulled his hat low on his forehead and pushed his horn-rimmed glasses up. "Tell them how you know it's true."

"The source?" Lieutenant Konig said.

"Yes," Army Brian replied.

"Go 'head, Dan," Beau said too.

Captain Cales folded his hands in his lap. He said to men at the table, "This source's true name can't leave this room."

Dan swiped his tongue over his teeth and took off his baseball cap. The picture of Haji Hyatullah, MHK, and Maziullah gleamed. He pulled it from the lining and pinned it to the table with his finger.

"Colonel Maziullah's our source. He wants MHK in prison for corruption. Haji Hyatullah is a direct link to MHK."

The others stood to look at the picture. They had all worked with Maziullah before in official capacities but never suspected he was a spy.

"Well, hot damn," Commander Russo said. "Any complaints now, Lieutenant? Chief?"

Lieutenant Konig and Chief Nunez shrugged.

"Looks good to me," said Master Chief.

"But the Colonel has to come on the raid to personally identify Final Blade," Commander Russo said. "That way we know for sure that we got Final Blade."

Dan frowned. "He's too well-known, sir."

"Can he wear a mask?"

"I'm concerned, sir."

"You want to go on the raid, right? He needs someone to babysit him."

Dan had never seen the real Afghanistan, all the strange things Toor Jan had described. This was his chance. "He'll come," Dan said. "I'll make it happen."

"Good," Commander Russo said. "Then Objective Final Blade is a go."

MIR HAMZA KHAN:
THE SUCCESSFUL HUNTER

Provincial Police Headquarters, Tarin Kot District, Uruzgan Province, Afghanistan, 05 February 2013—

All of Mir Hamza Khan's lieutenants were in his office. It had taken Maziullah two hours to gather them. Some wore their uniforms but most were in a *kameez* and vest because they hadn't been at their assigned posts. They were the sons of important men. None had earned their jobs, but they collected Khan's dole every month. His office was the hinged door in the tiger cage and they lined up to be fed. *Animals.*

Maziullah stood before Khan's desk. "The Barakzai people are revolting. Take your companies and set up checkpoints around the city. Stop them any way you see fit. Protect your General."

Khan raised his hand. "Go do it now." They turned and pushed out of the room. "Ali Muhammad," Khan called. Captain Ali Muhammad turned from the crowd. He was a fat man whose great belly strained against his thick leather gun belt. His father was a proud fighter and his entire family could be trusted. Khan often stationed him on the Teri Bridge to stop bombers and collect tolls from crossing vehicles. "Sit with us," Khan said, pointing to the carpet.

Maziullah scowled. He'd originally come to Khan's office to tell him urgent information, something important, but Khan made him find the lieutenants first. Khan squatted beside Ali Muhammad and pointed to the pot of *chai*.

"Pour, Maziullah." Maziullah poured for the three men. He replaced the pot on the desk. "Now, let us sip." Khan slurped. "There's always time for *chai*, Maziullah." Ali Muhammad smiled and raised his glass. Maziullah stared at the carpet. "Did you ever go to the old zoo in Kabul, Captain?"

"Yes, General," Ali Muhammad said. He was sweating from the strain of squatting. "I didn't like it."

"Why not?"

"My father was there on business and we were rushed." He wiped his forehead with the sleeve of his uniform. "I prefer animals in nature."

"As do I," Khan said. "But sometimes they are so sick or weak and must be cared for by others."

"That kind of life must be difficult for a wild thing."

"The cage?"

"Yes," Ali Muhammad said. "It's sad."

"But see?" Khan said and glanced at Maziullah. A phone fell out of the vest. Khan picked it up and put it back in its pocket. "It's the cage that saves them."

They finished the pot of *chai*.

"What was it, Maziullah? That you needed to tell me."

"It's better if we're alone, General."

Khan stood, went around to his desk. "No. Please. If it can't be said around Captain Ali Muhammad, then it doesn't need to be said at all."

Ali Muhammad stuck his chest out and moved closer to Khan.

"General, it's our vital business."

"Tell me or don't. Captain Ali Muhammad stays." He squeezed his new friend's hand. "*Major* Ali Muhammad, actually."

Ali Muhammad gasped, a bit too feminine, at the snap promotion.

"If I must, General." Maziullah licked his dry lips. "I know who's giving up our men to the Americans. I found out this morning."

Khan pretended to be bored, pushed around a few papers on his desk. "Who?"

"Toor Jan, from Safad Khare."

Khan turned around to the wall with the photographs that told the story of his life since the end of *Taliban* times. He had been a successful hunter with the help of Americans. Together they had built this zoo to control the animals. "What else do you know?"

"That they will capture Haji Hyatullah sometime soon."

Khan dropped Ali Muhammad's hand. His finger trailed to the empty spot where the worn photograph of Haji Hyatullah had been. The one he'd given Toor Jan. "Your American friends told you this?"

"No," Maziullah. "Toor Jan asked me how to find Haji Hyatullah."

Khan faced Maziullah. "And what did you do?"

"I sent him. We can pack up the weapons and move Haji Hyatullah and his brother Byat out tonight. The Americans will never suspect it."

Khan pressed his finger to the empty spot on the wall. "Go. Get the weapons."

"Yes, General," Maziullah said and turned away.

"But Byat stays. We can't make it too perfect, or the Americans will think we're involved."

Maziullah started to argue but stopped. "And Toor Jan?"

"We wait," Khan said, returning to his desk. Maziullah turned again and went to the door. "One last thing, Maziullah. Leave the phones with Major Ali Muhammad."

"General?" Maziullah said.

"You're an elder and I must respect you, not burden you with hard work and heartache." Khan pressed his fingers to his lips, like a gabled roof, a gesture he'd seen in the Urdu-dubbed American crime movies on Aghala's new television. Lately, they'd both given up on religion, tradition, and sex to watch movies together. "Major Ali Muhammad is young and ready for the pressures."

Maziullah slid out of the vest, gave it to Ali Muhammad. Beautiful gun across his back, he left.

Khan took the vest from Ali Muhammad, laid each phone on his desk, and turned the vest inside out to show its many pockets. "Please, sit." Khan motioned him to the Queen Anne chair and pushed a dish of candies toward him. Ali Muhammad unwrapped several and ate the candy with his mouth open, sucking them to fragile disks and finishing with a crunch. "These are all of the phones I use. I must change them often because the Americans are listening. Please stand." Khan gave him the vest. Ali Muhammad could only thread his arms through. It wouldn't button over his stomach. Khan put the phones back into the pockets. "You work directly for me now. My deputy."

Ali Muhammad stopped eating candy and stared at Khan. "What about Colonel Maziullah?"

"Your father was a good man. We were in many battles. There's no one I can trust like you. Do you understand?"

"I do," he said.

"Maziullah has betrayed us. He works with Haji Daoud." Ali Muhammad's eyes opened wide. He shook his head. "I couldn't believe it either. But I've been very careful to find out and I'm certain that it's true."

The fat man sank into his chair and some of the phones fell out. He bent, with difficulty, to retrieve them. "What must I do for you, Haji Sahib?"

"I have papers here from Kabul." Khan dropped a sheaf of papers on the desk. "They are the budget for our entire force. Money is an issue now that the Americans are leaving. I need you to go carefully through these and tell me how much they plan to send us. I'd do it myself but I'm too busy." Khan pushed the papers across the desk to Ali Muhammad. The fat man leaned forward, chin resting contemplatively in his hands, and looked over the papers. He muttered quietly. "What is it, Ali Muhammad?" Khan stood. He needed to leave to review the checkpoints going up in the city to stop the Barakzais. "What can I do for you?"

"You've done so much for me, General," Ali Muhammad said, tapping the phones on his chest. "But I can't help you with this budget."

"Why not?"

"I can't read, my dear sir."

BYAT

Kotwal Village, Tarin Kot District, Uruzgan Province, Afghanistan, 08 February 2013—

Under the silver-dark sky, two lines of men moved across the barley field. Yeasty smells drifted out of the irrigation ditches. Somewhere, stray dogs snarled. The men couldn't see the animals in the attenuated green of their night-vision devices and they continued toward the compound, a set of musty buildings behind two walls.

Towering racks of cannabis screened their advance. A squad of men secured an orange Toyota Corolla left in the field as the rest of the murderous line slipped by. They unspooled around the compound, guns trained on doors and windows, breaks in the wall, the high roof. They made no noise, except the muted chink of metal fitted into metal or the surprised expulsion of air when someone tripped and fell.

Behind the compound walls, running feet, hushed speech, and the mincing cry of a child. Then quiet. Wind and a cow chewing cud. The men scanned with their infrared gun lights, a gentle swaying like long grass. A heavy stone fell and clattered.

Their infrared gun lights darted to the top of the wall. Another stone thudded, closer. The infrared lights—invisible to the hunted but not the hunters—held steady on the spot the noise came from. Someone was climbing over the wall.

A man lumbered up. His bald head crowned and the invisible beams danced on its paleness. He emerged, a set of black eyes, flat broad nose, untrimmed moustache, trembling lips. The infrared gun lights circled his face like gnats.

Blind in the night, the climbing man couldn't see the waiting danger. He pulled himself on top of the wall and ripped his long shirt. The infrared lights stopped and held. They fired. The man was hit twice in the forehead and thumped behind the wall quicker than he had materialized. A woman called to him.

"Byat!" She repeated his name like a penitent, "Byat, Byat. Oh Byat."

The slick body was dragged away. The order came to assault. The men blew the doors inward and the compound devoured them, encouraging the slaughter.

DAN HADN'T BEEN AS CLOSE TO TOOR JAN AS HE WAS NOW

Kotwal Village, Tarin Kot District, Uruzgan Province, Afghanistan, 08 February 2013—

Dan ran as fast as he could along the track the EOD Tech had made with orange chemlights to mark the way clear of IEDs. He leapt across a canal but missed its opposite bank and was dragged down by the weight of his gun, body armor, and helmet into the standing, shitty water at the bottom. Everything had gone wrong.

Dan had made Qais sneak Toor Jan onto the base after dark, the ski mask already stretched over Toor Jan's head and beard, so Captain Cales wouldn't know that he wasn't Maziullah. Captain Cales never came to check, but the lies, the sneaking, the stress, broke Qais. He told Dan that he'd stay for Dan's first mission to make sure he didn't get someone killed but he was quitting when it was over.

The SEALs had made Qais wait in the truck with Toor Jan and let Dan come on the assault on Haji Hyatullah's compound. On their approach they did kill someone: an unarmed man trying to climb over the compound wall. Everyone swore they saw an AK-47 but when they entered the compound and followed the blood-stained path to his body they found nothing. No gun, no knife. Not even a large threatening rock. An innocent man had died as he tried to escape.

Lieutenant Ramsey was the officer in charge of the mission. He was excited and wanted to find the bad guys in Uruzgan. But after they had searched Haji Hyatullah's compound, turning every cushion, pillow, and box over, took metal detectors to the courtyard, and bashed through anything that looked like a false wall, they found nothing. None of the guns or RPGs Toor Jan had reported. Certainly no mine that could destroy a tank. Definitely no arms dealer named Haji Hyatullah. Two women, three children, and a dead man they all called Byat. No one else.

"Get Dan over here now," Lieutenant Ramsey had said into his radio. Dan heard it in his headset and ran out of an enclosed garden on the south side of the compound, through a hole in the wall, to the angry SEAL Officer. Lieutenant Ramsey, tall, face obscured by his night-vision device, looked down at Dan. "Get Qais and your fucking source and tell him to show us where he saw the weapons."

So Dan was running and he had tried to jump across an irrigation canal but fell in the water instead. The white wristwatch was covered with mud. He climbed his way out, back to the top and scanned the road. Their trucks, blacked out, glowed in the tubes of his night vision. SEALs stood at intervals along the convoy. At a police checkpoint to the south, many police officers, their weapons slung, watched the assault from the run-down shack and turnpike.

Dan turned on the infrared strobe light attached to his body armor to avoid being shot by his own men, walked out of the canal, and found his truck in the line. Toor Jan sat beside Qais in the cab. Qais stared straight ahead into the impenetrable night. Toor Jan shook with fear.

"You guys murdered a dude," Qais whispered. He was wearing a radio and had heard it over the net. "I knew you'd fuck it up."

"I didn't even shoot my gun," Dan said and pointed to Toor Jan. "Did you tell him what happened?"

"Course not, bruh. I know how to do my job."

"Then get out of the truck and do your job." Dan looked at Toor Jan and motioned. "*Rassa, rassa.*"

Toor Jan stepped to the metal running board and pulled the eye slit of his ski mask nearly closed. He wore an Afghan Commando uniform and cinched the huge pants. Qais put his hands on Toor Jan's shoulders and nudged him off. Qais jumped down next and Dan closed the heavy armored door behind them.

They looked at each other in the darkness. Dan could see with the night-vision but Toor Jan poked his neck forward, blind. Dan put his arm around one shoulder and Qais did the same on the other side. They went forward into the barley field.

Dogs, all around but invisible, snorted in the high grass. Dan raised his gun to his chest and walked along the chemlight trail. He cleared the first ditch easily with Toor Jan and Qais following. Deeper in, Dan caught the ground and fell. Qais laughed and walked ahead but Toor Jan stayed close and pulled Dan up to his feet. They came to a thin tree line, leaped across another canal, all three sticking to the bank on the other side.

On the crest, a large SEAL stood against the moon.

"It happens to us too," he said to Dan.

"What's that?"

"Falling every ten steps." He pointed to a field of cannabis undulating in the windy night. "Be careful going through the ganja."

Toor Jan reached out to feel for the nylon straps of Dan's kit and used them as a guide. Out of the cannabis, a long mud wall rose from the ground. Afghan Commandos stood in the open space between the cannabis and the wall. Toor Jan looked at the ground, avoiding the Commandos. Dan went along until he found the door. They went through. Lieutenant Ramsey stood inside with four others. All of them turned.

"Ask your buddy where the weapons are," Lieutenant Ramsey said. The veins in his neck were swollen as thick as pencils. "We've gone over this shit six times."

A SEAL walked the courtyard with a metal detector.

"You've found nothing?"

"A bag of pistol rounds."

"That's it?"

"That's it."

More Commandos and SEALs entered the courtyard. It was crowded. In the corner, two uncovered women and a few kids watched. Byat, under a sheet, lay in front of them.

"Qais," Dan said and put his hands on his shoulders. He lifted his night vision tubes and Qais did the same. "Ask where the weapons are in the compound."

Toor Jan whispered his answer to Qais.

"He's never been inside," Qais said in Dan's ear. "What I tell you, man? This is all fucked up now."

Dan—in his mind, as if through glass—saw himself raising his rifle and shooting Toor Jan. Right there in front of everyone. Dan turned to Lieutenant Ramsey. "Did you check the manger?"

"We checked everything," Lieutenant Ramsey said. "Ask him again, Qais."

Again Toor Jan couldn't be heard by any of the others.

"He said they must've moved it," Qais said to Lieutenant Ramsey. He was lying. The entire time he looked at Dan. "He says it was all in the barn last time he was here."

"Dry hole, huh, Dan?" Lieutenant Ramsey got in Dan's face. "You know Intel nerds are never trusted again after they bring us to a dry hole, right? It's a reputation-killer."

Dan stammered and was told to shut the fuck up.

"What'd you pay this guy?" another SEAL said. "More than anyone here makes in two years, I bet." He grabbed Toor Jan by the collar and dragged him toward Byat. "At the very least this piece of shit should tell us who this turd was."

"Don't ever fucking touch my guy," Dan said and ripped the SEAL off of Toor Jan.

Dan and Qais walked Toor Jan over. A lazing black cow mooed nearby. Three Afghan Commandos stood over the body. Dan readjusted the mask on Toor Jan's face. The SEALS wheeled their flashlights over and Dan pulled the sheet away.

The man's dead eyes drooped. Two diminutive holes had been drilled above his left eyebrow. His beard, shining in the strong white light, was filled with blood that had been ejected from his mouth. The blood was thick and bright. The SEALs swung their lights toward the masked Toor Jan. He trembled. "That is Byat, brother of Haji Hyatullah," Toor Jan whispered to Qais. "The one who sold me my motorcycle."

"Great," Lieutenant Ramsey said. "Call in dry hole, uncuff them." He pointed to the women and children. "Let's get the fuck out of here."

Dan and Qais led Toor Jan from the compound. The SEALs and Afghan Commandos had lined up to patrol out. Dogs continued barking from far off. Near the cannabis, where the big SEAL had been standing, an Afghan Commando slapped Toor Jan in the chest to stop him from passing.

"Whoa," Dan said. He came within inches of the Tajik Commando's face and the tubes of his night-vision pressed into the Tajik's forehead. "What's your problem?"

"He's good?" the Tajik Commando said.

"He's mine," Dan replied and pushed Toor Jan to the front of their patrol.

They didn't reach the base until it was nearly dawn. Dan and Qais hadn't said a word to each other, Toor Jan sat between them and stared straight ahead through the slit of his mask. At their Conex box meeting room, the SEAL driving the truck told them to get out. They climbed down from the big vehicle. The sun gilded the drab base. Dan's eyes hurt, he was so tired. Qais was not. He was furious and he pushed Dan. Dan pushed him back. Toor Jan's eyes went wide in the mask.

"You got a dude killed for nothing!"

"Not nothing, you bastard," Dan said. He spun around Qais, went for a headlock, but lost control. Qais made him pay by chicken-winging his arm. "You know they were bad dudes, Qais."

"That was a Pashtun man," Qais said, wrenching Dan's arm harder. "He was one of my people."

"You're a fucking American." Dan stomped Qais's foot and escaped. "You left them behind a long time ago, you fucking scammer."

"Scammer? Then take your *talib* friend to the gate by yourself." Qais pulled the 4Runner keys from his pocket and ran to the vehicle parked beside the Conex box. Dan tried to chase him but the truck pulled away in a curtain of dust.

"No!" Dan said. He kicked the ground. "Goddamnit."

Toor Jan came over to Dan. Without Qais they were speechless. Toor Jan's regular clothes were in a bundle in the Conex box. Dan gestured him inside.

Inside, Toor Jan shivered. It was cool but mostly damp. Shirtless, his ribs peeked from his chest and goose pimples dotted his skin. Dan turned away as he changed into his baggy pants. Toor Jan took the mask off, putting his hand inside to give it shape. He smiled and handed it to Dan. Toor Jan was thinner than Dan had realized. His hands were large, fingers thick. Fingernails trimmed and colored with henna. They couldn't talk but Dan hadn't ever felt as close to Toor Jan as he was now. He wasn't Dan's pet. Toor Jan was a man with a son.

"You did good, Toor Jan." Dan handed him his black knitted cap. "We tried."

The Conex box opened. Qais came in first, his face redder than hell, then Captain Cales. Toor Jan smiled and waved. He looked to Dan for an introduction. Dan swallowed a surge of puke in his throat.

"Dan?" Captain Cales pointed at Toor Jan. "That's not Maziullah."

MIR HAMZA KHAN FINDS THE CIA MAN

Tarin Kowt City, Tarin Kot District, Uruzgan Province, Afghanistan, 09 February 2013—

Mir Hamza Khan had decided not to go Mumbai for treatment and was paying the price. His head ached. He had vomited twice into a bucket and it needed to be emptied. Khan sat up from the blanket roll spread across his spot on the roof. Azzam, the manservant, clopped across the tiles below. Guards' boots thudded across the walls. Little Maziullah, now called Zayn, sang in Naghma's home. Her windows were open, even in the morning cold, and his thin, sweet voice came through. He could smell her cooking breakfast for him. Khan stood. Tarin Kowt City pulsed. People milled stupidly near the *bazaar*. Khan tossed his puke into the street.

At breakfast, he ate silently. Naghma watched him. "What is it?"

"I was called this morning," Naghma said and bit the corner of her mouth.

"What do you mean called?"

"My uncle called and said Haji Hyatullah was attacked by the Americans. They killed Byat." Naghma searched his face for an answer. "Why would they do that to you?"

"Because they're stupid animals," Khan said throwing his bread on the ground and rising. Zayn watched him. "Where's Maziullah?"

"Here, *baba*," Zayn said.

"What did I tell you about that name?" Khan touched his shoulder. "You're called Zayn now."

"Maziullah is outside," Naghma said. She collected the dishes from the floor and shooed Zayn away. "He doesn't look well."

Khan punched through the doors to the courtyard. The traitor sat slouched against a wall, his hands over his face. His shining gun was leaning, muzzle up, beside him. He didn't look at Khan. "What is wrong with you?"

"Nothing, General."

Khan ripped his hands away. His lips were swollen and he had a cut over his left eye. Khan shouted Azzam over, ordered him to bring a wet cloth. "What happened?"

"Barakzais stopped my car as I drove here." He spat blood onto the ground. "They beat me."

Khan stroked Maziullah's sweaty hair. Azzam brought the towel and pressed it to his face. Khan's personal doctor came to stitch the cut. "The Americans killed Byat last night," Khan said. "That was a great mistake on their part. Now we can control them. We must go to their base for a meeting."

The doctor finished the stitches. Maziullah hadn't winced.

"We? What about Ali Muhammad?" Maziullah said.

Khan looked down at him. Blood crusted the slash in his eyebrow. Maziullah was always small but now he looked weak. "I need you to come with me. I have an important thing for you to do."

"What is it?"

"I'll tell you when we're there."

Maziullah stood. "Have you called the President to tell them what the Americans have done?"

"I will in the car." Khan stood, brushed off his knees. "Separate cars. It's too dangerous to be together."

After the new American Commander received a call from President Hamid Karzai scolding him for the raid on Haji Hytaullah's home, he allowed Khan and Maziullah through the base's gate. Maziullah whipped his armored Hilux through the gravel in front of the Special Forces headquarters building. Khan followed behind in the cherry-red Mercedes. The new American Commander's gray-haired deputy stood outside and watched them as they got out of their cars. He had no *tajiman* with him. Khan pointed at the headquarters building. He walked them inside.

The meeting room was packed. Americans sat at a long table and many more lined the walls. The new American Commander was already in his seat, his *tajiman* alongside. He rose, the others too, when Khan and Maziullah entered the room. They took seats at the far end of the table. The new American Commander spoke, gruffly, to his men in English.

Khan leaned over. "Who is the one you speak to, Maziullah?"

Maziullah shook his head, confused.

Khan flipped his cell phone open. He scrolled to the picture Toor Jan had given him of his American CIA handler. He showed the blond, curly-haired man to Maziullah. "Is it this one? I don't see him here."

Maziullah raised his chin in the air, nose high as if he was sniffing for the CIA spy. He looked at an American, squat, bearded, wearing a faded blue baseball cap, in the corner of the room. "That one. Right there. In the regular clothes. With the white watch."

"How are you, General?" The new American Commander finally said through his *tajiman*. "How is your house? How is your family? How is everything?"

"Is your intention to trap me, Commander?"

"Sorry?" The new American Commander said. The other Americans stiffened.

"Is this another trick?"

"I don't understand, General. Why would this be a trick?"

"I will not speak until your CIA man is out of the room. The one who used a criminal liar to launch your illegal raid last night."

The Americans whispered. The new American Commander looked around the room.

"That man." Khan pointed to the stocky American. "That one. I don't sit in the same room as CIA." The new American Commander's gray-haired deputy spoke to the CIA man in English. The CIA man shouted at him. Another American, thin and boyish, pointed to the door. The CIA man stood and shouted at both of them. "Go, Maziullah," Khan said, quiet so the *tajiman* wouldn't hear. "Find Toor Jan and bring him to the prison. Wait for me there."

The CIA man had been convinced to leave. He stared at Khan with a hatred reserved for true enemies. Khan stared back. Both Maziullah and the CIA man left the room at the same time.

"Now we can fix this horrible mistake you've made," Khan said and pressed his fingers to his face. "Then we can discuss how to keep these Barakzai animals from ruining the peace we've created."

THE GOOD AMERICAN WASN'T TOOR JAN'S FRIEND

Safad Khare, Tarin Kot District, Uruzgan Province, Afghanistan, 09 February 2013—

Shaheen prodded Toor Jan's thigh. "Toor *Janna*. Please wake up. I know you said you needed to sleep but please wake up. Your phone hasn't stopped ringing."

His phone buzzed in her hand. He cracked his eyes open and groaned, took his phone. He wasn't sure what had happened with The Good American but he knew something was wrong. Qais and the other American had taken Toor Jan to the gate without The Good American. They let him leave without a word. Toor Jan had done what he had been asked and found Haji Hyatullah. It wasn't his fault that he wasn't there.

Toor Jan answered the phone, "*Bale, a-salam u' alaykum.*"

"Enough of that, Toor Jan," Maziullah said. "We have important business for the General today."

"What kind of business?"

"Work that cannot be discussed on the phone," Maziullah said.

"What must I do?"

"Where are you?"

346

"What does the General need me to do?"

"Are you in your village? I'll come meet you there. This is very important, Toor Jan."

Toor Jan sat up and pushed Shaheen away from him. He leaned into the phone. "Colonel, please explain this to me."

"It's no problem, Toor Jan. I'll meet you soon."

"But I'm not at home."

"Where are you?" Toor Jan pointed at their wood chest. Shaheen looked at Toor Jan, puzzled. He kicked at her. She went fast toward the wood chest. "It doesn't matter, I'll find you, Toor Jan." Maziullah hung up.

"What's the matter?" Shaheen said. She stood over the wood chest. "What's happening?"

Toor Jan went over and pulled fistfuls of clothes out of the wood chest. They needed warm shirts to ride the motorcycle through the cold. Beyond that he couldn't think of anything else. "Get the baby ready to ride."

Shaheen stared at Toor Jan. "They are coming for us."

He stopped, turned to his wife. "Yes, Shaheen *Jo*. They are coming for us."

The girl went to the baby's crib. Ibrahim reached up, hands clasping at something invisible in the air. Shaheen began dressing him.

Toor Jan went outside and passed Abdul Hakim—bruised face green with healing—and went to his motorcycle. He checked the gas, the lines, started the engine. The bike worked fine. Toor Jan ignored Abdul Hakim and went back into the house.

Shaheen stood with a bag, the baby, and her sister.

"What does she do?" Shaheen said to Toor Jan.

Both women stood tall and pitiless. Both wore their *burkhas*, pushed off their faces. They were ready. Toor Jan walked around them and found his knife. He took his cell phone from his pocket and went outside to dial.

"Is this the *tajiman*?" he said.

"Yes, it is, Toor Jan," Qais said.

Toor Jan paced around Abdul Hakim. "A man named Maziullah is coming to kill me."

"Mir Hamza Khan's Colonel?"

"The one with the blue gun." Toor Jan squatted. He traced his finger through the dirt. "He's coming to kill me. Can Commander come get me and my family? With a helicopter? Like he did when he saved my life."

"Why would Maziullah kill you?"

"Because I stole the picture of Haji Hyatullah from the General. And I asked him to tell me where Haji Hyatullah lived."

"Toor Jan." Qais cleared his throat. "You were tricked. The American tricked you. He won't come get you."

"Of course he will. He saved me when I was wounded. Where is he? Put him on the phone."

"Listen to me, we're both Pashtuns. I'm telling you the truth." He sighed. "You must leave on your own. Where can you go?"

Toor Jan thought for a moment. There was only one place he could go in Uruzgan. It

was the last place he wanted to be. "My uncle's house. The Big One."

"You must go there now. You have plenty of money. Leave now. Talk to no one." He paused for a moment. "The American isn't your friend.

He was never your friend."

Toor Jan clung to the words: *the American isn't your friend*. He hung up without replying and cut the rope away from Abdul Hakim's leg. They stood before each other. Toor Jan stroked his brother's bruised face. "Do you remember what I told you? That you must take care of this house?"

"Yes, brother," Abdul Hakim said. The women had joined them and watched the brothers speak. "I remember."

"You must leave," Toor Jan said to Mina.

She frowned. "How? Who will go with me?"

"Abdul Hakim. He'll walk you to our uncle, to The Big One's house. Tell The Big One that the police are after us and you need to wait there for the afternoon." Toor Jan took Abdul Hakim's face in his hands. "You must speak for her to the men. Speak as clear as possible. If they ask about your face, tell them you were in a fight. Nothing about being stoned. Do you understand?"

"Yes, brother."

"Mina will show you the way. When you get close get to Sarkhum Valley, ask for directions the rest of the way. We will meet you there later." Toor Jan turned to Mina to make sure she understood. "If we aren't there before the fourth prayer come back here. Make sure nothing happens to our father's house, Abdul Hakim."

Toor Jan hugged Abdul Hakim. The two sisters held each other. Mina took Ibrahim. She kissed him and her tears ran down his forehead before handing him back to Shaheen.

Abdul Hakim grabbed Mina's wrist. "We must go, sister." Abdul Hakim's swollen lips quivered but he stood proudly. Toor Jan gave them a stack of money. Mina pulled her *burkha* down and they went out, through the gate, together.

Toor Jan strapped their bag to the motorcycle's crate and Ibrahim to Shaheen and Shaheen onto him and they burst outside. He steered the motorcycle down the hill, around the white schoolhouse, wall still scorched from the attack. Behind them, the compound built by Haji Izatullah, grew small. Deeper in the valley, Safad Khare faded to a smudge of brown against the far mountains.

Shaheen's fingers dug into Toor Jan's ribs. He avoided bumps, rocks, holes, anything that could spin the bike out from underneath them. As he came out of the valley, on the road owned by the General, he began to think that they might escape without detection.

The road turned barren. A desert opened around them and Toor Jan's hands froze. They continued, through two prayers, on the road north toward Chorah. A camouflaged police checkpoint appeared in the distance. Without the green Ford Rangers parked nearby, Toor Jan might not have seen it.

He stopped. Shaheen asked what he was doing but she didn't finish. The trucks came screaming forward. Toor Jan couldn't turn the bike fast enough with the load of his wife and the baby. Police officers surrounded them with guns. The uniformed men were angry and breathed heavily, their rifles bobbing with each inhalation and release.

A young police officer came over. "Why do you run, friend?" he said and hiked up his pants.

"I'm not running," Toor Jan said.

"Give me your *taskera*." The young police officer rubbed his fingers together for Toor Jan's official identification. "Now."

Ibrahim began to cry.

"I don't have one," Toor Jan said.

"What's your name?"

"My name doesn't matter."

The young police officer threaded his thumbs through the belt loops and pulled his blue pants up again. He walked around the motorcycle to the baby hanging from Shaheen's back. The slide of his Makarov pistol clacked.

"What's this man's name, sister?" The young police officer pressed the pistol against Ibrahim's screaming face. "Tell me." The cold metal startled Ibrahim into crying louder. Shaheen dug her fingers into Toor Jan. The young police officer put the gun into the baby's mouth. Ibrahim gummed the metal and then cried so loud it drove into Toor Jan's bones. "What's his name?"

Toor Jan screamed, like a caged animal. "I don't have a name. No one remembers what I was called when I was born. But I am Toor Jan, son of Haji Izatullah."

The police men ripped Toor Jan from the motorcycle. Shaheen fell and Ibrahim spilled from the papoose onto the hard road. The young police officer picked the baby up, wiped his face, and handed him to Shaheen. The police officers stuffed Toor Jan into a truck and sped toward the city. His family diminished in the rear window. As the distance grew, they became lost against the darkness of the far-off mountains.

DAN IS BANISHED

Multinational Base Tarin Kowt, Tarin Kot District, Uruzgan
Province, Afghanistan, 09 February 2013—

MHK walked out of the meeting first. Dan was sitting, as ordered, on a bench outside the room. Four feet away—close enough for Dan to see that the hem of the General's long shirt had frayed—the two men stared at each other, connected until death by the ancient animosity of losing a friend to the other. MHK left the headquarters building. The rest of the staff filed out, except for the SPU and Intelligence sections.

"Petty Officer Bing," the Master Chief called. "Come back in here." Beau, Captain Cales, Army Brian—none of them looked up as Dan sat at the table. Lieutenant Konig and Chief Nunez grinned. Commander Russo motioned for the Master Chief to continue. "Do you have anything to say?"

Dan leaned against the table. "MHK was always a step ahead of me."

"Enough," Captain Cales said. "That's not what he's talking about. You know it. We all know it."

"Beau," Dan said. The big man stared at his hands. "Tell 'em."

"Petty Officer Bing," the Master Chief said. "Let's not—"

"Tell them what, Dan?" Beau raised his head, wiry hair silhouetted by the light. "That you fucking embarrassed me after I stuck up for you

352

every single time?" He spread his fingers on one hand. "Two times? Three? How many times did I go to bat for you? You used a compromised source and lied about it. MHK outed you. He was behind Toor Jan's picture. Clearly."

"I did what I needed to win, Beau."

"You didn't win," Lieutenant Konig said. "But at least we can go back to relying on MHK instead of undermining him. He's the only one who can get us out of this whole Barakzai mess."

Commander Russo cleared his throat. Everyone turned to him. He tried to look Dan in the eye but Dan watched his feet under the table. "We're going to send you home, Dan."

"Yes, sir," Dan said.

"You take some leave, and then—what was it, Robert?"

"Instructor duty at interrogator school," Captain Cales said. "We already got a plane for you. Leaves in two hours. Go pack a bag of whatever you need for the trip and we'll mail the rest."

Dan felt like he might shit his heart out.

"Will you get him to the terminal, Sergeant Chenko?" The Master Chief asked Army Brian.

"Yes, Master Chief," he said and stood. Dan stood too.

"And shave," Chief Nunez yelled as they left the room. "Put on a damn uniform and act like you're in the military."

Back at the SPU, Dan told Army Brian to fuck off.

"I don't need help packing," he said and stormed into his hut. "Just give me that ride to the fuckin' airfield." Army Brian followed him inside. He tried to help anyway. "Stop touching my shit," Dan said. He opened a canvas flight bag and stuffed it with shirts, pants, and shoes. He searched around. "Goddamn it. I lose fucking everything."

"Laptop?" Army Brian said.

"Yeah, man," Dan said, lifting the mattress from the plywood platform and throwing it on the floor. "Not here. Let's see where else it could be." He bent back a piece of plywood wall, already pulling from the stud, and ripped it off. Dust filled the air. "Nope. Not there either."

"It's on your desk." Army Brian pointed. "Beneath the stack of underwear."

"Goddamnit." Dan said. He put his laptop in the flight bag and sat on the floor.

"Relax, Dan. It's fine."

"No, it's not. I was right." He exhaled powerfully. "I know I was right."

"Maybe." Army Brian picked up the MP5 from the desk. He sighted down the barrel to the opposite wall. "But it doesn't matter."

Dan stood. "I didn't know you were a sergeant."

"Yeah." Army Brian closed one eye and held the gun steady. "I don't like to talk about it."

"What do I do with that thing?"

"What do you mean?" Army Brian said, dropping the MP5 to his side. "Oh, that's right."

"Yeah, Aaron signed it over to me. Who do I sign it back over to?"

"I can take it."

"You sure? You're not going to take it back with you to upstate New York, wave it at a bunch of grandmas, and start flying Don't Tread on Me flags from your pickup truck or anything?"

"No, sign it over to me. I'll take care of it." Army Brian slung into the MP5.

Dan worked faster, packing the essentials he'd need for the fifteen-hour flight. He finished and put on his hat. The glossy photographs cooled his forehead. "Will you do something else for me?" he said, taking off the hat. He pulled the picture of baby Charlotte from the lining but left Haji Hyatullah's. "Send this to Aaron's wife." Army Brian took the picture and looked at Dan strangely. Dan took off the white wristwatch—still caked in mud from the irrigation ditch at Haji Hyatullah's compound—and put it into his pocket. "Let's go."

At the terminal, they shook hands inside the 4Runner.

"How about Maziullah, huh?"

"I always knew we'd never win him over," Army Brian said. "Not really."

"What do you think will happen to him?"

Army Brian pulled a cigar from the 4Runner's ashtray and put it in his mouth. "Deader than dead, Danny boy."

Dan got out of the truck with his bag. Army Brian watched him go inside before driving away. The terminal was a plywood and cinderblock building. It was empty and unadorned except for a large chalkboard detailing incoming flights from other bases, and a flat, long bench across the middle of the room. There was no ticketing or attendants. Only the air-traffic controlmen, watching TV in an alcove, waiting for planes to signal their descent to the runway.

Dan almost waited outside after he saw Qais, three Louis Vuitton bags at his feet, sitting on the bench. But he went inside anyway, sat on the far side of the bench. The plywood walls popped as they expanded in the afternoon heat.

After twenty minutes Dan spoke. "So, you were serious about quitting."

"Hell yeah," Qais said, as if he'd been waiting the entire time to be asked the question. "I'm done with this shit."

"What are you gonna do?"

"I'll figure it out." He'd shaved but left a moustache. A gold chain fell out of his button-down shirt. Red suede slip-ons were loose on his feet. He was dressed like he was traveling first-class. "I can't do this anymore."

"Why are you *really* quitting, Qais?"

"Because, bruh."

"Because you hate me?"

"Shut up," he said. He slapped the flat bench. "You know Toor Jan called me this morning?"

"What?" Dan slid over close. "What'd he say?"

Qais shook his head. "He's gone, man."

"How? I mean, like how?" Dan pressed against Qais. "Where is he?"

"Probably dead." Qais stood, gathered his bags. "Entire family too."

Qais walked out of the terminal and waited on the sunny tarmac alone.

MIR HAMZA KHAN'S ZOO

Tarin Kowt City, Tarin Kot District, Uruzgan Province, Afghanistan, 09 February 2013—

As Khan left the meeting with the Americans, he called Ali Muhammad and ordered him to the Tarin Kowt Prison to lock Maziullah in the same cell as Toor Jan. Today all of the animals were going into their cages.

Khan went home and changed into regular clothing. He put a scarf over his face. He purposely smeared motor oil—from a drip pan under the idling Ford Ranger—on his shirt to look like a filthy, common person. He left his compound and pushed a beggar kid down so hard that he bloodied the kid's knees. The kid threw rocks at the disguised Mir Hamza Khan. Two heavy stones found their mark, hit his back. But he continued to walk.

The safe house with the bombers was two streets away. Khan dipped his head as he moved through the crowds, overhearing their conversations about the Barakzais and Haji Hyatullah. Everyone spoke of it. He sneered under his scarf. Stupid animals trapped in a great cage. He came to the safe house and swung the gate open. Several green Ford Ranger police trucks were parked in the large yard. Trash was heaped against a wall and the entire space was covered in goat shit. One of the dumb animals trotted over and rubbed its muzzle against Khan's leg. He kicked it and walked inside the safe house.

The room was filled with human stink. Ghastly figures languished, as if chained to the floor. Their tired whispers sounded like moaning. In the dark, Khan could see their blinking eyes, gleaming teeth, but nothing else. These were the bombers.

A well-fed man came over and put his hand on Khan's chest. "Who are you?"

Khan took the scarf from his face and pinned the well-fed man against a wall. Two of the bombers scurried out of their way. "This is my house. I hold these people for the young *talib* commander you work for. Tell him to use them against the Americans now. I will not stop him. He must strike his targets."

Khan left for the prison.

When Khan met him on the top floor—the one reserved for spies—Ali Muhammad was panting. His uniform tunic was untucked. Dark stains covered the front. He held Maziullah's blue rifle. A canvas bag was over his shoulder. "Toor Jan and Maziullah are over here, General." Ali Muhammad pointed to the cell. "We found Maziullah with this." He showed the canvas bag to Mir Hamza Khan. Inside was twenty thousand American dollars, the money that the old American Commander had given Khan to distribute to the elders in Safad Khare after the attack. The money Khan had given to Maziullah to keep for himself. "He was running away," Ali Muhammad said.

They entered the cell. Both men sat upright with their legs locked straight ahead in shackles bolted to the floor. Maziullah's face was oozing clear liquid and blood. One of his eyes was completely swollen shut. "Did you beat him more?" Khan said to Ali Muhammad.

Ali Muhammad shook his head.

Khan crouched down to Maziullah and slammed his head against the stone wall. Toor Jan looked at his feet in the shackles. Khan paced the cell a few times and stopped between the two men. Maziullah stared at him. He wasn't scared.

"You were born a dog, Mir Hamza. You'll die like one too," Maziullah said and tried to spit at Khan. The saliva dribbled down his own busted face. "Don't forget it."

Khan turned to Ali Muhammad. "Give me the rifle."

Mir Hamza Khan held the front sight of the blue rifle against Maziullah's forehead. The fiend, the traitor, the old, traditional, brave man didn't move. Khan jerked the trigger. The rifle clicked. He racked another round and jerked again. Nothing. He jerked again, again, still again and the blue rifle refused to fire. Toor Jan jumped at each trigger pull. Even Mir Hamza Khan started to flinch.

Khan threw the rifle down and drew the Makarov from his belt. He squeezed the trigger and his best *andiwale's* brains splashed onto the wall. Maziullah slumped back. He didn't lean and fall over as they often did. He remained upright and proud as always. His toothbrush hung from his pocket.

Ali Muhammad picked the blue rifle up from the floor. "Finish it, General?" He said and raised the gun at Toor Jan.

Khan looked over Toor Jan, trapped in the zoo of his birth, family, history. It made Khan sick. "Unshackle him."

Ali Muhammad freed Toor Jan. He jumped up. Khan opened the cell door and Toor Jan ran out of the prison. As Khan and Ali Muhammad left, two police officers came running by with wet rags and a bucket of water to clean the bloody cell.

"And the money, general?" Ali Muhammad said, hands gripping the strap.

"Yours now," Khan said with sickness in his heart. They left the prison together.

TOOR JAN,
SON OF HAJI IZATULLAH

Toor Jan had walked for an hour. Hands behind his back—clasped at the elbow—eyes down to the road, one foot after the other. He was going home. Toor Jan didn't know what he would find. *My father's house*. But would anyone else be there? The fourth prayer had sounded but Toor Jan walked through it. He didn't feel bad about missing the call. Toor Jan's deliverance from death felt like one great prayer to God.

The sand hill that overlooked Safad Khare loomed ahead and Toor Jan ran up to it. He fought the incline, bending to all fours, and reached the crest. He almost collapsed. Ahead, Safad Khare spread across the saddle. Men were talking with each other in their courtyards. Two yellow dogs chased each other along the path, each nipping the other's tail. Dinner had been eaten and the smoke dwindled to a thin wisp.

In the distance, near the end of the village, the gate to Toor Jan's house flapped open. Abdul Hakim stalked out with the rifle and stood there. He scanned up and down the road. Toor Jan's heart jumped. He started to run. On the roof, Mina, in her blue *burkha*, saw him and pointed. She shouted to Abdul Hakim. He turned and saw his brother, thrust the AK-47 in the air. Toor Jan sprinted across the flat. Behind Abdul Hakim, Shaheen came out, green *burkha* concealing her, and ran toward Toor Jan. They met, out in the open, holding each other, kissing each other through the mesh covering her face.

"You're here, Shaheen *Jo*. You're here."

They walked the rest of the way, taking Abdul Hakim with them through the gate and locking it behind them. He'd gone home. Toor Jan promised God that he would never do anything that might cause him to lose it again.

BOMBERS

Tarin Kowt City, Tarin Kot District, Uruzgan Province,
Afghanistan, 10 February 2013—

The room of the safe house wasn't lit but they knew each other in the darkness. Their two-week passage through the training camps and their two-month wait in this city had been long but—as they wrapped themselves in the purest white—they knew it was finally over.

They pulled prayer caps over their heads and delicately donned their explosive vests. Some shifted until the device fit properly over their thin frames but the others, terrified of setting it off without facing the enemy, stood stiffly and waited.

The light from the day filled the doorframe when the truck came. The Big One, commander of all of Uruzgan, stepped out and stood in the courtyard. He had a fierce look on his grim, set face. "Say your goodbyes," he told them.

The bombers smiled sadly at each other and said that they wished and hoped to meet again in paradise. The Big One began to divide them in the courtyard by target.

"You two to the National Bank and you two to the invader's base. Get in the truck." The four bombers got into the truck and stared straight ahead. The last two looked at The Big One. "I have a very special mission for you." He snapped over his driver. The driver came over with police uniforms. He handed them to the bombers. They put them on over their explosive vest. "You will rush inside of the criminal Mir Hamza Khan's walled mansion."

The two bombers looked at each other. "Isn't this his house?" one asked The Big One.

"Yes," The Big One said, impatient.

"Isn't he our friend?"

The Big One pointed to the two bombers and his driver prodded them to the truck. The Big One followed. The driver stuffed the bombers in and closed the door.

"Aren't they right, commander?" the driver said. "Didn't he give us this house?"

"Yes," The Big One said. "But he tried to kill my nephew and his family. I can't allow that." The Big One waved his hand and the driver got into the truck. He watched the procession exit the compound and split off toward their appointed places.

The bank exploded first. One bomber followed the other inside and screamed "God is the greatest" before detonating. All twenty patrons were killed.

Two bombers approached the gate of the invader's base, but the guards had heard the booming from the city and were on alert. They chopped the bombers down with machine guns and the men exploded in the cement causeway, killing only themselves.

The last two went into Mir Hamza Khan's mansion, let in by a guard who'd been sleeping when they approached. He opened the gatehouse door and went back to his rest on a stool. The house was palatial, grander than any building the bombers had ever seen. An uncovered woman, aged and beautiful, stood like a queen in the garden. A teenage boy—book in his hand—was beside her. They didn't see the bombers.

The aged queen called up to someone on the roof, "We are lucky with this warm weather, *Mira Jan*. The roses will be good this year."

A tall man, large hands, skin yellowed, stepped to the edge of the roof. A blue rifle hung from his back. He smiled down at the aged queen, then saw the bombers, explosive vests sagging on their chests. "Run Naghma!"

The aged queen and the teenaged boy saw the bombers and ran. The bombers chased—driven by rage—and overtook them. They detonated in unison.

Only the queen, the boy, and the two bombers were killed.

DAN THE INSTRUCTOR

Marine Corps Interrogator School, Virginia Beach, Virginia, United States of America, 20 May 2013—

Dan finished his Starbucks latte and checked his cell phone. *Time to go.* He put the white wristwatch on. "Jones," he called down the hall.

Jones, a Marine Corps Staff Sargent, stuck his head out of the Fish Bowl, the room where the instructors watched, through closed-circuit cameras, the mock interrogations going on in the rooms lining the hall. "What's up, Bing?"

"Take me in there." Dan put his hands out and Jones cuffed him. He led Dan into a small, cold room. A student was already sitting at the desk.

"Any information, Staff Sargent?" the student asked about Dan. It was a role-playing exercise. Dan was an enemy captured on the battlefield of a country they called Afraqistan. The student was to interrogate him. If he listened to the clues Dan dropped and used them, Dan would break and spill his guts. If not, the student failed the exercise. "Any information from the capturing force?"

"Nah," Jones said. "Except that he had an AK-47 on him." Jones forced Dan into a chair across from the student. "Oh yeah," Jones said, before leaving. This was the first clue. "He keeps asking if we'll let him call his sister."

A blank notebook and several colored pens lined the desk. They were arranged in perfect rows. The student wore a watch on his wrist and started a timer. His haircut was faded to precise Marine Corps standards. "What the fuck is your name?"

Dan laughed.

"Don't fucking laugh at me, faggot. What's your goddamned name?" He stood, leaned into Dan. He'd had too much coffee at breakfast. "Huh? What the fuck is it?"

Dan looked up at the camera in the upper left corner of the room. The other instructors were watching. "All right sit down, Sergeant Jenkins."

"You don't fucking tell me what to do!" Sergeant Jenkins said and slammed his fist on the table.

"No, dummy. I'm breaking character."

"Oh," Sergeant Jenkins said and dropped into his chair. He sat straight. "My apologies, Petty Officer."

"Cut the squared away, bullshit. Why are you screaming at me?" Dan put his cuffed hands on the table. "Get these off."

Sergeant Jenkins slipped the zip ties from his wrist. "Because I'm interrogating you."

"You think so?"

"Yes, Petty Officer." He shrugged. "Maybe."

"I've seen you in your Class-A uniform. You got a Combat Action Ribbon. Iraq Campaign with a star. Right?"

"I was infantry."

"Where you been?"

"Tel Afar. Mosul. Ramadi."

"Lots of firefights?"

"In Ramadi," Sergeant Jenkins said. "Especially during my first deployment."

"See," Dan said, glancing at the camera. "I've always been an intel nerd. So I don't know anything about *the* shit. I'll never know what you've been through." Dan leaned forward. "But do you think yelling would work on you? After all you've been through?"

"I wanted to establish control. Like we were taught."

"That's adorable." Dan wiped his face with the back of his arm. "What if every day of your life was like Ramadi?"

"What do you mean?"

"No coming back home, movies, fast food, iPhone, beautiful girls with pillows for tits. What if it was Ramadi all the time?"

"That would suck."

"Yeah, it would. And I'm from Afraqistan. My entire life is Ramadi. Did you listen to what Staff Sarn't Jones said? I'm worried about my sister. If I'm asking the Americans about her, she probably means the world to me. That's the scenario at least. Why the fuck would I care if a dumb-looking redneck was yelling at me? Is he going to find my sister? No? Then fuck him." Dan tapped the table. "You gotta make a connection. You're not in infantry anymore. You can't use hate and discontent."

"I know, Petty Officer."

"You ever kill anyone?" Sergeant Jenkins gave Dan a dismissive look, the first time he'd broken his military bearing. "I don't mean it like that.

I know I'm a desk jockey. I'm not talking shit. What I'm saying is that you're going to kill people doing this job, in a different way." Dan swallowed. "Do a good job, you'll save some Americans but your source dies. Do a bad job and those Americans die. Source still dies. Your fault, every time."

Sergeant Jenkins stared at him.

Dan changed his approach. "Look, do you read?"

"Some."

"I can't read. Only rich people can read in Afraqistan. But I know my lineage back to Babylon. What about you? What was *your* great-great-grandfather's name?"

"I don't know."

"My point. See, I'm a proud Afraqi. I know every civilization and invader that my people have ever beaten. It's so close to me that I feel like I've beat them myself. Have you heard the Iskander story?" Dan had told Toor Jan's Iskander story so many times that it was practically part of the course's syllabus. "I asked the guy where the Taliban leader lived and he said near where *we* beat Iskandar. Iskander is Alexander the Great. Have you heard me tell it in class?"

"Yes I have, Petty Officer."

"Good. You have to break me with a connection, right? But how do you beat all of *that* with words? What do you do?"

Sergeant Jenkins looked at his watch. He turned to the camera, then back to Dan. "I don't know how to beat that."

"Now you're learning," Dan said. "*Dummy.*"

THE QUIET BEFORE
MIR HAMZA KHAN

Mir Hamza Khan's mansion, Tarin Kowt City, Tarin Kot District, Uruzgan Province, Afghanistan, 01 June 2013—

Mir Hamza Khan balanced the blue rifle across his legs. It was dusk. The tarp, torn down the middle, flapped in his face. He held it still with his hand. Ali Muhammad, thin with the work and lack of food, sat beside him. They watched the last American plane taxi down the runway of the American base.

The Americans had spent the last four months flying everything out: their men, shipping containers, vehicles, water tanks, even the motors they used to grind their sewage. All of it gone. The Americans had destroyed most of their buildings and the ones they kept were now in the hands of the Afghan Commandos. The Afghan Commandos' tan Ford Rangers lined the airfield as the last American plane lifted from its wheels, glided toward the sun and was gone. Their cheer carried all the way to Khan on the roof.

"Here," he said to Ali Muhammad. He passed the blue AK-47 to his deputy—a position that no longer meant what it once did—and stood. He had to be dying, he was sure of it, his disease not treated. "You carry it from now on."

Ali Muhammad, hardened by the last four horrible months, said nothing. He watched the base and the setting sun, chewing on his *naswar.*

The mansion was empty. After the bombers burst through the gates and took his life away, Mir Hamza Khan sent the rest of the guards to their homes. He even threw one loyal man off a parapet after he had refused to leave his General. Fatima and Aufia left on their own, with a simultaneous declaration of "I divorce you, I divorce you, I divorce you." Fatima's uncle came and drove them away in Khan's white Corolla. Khan did nothing. Aghala, with her recovered television, stayed in her house for a month. Khan went there often and watched movies. The two didn't speak a word. One morning, Ali Muhammad came up the steps to the roof and told Khan that Aghala was packed and standing on the cement pad with the three remaining cars. Khan waved his hand at Ali Muhammad. The cherry-red Mercedes disappeared after that.

"Should we call the Commandos for a *shura*?" Ali Muhammad said to Khan. He opened the vest for the orange phone they used to call the government. "It's the proper way."

Khan rubbed his head. It ached. Even Azzam, the old manservant, had died—naturally. Khan didn't replace him. "Do you know what an American commander once told me about Uruzgan?"

Ali Muhammad looked up from the orange phone. "What did he say, General?"

"He said Uruzgan looked like the end of the world."

Ali Muhammad clicked his tongue.

"I never thought he was right." Dark was coming down on the city. Cooking fires sawed in the distance. To the west, a string of red tracers fell through the sky like the sad arc of a meteor. "He was from America, what could he know? Uruzgan isn't what the world looks like in the end." Ancient Tarin Kowt City surrounded the mansion—a terrible zoo. "It's like the quiet that comes just before it."

ACKNOWLEDGEMENTS

I'd like to thank my mentor, Tom De Haven,
for his selfless dedication to this book, Addie Johnson,
whose assistance, council, and hard work was vital to
make it real, and Ashley, who said I can, and should,
do this.

Matt Cricchio served in the United States Navy
and deployed to Afghanistan with Special Operations.
He currently lives in Richmond, Va.

Printed in Great Britain
by Amazon